]

of the

FORESTLANDERS

Book Two

Halfgrown Heroes

Written By

James Kelton
And
Dennis Harold

(Created by James Kelton)

HALFGROWN HEROES dedications page

To Joanie & Mac

~JK

*To my parents Bernie and Caryl. To my Gabrielle,
Sean and Genevieve. To James and Andy.*

~DH

Follow Thru Productions
PO Box 2171
Overton, NV 89040
general@followthrupros.com
www.Followthrupros.com

Published by Follow Thru Productions 10/01/2020

First Edition

ISBN: 978-1-7359084-1-0
Library of Congress Control Number: 2020919351

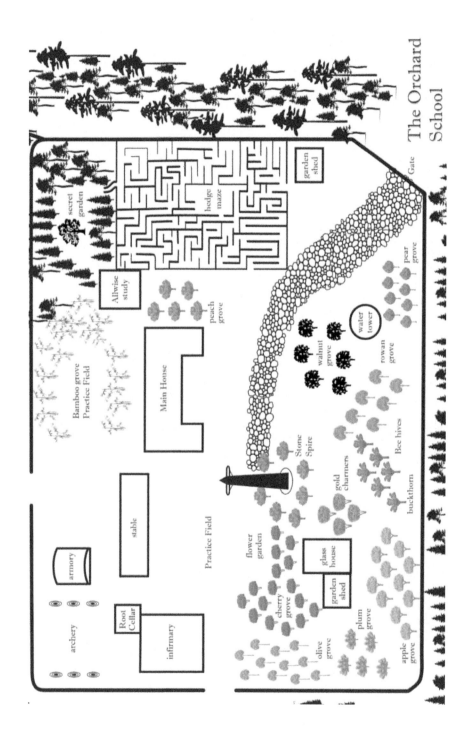

The Orchard School

Tribal Map # 1

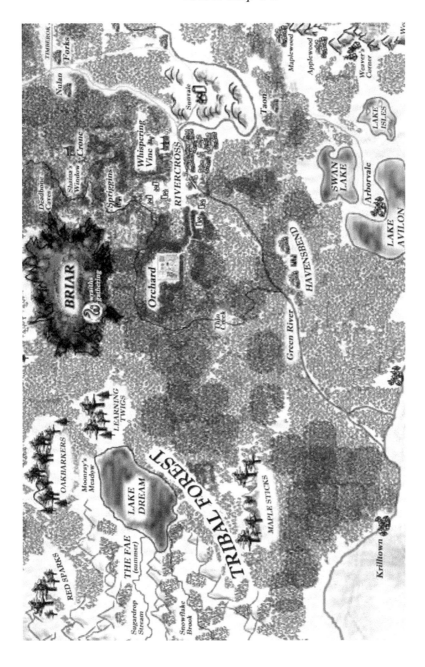

Chapter 1

SPIES

The main difference between an elfling of the Tree Tribe of Learning Twigs and a teenage boy from the Forestlands was about two and a half feet, but Jack Spriggins did not see it that way. Even at fifteen years old, he was still angry over the many times he had been caught off-guard by an elf while cooling his heels in the woods.

"Wild varmints!" he said, through clenched teeth. "Elves sneak up on folks. They thwack yeh with a mudball or hard acorn, only to laugh at yeh." He patted the small crossbow hooked on his belt. "Not me! Never again."

It was a midsummer morning and he was hot. His buckskin shirt and trousers, borrowed from his bunkmate, Redvere, helped him blend into the trees but felt clammy against his skin. To be assigned a task off school grounds seemed like a stroke of luck, until Jack had learned it involved *elves.*

A Fire Dance was to be held at the camp of the Learning Twigs, where the elder tree elves would choose a young one to return to the Orchard with Jack. It was as an assignment he dreaded, which was probably why Allwise gave it to him in the first place.

"Why elves?" He chomped on a hunk of jerky and washed it back with water from his flask. Allwise had called it *a lesson.* "It's really just a kick in the butt for all the trouble of teaching me. So, sure, 'Let's stick Spriggins with the elves!' Yeaah."

Once known as the yellow-eyed thief from Thin Creek, (actually his eyes were bright hazel) Jack had spent the past two years as a student at the Orchard School, near Rivercross. Allwise was a demanding headmaster under whom Jack had improved his reading skill, learned to chart maps, do arithmetic, and learn history. The fight instructor, Perdur Galles, helped him brush up with his crossbow, lassoing, and wrestling maneuvers. Jack truly loved to learn and did his best to shove his stubbornness aside to be taught.

He wiped his sweaty neck with a handkerchief, given to him by Rose Red, the only girl student at the Orchard. For the moment, he knew his bearings thanks to *Tom Tailor's Trail Guide,* a rare travel manuscript that he had paged through in the school's library.

"Now I gotta sneak around the Briar," said Jack.

Any halfwit knew to avoid it, but since the route to the Learning Twigs camp skirted this dangerous maze of brambles, Jack trekked cautiously. Boughs creaked above. Something sprang from one tree to another. His hackles rose, so Jack crouched low in a shadow, aware that he was being tracked.

"That ain't heavy enough to be a person. Ain't smooth enough to be a cougar. Aw, jits! It's gotta be an elf."

(Jack had a gut feeling about which one, too.)

"It's that copper-headed runt that tracks my moves whenever I set off in the deep woods. Where is he? The little coward never gives me a chance to shoot back. Always yelling out his name. What was it again? Tied-Toe? Tiky?"

"TYLO!" shouted the wily tree elf.

The name was howled at Jack in a shrill giggle accompanied by the elfling's battle cry of "Hee-Yo!"

Yes, the name was Tylo.

The imp could be seen crouching on the bough of an elm. Tylo was a runt. He was half a head shorter than other tree elves — mostly limbs, clothed only in a raggedy loincloth. His lank little arms and legs stretched more like a primate, and less like a boy. A mop of tawny hair hung down over his grin but did not hide from his bright eyes that the sole purpose of his life was to torment Jack Spriggins.

Over his head, Tylo spun a crude sling and with a flick of his skinny wrist, let loose.

Jack sprang aside, only being grazed by the nastiest spatter of muck ever thrown. By the time he repositioned and took aim with his crossbow, Tylo had skittered off into the trees.

"I hate yeh, elf!" said Jack. "I hate yer whole nasty breed but yeh most of all!"

He was being too loud, in a place where he should have been dead silent.

"Leave it to an elf to risk somebody's life for a lark! I wish the ogres would clean out the whole lot of them."

Ogres were the bloodthirsty army of men from the neighboring Desertlands. They brought war and terror to the forest, going on three years at this point. Mostly it was the northern villages they had ravaged and burnt without mercy.

The forest army held fast behind General Ardus Camlann. He was a popular ranger who marshaled their defenses smartly, even though his men were always outnumbered. They had muscled the ogres into a battle line along the upper Timberock Road, preventing the enemy from advancing south. Every stretch from Murkwell to Rudd had dug in but the ogres relentlessly sought to break through, and Camlann's forces were being stretched too thin.

"Only old men and boys are left in our villages now." Jack wiped the mud spatter off his buckskin shirt. "Our army needs more trained types, not elves."

Nevertheless, Allwise had gotten the chuckleheaded notion that elves would make good recruits for fighting ogres. Jack knew better.

"I'll just bite my tongue," he said. "That's how a soldier follows orders, I reckon."

Then, a salvo of drums rumbled from deep within the Briar. It had been faint, but Jack's keen ears caught it and he froze mid-stride. Another round thumped. The rhythm was deliberate and foreboding. Was it an ogre war party *in the bramble?*

"Even elves know better. "

Peering through a jagged gap in the Briar thorns, he found a twisted footpath.

"There's footprints on the ground. More than one set." Jack secured the beanstalk lariat on his shoulder. "Learning Twigs will have to wait. Something's afoot and I gotta know what. "

So, he slipped through, carefully navigating the twisted path of black limbs and knifelike barbs. The forest grew so thick in this place that daylight did not enter. The bramble eventually opened enough for him to observe the ruins of an ancient shrine. The roof had collapsed and only a courtyard of crumbled stone pillars was left.

"This must be part of the old kingdom that the forest grew over. Allwise lectured about that last term. Lots of crazed things went on at these altars. None of them good."

Smoke burned Jack's nostrils. He ducked.

Six eerie figures gathered amid the ruins, their torches illuminating the dark, unholy place. Leaves rustled. Jack huddled against an old oak, but caught sight of Tylo up in the boughs. The bothersome elf was also transfixed on the sinister group.

Their torches were laid upon a stone altar and now burned as one pyre. The members wore long black robes with wide hoods that masked their identities as they thrummed a baleful chant. The tallest of them pounded the summoning drum. Another was stooped, leaning on a white wooden staff. A female swayed with her graceful arms outstretched, as if collecting the darkness. Two in the circle stood side-by-side like twins. The last member, continuing to stoke the flames, was very short – the size of a child or an elf.

The one with the staff spoke. He was probably their leader. "Time is fleeting," he said. "Like souls of the departed. Let us account for our deeds and be gone."

The drummer gave a final wallop and the chant came to a charged halt.

"Where is the snake?" said the female.

A rasp seeped through the thin air as the bramble crunched and parted. Jack covered his mouth and nose from the awful stench. A massive black serpent brushed by him. It had a girth thicker than his body and uncoiled for yards to join the gathering. The hooded figures allowed the serpent to slither its demonic coils about their feet.

"League of Wraiths," said the leader, "Our chaos has spread, war thrives, and the woods grow heavy with fear. Tell me, has the last remaining grace – the Fae – been destroyed?"

"Splendidly dead!" said the short Hood. "All but one."

"The faerie bands should all be dead," said the female harshly. "How is it a single one survived?"

Reacting to her tone, the snake spiraled around the small wraith with tightening coils, and bared its oozing fangs.

"No! That was not my fault!" grunted the short one, whose voice squeezed to a higher pitch. "I am not to be sacrificed. Hear what I have to say."

The leader struck the cracked pavement with his staff. "Retract your fangs. Let him speak."

Released by the viper, the short one gasped for breath, regaining composure. "I poisoned the band of Faeries by the tainted streams of Lake Dream, which had sustained them. Ogre men will never be ensnared by their charms after what I did next." He made a slurping sound, licking his lips. "The Desertland army can now march on the southern woods."

Jack shuddered. Fae were a favorite subject among teenage boys. Could every one of them have been killed?

The drummer spoke in a thick *sartyrian* accent, which gave away that he was a Desertlander. "One faerie female is as much a risk as the entire sisterhood."

"I know, I know," said the short hood. "But this one is merely a child, the youngest of the band. Her allurement has not blossomed and there be none left to guide her when it does."

"Such innocent prey," said the female. "Then she should have been the first to fall."

The twin wraiths spoke together as one shared voice. "An elf tribe called the Red Sparks had a hand in the matter. We saw to it that an ogre infantry tracked and scalped them. The girl was no longer with them."

"How are you more useful, short one?" said the leader. "As an assassin or as snake food?"

The serpent lashed its forked tongue at the short one and raised its head to strike.

"Wait! I will track her down. I'll overturn every stone until I find this last faerie and devour her, scream by scream."

The female interjected. "No. I will kill her, not this pint-sized failure. I want to see her suffer. And I want to see it gets finished."

"Don't forget, I killed the others," said the short hood. "All of them. And I am still hungry for more."

He hissed. She hissed back. The snake hissed.

The leader clapped for silence. "I am not opposed to a race between you, so long as the faerie breed is extinct when it ends. What is the child's name?"

"Snow White," said the short hood. "Hair as black as ebony, lips as red as blood, skin as white as snow."

Silence swept over the gathering as the description sunk in. Then the female spoke. "I will consult with water and glass. Darkness will guide me to this Snow White."

The leader pointed his wooden staff at the tall drummer and said, "How is the anticipated assault in the south looking?"

"The Forest Army does not suspect it," said the drummer, "They are stretched too thin, and cannot fight on two fronts. We will strike fear into the heart of the forest."

"Take heed," said the leader. "The sheriff of the southern farms, Count Corrobis, is a formidable swordsman. His rangers are loyal to the woods."

"They are nothing," said the drummer. "Without Camlann's forces behind them, nobody can stop us."

The leader waved his walking stick. "Allwise's Orchard school concerns me more. His latest crop of students is a threat. Particularly young Spriggins."

Jack flinched upon hearing his own name. "The leader knows me?"

"Perhaps we can convert him," said the twins.

"Or kill them all," said the short hood.

"Or have them kill each other," said the female.

Not a face of the six could be seen, but Jack got the sense that dreadful smiles were curling beneath their black hoods.

"Our tasks are clear," said the leader. "Speak your oaths, Wraiths"

With a final wallop, the drummer pledged, "Sound the war drum for the southern invasion."

The twins pledged. "Divide the forest races. Keep the wilds wild."

The leader chimed in. "Break the Orchard School."

The short one said, "Find Snow White."

The female added, "Kill Snow White."

"Perfectly crazed oaths," said the leader. "Steal forth, Wraiths. Sit behind the seats of power, not on them. Keep your faces cloaked, your oaths, secret."

The six placed their hands upon the torches. United as one fire, they closed the gathering with a grave and bloodless chant: "ACHIX-SKRIIT-OTAAK-ACTIS."

"*Palagot*, the witching tongue," reckoned Jack. He was not one to get easily spooked, but the effect of it turned his blood cold. "Only demons use curses like that."

He spotted Tylo in the trees. The trembling elf turned and skedaddled.

The cloaked group disbanded. The serpent slithered back into the bramble. Jack did not linger to see what directions they all took, but scrambled out of the passage like he was ditching a nest of hornets.

Hearing his own name mentioned made his neck hairs stand straight. "That was a dark group of rabble-rousers. *Wraiths* must have hateful eyes everywhere."

He squeezed out of the briar, back into the woods.

Tylo gently swooped down from the trees, like a crazed squirrel. He stumbled closer to Jack, every step a quivering effort.

"Wonder how much of the wraith plots yeh understood?" said Jack. "If any."

The three and a quarter foot elf turned away, as if in shame.

"Miserable elf," said Jack. "I figured there'd be more to yeh than this."

Tylo turned with a grin, lifted up his ragged loincloth and wiggled his freckled backside. "Here's more!" The imp howled in delight as he bounded on all fours up an elm and leapt to a neighboring spruce, then off into the woods.

"Bunk!" said Jack. He had let the elf get up close and missed another chance to have at him. A flying dirt ball hit him smack in the face.

"Hee-Yo!" shouted Tylo.

Jack boiled in rage. "Run, yeh nasty little chickabee! Ogres can't scalp yeh fast enough. I'll do it myself next time."

As he smeared the clod off his face, the notion of meeting a whole tribe of these filthy pranksters only made his mood worse. Of course, his mission to the Learning Twigs took on a new purpose after what he had seen with Tylo.

The *palagot* curse still rang in his ears. All of the wraith's plots were almost too devious to reckon with. "Maybe it was a pack of lies? If I were a better spy, I'd know the difference."

* * * * *

From an unfinished note of Allwise written in his own hand to General Camlann – found at his Orchard desk, dated a month before Jack Spriggins was sent to the tribe of the Learning Twigs.

"I have suspected for a while that my longtime adversary has risen again and is the true architect of this recent war. While ogre-kind is combative by nature, they seem senselessly prompted to destruction by the same chaotic forces I battled in my youth. Evidence that this influence also whispers in our own ears becomes apparent as men turn their backs on other Forestland races and adopt defensive tactics to preserve what is theirs – and covet what is not. No one is safe as long as this foe thrives. I can only blame myself for showing mercy so long ago and assuming my order would be not become challenged. Now, here we are with new wraiths pulling strings like puppeteers and I am late to the game, too old to lay bare their mechanisms. I must rely on my halfgrown heroes – the junior soldiers and students of the Orchard – to end both the bloodshed and the madness that grows like wildfire."

E.M.B. (Allwise)

Chapter 2

FIREDANCERS

Of the eight Great Spirits known in the Forestlands, the elves worshiped the Fire One. It made sense since no other force in nature embodied their friskiness more than the Flickering Spirit, whom they fondly nicknamed "Sparky".

Jack was getting close to the elves' camp. Over the rustle of wind, a clamor of yelps and whoops travelled to his ears. It was the sound of elves – *a whole tribe of them* – up to their usual no-good antics.

"Jits! I've heard barnyards quieter on rodeo day," said Jack.

He stole into the glade of the Learning Twigs. Hundreds of elves – none over four feet – turned from every leafy branch and stared at him. Moments before, they had been screaming across the trees, squabbling for which feathers to wear on their loincloths, and passing dry branches down to a pit where a fireball was being constructed. Now, their countless beady eyes were all focused on Jack.

He felt an itch on his trigger finger and tapped it against his crossbow.

"Never seen so many shades of rusty red hair," said Jack, stepping cautiously forward. "Who's in charge?"

He looked around. The camp was actually impressive. Towering limlok trees framed a meadow, which was wide and ring-shaped around a marshy pond. Above it, ropes of black twine were suspended from the trees some sixty feet up, harnessing a web across the clearing. Elves stood on the mesh, gently bobbing as it supported them. Platforms and dwellings honeycombed the trees.

He-elves wore skimpy loincloths, aiming their loaded flings at Jack. She-elves wore threadbare drapes, aiming their loaded flings at Jack. Even toddlers (who wore nothing), aimed their loaded flings at Jack.

"I'll ask once more," he said. "Which one of yeh is in charge?"

A flurry of wooden flute notes broke the tension.

One of the elder elves lowered himself to the forest floor on a rope swing. "A lunkhead like you should know better who the Guide of the Learning Twigs be. And that be me. Call me Geyo."

He looked as ancient as the limlok tree from which he had descended with wrinkles like knotted bark.

"You be the teach-ling of Allwise Old Eyes?" Geyo's man-speech was surprisingly clear.

"Reckon so," said Jack.

"Offer proof," said Geyo, "Or suffer a fate of endless tickles."

Jack answered him in elf-speak: a series of intricate tongue and cheek clicks. "*Ki-ki nik All-wizen ooo nok-ka Jaa-ak Sprig-gins* (whistle, whistle) *wi kok zing ki-ki* (chest thump) *bik bik,* (knee slap)*, ko loko nok kha wi kok.*"

When translated, this meant: "Allwise, the Grand Lunkhead of the Orchard, has sent me, Jack Spriggins, to fetch an elfling chosen from among your tribes to take him back with me to our school and learn lunkhead ways and prepare your kind for warfare with the Desertlanders."

A reaction of surprise spread through the camp until every elf was chirping and whooping. They gleefully flipped on the boughs and made such an uproar, that Jack smugly folded his arms and jutted out his chin.

"That proof enough?" he said.

Geyo slapped his chest in amusement. "You speak the Learning Twigs rhythm better than my man-speak. Did Old Eyes teach it to you?"

"I was taught and I learned," said Jack.

Two more elders swung down from the trees. One of them, a female, waddled over to size him up.

Geyo made the introduction. "This be Neia, honored elder from the Birdsongs Tribe."

Neia wore blue-green peabhen feathers and little else. She brazenly wrapped an arm around Jack's legs and looked up with inquisitive eyes.

"My tribe was once welcome in man's villages to sing and act out stories," she said, "But the war for the woods has strained our relations. We must renew our good favor as Old Eyes says."

Jack gritted his teeth. "I just came to fetch an elf."

"My pack's finest youths are ready to compete," said Neia.

The other male elder, with very few streaks of red left in his hair, sprang forward. "My name be Kreo. I am Guide of the Maple Sticks. You be Jack the Giant Killer?"

Jack hated that name. "Just Jack."

Kreo addressed the tribes. "It's Jack the Giant Killer! Jack the Giant Killer!"

The elves wisecracked with chitters and cheek-pops.

"He's not big for a lunkhead," said one.

"Should not his voice be lower?" said another.

"Where be the ax he used to chop off the giants' heads?"

"Where's the fur coat of the Wolf Master he killed?"

"I thought lunkheads grew whiskers on their chins?"

Jack rolled his eyes. Different race, same questions. Tales of his adventures never came close to the truth. He let the elves jabber on and took a closer look at their dwellings.

Far from being crude, primitive nests, the Learning Twigs lived in round huts that clung to the trees. Dozens of tiered platforms were built right into the boughs, masked by foliage. The houses had walls, shelving and hammocks. Twine pulleys were strung between them so their feet never had to touch the ground.

It would have been tempting to explore the entwining tree world had a toddler not yanked on Jack's boot.

"What be this green coil on your shoulder, Giant Killer?"

Jack pulled away. "They're my beanstalk vines for climbing and roping."

"How tall be the biggest giant you have roped? As big as a limlok tree?"

"I didn't rope any. Giants are bigger than me, just not tree-big."

"*Zi kah woo hoot* (chest thump)," challenged a bold elf, implying that Jack couldn't rope a giant. The elflings thumped their chests in agreement.

Kreo of the Maple Sticks flicked their ears and shooed the wily bunch away. "You will not see our Fire Dance if you cannot reach a higher perch. Let us see you climb."

Jack nocked his climbing arrow and fired the beanstalk vine over a bough, some sixty feet up. The eyes of many elves flit in disbelief as he scrambled up faster than they did to reach the high platform.

Elflings pulled the elders to the landing.

"Take a seat," said Geyo.

The stump Jack was offered seemed to be a place of honor. Guides of the Oakbarkers, Featherfeet, Birdsongs, Maple Sticks, and Learning Twigs also sat. One stump was empty.

"It be odd" said Geyo, "That the Red Sparks tribe be not here."

Jack swallowed hard. If what he had heard the wraiths say was true, the Red Sparks would be no-shows.

Neia of the Birdsongs handed him a small wooden bowl of a pasty mixture. "Eat," she said.

Jack was hungry so he scooped the paste into his mouth. It had a mealy texture and tasted sweet. "Grits?" he said, chewing.

Neia shook her head. "Mashed wood grubs and maple sugar."

Jack forced the bite down, even though it made his stomach flip-flop.

As the sun set through the trees, the round huts began to glow with amber lanterns. The huge ball of plastered sticks was hoisted over the clearing. It reminded Jack of a hot air balloon he had seen at a festival in Havensbend. The elves winched the ball to the webbed overhang until it was suspended forty feet above the glade.

The tribes chanted:

"Sparky Red Sky show your smile,
Sparky Red Leaf show your wile.
By your flicks we dance in turn,
Sparky Red Flare, play and burn."

Twig arrows were lit but not by matches. There was a special trait elfkind possessed: their calloused fingertips could snap sparks out of thin air. A brush of three fingers and POP! Flickers would dance off the tips of their blackened thumbs. (Jack would not have minded possessing such an ability.)

From the judge's platform, Kreo of the Maple Sticks blew a loud wood horn. Archers with crude bows shot flaming arrows over the meadow. The fireball ignited. Its blaze was spectacular, the heat intense and exciting.

Music began. Elves plucked circular harps made of yew wood that made twangs like banjos, only higher. Reed pipes were blown with clear, bewitching notes. Heads bobbed, feet tapped, rears wagged.

"Let the fire-dancing begin!" said Geyo.

The younger elves swooped down on vines, circling the burning ball and hooting wildly. From high and low, they flew over, under, past the flames, and landed on limlok branches only to jump again.

"So many at once," said Jack. "They're gonna smack into each other."

There was a second horn blast. The elves swung back to the trees and waited. The elders pointed in judgment, cutting the candidates down by half. Five target wreathes were hung from trees around the circle of the arena. The players were handed twig bows. The oak horn blew again, signaling the next stage of the Fire Dance.

Arrow shafts were still sticking out from the fireball. The boldest (and looniest) elflings swooped down to grab and shoot them into the targets. The champs with the most bullseyes before the horn would be declared finalists.

"Hoo-wee!" shouted Neia of the Birdsongs. "One hit for Fato of my tribe. No, two."

"I would say watch my Maple Sticks, but they are too fast," said Kreo. "Two hits for Aira. You can feel the breeze as she zips by."

"Ooh! Ooh!" said Neia. "Who be that tiny elfling with his britches on fire?"

Geyo snorted, "It be Tylo."

"Tylo?" Jack's eyes widened with recognition, then rage. "It can't be!"

"Three times round," said Neia. "Perfect hits. He looks like a falling star."

Tylo received the loudest thigh-claps from the crowd (and a good deal of chest thumps) as he continued to notch bullseyes. His unmistakable grin widened as he struck his fifth target.

"Hee-Yo!" shouted the tiny overbold elf patting smoke from the backside of his loincloth.

"Tylo! Tylo!" chanted the Learning Twigs.

He banged his chest and took another spin around the fireball.

"What cheek," said Neia of the Birdsongs. "See how he twirls his bow round his fingers."

"Look at him smirk," said Geyo.

"What a shame he be so teeny," said Kreo. "Allwise Old Eyes would be displeased if we sent him a peewee."

Geyo agreed. "He be too small. We must consider others."

The elders gave a thumbs down judgment. Tylo's shoulders drooped. He swung away and hid behind the wide leaves of a limlok.

Jack unfolded his arms with relief.

When the round finished, Kreo of the Maple Sticks declared, "Six champs be left. It be time for the best teasing."

"My favorite part of a Fire Dance," said Geyo. "Matters of cleverness and buffoonery make our truest champs. Show off your wits, elflings!"

The six contestants stepped onto the crisscross web like clowns in a traveling circus. A she-elf donned a mask of plastered brown leaves and began to perform.

Neia whooped. "Hoo-wee! That be Che-Bee from my Birdsongs, acting just like a brown bear with two left paws."

Another elfling donned a hat of woven leaves and paraded out to the center.

"See? See?" said Kreo of the Maple Sticks. "It be Luko of my tribe showing us a fat lunkhead farmer who ate too many beans."

Luko bent over and mocked a loud fart. The crowd went crazy, yipping and laughing.

Jack slumped, growing impatient.

"Look at Togo," said Neia of the Birdsongs. "See how he hops by like an ogre with itches in his britches."

Geyo pointed. "And is that not my own offspring, Jiro, playing both harp *and* pipes to a beloved song?"

"Sing along, my Birdsongs," said Neia.

The whole camp crooned like sparrows. Jack had heard the anthem before sung by elf troupes in front of Rivercross taverns.

"You'd like if all could dive off boughs into a windless sail?"

"No, we sure would not."
"Or strike a dot from far away by using just a flail?"
"No, we sure would not."
"To find a laugh where no joke lives, would that be such a fuss?"
"No, for then all would be elves – and where's the fun for us?"

"If everyone could climb up high and sleep in beds of trees?"
"No, we sure would not."
*"Spy hornets' hives with sharpest eyes and drop them when you
please?"*
"No, we sure would not."
"How 'bout sharing ears, keen to sounds like any beast?"
"No, why give up all that's elf – when we just dance and feast?"

Tylo swung back into the arena in full view of the elders.
"Him again?" said Geyo. "We said 'no'."
The little showoff draped a garland of leaves over his head and
began a perfect imitation of the short wraith from the Briar, spoken in
verse.

"Bedlam! Bedlam be I! With words I say, I steal your days
I chew, chew, chew – you cry for all,
The dead and small, the weak and tall.
To you that say, the small can never rise to height.
Bedlam! Bedlam be I!
For the gobs that rob the day of night,
I chomp, chomp, chomp – and eat them all,
The dead and small, the weak and tall.
A little voice I be, who speaks, O Sparky's light!"

Geyo raised his brow in doubt. "What be this clever tale?"

Tylo stuck out his chest and uttered the terrible *palagot* hex. "ACHIX-SKRIIT-OTAAK-ACTIS!"

Jack paled.

The fireball burned through its cords and crashed on to the marshy pond. Embers scattered into the night air. The camp fell dead silent.

Tylo dangled from the web. "Why does no one make a peep?"

The elders put their heads together. When they rose, they clicked in praise.

"Winner," said Geyo of the Learning Twigs. "Tylo be winner."

"Winner," said Kreo of the Maple Sticks. "For one so small, he japes so swift."

"Winner," said Neia of the Birdsongs. "His decayed words be the keenest prank of all."

The Oakbarkers and Featherfeet agreed. Rowdy cheers erupted across the glade.

Jack stepped to the edge of the judges' platform. "Wait a blarn sec!" he said. "Do yeh have any idea what this little goblin just blurted out?"

"Ooh!" hissed the elves, pelting him with acorns.

Kreo of the Maple Sticks raised his arms. "Never call an elf a goblin," he said, severely.   Geyo added, "And yes, we elders know the *palagot* word that Tylo used."

"How do you know it, Giant Killer?" said Neia of the Birdsongs.

"I heard it the same time Tylo did," said Jack. "We were in the Briar. It was spoken by six hooded wraiths."

"*Palagot* means trouble," said Geyo. "You should both share what you heard with Allwise."

"Naw," said Jack. "Tylo got kicked out of the game. Yeh can't send this runt back with me. That's no good."

"Though he be small, Tylo shows he be the best Learning Twig."

Tylo crowed. "Hee-yo! From my wiggling toes to my freckled nose, I be the best."

The crowd trilled, "The best! The best! The best!"

Jack folded his arms in defeat. "We'll leave tonight."

Tylo's grin sank. "Leave?" He searched the elders' faces for a prank. "Naw-naw. I be taught *here* and will taunt this lunkhead 'til he runs off."

"No, Tylo," said Geyo. "You will go to the man's village. You will show yourself to be best of the elflings, like you did this night. You will learn, as they will learn from you."

An elfin couple mounted the platform. Tylo ran to them.

"Mam! Pap! Don't make me go."

"This is what Sparky has declared for you," said his pap. "Where you lead, others elves will someday follow."

"Naw-naw!" said Tylo.

His mam slipped a strand of red feathers around his neck. "This be our best robin's collar, Tylo. Wear it. Proud we are, my Tiny One."

Pap gave him a handful of twig arrows. "These be from your brothers and from me. Show the lunkheads that we elves shoot best."

Tylo tried to stand straighter and taller. If he cleared three and a quarter foot, it was a generous measurement. "By Sparky's flame, let me stay."

Geyo smirked. "Sparky has a new path for you, young fire-spitter. Do not let the smoke of fear blind you."

"Y'all sure there ain't a better elf?" said Jack.

"You are right to leave now while it is dark," said Geyo. "I will pray to the Fire One for both of you, Giant Killer Spriggins."

Jack frowned. "Yeh don't need to pray for me."

"But I do," said Geyo. "Anyone can see the growing light in you, young lunk. But it can blow out. Hate be more deadly than any ogre, any hooded wraith, any war."

There was a ring of truth to Geyo's words.

"You had best go and fetch Tylo then," said Geyo. "He has run off."

"Aw, jits!" cursed Jack. Indeed, Tylo had given them the slip.

He shot the elders a sour look and lowered himself off their platform to track down the *chosen one.*

"That be a good trick, eh?" said Geyo with a laugh. "Think how much you two youths will learn from each other."

* * * * *

From "A Handbook to the Forestlands" 2nd Edition

ELF – Any of a race of forest dwelling people that reside in trees or earthen trenches. They are small in stature, averaging a height of 4'0", possess impressive agility and worship the Fire Spirit exclusively. A tendency towards mischief may also noted.

Chapter **3**

PRISONERS

"You did catch me, Giant Killer," said Tylo. "That be the best joke on me ever."

Jack had him leashed by the wrists with his beanstalk vine and yanked him along.

"Tracked and hunted yeh just like any critter in the woods," said Jack. "Now quit stalling."

He trotted Tylo forward with each tug of the leash.

"I be no ground elf," said Tylo, lifting his hands. "Set me free and I will stay close. I promise. The ground be not safe for tree elves. I am better up in the branches."

"I ain't cutting yeh loose, runt," said Jack. "Keep up."

For a while, Tylo limped like a chained prisoner. Then, he skipped around Jack making faces. Finally, he prowled on all fours like a hunting dog. Jack kept on marching.

"Bugs, bugs, bugs!" said Tylo. "I need to play jokes. I need to tweet my elf-pipes. I need to un-bunch my loincloth. Why do we not stop?"

"There's still a day's trek ahead of us, so shut up, will yeh?"

Tylo dug his heels into the dirt. "I cannot go another footstep without a morning meal in my acorn pouch," he said, pointing at his belly.

"Have it yer way." Jack reclined against a fallen log and stretched his arms over his head, circling one foot over the other. "Reckon I'll eat."

He took some jerky from his pack and chawed, offering none to Tylo, then drank from his canteen.

The peeved elfling switched to a look of playfulness. "How good of you to scout my favorite food."

Tylo scooted underneath the hollow of the log and soon emerged with a handful of squirming grubs and beetles, which he shoved into his mouth. After chewing it up, he gaped at Jack, giving him a full view of the squirming mash on his tongue.

"Ew-ack!" Jack turned away.

"I be thirsty," said Tylo. "Be that water, kind sir?"

"Cup yer hands," said Jack.

He poured the flask into the elf's open palms.

Tylo slurped noisily. "It has come to my attention you do not like elves."

"Sure don't."

"Why?"

"Yer a pack of mean, selfish pests," said Jack. "Yeh pick a fight for fun, then run off like scaredy-cats."

"What if an elf told you he did not like those same things about his own kind?"

"I'd say he was full of bunk."

"You would be right!" said Tylo, giggling. "Elves be elves. Lunks be dull and slow!"

Jack pulled another bite of jerky. Tylo watched him, then started to sing.

"Tender rabbit, pig, or deer,
Romping in the forest near.
Did you dream that you'd grow up,
To be a bite of Jack's late sup?"

"Elves don't eat meat?"

Tylo picked a centipede off the ground with his toes and flipped it into his mouth. "No, Giant Killer, we do not."

"Mmm," said Jack. "Cured bacon. Yeh don't know what yer missing."

"Be this 'ba-con' something I will learn from Allwise Old Eyes?"

"Dunno. Everyone gets taught different things at the Orchard School."

Tylo's brown eyes widened, "He will make what be good about me better?"

Jack got up and hooked the flask to his belt. "Yeh ain't gonna last, elf. Teaching yeh to sit for a lesson and not pick things up with yer toes – it just ain't gonna *take*. Yeh'll hightail back to yer mam and pap inside a week."

"If your noggin thinks so, Giant Killer, then why did you come to the Learning Twigs?"

"Cause if I've learned anything at the Orchard, yeh don't always like yer lessons but they usually leave yeh smarter," said Jack. "I've also learned if something don't do yeh good, then ditch it."

Tylo reached over with his left foot and somehow looped the vine around Jack's foot, pulling it taut. Jack fell face-first in the bug riddled dirt. When he looked up, Tylo chucked a ball of tree sap into his face.

"You shall sing a changed tune about me," said Tylo. "The very *Best Elf*."

Jack grabbed Tylo's feathered collar with his fist. "I don't sing or even talk about yer kind if I don't have to. I'd be just as happy leaving yeh for crow-feed, elf." Thoughts of pulverizing Tylo's skinny freckled bones came easily as he scraped the muck off his face. "Yeh dirty goblin".

The elf snarled angrily. He drew his twig bow at Jack.

"Your lunkhead mouth will take that back!"

Jack drew his crossbow. "C'mon then!"

The two circled each other in a standoff.

"There be nothing," said Tylo, "Nothing more terrible than to call an elf a 'goblin'.

"Why's that?"

"Do you not know what they be, Giant Killer?"

"A bunch of made-up scare stories for tykes."

Tylo lowered his weapon. "Goblins were once elves," he said, his little freckled face shaking with rage. "Then they started eating other elves."

"Yeh mean, cannibals?" said Jack. "Ain't nothing like that in the Great Forest."

"Not anymore," said Tylo. "All elf tribes, both tree-climbers and groundies, banded as one and forced them out, long ago."

"How?"

The elf snapped his rough fingers. POP! A spark danced off his thumb. "We burned the gobs out with Sparky's gift."

There was no jest in Tylo's eyes just the vengeful glare of one ready to fight.

"Do all elves get so serious?" said Jack, trying hard not to show he was impressed. "Or do just the crazed ones, like yeh?"

Tylo began reciting an angry chant.

> *"Goblin!* (spit) *Goblin!* (gag)
> *Be elf kin and be elf size,*
> *Dance elf fires and blink elf eyes,*
> *But stay away if ye be wise!*
>
> *Goblin!* (bleeah) *Goblin!* (aack)
> *While ye munch on some elf's bone,*
> *Laugh at screams with heart o' stone,*
> *Know ye breed stands alone!*
>
> *Goblin!* (splack) *Goblin!* (harf)
> *Cast ye now from Forestlands,*
> *Forced to gnaw on other strands,*
> *This elf, O ye, doth wash his hands!*
>
> *Goblin! Goblin! Goblin!"*

The imp walked up and stuck out his little chest to Jack. "Elves saved our tribes, man's villages, and the Fae by ridding the forest of the worst of ourselves. Never call me 'goblin' again."

Jack bitterly swallowed his pride.

"*Ki bik* (chest thump) *kaw na ga-ab*," clicked Jack in elf-speak, (meaning, "I won't call yeh *goblin*, if yeh let me guide yeh to the Orchard in peace.")

The elf stuck out his rough little hand and Jack shook it. Orange sparks popped in their clasp.

"Ow!" said Jack, yanking away. "Another blarn trick."

"It be no trick," said Tylo. "Lookee."

Both had small blisters on their palms. "It is Sparky's Blister Promise."

Tylo leaped in delight, his fury forgotten.

"Jits!" Jack blew on his hand. "Even yer promises are a pain."

"Now, Giant Killer, free me of this green rope that no sparks can burn through?"

Jack pulled a white blade from his boot. "Bone knife. The only thing that can cut the bean vines. Don't ask me why. I get my lowest marks in science."

"Sci-ence?"

A screeching woodland thrush suddenly flapped away from the pines above, distracting them.

"Just a sec," said Jack. He crouched low, pressing his ear to the ground.

"Don't leave me tied to a log!" said Tylo. His eyes flit this way and that. He clearly sensed trouble.

"Shut yer yap," said Jack. "We're being hunted. Half a dozen men or so."

"Cut me loose."

"If I do, yeh better not run off."

Tylo showed his blistered palm to Jack. "I will not."

Jack cut the vine.

Tylo shook out his arms. With a cheeky wink, he turned-tail and shimmied up the nearest ironwood, turning on its lowest branch to Jack. "I promised not to run off," he said. "But I may run *up.*" Then he fled out of sight.

"Why, yeh puny, lying —"

Jack could not finish. A cold, curved blade pressed to his throat and the crossbow was ripped from his belt.

"Aw, bunk," said Jack.

He turned to face his captors. It was a band of six ogre soldiers, wielding jagged swords and cumbersome pistols. They were men, much bigger than Jack, baring tanned muscles beneath bronze chest plates and greaves. Their skin was covered with blue tattoos that resembled reptile scales. One wore a snake head helmet.

"*Shlo lerk dohl mongr al khanka Ka Bur!*" said one of his captors.

Their *sartyrian* speech was thick, spoken through teeth that were filed to fangs. Thanks to his schooling in the language, Jack understood they would not slit his throat just yet, but would take him to their commander.

"What're y'all doing this far south?" he said.

One of the ogres thumped him hard on the skull. His answer was darkness.

* * * * *

From "A Handbook to the Forestlands" 2nd Edition

OGRE - Slang word for persons of the neighboring Desertland located to the west of the Great Forest, which is derived from their worship of the Ogrelund – the symbol of a snake devouring its own tail.

Chapter 4

OGRE PAWNS

Jack opened his eyes with an awful headache. It was sundown. Torches were flickering. He wanted to rub his noggin but his hands were tied behind his back. Strapped to a post in a makeshift coop, he was disarmed and uncomfortable. The ground was soggy and reeked of rotting fish.

Two, armed ogre sentries sat by the door swigging flagons of ale. Beyond them, village homes and piers were smoking. Jack spotted a fallen sign that read: Krilltown. It was a fishing village of the south forest – or it used to be. Embers from the burnt buildings flittered in the sky. The charred remains of an unfortunate man's body lay on the road.

A foreign ship was moored in the cove, looming above the smaller fishing boats, which had been set ablaze. The ship was large and heavily armed with cannons.

Jack was surprised to realize, "The ogres got a boat." Desertlanders had not been known as seafaring folk, before now. "I gotta get word to General Camlann. Of course, I need to get out of here alive first."

A frog hopped over his leg and leapt off through the mesh. Raised voices came from the army tents erected in the ogre encampment. Jack could see dark silhouettes of the warlords meeting inside, against the glowing canvas. He knew enough *sartyrian*, the Desertland tongue, to grasp what was being said.

A commander spoke with a deep voice. "The raids will draw Camlann's forces away from the north, further weakening their strength."

"We are only two hundred men," said an officer. "He will not take the bait."

"He will," said the warlord. "When he learns the Fae were defeated."

"It is rumored, my liege," said the officer. "They were not all destroyed."

"You fear one little girl!" said the warlord, with an insulting laugh. "Ha! Trust my instincts, Gutfaar."

"What is our next move?"

"To kill her. Strike Camlann where it hurts most."

"Jaa of Fantash is our appointed leader," said Gutfaar. "You cannot simply violate his orders – aargh."

Gutfaar gave a dreadful groan. The warlord had plunged a curved blade into his innards.

"*I* am the only superior officer you should have been concerned about," said the warlord, wiping his blade. "Who do you serve, men?"

"Ka Bur!" shouted the other officers with raised weapons.

They exited the tent and approached Jack's cage. Warlord Ka Bur struck a threatening figure, outfitted with blades and polished guns. His body was even more daunting than those of his burly officers. He moved with swagger, flashing black eyes under sharply arched brows. His strong jaw-line was covered with blue tattoos, which resembled a close-cropped beard.

Ka Bur motioned the sentry. "Open the cage door."

A gloating smile revealed canine teeth filed to perfect white fangs.

"I am Ka Bur," he said to Jack. "Overlord of B'Ashabir, Night Screamer of the Stoelyn Empire, and Raider of the Woodland Realm."

"I'm Jack."

The warlord chortled, "A small name. You were captured leading an elf prisoner through the woods, but let it escape."

Jack tried *sartyrian* on for size. "*Tamedna molta mothenya jinspa,*" he said, meaning: "It's a waste of rope to hang an elf."

Ka Bur raised a brow. "He attempts to speak our tongue, Simbor'Ash."

"Crudely," said Simbor'Ash, another imposing warrior with long black hair and tattoos that formed a blue "S" over his right eye. "We left the scalp on his head until you could see him for yourself."

The warlord ripped a flagon of ale from a sentry and downed it with a single gulp. Another sentry gave him Jack's crossbow and beanstalk vines.

"Tell me," said Ka Bur. "Can you actually be the Giant Killer, Slayer of Wolfmen, and Savior of the Red Hood?"

The soldiers laughed mockingly.

"Told yeh before, I'm just Jack."

"A boy proves himself a man through acts of courage, not years. I, myself, am younger than many princes under my command." (The warlord appeared to be in his mid-twenties.) "Yet, Ardus Camlann denied you a post in his army. How does that make you feel?"

The truth was, it stung. Jack looked away.

Ka Bur cut Jack's binds with his dagger. "Such a slight as you have received does not happen among the desert lords of B'Ashabir. Perhaps your humiliation is enough to share some information?"

Jack rubbed his sore wrists. "Yeh want me to snitch?"

"It would prolong your life."

"I ain't got much to tell yeh."

"Not even the whereabouts of Camlann's daughter?"

"Daughter?" said Jack. "The general don't have a daughter."

The warlord slugged him in the gut with a ring-covered fist. "Liar! By the Serpent's Venom, we shall scalp and hang you."

Jack bent forward coughing. As he did, he lifted the saber from a soldier's scabbard and hurled it at Ka Bur. The warlord dodged the blade and it struck another guard, who fell with a groan.

"Stop him!" ordered Ka Bur.

Jack ducked out of the cage and bolted for the woods. He slipped between the war tents and then leapt over a campfire; but a stunning blow from a throwing club knocked him down. He was quickly bound by two sentries.

Ka Bur was amused. "A noble effort, boy," he said, waving the purloined saber near Jack's face. "Whose blade is this?"

One of the guards stepped from the ranks, his head lowered in shame.

"Mine," confessed the warrior.

Ka Bur handed the saber back to the warrior and challenged him with his own. For a tense moment they stared at each other. The guard hastily drew his weapon. Ka Bur overpowered him and drove his blade through the man's chest plate, instantly ending his life.

"I have no use for warriors who are so easily disarmed."

Jack had never seen such a cold-blooded disregard for life.

Simbor'Ash signaled other guards to haul the body away.

"A generous punishment," said Ka Bur. "The next warrior who gives up his sword will have his eyes burned out. Now, take the *legendary* vines and hang Jack Spriggins."

A chirpy voice rang out from the trees, "Hee-Yo, Bluebeard!"

Blades were drawn as Tylo leapt down beside the campfire, warming his hands and smiling as if he had dropped in for tea.

"Why do the desert lords toss away all their chances for fun?" said the elf. "You be bigger bores than lunkhead Jack Spriggins."

Ka Bur smiled. "What was that name you called me?"

"Bluebeard," said Tylo. "In honor of the snaky blue whiskers that color your chin."

Stroking his jaw, Ka Bur laughed. He translated his new alias to the warriors. They roared with amusement. Tylo clapped and roared with them.

"Bluebeard!" repeated Ka Bur. "The name has a dashing quality, don't you think?"

"Aye, my liege," said Simbor'Ash.

"It suits your mighty blue-jaw," said Tylo.

"Very well," said Ka Bur, raising his sword. "I shall conquer the woodland realm by this new name. Who do you serve, men?"

"Bluebeard! Bluebeard! Bluebeard!" shouted the ogre warriors.

Jack knew no one in the forest would ever call Ka Bur anything else.

Bluebeard turned to Tylo. "And what shall I call you?"

Tylo bowed low with a flourish of ridiculous hand gestures. "Tylo of the Learning Twigs be your servant, sir-sire-sir."

"We shall see, jester," said Bluebeard. "So, what is more fun than a good hanging?"

Tylo put one hand to his chin, deciding. "Hanging ends the fun too quickly. When you have famed Jack Giant Killer, friend of Ardus Camlann, you need to do more."

"What would you suggest?" said Bluebeard.

"Drinking! Games! Teasing!" said Tylo.

Bluebeard seemed encouraged. "Guards, bring a barrel of molasses rum. Let us be entertained."

A barrel was rolled from a supply tent. Tylo poured out flagons as he recited the rules of his game:

> *"Make Jack skip! Make Jack run!*
> *Make him dance for a jug of rum,*
> *Drink once first, then twice again,*
> *Throw best mud ball, straight at him.*
> *Put Jack in a sack for shame,*
> *Give him eyes to watch the game.*

Drunkest man who keeps his aim
Walks Jack to the plank to hang."

"Excellent sport," said Bluebeard. "I may slit your throat and take credit for it myself."

Tylo covered his neck. "All my thoughts be free of charge."

Bluebeard motioned at Jack. "Stand him up."

Jack glared at Tylo. He was hooded with a rotting potato sack with eye holes cut into it. "Dirty, double-crossing, tree mite."

Bluebeard shoved Jack towards the rowdy warriors. "Another round of drink then Jack dances."

They drank and guffawed. Bluebeard clapped his hands as the warriors kicked Jack on backside. Dancing was not one of his talents.

"Bah!" said Bluebeard, with annoyance. "No rhythm. Give him a dance lesson."

Jack felt a burning on the seat of his pants. Tylo had lit a torch under his rump.

Bluebeard laughed uproariously. "Jack be nimble now! Pour more rum."

The ogres delighted in roughing Jack up while he hopped around.

"It is time to see how smoothly Jack's scalp parts from his skull," said Bluebeard, starting to slur his words.

A lean warrior came forward wearing a bronze serpent helmet. He was armed with a dozen gleaming blades and many pelts of hair, mostly elfin red, which hung from his belt.

"Ah, Scalper," greeted Bluebeard, indicating Jack. "Your canvas awaits."

Scalper pulled a curved sickle from a sheath and began to hone it on a leather strap. He stared at Jack with a dead gaze.

"So, this be Scalper?" said Tylo. "Small for an ogre, so close to Jack in size, but with so many more kills."

Bluebeard clasped Scalper's strong, wiry arm. "Scalper is the finest executioner in the Desertlands. What he lacks in stature, he makes up for with the surest cuts."

The warlord handed the executioner Jack's crossbow. "Add this weapon to your war trophies. Fair trade for the lad's skin."

Scalper nodded. Tylo thrust a mug of rum at him and he helped himself to a long swig.

"Good, good, good," said Tylo. "But be not the flesh of Jack Spriggins too clean? Should he not be covered in mud?"

He blew notes on his reed pipe and then sang:

"O ye of sharp wits and aim,
Here's a weapon for your game.
For each toss that strikes Jack true,
Another round of rum for you!"

"Very well," said Bluebeard. "Let the mudslinging begin."

A mudball firing squad of drunken ogres warriors wobbled into position.

Bluebeard led the contest. He squinted one eye and hurled a muddy wallop into Jack's face.

"Direct hit," he said. "We drink. A fresh cup for every filthy mark."

Warriors took aim and pitched. Rounds of drink followed. Tylo flitted about, merrily filling their mugs.   He seemed especially attentive to Scalper. The creepy butcher always had more to drink.

Jack got as dirty as a pig in slop. Not surprisingly, the ogres were getting so drunk they began to miss.

Simbor'Ash cautioned Bluebeard. "Have the men not had enough leisure?"

Tylo bowed to Simbor'Ash. "Am I mistaken? My dizzy elfin head thought that Bluebeard was the leader, not your noble self."

Bluebeard smashed his goblet. "*I* give the orders. Not him!"

"Truly?" Tylo glanced from one to the other.

The warlord grabbed Simbor'Ash by the chin. "The elf-rat makes a point. You overstep yourself. Should I have Scalper slice off your tongue and send it back to your wives?"

Simbor'Ash bowed. "Forgive my impertinence. I will tap another barrel of rum in your honor, my grace, and serve the men myself."

"Do it!" said Bluebeard.

"Do, do!" repeated Tylo.

The ogre troop had become dangerously rowdy on the Krilltown docks, firing pistols in the air. Bluebeard drew one of his own pistols and fired a shot into the sky. He sang with the troops:

> *Down a goblet to the serpent,*
> *If be venom, die you will.*
> *Drink with courage, drink with fire,*
> *Drink with pride for all you kill.*
> *Let the blood flow red as wine,*
> *Laugh and swallow fast.*
> *Drain the goblet. Every drop*
> *Will likely be your last.*

Tylo sprang on top of Jack's hooded head and steered him through the throng of drunkards. Jack rammed into Scalper who had downed so much rum, he was barely able to stand. The three toppled into a supply tent.

There was a scuffle as they rolled in the dirt. Jack expected to be stabbed any moment when a twanging *thump,* like a muffled dinner gong, rang out and the fight ended. The potato sack was torn from his head. Scalper lay unconscious in the corner. The elf had whacked him in the skull with his own snake helmet.

"Time! Time!" said Tylo, cutting Jack's binds with the bone knife. "We have none. Swap your clothing. Put on Scalper's steel skin, his sharpies, and his belt of scalps. Do it now. Be quick, be quick!"

Jack wiggled out of his buckskins and strapped on the ogre's armor. He put on the snakehead helmet, which covered his face. They dressed Scalper in Jack's muddy duds and crammed the sack over the executioner's head.

"Remember," said Tylo. "Scalper be drunk, so you be drunk."

"I ain't no actor," said Jack, "But I'll try my best."

They parted the tent flap and Jack wobbled out. The ogres' bawdy song had just ended. Bluebeard and his warriors raised their goblets.

Tylo patted Jack's chest plate. "Scalper be ready, sires."

"What have you done with Jack Spriggins?" said Bluebeard.

Jack peered through the slits of the snakehead helmet and pointed at the tent.

Tylo explained, "The Giant Killer did faint and toppled in there."

Without a word, Bluebeard barged past them fingering his razor-sharp dagger as he skulked into the supply tent.

Simbor'Ash gave the warriors a violent shout of command. "*Han! Karta! Banmu!*" There was a wave of military discipline as the carousing men snapped to attention, forcing sobriety as they awaited orders.

Bluebeard reemerged, wiping blood from his knife with Jack's deerskin shirt. "I have slit Jack Spriggins' throat."

Tylo glanced back at the tent. "Then that be that. Mighty Bluebeard's army be taking the Forestlands. My tribe of Learning Twigs will help you win the war. Allow me to go tell them."

"Of course," said Bluebeard. "If one of my men goes with you."

The elf eagerly pointed to the snake helmeted soldier (who happened to be Jack). "I will take Scalper," said Tylo.

"Perhaps, we've misjudged your value," said Bluebeard, who folded his massive arms. "So be it. I shall allow Scalper to escort you. Return with your best warriors and serve me."

Tylo saluted the leader. "You be as true as you be wise, sir-sire-sir."

Bluebeard stayed beside them to the edge of Krilltown. He took Jack by the arm. "A brief word in private, Scalper."

Jack tensed every muscle.

"Find where the elf tribe dwells," said Bluebeard in *sartyrian*. "Then bring me Tylo's scalp. We shall clear out the lot of them."

Jack saluted. "*Hyn Pythava*" ("*Hail Serpent.*") He must have hit the accent perfectly because Bluebeard nodded and sent them on their way.

Once in the woods, they ran like jackrabbits.

"Don't look back!" said Jack.

"Up, up, up!" said Tylo, clambering up the elms.

For once, Jack felt that the elf would not ditch him. For better or worse, they were stuck in this adventure together.

"Keep heading into the thick," he said. "Ain't gonna be long before Bluebeard sees he killed Scalper, not me."

Tylo stooped on a bough, tossing Jack's bone knife from hand to hand. "With all the elf pelts on Scalper's belt, getting a slit throat could not have happened to a better og. Yes?"

Jack did not answer but decided to let the elf keep his bone knife.

* * * * *

From the war journal of General Ardus Camlann.

"Of all the Ogre warriors I have faced in battle, none are more dangerous – or capable – than Ka Bur. We faced off in combat when he was a new lieutenant at the battle of Fort Delden during the early campaigns along the Timberock. He nearly bested me with his lightning fast saber. He has a passion for the fight –treats it like an art – and strikes like an entitled viper. I've heard in civilian life, he is regarded an expert sculptor, well versed in complicated poetry, and a charmed "ladies man". Yet, I only see a warrior with the blue-tattooed jawline who seemingly butchers for sport. In the times we've crossed paths since Timberock, Ka Bur has risen in rank and talent, is a terrible challenge on the field and he always welcomes the fight. I wish more of my men had half his confidence – myself included."

Chapter 5

CAT NIPS

Night turned to morning. Dangerously worn out, Jack leaned against an elm, huffing and puffing.

"Jack Giant Killer moves fast for a lunkhead," said Tylo, perched above. "Why stop?"

"If the ogres were gonna catch us, they would've by now," said Jack. He rubbed the knot on the back of his head. A string of elf scalps still clung to his ogre armor. Repulsed, Jack wiggled out of Scalper's wear, down to the leggings and boots, keeping only his crossbow.

He was grateful to be alive.

A strange gust shook the leaves. This was no summer breeze. It carried a lulling chill. Tylo must have felt it too, because he became un-elfishly still.

An eerie twang of harp music passed through the copse of elms. It was a tune Jack recognized; one he had expected never to hear again. Lell, the Dark Spirit, passed through the trees like a ghost. She was a tall and thin lady, with a black gown and a veil that covered her from head-to-foot.

"Hello, Lady," said Jack cautiously.

Lell did not answer. She plucked two apples from the branch of a black tree. Their golden skins gleamed, even in the shadows. Then the apples fell from her grip and split open. A dark red stream of blood seeped from their seeds and puddled at Jack's feet.

"Yer warning me, ain't yeh?" he said. "Like before."

The tree revealed a third apple which Lell took between her fingers. It was larger and brighter. Jack felt a surge of dread. He knew if that last apple dropped, all that was worth living for would die with it. He ran to catch it but his body felt heavy as lead. Screams from all sides came, of wraiths, ogre warriors, dead elves, and the Fae. The forest enveloped him in a swath of frost. Jack could not see. He could not breathe. Lell vanished with the mist.

"Brrr!" said Tylo, giving him a shake. "Best get off the ground and stretch your lunk arms and legs. There be chills here not of summer. It's near snow-white cold."

"Snow white?" said Jack, his eyes still shut as he regained his senses. "What made yeh say that?"

"I do not know. Never have I seen snow unless it be capping far off hills."

Jack looked up, his head smarting as if he'd eaten too much ice. There was no blood river, no apple, no lady. "We the only ones here?"

Tylo nodded innocently. "Just you and me and the wind."

Whatever spirit had just visited, the elf was not aware of it. Tylo stretched up on his tip toes and watched the woods. Jack took in how small he was, yet as fearless as an eight-foot giant.

"Yeh might've just run back to the Learning Twigs and left me to rot," said Jack. "But yeh didn't. That's something I never thought an elf'd do."

Tylo crawled over a fallen log, leaning his head on his hands like a romantic goon. "You want to rub noses?"

"I'm trying to thank yeh."

Tylo thumped his chest. "Giant Killer would do same for best Learning Twig?"

Jack had to think about that. "Reckon so."

Tylo tapped Jack's weapon. "So this shooter be as good as my twig bow?"

"By far."

"And be you a fine shot?"

"Better than fine, I reckon."

"Jack Giant Killer does not miss?"

"Usually not."

"Then you be almost as good as me."

If Tylo wanted a challenge, Jack saw no harm in putting the little big mouth in his place.

"Line up yer mark," said Jack.

"We can shoot from up this tree," said Tylo as he scrambled up the elm and wriggled his elfin twig bow off his shoulder.

Jack clambered up the trunk, settling beside him. The elf pointed to a cluster of acorns dangling from an oak sixty paces out.

"Acorns," said Tylo.

"I see em," said Jack.

Tylo leaned out and pulled his bow, letting the bolt fly. PWING! The swift dart struck the cluster, rattling it like a dancing peacock.

"Hee-Yo!" said Tylo, handing Jack the bow and a new dart.

"Yeh want me to shoot with yers?"

"Too easy for you to miss?" said Tylo.

"Give it," said Jack. The elf bow was toy-sized in his hands but Redvere had versed him in all manner of weapons at the Orchard; longbows, pistols, muskets, and blow-darts. Jack knew how to manipulate this one.

"Let's not make it too easy," he said. He lay sideways across the branch. With a smirk, Jack fired the dart. FWOP! The acorn cluster was torn free and fell from the branch.

Jack flexed his shooting arm. "Who's the best?"

Before Tylo could answer, a forest man's loud yell echoed through the trees.

"Ouch! Who in Green Mother's fury shot that knot of acorns at my head?"

Tylo retrieved his bow and scrambled up the tree. "You be best, Giant Killer."

"Yeh swindler!" Jack warily loaded his crossbow.

A broad bearded man with a tight-fitting ox hide helmet and leather armor, rode into the thicket on a brown steed. He was armed with a musket. His armband was colored two shades of blue for sky and lake, divided by a stripe of purple. He was a guardsman of Havensbend, the most prosperous region of the south forestlands.

"If you be not ogre," said the man, "Speak now or prepare to feel the blast of my gun."

"I ain't no ogre," said Jack, who jumped down from the tree and lowered his crossbow.

The rider lowered his musket. "Who are you, boy?

"Jack Spriggins."

"You alone?"

"Nope." Jack indicated Tylo in the upper branches. "Got an elf with me."

The rider looked again at Jack. "Why are you wearing ogre leggings?"

It was a fair question.

"Got myself captured by a troop yesterday. They hauled me to Krilltown. It was all burnt out. I would've been a goner too til this elf made a trade for me."

"A trade?" said the rider.

"Long story," said Jack, tugging at his Desertland pants. "But I got the better end of the deal."

"We heard Krilltown was destroyed," said the man. "Word was brought to our troop. I serve the Count of Havensbend."

"Count Corrobis," said Jack. "I've heard of him."

He gestured for Tylo to climb down. The elf slinked down the elm, keeping his distance from the plodding horse.

The man extended an arm. "I'm Brion Bellows of Arborville, former blacksmith now Guardsman to the Count. The ogre intrusion caught us off-guard. They weren't supposed to get this far south."

"They done it with ships," said Jack.

"That's ambitious for desert-kind," said Bellows. "How many ships do they have?"

"I saw only one at anchor."

"Were there other survivors?"

Jack shook his head. "None I could see."

Tylo finally jumped down and pivoted around Brion Bellows, sniffing, imitating, and puffing his cheeks to see if could make them as wide. "Whiskery be a curious trait of many lunkheads."

Bellows pointed. "You're not the first elf we've come across today, little scrapper."

"We?" said Jack.

"I'm just the advance. Count Corrobis and a dozen more riders are half a league out."

It was a thrill just hearing that name: Count Corrobis was a recounted hero of the war.

Jack gushed. "Heard that he rescued the old Count's daughter from being kidnapped by cutthroats and beat them away single-handedly. He also kept a passel of ogre soldiers from taking Millerstown with just a pet cat by his side. And, of course, how he saved General Camlann's company from ambush in the Swamplands."

"With just his cat," added Bellows.

"*That* Count Corrobis?"

"The very same."

Tylo nudged Bellows proudly as he nodded towards Jack. "This be Giant Killer Spriggins. Even the ogs know about him."

"Yes, I know of Master Spriggins too," said Bellows. "I saw yeh once in Rivercross. Even grabbed a mug of bean brew at your mother's inn. I'm sure Count Corrobis would want to be meet the famous chap who toppled Giantdom, hero to hero."

The elf leapt onto Jack's shoulders. "And Count Cory-bis will get the honor of meeting Tylo of the Learning Twigs. That be me. Hero to hero to hero."

Jack swatted him off.

Bellows turned the reins of his horse. "Then stay put, they're coming."

An earth-shaking rumble shook the wilderness. Tylo scampered back to Jack's shoulders. "H-h-hoofs!" said Tylo. "Elfkind gets jittery at big hoofer stomps!"

Sun rays spread on the trail, bathing it with golden beams. Into the light rode an eighteen-year-old man on a chestnut steed, with a dozen armed troops astride magnificent stallions. The riders surrounded them as Bellows raised a hand in greeting. The horses filled the air with steam from their nostrils as they stamped and huffed from a hard ride.

Jack was impressed by their banners and bright colors. The men were fit like champions but none were as impressive as their leader, Count Corrobis.

With a head of thick, wavy blonde hair and cleft chin that framed a perfectly molded nose, Corrobis seemed to have been blessed by Shaina the Light Spirit. His sky-blue eyes dazzled in competition with a mouth of straight white teeth and unblemished skin (unlike Jack's). His leather breastplate and tailor-cut breeches fit snugly against his form. Statuesque in the saddle, Corrobis wore unusually high boots of an old-style that ran up to the thigh.

The most fascinating feature of the Count, however, *was his cat.*

The sleek white tabby was puzzled with patches of brown and black and a long, curling tail. It rested casually on the Count's shoulders, and with wide amber eyes, examined Jack and Tylo as it licked its paws nonchalantly. It seemed to possess more intelligence than a regular farm cat. Perhaps even more than a regular farmer.

One of the riders spoke out. "Bellows, you've scrounged up another elf? And who's that?"

Bellows replied. "An unexpected hero, Segamor. This is Jack Spriggins."

The men turned with curiosity, many nodding their heads.

"He wears interesting attire for a giant killer," said Segamor.

The cat rose and crossed over Corrobis' shoulders, nudging and purring into his ear. The Count looked intrigued.

Tylo parodied the cat by crossing Jack's shoulder and clicking in elf-speak, with a good measure of disgust. "There be something strange about the cat and his count."

Jack guessed the elf did not like cats any more than he did horses.

"Your name is well known, Jack," said the Count, his voice a tad boyish, yet pleasant.

Bellows added, "Jack escaped the ogre camp at Krilltown."

"Are the ogres still there?" said the Count.

Jack nodded. "A couple hundred, heavily armed. They're led by a maniac called Ka Bur."

"*Bluebeard*," corrected Tylo.

Jack resumed, "He was fixing to draw General Camlann south by staging raids down here."

"That's certainly of interest," said Bellows.

Tylo puffed out his chest, adding, "Bluebeard didn't expect Jack Spriggins to escape with a too-smart elf. Hee-yo!"

Jack shook Tylo off his noggin, "I'm supposed to deliver this elf to Allwise at the Orchard. The sooner the better."

Once more the tabby snuggled Corrobis, elegantly pawing round the back of his neck with a soft *"mrrr."* After a moment, the Count said, "The Orchard, yes. A wise decision."

Bellows suggested, "Allwise should learn of the ogres' plan. Word should be sent to the Rangers up north."

"I agree," said Segamor. His fellows nodded with a round of "Aye".

Corrobis watched them and awkwardly agreed. "Thank you, Bellows. That's it exactly."

The cat mewed.

"That is why we are here, Jack," added Corrobis. "We do not number two hundred, but we've taken on far more with worse odds. We'll rid the woods of these villains and keep your homes safe and free."

"Yeh gonna take on two hundred ogres?" said Jack, incredulously. "Just the bunch of yeh?"

Tylo snorted a skeptical "Phfft!".

The nobleman did not reply. He appeared confused as the cat leapt off his shoulders and strolled over to weave between Jack's legs. Perhaps Corrobis, for all his reputation and fine looks, did not have the wits to complete the picture.

Bellows spoke up. "We're to rendezvous with Bors Celot, Chancellor of the Horse Province."

Jack felt reassured. "I know his son, Redvere Celot, from the Orchard School."

"Then they definitely should learn what you know," said Bellows, dismounting. "You can take Smoke. He's a good steed."

Segamor dismounted. "Since you're going to the Orchard. We have a favor to ask."

"What favor?" said Jack.

The man gently unfurled a blanket on the ground. A black-haired elf, bloodied, injured and wheezing, lay inside. The creature was bruised with twisted limbs. Jack was speechless. The horses paced nervously hearing the moans of the little victim. Even the cat drew back at the pitiful sight.

Tylo scurried up for a closer look. "He be a groundie."

"None of us speak his language, of course," said Segamor.

The injured ground elf tried to speak, "*Ebba siik ebba ebba koolt.* (cheek click) *siik.*"

Jack did not understand him but Tylo did.

"His name be Mysslo," the Learning Twig translated. "He be a full year older than me. His tribe was the Claytoes. They be rooters and buriers."

"What got him so beat up?" said Jack.

"Ogres," said Segamor. "He probably dragged himself to the road. We heard that elf tribes and Fae bands were brutally attacked so we went to investigate. Riding hard, we found the little fella at the side of the road. It's unbelievable he was still alive."

"What about the Fae?" said Jack.

Segamor rubbed a hand through his white hair. "Killed. Poisoned by the water of Lake Dream."

Jack could hardly believe it. "But weren't the Fae bowers protected?" he said. "Don't they got power over men? I thought that none could enter."

"The ogres found a way," said Bellows. "The lovely faerie lasses are dead."

"Except Snow White," Tylo whispered to Jack.

The Count's Men lowered their mournful heads.

"*Ebba— ebba,*" said Mysslo, raising his battered head, but he collapsed into the folds of the blanket.

"This groundie is the last of his kind and will surely die out here with us," said Bellows. "Only by the healing methods of Allwise at the Orchard does Mysslo have a chance."

"Rose Red can help too," said Jack. "She's a girl student from Zan who's good at fixing folks of their ails."

"Count Corrobis?" said Bellows.

Corrobis' eyes never left his cat, which was strolling playfully at Jack's feet. It mewed.

"Yes. Do that, Jack," said the Count. "I mean, take the elf. Both elves. To the Orchard. When you go."

Any admiration Jack had felt for Count Corrobis was fading.

Mysslo was gently strapped onto Smoke's saddle. Jack downed some vittles and was outfitted with spare clothes from the Count's Men. They said their goodbyes.

"I'd give you my boots," said Corrobis, "But these belonged to my father. They're sentimental to me." He flashed a perfect smile and trotted his steed to the head of the company. "Puss?"

The cat waited until the last moment before it ditched Jack's side and bounded up his master's leg, settling in front of the saddle.

Brion Bellows sat behind Segamor on one steed. "Good luck, Master Spriggins," he said. "May we meet again."

The horses stamped by, tearing divots in the ground as they trotted to a gallop. Only after their hooves faded did Tylo release his grip on Jack's leg.

"So that was plucky Count Cory-bis?" he said.

"What of it?"

The tawny-headed elf climbed one of the taller oaks. "He be dashing to look at, but when it comes to thoughts, puss wears the boots."

Jack stroked Smoke's black mane. "Yeh best climb on the horse here. We'll get the ground elf to the Orchard more quickly."

Mysslo gave a tortured cough from beneath the blanket.

"Elfkind do not ride on big hoofers," said Tylo. "And a groundie be not *a real elf*, like we tree-climbers. No big loss. Hee-yo."

It was the last thing Jack had expected to hear.

* * * * *

From "Mistress Muffet's Web Spinner", a newspaper column in the *Daily Coastland Gazette*.

"Devoted readers, while it is not my usual practice to gossip about commoners from the socially backwards backwoods, an exception must be made for the gallant vision of manhood that is Count Corrobis. While it may be tempting to believe such a specimen yields from our own coastal cities or is even a lost Baron of Thunderer wealth, this handsome, golden-haired hero actually comes from much humbler origins. Straight out of the wood-chopping, bear-hunting, bug-bitten wilderness, if you will.

Corrobis was born the third son of a simple working-class miller, who ground wheat into plain flour in a region of the Great Forest known as Sunvale. Yes, Sunvale. Not even the richer, closer-to-civilized Havensbend. As basic as basic can be. It seems when the father died, he willed his shabby mill and its entire works to the two older brothers, leaving the youngest, 'Cory', with nothing except a pair of old tan boots and the family cat. How, you might ask, did such a majestic figure rise to greatness from a dour inheritance?

I credit natural gifts from the Eight Spirits and tremendous luck. Corrobis caught the eye of Havenbend's rich heiress, Ethyline, early in his adventures and she married him before other eligible (and, to be frank, younger) maidens had the chance. This gave the famed head-turner stature and funds to build his Count's Men, who provided so much protection during the savage Forestland wars. One would think Corrobis Miller's head would have swelled, but it always remained level, demonstrated in large part by the ever-present pet cat on his shoulder; a reminder of his shockingly modest beginnings. Such a-mew-sing inspiration for one who inspired so many female hearts to beat faster."

Chapter **6**

ROSE RED'S PATIENTS

The open gates of the Orchard had never looked as welcoming as when Jack entered astride Smoke, the horse lent by Brion Bellows. Woozy from exhaustion and the steady throb of pain on the back of his head, Jack slumped in his saddle. Days of tree climbing and elf tribes; enemy soldiers and wraiths; spirit visits *and Tylo,* had taken their toll.

Jack did not view Allwise through his bleary vision, but the old man's assured, well-known voice said, "Take Spriggins to the infirmary. I'll tend the elflings."

Jack was tugged off the saddle and carried to a snug cot under a tent of stretched canvas. Comforting sounds and scents swirled about. Cold cloths and pungent balms were applied on his skull and neck. He sighed and stretched out his legs, grateful to be back among friends.

Then he drifted off.

"Hello Jack? Can you focus your eyes?" Rose Red's calm, measured tone brought him back.

She was peering down at him, her dark skin the shade of cacao, her black curly hair woven with neat braids. He saw that her large, brown eyes were absorbing as much of his condition as could be judged. Dressed in a gray work coat with rolled-up sleeves over a shirtwaist and overalls, there was no other girl like her. Not because she was the only one at the Orchard school or because of her dark skin, but because she had smarts and a bedside manner that made anyone feel cared for.

"Hey there, Rose," said Jack mildly.

"The lump on the back of your head went down," she said, rubbing it. "It wasn't a concussion, thank goodness, or I would've been forced to keep you awake with buckets of icy water. That wouldn't have been easy considering how ornery you get."

Jack raised himself up on his elbows. A fresh school uniform (shirt, vest, and breeches) had been laid out beside him. Rose Red stood up a privacy screen beside his cot.

"Get yourself out of those filthy clothes," she said.

Jack shimmied into the fresh duds.

A light breeze shimmied through the open sides of the pavilion, carrying with it the smell of summer blossoms and timbre of wind chimes. The large infirmary tent was elevated over a floor of pine boards. It held a surgery table, medical supplies, and many cots that were regularly occupied by soldiers returning injured from the warfront.

As much as he wished to move about, Rose Red placed another damp cloth on Jack's forehead, easing him back down on the cot.

"That was some entrance you made," she said. "Slouched over that huge horse in borrowed clothes with a pair of elves. We hardly recognized you."

"Where are the blarn elves?" said Jack.

"The beaten one is resting down in the root cellar," she said. "Since he's a ground elf, Allwise thought he might respond better to medicine there."

"He's called Mysslo," said Jack. "Think he'll get better?"

"If you asked me last night, I would've said 'no'," said Rose Red. "His bruised bones and injuries are severe but he shows a will to survive. Allwise is treating him with powerful manna-root herbs."

Jack hesitated asking about *the tree elf.* "What about—?"

"Hee-Yo!" crowed Tylo from somewhere out in the orchard.

Rose Red chuckled. "Tylo? Oh, he's in fine fettle."

There was a sound of whooping and hollering outside.

"Chee!" said Jack. "Is there a stampede chasing after him?"

He rose from his cot and then staggered out to the main lawn. Tylo was racing around the pear grove swinging a ring of keys. Half of the student body, probably locked out of their rooms, were chasing him like hounds after a fox.

"Little rabble-rouser," said Jack. "The first-year boys are just encouraging him."

Rose Red stepped beside him. "He's the only elf they've seen up close."

"That's one too many."

"Come now, Jack. Back inside with you," said Rose Red. "Rest a bit longer."

"With all this ruckus?"

Jack spotted a pair of soldiers playing cards on their cots. One had lost a leg, the other had a bandage wrapped round his head. Next to them was a bow and quiver of arrows.

"Can I borrow these?" said Jack.

The one-legged soldier laughed. "To see the famous aim of young Jack Spriggins? Yeh bet!" He gladly handed them over.

Jack nodded thanks and ducked under the pavilion flap. He grabbed a coil of beanstalk vines from a supply chest.

Rose Red stayed on his heels. "Whatever you're up to, Jack, I don't have room for any more patients."

"I ain't gonna shoot the runt," said Jack.

"You should learn to respect your superiors, Know-It-All," said Rose Red, sighing.

Jack smirked. "Yeah, yeah, Smarty. Yeh only got half a month on me."

"And about eight years of schooling," added Rose. "Y'know, that head wound may be worse than I thought."

Jack strung the arrow, aimed and fired the bow.

The arrow flew across the yard with a streaming tail of vine, until it pierced the trunk of a pear tree. Jack drew in the slack and waited.

Rose Red shaded her eyes from the midday glare. Jack watched Tylo dodge the furious schoolboys. The elf charged from the blueberry bushes with them hot on his tail, and turned toward the pear grove.

"Here we go," said Jack.

Tylo was taunting his pursuers with the key ring, looking back, when Jack yanked the line tight. It caught Tylo's feet mid-stride and he tumbled to the ground. The first-year students delighted as they reached the little scamp. He proved much too quick to be caught in their grasp and scrambled through their legs. This was when Jack closed in, swinging a lasso. He snared the elf's tiny feet and gave another hard yank. Tylo squealed. Jack turned and hauled the elf kicking and screaming back to the tent.

"Let me go, Giant Killer!" said Tylo, clawing at the dirt with his little arms.

"Give it," said Jack.

Tylo grinned and tossed him the keyring. "Please show me how to weave twisties like this? It is a good joke for me to use on you some day."

Rose Red put a gentle hand on Jack to stop. "That's enough. Don't hurt him."

"He ain't hurt," said Jack. "I've seen this runt dive over a ball of fire and go back for more."

"I did, I did!" said Tylo. "Tylo be the best."

The first-year students had clustered together, panting and wide-eyed.

Jack shook the ring of keys. "I don't care which one of yeh tenderfoots lost these. Y'all should run legs in stable-muck with yer boots tied together. It's downright embarrassing."

The chaps kept huffing with their arms akimbo, all except Frog, a bright-eyed student who never seemed to run out of air.

"I swear I was just about the catch the tree elf myself," said Frog, his straggly bangs drooping in his face."

"Sure yeh was," said Jack.

Frog was an eleven-year-old Crokee bogtrotter from the Swamplands. He got the nickname because he could hold his breath in the Orchard pond longer than anyone, including Jack. He swam so well that the boys teased he had webbed feet. (It was not true.)

Jack tossed Frog the key ring. "Don't give these up again."

"Naw, we won't, Jack," said the boys, overlapping in hero worship. They ran off towards the main house tossing the keys between them.

"K-keys," Tylo sounded out, unweaving his legs from the strands. "That be what those janglies be called? What do they do?"

Rose Red helped untangle him. "They lock and unlock our doors."

"Hmm," said Tylo. "I was sure they be little chimes."

The breeze stiffened. Broken shadows from an approaching summer rainstorm carried across the yard. Above the towering stone spire in the center of the garden, a rainbow had formed.

Tylo put his nose to the ground and clapped. "Rain will bring Tylo's favorite meal – snails!"

The light patter of raindrops began to fall. He lifted his reed pipes to his lips and played a strange melody.

"Drop drip, take a sip,
Quickly while you can.
Green Mother's tears come sweet and clear,
And smile where they land."
Rat-a-tat, what was that,
A drink where wormies squirm?
Hee-yo, the snails come,
Crawling on the ferns!

Rose Red complimented him. "Your grasp of man's speech is remarkable, Tylo. I don't know much about the Green Mother Spirit but I do love rain. You're quite the song-spinner."

"Spin, sing, spin." Tylo sidled up close to her. "I will spin another song about your beautiful dark skin. Why do not all lunkheads look like you, pretty girl?"

"They do in Zan where I was born," she said, unruffled by the flattery. "If someone like Jack were to go there, he'd stick out as much as I do here."

Tylo cooed. "Will you go back to Zan?"

"No," said Rose Red. "The Orchard is my home."

She removed a pocket watch from her coat and, noting the time, proceeded to measure out medicine from a brown glass vial onto a spoon.

"Aw, bunk," groaned one of the wounded soldiers, recognizing the bitter smell of the elixir. "Time for another dose already?"

"Sorry to interrupt your cards," said Rose Red.

"Obliged, ma'am," said the one-legged soldier. "But I got a question. What's an elf doing here among regular folk?"

His bandaged companion grumbled. "Imps! They ought to be flushed out of—"

He would have finished but Rose Red stuck the medicine in his mouth. She shot him a look that put an end to his gripe.

Jack wanted to agree with the soldier. He ducked inside and punched his pillow, trying to get comfortable on the cot. The fact that the elf had saved his life was probably causing his head to ache even more than the ogre club had.

The tent flap opened and Humfrey, a stocky, bald little man, strut in with a basket of fruits and vegetables. He was an odd genius who tended the gardens and crops. He flashed blue eyes and a good-natured smile as he emptied the basket on Rose Red's medical desk.

"Rooty-red-ruddya-rooties-ripe-reds," said Humphrey, in his unique gibberish.

Humfrey only grew crops one color at a time. This crop were all luscious shades of red.

"Red-red-red-must-be-ready-red," he said.

"Let's see," said Rose, sorting through them. "Summer cherries, beet roots, red leaf lettuce, pomegranates, rhubarb, radish, cranberries, and red cabbage. A bountiful harvest."

Lastly, Humfrey presented her with a large tasty-looking strawberry.

"Thank you," she said, biting into the fruit.

Tylo could not stop staring at the peculiar fellow. Jack was ready to kick the elf if he poked fun at the gardener's expense.

"Mister Humfrey," said Tylo slowly, straightening like a small gentleman. "I am happy for you to meet me. I be Tylo." He held out a palm of friendship. The two were close in height except Humfrey more than doubled Tylo's weight.

"Tylee-lolo-loty-lo," said Humfrey. He slapped his chubby hand against Tylo's and they shook for nearly a minute.

"The red seedlings give you a sturdy grip," said Tylo.

Humfrey tottered out of the tent with a satisfied air, dropping stray red lettuce leaves in a trail behind him.

Tylo gestured with a bow. "That be the finest lunkhead an elf ever did meet." He lifted one of the fallen red leafs and nibbled on it. "It needs a red bug or two."

Jack at-eased. "Yeh didn't try to play tricks on him like yeh always do to me."

"You be not best lunk," said Tylo. "Just Tylo's best lunk friend."

"I sure ain't," said Jack.

"Bunk, if you not be, Giant Killer." Tylo flipped on to his hands and arm-walked on the table past Humfrey's pile of roots. "We fire-dance together, we fox-smarted ogres together, and we hear evil hoods when they go—"

"Don't say it!" said Jack.

Tylo crowed, "ACHIX-SKRIIT-OTAAK-ACTIS!"

Ravens cawed outside and horses neighed from the stables; the hounds bayed and the tent flapped with a sudden gust. Rose Red covered her ears, the wounded soldiers groaned. One even vomited. Jack felt the knot at the back of his head throb stronger as the wraith curse passed over all.

"I'm gonna throttle yer scraggy neck, elf!" he said.

He did not have to. Allwise and Redvere entered the sick bay tent – the first aged and crabby, the second twenty-years-old, good-looking and dependable. The old man's eyes fell upon Tylo like a branding iron on a spring calf.

"That will be the last time vulgar *palagot* is spoken here," said Allwise. He had a rolling timbre of speech that could make anyone, man or elf, tremble without raising his voice.

Tylo flipped to an upright-seated position and shrank beneath the sage's stare. Jack knew what that felt like. To the casual observer, Allwise's large belly, dirty smock, and gray-whiskered jowls suggested someone much less intimidating.

The elf cocked his head in suspicion. "Be you the sharp Old Eyes that the elders of my tribe talk of?"

Allwise's silverish eyes narrowed. "Be you the Learning Twigs' finest, sent to train and help advance relations between our races?"

Tylo was content. "You be as wise-worded as your name."

"Names and words, I have many," said Allwise.

Redvere rubbed his temples. "What horrible word did you just use? Hearing it made me near sick."

"It be a man-word, Master Tall-n-Dark," said Tylo. "Your ears make it badder than it has to be."

Allwise raised his brow. "The elf's basically correct. *Palagot* is ancient and those who assigned it meaning did so to evoke chaos and hatred. Speaking it carelessly is ignorance."

Tylo let out a yip. "It be a terrible good trick and Tylo be best trickster in the woods! I will use it as a game."

Allwise interrupted him in offhanded, crisp elfspeak:

"I know many phrases and sounds of the goblin that make elflings cower with dread, Tylo, and will not delay to utter them if that ugly curse ever rolls off your tongue again."

Tylo eyes grew wide. He said no more.

Allwise acknowledged Jack with his usual down-to-business manner. "Spriggins, I'd like to know where he heard that curse. Was it the desert lords you encountered?"

"The ones that used it were worse than ogres," said Jack.

"Hoodies," said Tylo.

"Let us adjourn in private, halfgrowns," said Allwise. "There are many topics we need to speak of. Come along and bring Tylo."

Rose Red blocked their way out of the tent. "No," she said.

Genuine affection softened Allwise's tone. "Why not, my dear?"

"Jack has a huge bump on the back of his head. He needs to be cared for."

Allwise nodded. "How about if I tend to him with a healing balm of wixleaf and burba oil? That should help."

Rose Red eased her stance. "Fine. You taught me such things, after all. But then he must rest."

"Agreed," said Allwise, taking a whiff as he passed Jack. "I'll have him bathe as well. A few days in the woods and the backwoods-pickpocket stench returns."

The old man moved out to the lawn.

Rose Red whispered to Jack. "He missed you."

"He missed making jibes at me," said Jack, who gave Tylo a helpful nudge through the flap.

The three youths walked behind Allwise on the garden path. The Orchard was open and ample, a sharp contrast with the deep woods. They passed the main school buildings, then the towering stone spire and flower gardens. A purple-breasted hummingbird flew by as they approached a gardening house made of paned glass.

Jack caught up to Allwise. "If yeh think yer gonna rub rotten glop on my head, think again."

Allwise exhaled in irritation. "I am not about to lie to my Rose Red." He looked back over his shoulder. "She *has* become somewhat commanding of late, though, don't you think? I wonder if that happens to all fifteen-year-old girls? I really don't know."

Redvere laughed. "All fifteen-year-old girls who grow up *here*, perhaps. You know we'd be lost without her."

"True," said Allwise. "She's given us all her skill and devotion since she toddled through the gates, hanging on to Ootan's hand. It was fatherly love at first sight, for me."

Tylo sprang forth with leaping bounds then clambered on top of Redvere's shoulders.

"What be red about Rose Red?" he said. "She be lovely but that is not a shade my eyes see on her."

Allwise smiled. "I named her that myself. Her Zan name is Korari Mwenje Gamu, which translates to 'Gleam of Ruby'. We don't have gems like that here but we *do* have hearty red roses, which capture her brilliance perfectly." He plucked a red primrose from beside the path. "See?"

"I do see," said Tylo. "But how came she to be your flower to tend? Did her people have a Fire Dance?"

Redvere chuckled. Jack grimaced.

"It's a sad tale, Tylo, but one you should hear," said Allwise. "I visited the country of Zan as a young adventurer sailing the Sunrise Sea. There I befriended Rose's grandmother, whose family ruled the jungles much like elder elves do your tribes."

"What be 'jun-gles'?" said Tylo.

"Woods," said Redvere, helpfully. "Only hotter and wetter with less wolves and more snakes."

Allwise resumed. "When I settled here many years later, I learned that Rose's parents had been overthrown and murdered by usurpers. Their loyal guard, Ootan, rescued the baby princess and brought her to me because he knew I'd protect her. So, you see, young elf, Rose was an outsider who became a vital part of our family. As will you."

Jack had heard Rose Red's story before. It always reminded him how much of a home the Orchard School had become to him as well.

He paused to listen to the clang of sword practice and chatter of the second-year students in combat class. The fight master, Perdur Galles, was teaching them on a cleared field near the cherry orchard about the progression of moves in their swordplay.

Combat exercise was one of Jack's favorite subjects; it certainly came easiest to him. He was tempted to run off and join them, but that would have to wait. Too many questions needed to be answered.

Humfrey waved energetically from a patch of scarlet ferns. He had company. With him was an older woman in a long green dress and wide-brimmed sun hat that rose to a tall cone. She was very plump with round, waxy cheeks that shined when she smiled.

Jack knew who she was at once. "What's Mother Goose doing here? Ain't she needed in Arborvale?"

Allwise corrected him. "*Lady Viviyann Greygeese*, as she's properly addressed, came for a day's visit at my request. There's been a challenge with one of our charges; never mind who. She gave her expert advice on how to handle it. That's all. She'll be on her way home as soon as she takes in Humfrey's handiwork."

He gave a respectful nod to the notable woman, received one in return and stepped into the greenhouse.

There was certainly more to Mother Goose's stopover but Jack knew better than to press. Puffing for air inside the heated glass conservatory, he trailed the others inside and pulled the glass door shut behind him.

* * * * *

From *"A Handbook to the Forestlands"* 2nd Edition

ZAN - A temperate eastern country across the Sunrise Sea that is known for its vast jungles, rich mineral exports, and colorful culture. Matriarchal in rule, the citizens are generally dark-skinned intellects, at once famous for superior athletics and for their advanced technology. Unfortunately, recent military revolts have closed Zan's borders, cutting them off from the global stage. Its current status is unknown.

Chapter 7

HOTHOUSE SEEDS

The heat inside the hothouse always made Jack wish he was someplace else. Watching Tylo burst into a gleeful frenzy only made that wish grow stronger.

"Hee-Yo! Yellow and pink featheries," said the elf.

He scaled the trees to chase warbling birds, skimmed the fish-life in the long salty tanks, and pressed his nose against the glass-encased insect farms. The variety of exotic life forms that Allwise grew here was impressive and the elf was obnoxiously taken with it all.

"Leafy wonders and crispy bugs to be tasted!"

The old man led the boys along rows of interesting plants to the rear of the conservatory. "So, tell. First about Krilltown. The accounts I received were varied."

"Well, it's simple and ugly," said Jack. "They burnt the village. No survivors. They had a warship anchored in the cove."

Redvere was startled. "But Desertlanders have never been seafaring."

"I reckon that's what a surprise attack looks like," said Jack. "They had about two hundred warriors fixing to strike more villages."

"And you know this because the enemy spoke freely in front of you?" said Allwise.

"Yep. None of them figured I could pick up their ogre talk."

Jack waited for Allwise to say "I told you so" but the mentor merely gestured for him to keep speaking.

"Their leader is called Ka Bur," said Jack. "He's as bad as they come. His men had elf scalps on their belts. It was a party of elf-raiders who grabbed me."

Allwise took in the news without emotion. "Their invasion has come sooner than I had calculated. Hopefully, Count Corrobis' men can stop them. They're stout defenders even when outnumbered, much like General Camlann's Rangers."

"They sure proved that. When did Count Corrobis rescue you?" said Redvere, drawing an awkward conclusion.

Jack twitched at the assumption. Tylo watched in purposeful silence, which made him even more annoying. Allwise and Redvere waited as Jack had no choice but to fess up.

"We ran across the Count's Men later," he said. "It was the elf that sprung me from the ogres. And I ain't never gonna hear the end of it."

"Bluebeard be not as smart as I am," said Tylo, chittering from a palm trunk like a preening chipmunk.

"Bluebeard?" said Allwise, "Sounds like a pirate's name."

Jack shook his head. "Ain't hearing the end of that, neither. Ka Bur *is* Bluebeard. The elf nicknamed him. Won them all over, then double-crossed the lot to save my neck."

Tylo thumped his chest. "So, you see how wisey-head I be! There be nothing Orchard lunks can teach me. Yes?"

Allwise sized Tylo up. "It is promising. Perhaps Geyo of the Learning Twigs chose correctly. I wouldn't have known by the uproar this elfling has caused since his arrival. How many days has he been here now?"

"It's been *hours*," Redvere corrected.

"Really?" said Allwise. "Then it appears *one elf* is quite enough to begin our experiment with. Redvere, would you slice me some fresh wix, please?"

The old man pulled a jug from behind a workbench and poured oil into a stone mortar. Redvere squeezed through the narrow columns of flora in search of wix.

Allwise pressed further. "So Spriggins, what other information did you steal from the ogres?"

"Nothing useful," said Jack. "Bluebeard raved on about a missing girl, who he thought was General Camlann's daughter. Ain't that a lark?"

Allwise paused.

Jack's gut (or maybe the punch he had received from Bluebeard) told him this was dicey territory. "I reckon Bluebeard wanted to kidnap her. But, of course, she ain't real. Is she?"

"She is very real," said Allwise. "A thirteen-year-old girl."

Stunned and feeling a bit cheated, Jack plopped down on a pot of slotted earthenware.

"Be careful, don't sit there," said Allwise. "I've got rare peppers from Lir growing in that pot."

Jack stayed put.

Redvere sidestepped back through a wall of plants holding a sickle and a bunch of orange leaves, which he handed Allwise. "Fronds of wixleaf, sir."

"Ah, good."

It was not easy, but Jack kept his cool. "How come I never heard about Camlann's daughter before?"

"Because it was a secret," said Allwise with a resigned sigh. "Ardus wasn't much older than you are now when he lost his head to a fair maiden. They fell in love and there was a ceremony. The child followed within nine months."

"Well, jits," said Jack. "Does the girl have a name?"

"For her safety, and yours," said Allwise. "Her identity shall remain undisclosed. The same as her whereabouts."

"Wait a blarn sec!" said Jack. "Y'mean the girl is here? At the Orchard?"

"*You will* make a decent spy someday," said Allwise, rubbing his brow. "Yes, she is here. Hidden safely from view."

"Even I don't know where," said Redvere, plopping down beside Jack.

"My peppers!" protested Allwise. The old man tossed up his hands in abandon and returned to the matter. "You boys can imagine how many enemies she has being Camlann's only child."

"What of her mother?" said Redvere.

"Perished," said Allwise, mashing the wix leaf in with the oil.

"Well, young Mistress Camlann is certainly protected here," said Redvere. "No one gets into the Orchard grounds without an invite. Our walls are booby-trapped with shooting darts, poisonous ooze, bone-crunching snares—"

"I climbed over them when I was barely thirteen," said Jack, cracking his knuckles. "I'm betting Bluebeard could too. Seeing how he's got this girl in his sights and Krilltown is so close."

Allwise finished the thought. "Then it will not be long before the ogres connect the dots and are banging at our gate. We are not the safest place for her after all."

"Where else can she go?" said Redvere.

"I had considered Viviyann Greygeese's Orphanage in Arborvale," said Allwise.

"Mother Goose?" Redvere laughed. "Is that why *you*, the last word on reason and science, consorted with one of the three witches today?"

"Well, Viv is the *good one*, after all," said Allwise with a shrug. "But she herself convinced me that sending the girl to the Dwarf Domain is a wiser option."

"Dwarfs!" said Jack.

Redvere chimed in. "With respect, sir, is that a joke? Dwarf clans shut their borders long before the war. Even if they hadn't, their mines are north of the battle front. Nobody can reach them."

The old man gave a level stare. "There are always routes, Redvere."

"But dwarfs ain't exactly friendly," said Jack. "Especially to men."

"Sheltering *this* girl will be of particular interest to them," said Allwise. "And I may be persuaded to offer up the Deed of Dynadin as further incentive."

Redvere spoke tentatively. "If that deed is even genuine, it would end the dispute that alienated the dwarfs in the first place."

"Oh, it is genuine, seal and all," said Allwise. "But revealing it will outrage the land barons of Breymen. The Forest Army needs their continued alliance. I must sort out the politics before making a final decision."

"And until then?" said Redvere.

"We keep the matter between ourselves," said Allwise, looking up at the elf. "Not one peep."

Tylo lowered himself down from a curly vine and gestured that his lips were locked.

"Moving on to other topics." Allwise scraped a gray paste from the mortar on to a strip of cloth.

"I told yeh, I don't want any mediciny stuff on me," said Jack.

"Nonsense," said Allwise. He tossed the wrapped balm at the boys. Jack ducked but Redvere caught it.

"We promised Rose Red," said Redvere, shaking the balm in his hand.

Jack tried to dive clear. Redvere, being taller, stronger, and an expert marksman, pitched the glop smack on to Jack's knotted head.

"Jits," said Jack, rubbing the gunk in his hair. "Lucky shot."

"I catch you with that move every time," said Redvere.

"Hee-Yo!" said Tylo, rattling the panes of the hothouse. "Master Tall-n-Dark, let us grab more muck and hurl it at Giant Killer Jack."

"Enough horseplay," said Allwise. "Now, kindly share where Tylo learned that loathsome *palagot* curse?"

"It be spit out by hoodies with a big pet snake," said Tylo.

Allwise tilted his spectacles off his nose and rubbed his eyes. "Let me guess. They called themselves something like the 'Commonwealth of Wraiths'?"

"Wraiths it was," said Jack. "How'd yeh know?"

Allwise poured a flask of water into the mortar, calmly cleaning it. "This entire war was likely prompted by their deeds. Tell me, how many were there?"

"Six," said Jack. "Plus, the snake."

Allwise shook his head. "Well, it's anyone's guess who he has inducted this time."

"Who do you mean?" said Redvere.

"Their leader; a purveyor of lawlessness whom I thought I had rid the Great Forest of decades ago." Allwise glanced at Jack. "Did they see you or Tylo?"

"Naw," said Jack. "We'd probably be dead if they did."

"You're right, they would have killed you without hesitation."

"What sort of people are the wraiths?" said Redvere, "Ogres?"

"Not necessarily," said Allwise. "Ogres may be among them, or forest men, elves, dwarfs; whoever he can recruit to stir up hell. Believe me when I say, wraiths are effective despite having a small inner circle. Their leader concocts elaborate schemes and he has a long reach."

"It sounds almost personal to you," said Redvere.

Jack thought so too.

"Any threat to order in the Great Forest is personal," said Allwise. Placing the mortar bowl under the workbench, he looked at Redvere. "Be ready to travel to Camlann's camp at the warfront with Humfrey tonight."

"Yes sir," said Redvere. "I figured that time was coming."

Jack stood. "Can I go too?"

Allwise shook his head. "I have other plans for you and Tylo before I turn you loose on the world, my halfgrowns."

Exasperated, Jack clenched his jaw. He was not sure what Allwise meant but he knew not to argue, no matter how rotten the answer.

Redvere gently nudged Jack with his elbow. "Your turn will come."

"Yeah sure. When the last musket's been fired," said Jack.

"Your word is sarcasm," said Allwise, who shot him a smug glance. "My word is final. Show yourselves out. Miss Linnie will handle Tylo's accommodations. See you all at dinner."

Jack huffed towards the door.

"Hey Jack," said Redvere, catching up to him. "Allwise treats you with more regard than you realize."

"Yeh kidding?" said Jack. "He treats me like a thief he took pity on. Always has. Always will."

"If that were true, do you think he would've sent you to the Learning Twigs?"

"For what? To babysit that obnoxious elf?"

"You did good. Really good. And admit it, so did the elf."

"I ain't admitting that. Elves are a waste of the air they breathe."

"Just be patient." Redvere slid the door open and left.

The humidity outside seemed much cooler after leaving the hothouse. Tylo had taken off and disappeared into the pear grove.

Jack brushed his hands together. "My job with the elf is done."

He looked up. The ancient stone spire jutted invitingly to the sky. Jack climbed the ladder to the platform on top, where he often fled to sort out his troubles. It had a full view of the Orchard campus and, at night, a clear view of the stars. Now, he crossed his legs and leaned his head on his hands, watching the students continue their combat practice near the cherry orchard.

It made Jack wonder. "My hero, General Ardus Camlann, has a thirteen-year-old daughter nobody knew about. She's here, right under our noses. Why keep her a secret? Shouldn't she be in school like Rose Red?" This raised other questions. "Does Rose Red know about her? Probably. Mrs. Linnie too. Seems everyone did except me. How can they think I'm gonna let that stand?"

The sweaty combat students finished with practice and were plodding along the garden path under the spire. They passed Allwise and Redvere who stopped beside the tower, continuing their talk. Jack scrambled onto his belly to eavesdrop on all they said.

"Jack's fully capable to accompany me," said Redvere. "Look how well he handled being captured. We now have valuable intelligence about the ogre maneuvers. And, even though Jack hates elves, he delivered us Tylo *and Mysslo.*"

"I admit, his attending the Fire Dance was a bigger test than I had originally laid out. He exceeded all expectations," said Allwise. "He's grown beyond the juvenile felon he was two years ago. But, no. I need Spriggins to stay here now. His skills are suited for other missions yet to come."

"If you say so. It might do Jack good to let him know he has a purpose."

"He'll know when I do," said Allwise. "As for *yours.* The intel, supplies, and weaponry you'll transport to the General's base at Fort Delden are invaluable. For security, you are to meet a detachment of Crokee foot soldiers that awaits you at Forks. Don't tarry. Ardus needs to know all I have shared."

Redvere sounded like he was dragging his feet. "You think I'm ready to go back to the front?"

"Well, no, I don't," said Allwise. "Nobody ever is. I do know you're a fine soldier. A fine leader. And I know you will do you duty."

"Yessir," said Redvere.

Jack rolled over to his back, feeling rejected like the dirty-handed kid he was back home on Thin Creek when he would lie on the thatch roof of Ma's shack hating his no-good life.

"Why ain't I a soldier?"

The afternoon passed. Jack climbed down off the spire and showered before supper. Rose Red helped him reapply the bandage to his squeaky-clean noggin.

In the mess hall, Mrs. Linnie served roasted duck with buttery mashed taters, peas and carrots. It tasted homey, as always. The boys were seated at two long pine tables. Allwise sat among the first-years, as he often did, exchanging small talk and jokes. Tylo, thankfully, was absent. It should have felt perfect, landed in comfort, but it did not. Jack could not shake the feeling that the shadows in the corners had grown and were hissing whispers.

"You alright, Jack?" said Tymmy Mason.

"Reckon I'm fine," said Jack, with a convincing nod. He liked this bright young kid and felt protective of him and Frog, like Redvere was to him. "Just wanna get back to classes tomorrow. I've missed nearly a week."

Tymmy did not blink. "I feel that way every night."

Jack grinned. There was a sliver of comfort, after all.

After supper, he skipped out on *music time* and went upstairs to his cozy dormitory room.

Redvere was reclined on his own bunk strumming a nine-string guito – a rural viola that he plucked with his fingers. They had roomed together for the year. Tristano, a third bunkmate and crackshot from Colterton, had left for the war when he turned eighteen last winter. Seeing Redvere's gear packed in the corner, Jack felt the same gloom he had felt then.

Redvere's tune carried the mood. He sang the lyrics in a pleasant tenor.

> *"Play not on your flute or silver moon strings,*
> *Only beating drums will I hear.*
> *Pack away satin vests and three-corner hats,*
> *Deerskin and a helmet are my wear.*
> *No more will I dance, pen, or speak soft in verse,*
> *Gone are nights of courting at your door,*
> *Yet, save me one last kiss and a murmur of love,*
> *Those I'll keep in pocket evermore."*
> *(Ever-more)*

> *"Nowhere are lilies I'd pick by the stream,*
> *Traded for a sword and gun of steel.*
> *Wait not for tender thoughts once shared secretly,*
> *The push to keep my land is all I feel.*
> *Time to plan tomorrow has fallen to the past,*
> *Ask not for tears or laughter from my core.*
> *Yet, lose not the gazes of your warm, sparkling eyes,*
> *Those I'll keep in pocket evermore."*
> *(Ever-more)*

As soon as Redvere put the guito aside, he resumed packing.

Jack struggled with what to say. "Jits, I wish I was going with yeh."

"Remember to be patient, Jack."

"Hey, yeh seen my bow?"

"Yep. Right there in the cedar chest. Perdur has restored it for the umpteenth time."

He handed Jack the small walnut crossbow; restrung, polished, and reinforced.

"Thanks, Vere."

"Y'know, there are newer models, right?"

"But none as good," said Jack, crinkling one eye shut to admire the calibration of his favorite possession. "Bet I could protect the whole school armed only with this."

Redvere smiled. "Before that happens, someone's going to have to take over teaching archery. I'm counting on that person being you."

"Reckon I'm the next oldest," said Jack. "And the best aim. How can I say 'no'?"

Normally, Redvere would have accepted the challenge but now he grew serious. "While I'm gone, Jack, I need a favor from you."

"If yer gonna say, 'be nice to the elves', save it."

"Ha! Tylo and Mysslo may prefer to face ogres after a few days with you. No, what I want is for you to check in on my betrothed in Rivercross."

"Betrothed?" said Jack, with a laugh. "By the hog's bacon, no one falls for gals more than you, Vere. Who are yeh hand-and-glove with this time?"

"Why, Ganzil. The golden beauty from your mother's inn. She's different from other girls. And yes, she is real easy on the eyes. I can hardly believe she's vowed to be mine."

"Ganzil?"

Ganzil *was different*. No female turned as many heads in Rivercross, or anyplace else. Her long blonde tresses and eyes as blue as Lake Avilon were hard to resist. She'd caught Jack staring more than once, and smirked like she enjoyed the power it gave her. Jack never trusted her, nor the cold twinge of desire she brought out. He did not share this with Redvere, however.

"Sure," he said. I'll check on *yer betrothed* when I go to see Ma."

Redvere looked lovestruck.

Jack wished to change the subject. "Yeh taking Blackberry to the front?" He did not admit to loving many things, but Jack loved that horse.

Redvere wriggled into a black suede pullover with a wide hood. "I knew I was forgetting something. Blackberry is yours now."

Jack was gobsmacked. "My – mine?" He gripped Redvere with a brotherly hug. "How yeh gonna ride to the front then?"

"I'm taking Smoke, the Count's horse. I know Blackberry will be in good hands with you."

They walked out to the yard. Allwise stood with Frog and Tymmy Mason who held torches while Rose Red and Perdur Galles waited with the horses, which were bridled to a loaded wagon. Humfrey was already seated on the riding bench.

"Ja-jack-be-here-be-here-jits-bunk," said Humfrey.

Jack nodded. "Yeh watch Redvere's back, Humfrey. There's plenty of trouble in the forest. I know firsthand."

"Fir-fir-first hand."

If Allwise was sad to see his students off to the bloodshed of battle, it did not show. "These weapons and provisions are important but not as vital as the news you carry." He handed Redvere a bundle of sealed papers. "Do not delay giving these to the General."

Redvere mounted the wagon. "Yessir."

Grainhoof glanced back at the drivers and tossed her head. Smoke, the warhorse, hoofed the pavement with a ready snort.

"Easy," said Redvere, settling the steed.

Rose Red reached up and gave a handkerchief to Redvere (like the one she had given Jack). "You might reunite with your father and brother at the encampment."

He reached down and touched her cheek. "You are all as much family to me as they are."

"Always the poet, Vere," said Perdur. "Remember to keep your heels down when you shoot."

The young men clasped each other's wrists.

"No one will be as challenging as you are in the training field," said Redvere.

Perdur chuckled. "That's the idea."

Humfrey leaned toward Redvere. "Red-red-reddy-red."

"Let's get going, Humfrey."

Redvere shot them a final nod and whipped the reins with "heigh". The rattle of the wagon shook loudly going out the gate and lasted awhile before it faded into the night.

Rose Red took Jack's hand. "Do you think Redvere will miss me?" she said.

"Yeh know he will," said Jack coolly.

He broke off and strolled over the mowed lawns toward the stables.

"Why do smart girls always fall for pretty-faced boys who only see them as sisters?"

Jack passed the cherry grove. A trill of elfin reeds made him stop. Tylo lay in a hammock tied beneath the arbor, blowing lazy notes from his pipe. Mrs. Linnie had found him the perfect sleeping arrangements, far away from everyone else.

"Giant Killer, Giant Killer, lunk-lurking in the night," said the elf. "Would you like a friend to hike with whom provides a light?" He snapped his fingers and a spark flickered off the end of his thumb.

"Not unless yeh wanna spook the big horses in the stable and make 'em trample yeh," said Jack.

"Hoofers? Stable? No, not me." Tylo resumed his lonely tune.

Jack lit one of the oil lanterns in the stable. He carried it past Thundersong, Sweetbrook, Cai's Hart, Greywick and other mares and colts until he came to Blackberry's stall, the noblest steed of all.

"Miss me, friend?" said Jack. Blackberry pushed his nose through the slats to let him pat his forehead. "Redvere has gone. I'll take care of yeh now. Is that all right?"

Blackberry playfully tossed his head. Jack removed a yellow apple from a stable-side feedbag. His hand suddenly blurred. Blackberry and the other horses neighed in fright. A troubling melody of harp chords stirred in Jack's mind. The nightmare of the three apples returned. Lell, the Dark Spirit, flashed before him. The black tree. The first golden apple dropped.

"The Orchard!" said Jack, gasping. "It's on fire."

Jack fell back. Blackberry's apple rolled on the hay. He shook off the vision.

"Lell's warning. Is the Orchard in danger? Who'll save the day? Not Redvere. Not the old man. Not the elf."

Jack clutched his head. The harp music faded.

"Reckon that someone is me."

Blackberry snorted. Jack got up and pulled himself together.

"It's alright, boy, I'm only Jack Spriggins," he said. "I'm here."

* * * * *

An excerpt from *"The Great Forest— Volume Four: Southlands"* by Professor Tymothy Mason.

THE CELOTS OF HORSE PROVINCE

*By the time **Bors Celot** became Chancellor, the prairie range of the Horse Province had gained world-fame as the finest breeding ground of modern day. Its wide ranges of grass were protected in a valley surrounded by meandering foothills. The place was idyllic for the ranchers. As the Horse Province grew in prosperity, only wealthy Havensbend in the south and Breyman in the north could boast more power.*

*Chancellor Bors Celot, the most successful rancher and breeder of thoroughbred racing horses, had hopes his sons, **Gilad** and **Redvere**, would one day succeed him as leaders. Both were handsome gentleman who excelled in horsemanship; but the eldest, Gilad, was cut more in his father's robust mold, while young Redvere was a dreamer and poet who pursued another destiny beyond the ranch. He was at odds with his father from an early age.*

*Matters grew worse when Gilad returned from a racing tournament at the Festival of Hearts with a bride – the renowned singer from Arborvale, **Gwinna Wren**. Redvere was only thirteen at* the time, but fell hopelessly in love with his brother's beautiful and talented wife. To keep peace (and his sanity), Redvere renounced his inheritance at fourteen, and left the Horse Province against his father's wishes, to study at Allwise's Orchard School. The patriarch was not happy with this second-born's decision but trusted that Allwise, a friend and ally, would redirect his son home.

Within a year, the Desertland invasion of the Great Forest changed everybody's reality. In an act that firmly bonded the Horse Province with its surrounding communities, Bors raised a cavalry of prime warhorses with skilled riders to face the invaders. It was his wish that Redvere, now seventeen, would return and lead the mounted squadrons alongside Gilad. Instead, the young man chose to join Ardus Camlann's Rangers, leaving his family conflict unresolved. Some historians claim the father and son made peace on the battlefield of Codger's Bog but others dispute if Redvere was ever there. Regardless, the courage, romances, and swift longbow of Redvere Celot, Horse Whispering Ranger, have never been disputed, delivering an unforgettable champion to the lore of the Great Forest.

Chapter 8

SEARCHERS

Allwise should have known better than keeping secrets from his master thief. Yet, finding one girl on a campus full of schoolboys proved more difficult than Jack expected. He knew all the buildings and classrooms, even the private study. He knew how to get over the booby-trapped wall. He knew Allwise was no magician. Yet, Camlann's daughter stayed hid at the school like part of a vanishing act.

"She's stashed somewhere I probably pass by all the time," figured Jack. "I just need a clue where to look."

He made daily jaunts to the top of the stone spire for a clearer view of the gardens and fields, dividing them into imaginary squares in his head as he searched (advice from *Tom Tailor's Trail Guide*). Not a shed, cellar, or grain silo were left unexplored.

Jack roved the Orchard at night, scanning for hidden forts in the trees and searching the walls for any chink that might give away a secret door.

"Allwise wouldn't keep her locked up like a prisoner. She'd have to be comfortable with lots of fresh air and sunshine."

He kept a constant lookout, even gazing out the study hall windows during Allwise's select discourses.

"Spriggins," said the caustic sage from his lectern during a biology lesson. "You're daydreaming."

"No, I weren't," said Jack.

"Then kindly educate us on the contents of page eighty-seven in your *Grimm's Insect Anatomy* text."

"Pretty much the same as page eighty-six, I reckon."

"More elaboration, please."

Jack looked to Rose Red in the next chair for help but she merely shook her head with an amused smile. He vaguely recapped the boring fundamentals. "Well, it's a lot of fancy terms to dress up plain, ordinary caterpillars, yeah?"

Allwise never broke his crystal stare. "Name some of those *fancy terms.*"

"Larvy. I mean larva. Lar —"

A chipper voice squeaked in. "*Cartipel or lep-is-op-terons that cocoon in larval stages with clades that include butterflies and moths,*" said Tylo, sitting leisurely in an open windowsill.

"You do not take this class, Learning Twig," said Allwise.

"I be best in it, anyway," said Tylo. He then quoted in an uncanny imitation of Allwise. "*It is not the molting larva worms we will focus on today but the phenomena of metamorphosis they so aptly illustrate versus unnatural interference."*

Allwise was unimpressed. "Meaning what, youngster?"

Tylo shrugged. "It be man-speak, Belly-Bounce. I do not know the answer."

Jack had heard enough. "C'mon! The runt's just repeating words he heard, like a parrot."

"And what do those words mean, Spriggins?" said Allwise.

"Well, yer saying a caterpillar's change to a moth is natural. Can't be helped."

"As opposed to?"

"Change that's man-made. Finagled." Jack's eyes fell on the sketch of a dangling cocoon in his text. "Change is order in nature but a crime when it's forced."

"Correct," said Allwise. "You're as subtle as a mallet and less artful but you always learn the lessons. Don't get distracted and someday maybe you'll be teaching."

Twenty-two boys still studied at the Orchard who had yet to be drafted into war service. Jack was now in charge of Redvere's archery class. Under his watch, they all improved at shooting the crossbow, rope and climbing skills, and even tracking game with longbows. He was not always patient but when the boys showed effort, he made sure they got an encouraging nod. It was enough.

Each of the young students had unique skills:

Varlan and Barlan Wood were fourteen-year-old twins from Tarnvil. The first ran like a deer, the latter had no equal in mathematics. Tymmy Mason, a Rivercross stonecutter's son, could read at age three, write at four, and was now chronicling Great Forest history at thirteen. Manawydan Daire, a braggart with wide shoulders, was Jack's age but an inch taller. "Manaw" had the muscle but Jack had the smarts, and whenever they squared off, the match went either way. Geoff Greens was a quiet boy of fifteen from Arborvale with a knack for botany. Frog, the eleven-year-old Crokee bogtrotter, swam the Orchard lake across and back in thirty seconds, holding his breath for five minutes a stretch. Rose Red excelled at languages and all things science. She had been expertly teaching classes since the war's outbreak.

Then, there was Tylo.

The Learning Twigs' puniest now wore gray school breeches that Rose Red had hemmed, and a billowy white shirt overtop his feather collar. He still pranked, cartwheeled, and crowed so often that Jack got hoarse just yelling at him. The elfling's aim with his little bow was remarkable. "Hee-yo!" became a victory cry for every student.

The boys started taking wilder shots themselves, spurred on by Tylo who mocked Jack's snarly voice. "*Strike where yer giant's gonna yelp loudest, Rangers. Then follow me to the wolf cave. Jits! Jits! Jits!*"

Whenever the elf outshot Jack, it felt like a kick below the belt.

"Why don't you learn Tylo's moves until you can do them better?" said Rose Red one afternoon. She added, "Unless you can't?"

"Yer just baiting me."

Just the same, Jack upped his practice, flinging himself across beanstalk vines in the bamboo grove, firing his crossbow in midair, and launching bolts from ridiculous angles to hit a target. After many humiliating misses, he started notching direct hits. FWAP! SNAP! FWIP!

"Hee yo, Jack!" shouted Frog.

"Teach *us* that," said Barlan and Varlan.

"Show-off," said Manawydan.

No one applauded louder than the elf. Between blasts on his reed pipes, he cheered, "Hee-yo, Giant Killer! You be the largest Learning Twig in the Great Forest."

Jack regained control of the class by instructing elf-inspired maneuvers. Training this way was unusual but it made everybody better shots with an element of fun that was motivating.

Mysslo, the battered ground elf, began recuperating. Tylo convinced him to leave the root cellar for an hour or two each day. He seemed out-of-place, all balled up with aches, but managed a grateful smile with his few crooked teeth. A natural digger, he unearthed long irrigation trenches in the garden that would have taken the boys much longer.

"M-mo-morning, mi-Mister Jack Giant Killer," the groundling stammered in elfspeak.

Jack was civil. "Glad digging is making yeh git stronger."

The pitiful elf giggled, which grew into a coughing fit and caused him to hide his face against the ground.

"Is that laughing or is it hacking?" said Jack to Rose Red.

The dark-skinned girl had a soft spot for the ground elf. "He's upped the boys' gardening skills by showing them how to cultivate plants around the tree roots. Apparently, he's also got some tips for removing weeds with his teeth."

Jack scoffed. "Life is simpler when you plow around the stump."

It was an exceptionally hot day and she was tutoring him in *sartiryan* (ogre-ese) under the shade of a willow by the lake.

"All should feel welcome here, Jack," said Rose. "Especially a guest who works to earn his keep."

"What about the Orchard's *other* guest?"

"Who do you mean?"

"General Camlann's daughter."

Rose Red was caught off guard and was at a loss for words (which was rare).

Jack rested his arm against the tree. "Yeh know about her too."

"Let's get back to your ogre dialect," she said, changing the subject. "It almost tripped you up when you were captured last month."

"C'mon, Rose," said Jack, persisting. "Allwise and Redvere told me all about her."

"Good," she said. "Then we don't need to talk about the poor girl."

Jack was pleased with himself. Whether Rose was aware of it or not, she had just given him a new lead in his hunt. She always took precise notes during her studies, perfectly penned and numbered by page. Yet, she drew doodles in the margins. Jack had snuck a look over her shoulder and saw many elaborate sketches: birds from the greenhouse; Tylo hanging from a lamp in the mess hall; his own yellow eyes and scraggly hair; Redvere seated handsomely in the saddle; Allwise lecturing; but, most notably, an unfamiliar pair of round black eyes with girly lashes. They differed from Rose's and were always set against a backdrop of ivy. The eyes *had to belong* to Camlann's mystery daughter.

"Do yeh think I'm addle-headed, Rose?"

"No, Jack. You're very smart."

"Untrustworthy?"

"Just the opposite."

"Then tell me where she's hid."

"I can't."

"It'll stay our secret. Yeh know it will."

"There are reasons why she's been kept from you boys," said Rose.

"What makes yeh so special that Allwise let's yeh in and not us?"

"Because I'm a—" Rose hesitated. "Never mind."

"Yer a what?"

"Because I'm a 'blarn' girl, I suppose."

"Huh?"

Rose looked daggers at him. "Stop fishing, Jack Spriggins. I'm not saying any more. Subject closed. Honestly, you're as bad as Tylo."

"Tylo?" said Jack. "He's been pestering yeh about her too?"

"At every turn," she said. "Especially during *study time.*" She pointed at the pendant around her neck (a watch given to her by Allwise).

"What are yeh teaching that whooping elf, anyway? Can he even read?"

"No, he cannot," said Rose. "His eyes move too fast to settle on a page. But if I read something aloud, he keeps it in his memory forever. You've seen it yourself."

"Maybe I have."

"He's scientifically amazing. He can recite the entire *Dwarf Rules for the Melding of Mines* after hearing it a single time."

"Why does a tree elf care anything about the Dwarf Ministry?"

"For the same reason we did. It's called *learning.*"

Allwise schooled his pupils in all the odd practices of Great Forest races: elves, faeries, dwarfs, and giants (although Jack already knew plenty about the giants, having dwelt among them himself two summers ago). The *Melding of Mines* was a gathering of the dwarf clans, called whenever the miners needed to resolve conflicts. As long as the purpose for a Meld Council challenged the tenets of dwarf security, anyone could call for it.

"That's a near dozen pages long," said Jack. "And the elf knows every word by heart?"

"After hearing it *once*," said Rose, smiling. Her brown eyes widened. "I don't know if all tree elves can do it but he's remarkable. Just like someone else I know. Any guesses who?"

"I don't know," said Jack. "Tymmy Mason? Geoff Greens?"

"*You.*" said Rose Red. "The thief prodigy from Thin Creek."

Jack got flustered. "Me?"

"Sure," said Rose. "I mean, maybe you don't recite literature word-for-word like Tylo does but you can recall languages and understand elf sounds just the same."

"Don't compare me to an elf, ever!" said Jack.

"Why, be so angry? I meant it as a compliment."

"Well, it ain't taken as one," said Jack. "Makes me feel like yeh do when folks say 'she's smart *for a girl.*'"

Rose put aside her notebook. "Your hatred for elves is *that much?*"

"Uh huh."

"Then I'll never bring it up again. Unless you want me too."

"I won't. Thanks."

"You're welcome. So, how do you feel about the Fae?"

It was a strange question. "They ain't around anymore," said Jack. "Even if they were, I don't know any. Why?"

"Actually, it's not important," she said. "We can both agree to despise ogres. Let's switch our focus to learning their sartyrian language."

"Fine."

Rose's nothing-to-nobody sense made it clear she would not spill the beans anymore. The most sensible place for the next leg of Jack's search was the "girl's floor" of the main house, where no Orchard boys were allowed. Mrs. Linnie and Rose Red both had rooms up there.

"Rose not only knows the Camlann girl, she's protecting her," Jack realized. "Makes sense they'll probably be rooming together."

At dinner that evening in the mess hall, Mrs. Linnie had cooked her popular chicken pie and asparagus. Following the meal, Tylo swung about the oil globes that hung from the ceiling, singing an ode:

> *"There sits Mistress Rose Red,*
> *Many thoughts dance in her head.*
> *What are secrets, do you suppose,*
> *That can't be found within a rose?"*

The boys and Allwise delighted in singing the hokey chorus along with Mrs. Linnie. Rose Red tapped the rhythm on a spoon to hide that she was blushing. Jack groaned. As the verse repeated, he moped outside with a second slice of pie, making sure anyone who saw him would guess he was bored. In truth, Tylo's tune was just the distraction he needed.

The sun outside was setting over the treetops. Jack climbed the ivy-covered chimney to the second story balcony. He snuck through an open window and treaded on the balls of his feet down the hallway, passing Mrs. Linnie's room to the very end. Rose Red's room was locked.

Jack fished an iron pick out of his vest pocket. "Ma would give me a licking, sure as sap, for rummaging through a girl's private lodgings. But it can't be helped."

He prodded the brass keyhole, remembering the technique Allwise had taught him for picking a bolted lock. (It pointed to a crookedness in the old man's past, which Jack had always suspected). He pressed an ear to the door, made a few tender twists, and *CLICK!* The bolt was sprung. He opened the door. Streaks of orange dust leaked in from the closed shutters. None of Rose's books were there. No desk. No wardrobe. Not even a bed.

"Rose Red ain't lived in these stuffy digs for weeks."

Jack grit his teeth and backed out, shutting the door. He spied a piece of red feathery down drifting on the hallway carpet. At a glance, he knew the fluff did not come from a pillow.

He snatched it up with a scowl. "Why is it red? Tylo's feather collar!"

The elf was there first. Jack realized the quest to find Camlann's daughter was now a race. Worse, he was already a step behind. He clenched his fists. By hook or by crook, he would flush the girl out before Tylo.

Later that night, while everybody slept, Jack snuck out of his room. He padded over the star lit yard, opened a storm door and descended to the root cellars below ground, lighting a lamp before dropping in.

Mrs. Linnie's fruits and preserves were stored on the cellar shelves, along with Allwise's medicinal roots. Jack was startled to find Mysslo sleeping in one corner, until he remembered this was where the ground elf bunked. The strange little wheezer had rolled off his bedroll and slept beside it on the dirt. His filthy little fingernails curled overtop of the blanket like claws, blackened by digging in the gardens. Jack poked around a bit, looking for any clues to an antechamber but soon gave up his search. The place was too cold, too damp. A fool's errand.

"Rose Red and the girl won't be here, especially with that groundie sleeping there."

Mysslo's congested snores came to an eerie stop. The elf did not flinch but Jack felt he was awake. A reflective gleam stared out from his droopy eyes. There was no need to tarry. Without a word, Jack snuffed the lamp and shut the cellar door securely.

He harrumphed at how quickly he'd fled. His heart was even beating fast. "What's the matter with me?"

Beside the water troughs was Manawydan smoking a quirley. He saw Jack.

"Manaw? Why're yeh lurking about?"

"Yeh should talk," said Manawydan, blowing out a smoke ring. "Gonna snitch on me for puffing my own makins?" He flexed his arms to show they were bigger and could pack a wallop.

"Naw," said Jack. "Yeh wanna choke on those coffin nails, go ahead."

"Take one," said Manaw, handing another to Jack. "Rolled it m'self."

For whatever reason, Jack took the smoke. Manawydan lit a match, Jack puffed. He gagged and started coughing.

Manawydan smirked, then spoke with plenty of mustard. "Ye ain't square, are ye, Spriggins?"

"I'll clean yer plow if yeh say that again."

"Sure. Just outta practice then."

"These things taste like dung."

"Ain't a soldier in the Forest Army that don't smoke 'em," said Manaw. "It's a man's taste."

"Reckon." Jack nodded, then walked off with it lit between his lips. The moment Manawydan was out of view, he snuffed it on the ground and stuck out his tongue.

"*Blargh!*"

He scaled the ladder of the stone spire for his nightly check of the grounds. A high-pitched giggle chittered down from the top. It was Tylo. The tree elf was crouched above the ladder where the moon shaded all but his bug-eating grin.

"Great," said Jack. "I ditch a nutty hick only to run into a hickory nut."

Tylo mimed smoking the quid. "Did Sparky's flame taste bad on Giant Killer's tongue?"

"Go taunt somebody else, runt," said Jack. "Why ain't yeh sacked out on yer hammock?"

"I be too busy searching for General's daughter, just like you. I shall let you know when I find her."

"Yeh can't out-track me," said Jack.

"Snip-snap!" said Tylo. "I do not need to."

"Yeah? So, how does a highfaluting tree elf look for her then?" said Jack.

"By having her look for me."

Tylo took up his reed pipes and started to play sweet, enticing notes. They drifted on the night breeze over the yard. If there were lyrics, they would have said: "*Come out, lovely child, come out.*"

Jack played along with Tylo's game. "Music ain't a bad way to snake a lonely girl out in the open."

He pulled a spyglass from his belt and scanned the gardens. The archery ranges were in view, as well as the the beehives. Micca the hound hobbled out of his doghouse near the stables, stretching with a yawn.

Tylo paused his flute, fascinated. "Where did that folding eye-branch come from, Giant Killer?"

"This spyglass? Uh, I borrowed it from Tymmy Mason."

"I believe your lunkhead word is 'hornswoggled'."

"I'm gonna give it back."

"How does it work? Do you see like a bird does? Like a raccoon?"

Jack tossed the telescope to him. "Have a look and stop pestering me."

The elf caught it, squishing one eye as Jack had done and peered through the lens. "Ooh-ooh! Small things got so big!" The elf clutched his tawny head and looked away. "It hurts my head with its faraway-closeness."

"Quit yer hollering then. Give it back."

Tylo resumed playing the flute. Jack resumed spying.

He aimed the telescope at Allwise's hedge maze located near the east edge of the Orchard. The maze was a complex network of hedgerows designed as a puzzle for the students to hike through. Sculpted bushes fifteen-feet-tall were spread over a full acre with differing paths that led to a central garden. Topiaries of beasts, dragons, and sea critters were recut by the students yearly to keep the layout ever-changing. They played games of flag-capture, or hunted each other in team scrimmages.

Allwise had boasted, "It's as fine as any topiary found in the imperial Dragonlands."

Jack swiped the lens past the maze's boxwoods, privets and ivy. Then, he spotted an odd glimmer at the north end, just below the pines. Panning back, something fluttered in the hedgerow. Jack twisted the focus ring for a clearer view. A portion of the garden maze had a cover of scrim-lace pulled over the top. It was hard to see because the scrim was woven to look like garden shrubs but when the breeze hit it just right, the cover waved gently.

Jack slowly lowered the spyglass. Tylo was still fluting.

"Uh, I'm gonna turn in for the night," said Jack, feigning a yawn.

"You are not going to search anymore?"

"Naw. I've been over every square inch of this place. Still no secret hiding place and no girl. Lemme know how yer song works out. See yeh in the morning."

Tylo bid him, "G'night." It did not sound snarky.

Of course, Jack had no intention of going to bed. As soon as his boots hit the ground, he snuck over to the hedge maze. Confident he was alone, Jack ducked inside.

"Turn left, then right. Left at the fork to the three-way split, then follow the middle."

Jack had mastered the twisting paths as a first-year student. He knew how to get to the north bower. On the way, he passed the central garden.

"Turn left at the grizzly-shaped boxwood, go straight for a bit – wait!"

Someone had trimmed the hedgerows into unfamiliar corners.

"Jits! Those trouble-making first-years."

A rustle like hurried footsteps went by as a shadow passed behind the grizzly-shaped boxwood.

Jack grit his teeth. "Whoever it is, is gonna get themselves caught by me."

He returned to the three-path split and put an ear to the ground. He could make out soft thuds moving down one of the rows. He veered right and followed a dogleg to a diamond-shaped portal had been cut in the hedgerow. Jack did not recognize it. He stepped through the diamond and discovered he was facing a dead end. The glint of moonlight bounced off a sculpted ivy rabbit, trimmed to appear as if it was fleeing a blue juniper badger.

"Aw, spit!" He was off course.

A clucking giggle trailed by with reed notes whistling through the maze walls. The tune was a humiliating taunt.

"Blarn elf! Jits!

Once more, Jack retraced his steps.

"*Turn left, then right, pass by the archway that goes north to the pines.*"

The pines above the hedgerow. "That's where I saw the rippling scrim."

He stuck a hand in the shrubbery to feel for a door or gate. Sharp branches scratched and poked him. They were too dense to push through. The wind picked up and swayed the prickly boughs. One small section, however, did not move.

"What's behind there?"

Jack reached through the spread of ivy, bumping against a solid barrier of wood. He felt the surface and found an oblong handle in the middle, shaped like a root sprig. He smirked. With a twist, the latch released and the fake wall swung back. A cramped passage ran through the shrubs with an inviting floral scent. Jack followed it. Then stopped. His face was met by another, poised inches away.

It was a girl.

A wild, yet graceful girl. She looked about thirteen years of age with pearly white skin. Her hair was long and black with uncombed bangs that dangled on her forehead. Blush-pink cheeks framed an innocent smile. Her brown eyes, huge as coins, seemed to be wells from a spirit realm. It was impossible to look away.

"Yer the general's daughter, ain't yeh?" whispered Jack.

She smiled and touched his cheek. The girl was barely five feet tall and stood on her toes to reach him. She playfully ambled backwards into a courtyard pavilion that was covered by the scrim canopy. With fluid steps she whirled into a spin, which seemed to inspire the summer wind to blow. The hedge walls trembled and the scrim wavered. Then she paused with a welcoming gesture.

"I'm Jack Spriggins," he said, "Friend of Ardus. Yer pa."

Her eyes widened (if that were possible) and she stretched out her hand, rippling the air with her fingers in a complicated yet graceful motion. She covered her heart, then took Jack by the arm and led him out of the passageway. For a moment he felt as if they were floating and could scarcely feel his own legs. His whole body tingled. The feelings added up uneasily in his head.

"Could she be a—?"

The girl was barefoot. Her white gown draped short and sleeveless, almost a wrap, bound with a sash of primroses that sheathed a telltale wand of yew wood. The girl's lithe, nimble form seemed in tune with nature. And then, there were those bewitching eyes.

"Yer Fae," said Jack, swallowing hard.

She guided him to a wide squat oak growing in the center of the pavilion. Crouched in its boughs was a small, tawny-haired, grinning menace.

Tylo.

"Glad you made it, Giant Killer," said the elf, swiveling from a rope swing and tooting his reed pipes. "It is good to meet the last faerie of our Great Forest, is it not?"

Being bested by the elf did not sting as much as it should have. Jack was too much in awe. The faerie's supple hands cut through the air with precise elegance as she tried to communicate the signing language of the Fae.

Tylo sighed. "Hee-yo. Snow White sees much in your yellow eyes. Be you certain you have not met before?"

"Snow White?" said Jack.

The familiar name had been spoken by the wraiths' in the Briar.

"Yer *the* Snow White."

The faerie traced Jack's face with her forefinger. Her eyes brimmed with such healthy curiosity that he smiled back.

"She weaves her charms on you," said Tylo.

"And she don't on yeh?" said Jack.

Tylo shrugged, his eyes drifting from Snow White in a way Jack's could not. "Elves be not weak-kneed by the Fae in the way lunkheads be."

"I ain't got so close to one before," said Jack. "I heard the Fae bedevil menfolk and put horns on 'em."

"Menfolk. Not elf-folk," said Tylo with a puckish snicker. "We do not lose our red heads over a faerie's sweet scent like you do."

Snow White gestured again with a spin of her hands.

Jack shrugged, not understanding. "The Fae ain't talkers?"

Rose Red entered the pavilion holding a tray with a pitcher and drinking glasses. Her brows were lividly knit and she spoke with vexed timbre. "Snow talks if she wants. She is human, after all, but prefers the hand language of her kin. Now, are you happy with yourself for barging in after being told not to?"

Jack was unapologetic. "Yeh could've told me she was Fae. I'd have listened."

"I have my doubts about that, Spriggins," said Allwise, who followed Rose Red. "But here you are."

Snow White affectionately clasped Allwise's hand. He twirled her in a fatherly fashion.   Jack watched the faerie's every move. "I only want to protect her. Especially now that I know General Camlann's daughter is so *different*."

"Really Jack?" said Rose Red. "That *difference* can control ogre soldiers and enfeeble men twice your age. Look at her hold on you already and she hasn't even reached womanhood."

"Bunk," said Jack. "Why bring a faerie to a school full of boys then?"

"She's alone and in danger," said Rose. "Her father is at the warfront and all her sister Fae were murdered. Elf scouts found Snow White barely alive in her mother's arms and brought her here."

"The Red Sparks tribe," said Tylo. "They be scalped by ogres."

Tears streamed down Rose's cheeks. "No place is safe for her."

Allwise put a comforting hand on her shoulder. "Calm yourself, my brave dear. Snow White has recovered because of your care. When the Desertlanders thought she was dead, the Orchard was the safest place to hide her. That has changed now that they know she lives." He poured Jack a glass of limeade. "Of course, we both knew that Spriggins would behave recklessly no matter what he was told."

Jack resentfully folded his arms. "So what?"

"Watch that stubborn attitude, young man. Snow White's power runs deeper than the beguiling of men. The enemy knows this. The balance of good in the forest is upheld by the Fae's presence in it. Destroy the Fae and he tips the balance in his favor."

"Yer talking 'bout the wraiths leader," said Jack, taking the cool drink. "Does General Camlann know his kid is in such danger?"

"Redvere will convey the message," said Allwise. "We'll move Snow White soon. Our foes are closer than I like but they haven't placed the girl at the Orchard, else they would be here already."

Rose Red sat on a stone bench. Snow White knelt and rested her head on Rose's lap. They could not have looked more different, yet they seemed like sisters.

"I suppose, in the meantime," said Rose, "We'll have to find another nook to hide her."

"Why, because I found her?"

Tylo chimed in pointing at Jack. "And because I did, because he did?"

Jack paced angrily. "Faerie or not, she's Ardus's daughter and I'll protect her. If y'all trusted me, you'd know that."

"Trust goes two ways, Spriggins," said Allwise.

Snow White jumped up with a flurry of hand motions, many of them gesturing towards Jack. Confidence lit her young face.

He resisted looking at her; not an easy practice but a first step. "She has nothing to fear from me. I'm the best one to keep her safe. Not an elf. Not a nurse. Not an old man. Me."

Allwise rubbed his tired eyes. "Check your pride, Spriggins."

"Check yer own," said Jack, gulping the drink.

He set down the glass and sidled out through the secret pathway. Tylo followed until both of them were out of the maze and back in the yard. Balmy gusts of wind cleared the befuddling faerie scent from Jack's nostrils but not exactly from his head.

"Look, elf, I'm going to stop yeh from teasing me straight off," said Jack, turning.

Only, Tylo was not there. The elf had skipped off and was hurtling past the beehives to his hammock in the groves without a single mocking word.

* * * * *

From "A Handbook to the Forestlands" 2nd Edition

FAERIE - (meaning "those of Fae blood") Extinct bands of female roamers from hidden bowers of the deep forest. They were known as athletic hunters, devoted worshippers of the Light Spirit, and for being few in number. The Fae, exclusively women, only gave birth to female offspring, but required taking husbands from mankind during a shrouded midsummer ritual. It has been suggested they possessed an alluring musk that invariably attracted all men, but evidence of their existence has never actually been verified. Most of their story is buried in rumor, lore, and mystery.

Chapter **9**

SNAKE WRANGLERS

A courier on horseback arrived from the north. "Letters from Rivercross, Arborvale, Havensbend, and the front!"

Allwise ordered the gate opened and students rushed forward to greet the rider. He was one of Bors Celot's cavalry messengers, trotting a sleek yet filthy chestnut roan into the yard. He drew a bundle of mail from his satchel and handed it to Perdur. Allwise tottered out to the yard. The schoolmaster sifted through the letters, doling them out to Tymmy Mason, Varlan and Barlan Wood, and even one to Jack.

"From Redvere," said Allwise coolly, tucking his own dispatches beneath his arm.

The messenger dismounted, stiff from the saddle. "The Timberok has been a hard road to travel these days."

"Come into the lodge, lieutenant," said Allwise. "Mrs. Linnie can fix you something to eat and I'll need to hear all the news from the battlegrounds."

Jack thought he'd tag along, invited or not, but then Perdur called out.

"Your ma's here, Jack."

Ludi Spriggins arrived without warning, as usual. She was stout and spry, flitting through the gates faster than a three-legged chicken and clucking twice as loud.

"Oh my, Jacky! Yeh seem twice as tall as yeh was two weeks ago." She affectionately pressed his cheeks between her hands. "Yer skin's clearing up. So handsome."

"Stop it, Ma," said Jack. It was good to see her, but embarrassing.

Ludi handed a large basket to Perdur. "There are bean grounds in there for Allwise and sourberry bread and jam for the boys. Yeh'll take care of 'em?"

"I sure will, Mrs. Spriggins."

She smiled. "Perdur, yeh should come to town more. The young ladies are always asking about yeh."

The fight-instructor blushed. "Aw, they've only got eyes for Redvere."

"He's showier but yer the sturdy one," Ludi defended. "Yer who girls'll want to set up house with. Trust me on that."

Geoff Greens timidly approached. "I'll tend to your wagon and mule, Mrs. Spriggins."

"Thank-yeh, Geoff," said Ludi, proudly. "Yer speaking right up, like we talked about. Good fer yeh."

Geoff beamed.

Jack never ceased to be amazed at how devoted the students were to his ma. She had come a long way from the shut-in he grew up with on Thin Creek. She was everyone's favorite; no longer Jack's down-on-her-luck ma, but a respectable innkeeper with a thriving business in Rivercross.

"How're things at the inn?" said Jack.

"Things're busy, son," she said, hooking a proud arm around his waist. "Yeh wouldn't believe how many travelers and soldiers need a bunk. Ganzil's so helpful, o'course, and Tilda's baking up a storm. We're near run-ragged and getting low on beans."

"I'll help yeh haul the heavy barrels soon."

"It's Green Mother's Day," said Ludi. "Why don't yeh come tonight? I always keep a room for yeh neat and clean."

Jack squirmed. "Got a lot on my plate here, Ma. I took over teaching archery, y'know. And there's a challenging new *student* that ain't making things easier."

It was difficult for Jack to talk to her. Perhaps he had grown up too quickly, perhaps she had grown too responsible. Maybe neither one had grown enough. Ma was never shy, though, which was a trait he dreaded and admired.

She winked. "Gossip says yer learnin' a tree elf here? That true?"

"Allwise is."

"That's a big step for the Forestlands. And could be for yeh, if yeh let it be."

"Maa—"

Ludi chuckled. "Never mind then. Where's Rose Red? I brought her a proper bodice from the dressmaker. High time the lass had one."

She dug a red corset out of a knit hand bag and waved it at him.

Jack was mortified. "Give that to Rose, not me! She's at the infirmary tent."

"Will do," said Ludi cheerfully. She mussed his hair and headed off with a bustle in her step. "Gotta hurry back to Rivercross soon, bye now." She waved over her shoulder.

There was a comfy rocker on the porch of the main lodge. Jack sat down and tore open Redvere's letter. It was scrawled in his friend's neat penmanship:

> *Greetings Jack,*
>
> *Humfrey and I arrived at the front in good form. He's a good travel mate and always sets a smart camp for us. I forgot how cold the nights get this far north.*
>
> *Oh, what a bloody business this war is. Our battalion has seen a lot of action and camp was disorganized when we first arrived. G. Camlann was happy for my return, gave me a platoon of archers. Ardus manages to dispatch troops as quick as Tylo's sparks. He has a knack for bolstering the lines and keeping the ogres from overrunning us. Plus, he knows every man by name. The troops feel spirit-blessed to have him as our leader. I must add, his face looks older than his days as a Ranger.*
>
> *I've enclosed a note for my beloved Ganzil. At your earliest chance check on her. Let her know I dream of her often.*

You and the other students are on my mind a lot too. With each young soldier that doesn't return from a skirmish, I "thank the Green Mother that Jack is watching over the Orchard." Allwise was right to hold you back. I'm sure the General feels the same with his concern for <u>everyone</u> who is there. You're our home-front hero. I hope you see that.

Ootan and Gwachmai send their regards (with a few new swears that I won't print here). Say hello to Rose and the boys for me.

Be strong & well,

Redvere

It was a good letter but got Jack riled when he put it down. "A hero – *sitting* at home. Chee!"

Tymmy Mason came out and sat in the rocker next to him with a grunt that sounded just as vexed.

"What's up?" said Jack.

"I can't get in the library before combat class to page through *Eubert's Crokee Battle Stances,*" said the serious thirteen-year-old. "The door is never locked but today it is."

"Why don't yeh pick it like I taught yeh?"

"Naw, I'd just get caught. I'm not a master thief like you. Just one of Allwise's halfgrowns. That's what he calls us now."

"Uh-huh," said Jack.

Tymmy glanced at the gardens. The one-legged soldier (the one who hated elves) was hobbling by on crutches. "There are so few

~ 111 ~

grown men nowadays," said Tymmy. "They're all off fighting the ogres."

Jack was done sitting. "C'mon, I know some Crokee moves," he said Jack. "Yeh'll learn faster from me than a book."

They left the porch and headed out to the practice field. Fight-instructor Perdur had just finished discussing the use of different weapons and he was putting aside lariats of rope, two pistols and a pair of longbows. Frog, the twins, Geoff Greens, and Manawydan were standing there shirtless. The boys started waving their arms to get loose. Manawydan was flexing his triceps.

Perdur must have seen Jack and Tymmy coming over to join them because he seemed inspired. "How about we make the first round of the afternoon an actual one-on-one combat exercise, chaps?"

Manawydan stepped forward. "I'm first."

"Hee-Yo!" said Tylo. "The smallest Learning Twig against the braggiest lunkhead."

"Ye aim to fight me, elf?" said Manawydan, flashing an overweening smile. "Ain't exactly a fair match."

Frog agreed. "Tylo *is* fast."

"Watch it, Crokee," said the bruiser, scowling. "I'll stuff yer face in the grass next to his."

"That's a sporting jest, if you can get past Tylo," said Master Perdur. He guided the tree elf to the starting position. "Set? Good. Havensbend Wrestling Rules apply. One, two, three and – have at it!"

Manawydan lunged but Tylo was too quick. He sprang aside, letting the northern bully's weight outdo him.

"Mark Tylo's action," shouted Perdur. "The elf turns square each time he moves aside. His body position and footwork are always ready to shift direction. Manaw has yet to land a blow and is already fizzling."

"Not so," growled Manaw. "Just pacing myself."

Each swipe by Manawydan only caused his face to redden with frustration. Tylo capped it off by sneaking between the bully's legs unscathed.

"Should not Burly-Boast try to toss someone his own size?" said Tylo. "If only there be a Giant Killer handy."

Perdur turned towards Jack. "Up for the next bout?"

Jack pretended to yawn. "Maybe tomorrow when Manaw finally catches his breath."

Manawydan rested his hands on his knees. "Spriggins is just afraid I'll clout him as usual."

Varlan and Barlan Wood hooted in favor of the new match. "Jack-Manaw! Jack-Manaw!"

Even Geoff Greens yelped a "hee-yo!"

Persuaded, Jack rolled up his sleeves. "Teeth are bound to be loosened."

"Yours," said Manawydan, straightening up.

The two youths squared off. Their fellow students circled around them. Tylo clambered up on Varlan's shoulders for a clear view.

Perdur dropped his arm with a loud, "One, two, three – fight!"

All the boys hollered loudly, like a gallery of grownups at a cockfight. After all, Jack and Manawydan were the only two students at the Orchard School who had faced actual ogres. (Manawydan had helped thwart an ogre invasion of his village a year ago.) Their matches always thrilled everybody, including Jack.

Manaw feigned a left jab then swung hard with a haymaker, which Jack deftly ducked, rising to deliver a swift thump to his challenger's gut. The big lug grunted and stepped back. With a furious scowl he lurched head-on, as did Jack; both locking arms in wrestling form. Manawydan torqued Jack to the grass with a flop but he managed to squirm free and roll to his feet. Both glared at each other with plenty of mettle.

"Knocked the wind from ye, didn't I?" said Manawydan.

"Hobble yer lip," said Jack. "I ain't even broke a sweat." (That was a lie).

They braced for another go when the match got interrupted. "Snake! Snake!"

It was Mysslo, whose ear-piercing scream broke over the lawn. A horrid rasp followed as a massive black serpent crossed the garden and struck its first victim, the one-legged soldier. When the coils released, the man fell in a pale heap. Blood ran down his neck from the viper bite. Rose Red dashed from the infirmary tent to assist the screaming man.

The snake was several yards long with gray scales. Jack recognized it immediately. He and Tylo exchanged panicked glances.

"The wraith's snake," said Jack. "We gotta stop it!"

That was not going to be easy. The reptile moved fast as it slithered across the grounds.

"Weapons, boys!" ordered Perdur who seized a pistol off the grass and gave chase.

Jack grabbed the lariats of rope and tossed one to Manawydan.

Mysslo sprinted across the yard as fast as his crooked little legs could carry him. He glanced over his shoulder at the viper, which was aggressively pursuing him. "Demon slither!" he cried, bolting straight into the hedge maze. "Snake! Help! Big S-S-snake!"

Tylo chased after them chittering a war cry. The tree elf sprung onto the maze wall, scaling its fifteen feet swiftly. Jack entered the hedge maze with Perdur. The other boys chased at their heels.

Ahead, Mysslo shrieked and dove into a hedge wall to hide. The snake passed him by and wriggled towards the north bower, its massive head probing the shrubbery. Then at once, it penetrated a hedgerow and its long body disappeared. Jack understood its purpose.

He clicked at Tylo in elfspeak, "*Snow White! The snake is here for Snow White.*"

Tylo leapt across the rows from above; his bone knife clenched in his teeth. Jack and the others had to follow the hedgerows.

"Jits!" he swore, angry for not having his crossbow.

He led them around the corner that ran to Snow White's bower. A violent rustle shook the ivy leaves as the serpent's tail disappeared through yet another wall. Jack's heart raced with panic, until he heard Tylo shouting ahead, "Hee-Yo!"

The snake suddenly undulated into the path with a flaming dart stuck in its head. Tylo rode its scaly back, giving Jack a fiery "thumbs up" before he leapt atop another hedgerow.

The black serpent twisted on the grass, trying to snuff out the fiery dart. Angrily, it reared its venomous head, looking to strike.

"C'mon, yeh fangy devil!" said Jack, swinging the lariat.

Perdur discharged gunfire from his pistol, causing the serpent to lurch upward, its mouth gaping with pain. Jack was impressed.

"I shot it where the main lung is," winked Perdur.

The snake dove away and curled underneath the hedge, slithering toward the central garden. Perdur and Jack burst through the gap in pursuit.

The big garden was an ideal, open space to coordinate an assault but also gave the serpent more room to move. The twins, Varlan and Barlan, bravely cut off its escape from the far side as did Geoff Greens. The boys drew their longbows as the reptile wound itself into a massive coil. Tymmy Mason and Perdur aimed pistols. Frog wielded stones with a slingshot. Jack and Manawydan twirled lassos. Tylo took aim from the top of hedge with his twig bow.

Mysslo popped out from the hedge he was hiding inside and found himself in the worst position, trapped beneath the writhing reptile.

"S-snake!" he cried, then desperately crawled under a boxwood topiary trimmed like a rabbit.

The looming reptile reared to strike Mysslo. Without a signal, Tylo jumped down and fired another flaming dart. The snake flinched and the twig arrow missed, leaving the tree elf vulnerable.

"Jits, Tylo!" yelled Jack. "Git clear!"

The creature expanded its hood then struck. With speed never imagined, Tylo leapt aside and jabbed the snake with his bone knife. Jack and Manawydan swiftly lassoed it with perfect tosses. The serpent recoiled with a hiss, cinching the nooses tight. Venom dripped from its fangs, burning the grass.

Tymmy and Perdur fired a fresh volley of pellets from their pistols. Beads of blood erupted from the scales. Varlan, Barlan and Geoff Greens fired three arrows.

"Great shots!" said Perdur.

Mysslo's wails drew the viper's focus and it plunged, dragging Jack and Manawydan to the ground. The snake captured the terrified ground elf and started gobbling him. The boys stood up, pulling their ropes in opposite directions. The throttled snake gagged; Mysslo fell from its mouth in a slimy heap.

Tylo shouted, "Sparky's Flame!". With grand imp fierceness, he fired a burning dart into the snake's nostril.

The viper rasped and twisted, exposing its underside. The boys open fired with longbows and pistol fire while Jack and Manawydan tensed until their arms shook. Tylo stabbed with the bone knife. The elf's exuberant cheers were muffled as the coils collapsed over him.

"Tylo! It's trapped Tylo!" cried Frog.

The snake was dead. The students pulled at the heavy carcass, rolling the limp form aside. Tylo lay in a heap, bone knife still clutched in his hands.

Frog shook him. "You okay, Tylo?"

Perdur shook him. "C'mon, tiny elf, wake up."

Jack shook him. "Think of all the jibes yeh'll miss if yeh don't."

Tylo sputtered and coughed, then opened his eyes. "Be this the Sleeping Beauty's bower?"

"Naw," said Jack, pointing at the snake. "Just the Sleeping Ugly's. But yer awake."

The other boys crowded in, heaping backslaps of praise on the elf.

Mysslo slithered out from under the shrubs. "Curse and bless," he said in elfspeak.

Jack exchanged a dog-tired look with Perdur who playfully head-butted him.

"That was the best combat exercise ever," said Barlan.

The students lifted their arms and hollered in victory.

Rose Red entered the garden wielding her own crossbow. Snow White stood several feet behind, peering at all the excitement. Fortunately, the boys were celebrating and did not see the faerie. Jack shooed the girls back. They left unnoticed.

Tymmy Mason carefully investigated the dead snake. "I've never seen a species so immense."

"There are constrictors in the Swamplands nearly this large," said Frog, giving it a poke. "But they don't look like this."

"How did it get inside the Orchard?" said Geoff Greens.

Perdur answered. "It must've come over the wall near the apple grove."

Allwise entered the garden. He shooed the students aside to view their handiwork. "Well done, boys. Dissecting this rare reptile will be a grand experiment for our biology studies. Manaw, kindly retrieve a bullock cart and haul the carcass to the hothouse tank. Geoff and the twins will assist you."

"Yessir," said Manawydan, who ran off trailed by the others.

Perdur gathered the strewn weapons. "I'm going to examine the wall and back arbors for breaches."

"Precisely what I was going to ask," said Allwise. "Take Frog, Tymmy and Tylo. Nothing will slip by their sharp eyes."

Tylo whumped his chest. "See how wonderful my shots and stabs be, Belly-Bounce?"

"I do, Tylo," said the headmaster. "But I am more impressed by how well you worked with the others. You've learned much in your weeks here. We should have more young Learning Twigs among us. And Oakbarkers. And Featherfeet. The lot."

"Yes, yes, yes!" said Tylo. "But I still be the best of them."

Rose Red had returned with a medical bag and was examining Mysslo. "You're lucky. I was sure you got bit but you only have some bruising."

Shaking and hiding his face, Mysslo could hardly speak. "D-d-dig now. Must dig."

He squeezed under the hedge wall and dragged himself away.

"Stop, Mysslo," said Rose.

"Let him go dig," said Tylo. "That be what groundies do."

"What about you?" said Rose, checking Tylo's ribs. "I'm going to rub witch hazel on these cuts before you search the grounds."

He nodded. "I think my cheeks need to be kissed as well."

Rose laughed, as did the boys. They followed Perdur out of the maze.

Two wild hawks circled the sky, scavenging the dead prey. Jack was left alone with Allwise, awaiting instruction. Neither said a word, pacing up and down the length of the snake.

"Have your own wounds tended to, Spriggins," said the old man at last. "Then go to my study. I'll be waiting."

Jack would have rather stayed with the dead snake.

* * * * *

A handwritten communication from General Ardus Camlann (date crossed out), hastily jotted on the back of a torn cloth satchel.

Master Allwise,

Redvere and Humfrey arrived, and we intercepted a package in route from a cloaked courier that was to be delivered to the

Orchard. It contained a pair a of a lady's shell hair combs coated in acid so noxious that whoever wore them would have been poisoned to death. One comb was engraved with the word "SNOW", and the other "WHITE". A scant note implied they were a gift from me but, of course, I had nothing to do with them. This is an assassin's handiwork and proves the enemy knows my daughter's whereabouts. Proceed with your intention to move her at once. I agree the Domain is ideal, if they will only grant her sanctuary. I caution you to use the "document" only as a last resort. If it comes to that, then let me deal with the backlash of Breyman. Please protect my Snow White.

Ardus

(stamped with the General's official seal.)

Chapter 10

LEFT BEHIND

Allwise's study was a cramped, dusty annex off the side of the main lodge with tall neglected windows that were blocked by stacks of books. Midsummer heat made it even more uncomfortable. Jack usually went there to get chewed out for poor behavior. A map of the Forestland was spread out on the oak desk. Allwise was redrawing lines with the aid of a compass, taking random sips from a cup of cold tea. He appeared worn and frazzled, not the sharp-tongued observer Jack was accustomed to sparring with.

The old man cleared his throat, still focusing on the map. "I'd ask you to sit, but you'd go out of your way to do the exact opposite, so I won't bother."

"Ain't nowhere to sit, anyway," said Jack.

Any discernible chair was stacked with books.

"Well, yes. Forgive the disorder," said Allwise, finally making eye contact.

"Look," said Jack. "If yer mad about me finding Snow White—"

Allwise blotted the fresh ink. "In truth, I'm impressed by that. It opened my eyes to how precarious her being here really was."

"So, this was another one of yer tests?"

"I suppose it was. You're becoming just the spy we need you to be."

"Sneaky how yeh left out that Snow White was Fae. That snake was sent to kill her."

Allwise's silvery eyes flared. "It *was* the wraiths' snake then?"

Jack nodded. "The same one me and the elf saw in the Briar."

"Yes, yes. You and Tylo, side-by-side. I don't suppose the experience has altered your opinion of elfkind any?"

"The more yeh bring here, the more I'll trip over on my way out the gate."

"Is that so?" said Allwise. "That sounds more like a backwoods boy afraid his narrow mind is changing, than a man who's able to accept it."

Jack tapped an hourglass on the bookshelf and said nothing.

Allwise continued. "Are you so prejudiced you'd deny our army the advantage of elf archers striking the enemy from trees? And does that hatred extend to faeries?"

"It don't," said Jack. "Yeh just don't get how it is with me and elves."

"Oh, I understand," said Allwise. "All your life the villagers looked down on you. That patch-poor hoodlum. That no-account thief. That *nobody*. But, as low as they made you feel, something was always lower than you. You could always say, 'at least I'm no stinking elf'. A desperate security, as false as it is."

"Yeh think yeh know me inside and out, don't yeh, geezer?" said Jack.

"I wasn't talking about you, Spriggins. I was talking about myself."

"Huh?"

Allwise stood and cleared some books from a stool. "Sit. I'd like to show you something."

The oil lamp flickered as he drew his finger across the map. A trickle of light danced around the etching of a small lonely island.

"When I was a boy, I grew up here, off the coast of Breyman. 'Stone Isle'. As bad as you think your home was at Thin Creek, this place was worse. A miserable, cold slab of brutality and slavery."

The old man went on. "My birth name was Emris Blood. My earliest memories are working as a child slave with my father in Bluurg Fortress, stronghold to the Winter Barbarians – or Berserkers – who split our family apart during a raid. They turned Stone Isle into their stronghold to pirate, to pillage, and to dominate the communities of the north seas. As you can imagine, the barbarians were not kind masters. We mined rock and built their fortress. When I dropped onto my straw mat each night, bruised by beatings for working too slowly and bone-weary from labor that made grown men buckle, I believed I was no better than a sewer rat."

Jack knew what it was like to feel that.

"There were some beacons," Allwise insisted. "Foremost was the love of my pa, who raised me to be smart. He kept his head low but his chin high. At night he would whisper tales to me of faraway places, where freethinkers lived untrammeled by oppressors."

The old man faltered. Jack held out an arm but Allwise waved him aside and steadied.

"I also had a best friend, whose name was Pels," he continued. "A cobbler's son. We were close in age, both sharp-eyed with dreams of escape. We even looked like brothers. Pels had snuck books from a library the Berserkers destroyed. We taught each other to read and write from them. There was no one I trusted more."

Allwise drew a long breath.

"I was only thirteen when our overlords said my father – a staunch servant – had gotten drunk on stolen ale. I watched the next morning as he was marched to a courtyard and bludgeoned to death before my eyes. The rage I felt never went away. It still burns me now."

Jack felt the rage as well.

Allwise swatted at the image of Stone Isle as if it were a stray fly. "Pels easily talked me into leading a rebellion of the servants. I planned it, he executed it. On the eve of winter solstice when wine overflowed, so did the blood of our feasting masters. No one was spared. We were as remorseless as the barbarians had been to us. Four hundred slaves were freed, the treasury appropriated, and the fortress burned to the ground. Pels and I then sailed off to new horizons."

The flame of the oil lamp flared as Allwise turned the valve for more light.

"We travelled the globe. The Dragonlands, Desertlands, Lir, Jungles of Zan. We gained wealth and knowledge, broke some hearts, and enjoyed a popular reputation. Pels forged the way as I steered. It wasn't until we reached these untamed Forestlands that I learned the truth."

Allwise paused for a sip of cold tea but his voice sounded as dry as before.

"All those years back on Stone Isle, Pels had slipped a toxic spider into my father's boot, the bite of which had made him appear drunk. My best friend set up my father's murder."

"Why?" said Jack.

"To fill my heart with hate, so that I would mastermind our revolt. Apparently, I wasn't acting fast enough. I was never as ruthless as Pels wanted me to be," said Allwise. "You see, Spriggins, I put blind faith in someone who appeared to be an exact mold of myself."

"And he turned out to be rotten to the core," said Jack.

"Hate is a powerful but blinding force," said Allwise. "Pels knew that."

Jack finally understood the sly old geezer. "So, yer saying if I judge by what someone seems to be, I'm liable to miss the real bad ones."

"*And* you're liable to miss the true heroes. Be they gardeners, harp thieves, or Learning Twigs," said Allwise. "You know, you *can* be very smart. Your own mother is quite open at appreciating others. Take a cue from her."

"Ma?"

"People of every sort flock to her inn in Rivercross. It cannot be for the ghastly bean tea."

Jack could only agree.

"As to why you're here now," said Allwise. "I am going to need you to step up and watch over the school with Perdur during my absence. Rose Red and I are going escort Snow White to the Dwarf Domain. The Orchard is no longer safe for her."

"Jits! Yeh'll have to walk her past the enemy lines," said Jack.

Allwise pointed at his map, tracing a line near Breyman in the east. "General Camlann suggests we follow this route."

"That's a lot of woods to travel, old man, with just a brainy girl and a faerie," said Jack, taking a closer look. "Even if y'all don't get captured by ogres or attacked by wolves, when yeh get to the Iron Hills, what do yeh plan on saying to the dwarves? 'Room please?' "

The old man reached into a small cherry wood chest, withdrawing a brittle scroll. A burgundy seal of the Earth Spirit had been stamped on the parchment. This was a symbol of Breyman, a powerful province of the north forestlands. "This might be the key. The Deed of Dynadin. It is nearly mythological. Thanks to Lady Greygeese, it is in my guardianship."

"Yeh talked about it in the glasshouse that day she was here," said Jack. "It looks old."

Allwise nodded. "It would mean a lot to the dwarf clans." He returned the scroll and snapped the chest shut. "But, believe me, Viviyann had reasonable fears to keep it stashed away all this time. It's risky and I abhor risk."

"I'd keep the deed hid my vest pocket," said Jack. "Like the ace in a card game."

"Yes, Spriggins, questionable ethics is exactly what you excel at. And I mean that as a compliment. No one can slip by locked gates and work up a hostile society like you can."

"Then why ain't I going on this blarn journey?"

"Because of Snow White," said Allwise. "You're a growing lad with healthy yens and she's a faerie. Even a *young* faerie exudes a dangerous lure. It takes tremendous will, or old age, for most males to overcome."

"I ain't most males. Snow White's just a poor kid. I ain't gonna forget that. If I run through all the languages and fractions and other lessons yeh taught me, there's no room in my head to get distracted."

Allwise considered a moment then with an amused smile, shook his head. "No. You're not ready."

"Yer always building me up just to knock me down," said Jack. "All I really want is to be a soldier. When's that gonna happen?"

"You'd be a terrible soldier. Having to follow orders without question? It would be a complete disaster. Manawydan is a soldier. Varlan and Barlan are soldiers. You, Spriggins, have a more important role to play in the Great Forest."

"Do *yeh* even know what that is? Because I sure don't."

"Wartime is confusing. Almost as confusing as being fifteen-years-old; stuck, halfway between boy and man and in a big hurry. You learn well, with a fervor that is inspiring. There are reasons I hold you back that are too difficult to voice."

"Just tell me what I need to know. Yeh always do."

"I am a very poor teacher if that's true," said Allwise. "When you can see yourself as the rest of us do, your education will be complete. Do I have doubts that will come to pass? Yes, I do. It is my greatest fear concerning the man you will become."

Jack could not hear any more. "So, I gotta sit around and babysit stinking elves while everyone else gets to fight for the forestland? Jits to that!"

He turned and marched out of the study.

"Spriggins," Allwise called after him. "There are more plans to discuss. Spriggins!"

Jack marched towards the stables. Rose Red was bandaging Tylo's bruised ribs on the lodge porch while the boys re-enacted their day's heroics in the yard. It was Green Mother's Day and the blessed aroma of green tea cake, a holiday favorite, wafted through the air. Mrs. Linnie twanged the dinner gong. Jack strode past them, deliberately not looking back.

"The old coot's never gonna see me as full-grown like Ma does. She sees what Allwise don't. Looks like I'll be visiting the inn tonight, after all."

After tacking Blackberry for the ride, he secured his crossbow and galloped the horse out the Orchard gate. With a spit, he followed the road to Rivercross before he realized the sting of humiliated tears on his cheeks.

* * * * *

Excerpt from an early journal of Emris Blood (commonly called "Allwise") dating back to the Stone Isle rebellion when he was approximately fifteen years of age.

"Pels and I set sail tomorrow for parts unknown. We'll travel down the coast from Breyman, then set off across the black sea, east towards the Dragonlands. I can't wait to leave this miserable rock yet, for the first time since relaxing my bloody dagger, I'm scared. How many times have I stood on the pier watching ships come and go, always being left behind – the worthless son of a manservant – certain my feet would never leave these shores? I chased away dreams of escape because they hurt too much to wake up from. Now, I'm off

but my knees are weak and my eyes are tearing up. It's stupid. There's nothing for me here. There never was. The one thing I could call home was the love in father's eyes and I'm taking that with me. So what hold does this stone slab fill? Why do I dread being on the ship and seeing the ghost of a lonely broken boy on the dock watching us go? I guess he'll always be there, no matter how far the future takes me."

Chapter **11**

REFLECTIONS IN A MIRROR

In the two years since the war, Rivercross had tripled in population. Always an active town, it was a watercourse hub for traders, farmers, hunters, fishermen, and, lately, ragtag men-at-arms granted leave from duty. On this holiday honoring the Green Mother, Jack had granted himself a *leave-of-study*. He trotted Blackberry along the road, revisiting old haunts from his childhood as a thief.

Nothing looked the same.

Docks stood jammed with ferries carrying soldiers instead of cattle. There were no children running about. Blacksmiths forged weapons. Tailors propped their shop dummies with military uniforms. A printing press had been set up in the old parishioner house and churned out daily newspapers. Local chorales had been replaced by ditties such as "*Sweep the Desert Sands, Boys*" or "*The Lonely Bridesmaid*" twanging from piano saloons. It was not unusual to hear the splash of someone falling into the Green River amid ruckus hollers and laughter, or stray musket blasts.

One place that had not changed was *Ludi's Bean Tea Inn;* the popular establishment owned and run by Jack's mother. It maintained a scrubbed, folksy facade that served uplifting bean beverages. Gleaming beanstalks on the stained-glass windows made patrons feel welcomed as they passed inside for a taste of the olden times.

Jack felt reluctant to hitch Blackberry to the roadside post alongside scads of snorting buggy and wagon horses, until he remembered that his trained stallion could handle himself with a well-placed hoof should any fool try and take his reigns.

"I'll be back soon," he said, patting Blackberry's nose. "Promise.

Townsfolk crowded the outdoor terrace, which was full of holiday hubbub. Heads turned as Jack passed them.

"It's Yellow-Eyes," somebody said in hushed tones.

"There's the Spriggins lad with the lasso."

"Jack the Giant Killer," said another.

It always took a while for Jack to get used to being noticed outside the school grounds. Folks had spread tales of his early encounters with such wild exaggeration that he felt he could never fill the boots of the hero he supposedly was. Ma explained that folks needed champions during wartime, real or not. Jack, being a local, helped fill hearts and mugs at the inn. He passed the gawkers without eye contact and pushed through the hinged parlor doors.

The inn was even more boisterous inside. Tables were packed with soldiers, farm folk, merchants, and drifters. They talked and cheered, munched Ma's famed sourberry bread, and celebrated Green Mother's Day. A piano man sang a sentimental favorite:

> *"Oh, for days of yore with simple goods,*
> *When the Beauty slept within the Woods.*
> *When we worked an honest day,*
> *For dinner and a coin in pay,*
> *Were we ever richer? I say 'nay'."*

> *"How do we go back to times of ease?*
> *Lead me and I'll follow, if you please.*
> *I'll not ask for land or gold,*
> *Keep your fame and I'll grow old,*
> *On the days of yore far from the cold."*

The pianist was Mister Scratch. He was the town shoemaker, a slight man with age and smarts that rivaled Allwise. His jacket was patched with velvet on the elbows and bottle green in shade; his brimmed felt hat was topped with a long quail feather; his trim white beard came to double points on his chin framing a bright, shrewd smile.

"Why, Master Spriggins," he said. "You've grown nearly a foot since I last saw you. Fled the Orchard School to grace Rivercross, eh? Look at your appearance, so well and accomplished. Are you?"

A little of this agitator always went a long way.

"I'm looking for my ma," said Jack. "She in the kitchen?"

Scratch sighed. "Oh, Jack. Your timing is so unfortunate it would be comical if seen on a theatrical stage."

"Is that a riddle, old timer?"

"Your dear mother left to fetch more of those magnificent beans, barely an hour ago." Scratch pressed a flat note on the piano. "If only she'd known you were coming, young sir."

"She asked me to stop in for the holiday."

"Your visits are so few and far between, she must've figured you would not come. Allwise keeps you very busy."

"I study hard. Ma's proud of that," said Jack. He figured if he raced Blackberry, he might catch up with his ma at the cabin on Thin Creek where the beans grew. "Thanks for yer—" (Jack wanted to say 'meddling') "*Concern*, Mister Scratch."

"Not at all, not at all," said Scratch. "Only, Jack, you shouldn't follow her."

"Why not?"

"It's nearly sunset and the local Rivercross guards put out a curfew for civilians your age to stay in the village. It is wartime, you know." The shoemaker gave a cunning wink.

Jack shrugged. "I ain't exactly a youngster."

"Not exactly a soldier either, not exactly," said Scratch. "We're all versed in your adventures, Jack. Only rules are rules and your ma may be fined by the sheriff. You remember Big Bill, don't you?"

Of course, Jack did. Big Bill was a bloated, bull-headed lawman who despised Jack as a young pick-pocket because he could never catch him stealing, but the idea of getting ma fined did not sit well.

Scratch's boney hand pinched Jack's shoulder. "Why not spare your loving mother the embarrassment?" he said. "Spend the night here at the inn. She keeps a room made up for you. Think how pleased she'd be if you actually used it, son."

Jack stalled. "It'd be a surprise to greet Ma when she gets back."

"And I won't lie," said Scratch. "You look in need of a good rest. That featherbed upstairs may be just what you need."

The shoemaker motioned across the rowdy parlor. "Ganzil? Oh, Ganzil."

The golden-haired beauty was wiping down a table with a flirtatious smile at a soldier. She was even more fetching than when Jack last saw her. Seventeen years of age and clothed in a tight purple bodice, her skirts swayed with a doe-like grace that not even a starched apron could hide. Soft-spoken but not shy, she welcomed any man's besotted stare be they farmer or army captain. It was impressive how coolly she handled herself despite every lovesick male patron who offered the moon for an ounce of her affection.

"What can I do for you, Mister Scratch?" she said, carrying a tray of empty mugs. She flipped her bright golden braids and noticed Jack.

"Here's Ludi's famous son," said Scratch. "He's planning to stay upstairs. Perhaps you'll see he gets settled?"

Ganzil exchanged an indifferent look with Scratch before returning her blue-green gaze to Jack. "My pleasure. Shall I find you a table, bring some bread and tea?"

"Naw," said Jack. "Ain't hungry."

"Go get settled then. I'll bring fresh linen and a basin to your room."

With a nod, she went to the bar and set the empty mugs on a mahogany sideboard. A wide mirror was mounted on the wall behind it. Ganzil admired her flawless reflection. Then she chirped beguilingly at a red cardinal perched inside a wicker birdcage. She fed a piece of sourberry bread to it through the slats. Jack was struck by a haunting notion that Ganzil had known him for a long time. He could not figure why.

"She's lovely, eh?" said Scratch, nudging Jack.

"Reckon she knows it."

"Surely, few girls carry as much charm."

"Faeries, maybe," said Jack. "Reckon all the pretty ones cast spells on yeh."

"When you're a grown man like all these noble soldiers, perhaps." Scratch smirked, tipping his hat. "There's still a healthy amount of juvenile in you after all, Jack." The shoemaker returned to the piano and roused the place with more music.

Scratch's clever innuendos could not have stung more deeply. Jack pushed through the din to the staircase and climbed to his room on the third story. He lit a tiny oil lamp, unhitched the crossbow from his belt, and jutted out his chin, checking it for whiskers in an oval mirror above the oak dresser. (Disappointedly, he found none).

There was a knock from the hall. It was Ganzil, holding a stack of bedding and a china basin with a pitcher of clean water. Rather than hand these to Jack, she walked into the room and shut the door.

"I can fix my own bed," said Jack.

Ganzil tossed the quilt aside and spread out the new linens. "Your mother has been very good to me. It wouldn't feel right if I didn't treat you as she would."

Jack caught a whiff of cinnamon and violet from her hair. He stepped back, trying to seem relaxed. "Fair enough, I guess." Then he remembered Redvere's letter and fished for it in his vest pocket. "Oh yea, I have a note for yeh from the front. From Redvere."

"Who?"

"Redvere Celot. The junior captain of the army. He just rejoined the ranks."

Ganzil acted clueless for a moment and then exhaled in recognition. "Oh. The Horse Chancellor's son. Always with a poem. It's hard to take him seriously."

Jack was glad Redvere was not present to hear that. He handed it to her. "He sure thinks better of yeh than yeh do of him."

"I can't help that. Most boys lose their heads when it comes to me," she said, crossing to the mirror, toying with the strings of her bodice. "But you don't, do you, Jack?"

It was best to be honest. "I see what they all see. But there are things in other girls I find prettier."

Ganzil spun around, white flashing in her eyes. "Who? What makes them so pretty? Tell me!"

"That's my business," said Jack. "Ain't yers, so back off, yeh little hepcat. Go play yer games on them slobbering fools downstairs. I'm fine here by myself."

With a hint of a grin, the serving girl calmed herself. "I'm sorry." Her voice gained a lilt as she reached into her apron pocket and pulled out a glass bottle of amber drink. "I almost forgot this. You must be thirsty."

Parched as he was, Jack made no move to accept it. "I don't like the bean stuff."

"It's cold apple cider," said Ganzil. "A gift. I made it myself."

She took two glasses off a tiny bedside table and filled them both. She took a sip and handed one to Jack. He tasted it. The cider was good, unexpectedly sweet-spiced with nutmeg.

Jack drew up a wooden chair and sat. "Most girls would keel over if a good-looking hero like Redvere wanted to wed them. What makes yeh so fussy?"

"I don't like personal questions any more than you do," said Ganzil, plumping the pillows on the bed. "But I'll share because we're alike – heartless and realistic."

It was not a comparison Jack liked.

Ganzil sat on the side of the bed. "I'm a princess, Jack. I should be a queen. My father, Gan, Warlord of the Winter Country, wanted only sons. So, he cast me aside. It doesn't make me any less royal, though."

Jack knew better than to laugh and kept a straight face. The Winter Country was a frozen landscape beyond the Iron Hills. Legions of barbarians had wandered its barren mountains and snow-covered fields for centuries before turning seafarers. Whatever royalty existed there had descended from pirates and outlaws.

"How'd yeh end up in the Forestland?" he said, guzzling his cider.

"Witches rescued me from being sacrificed by the norse priests," said Ganzil. "I was sent here to live with Viviyann Greygeese and Hepkatee the Crone. You know both, don't you?"

"Sort of."

"Meddling biddies," said Ganzil. "They claim to be charitable vessels of the Green Mother Spirit."

"They took care of yeh, didn't they?"

"No. They brought me up in musky cabins to be their 'maiden witch'. What they really wanted was my vision."

"Yer what?'

Ganzil stared at him. "I was born with the Norn's Sight. I see what others cannot."

"Like what?"

"Secrets. Thoughts. Dreams. I read the minds of others." She refilled his glass and held it to his lips.

Jack swallowed. "So, yeh didn't want to share yer tricks with them. I don't blame yeh. What then?"

She laughed. "I learned what I needed. Then I ran from them and came here."

The sweet cider made his head feel numb. He was tempted to leave but a swell of excitement kept him there.

"Well, good fer yeh," he said too slowly.

One of Ganzil's braids came loose. She ran her fingers through it, then unraveled the tresses like spun gold.

"Folks see my beauty, not my smarts. Not my royalty," she said. "You're held back too, aren't you, Jack?"

"Nobody thinks I'm good enough."

"You see?" She clasped his face in her hands and kissed him wildly on the mouth. Jack could have held his own against wild boars, ogre soldiers, and giant snakes, but at this moment he felt helpless. All he did was kiss her back.

Ganzil drew away and whispered, "Want to see how witchcraft works?"

He nodded, feeling sweat bead on his upper lip.

She took the oval mirror off the wall and laid it flat on the bed, silver side up. In a swift motion she threw open a window, letting the breeze blow out the lamp. Now, only the night sky lit the room.

"You've learned my truths, let's learn yours," she said.

The enticing young witch stroked Jack's face down to his chest with one hand as she poured water from the basin on the mirror with the other. The blood through his body ran hot and he breathed heavier.

Ganzil began a chant in forbidden *palagot*. The words did not translate easily but the gist was clear.

>*"Mirror, Mirror. From the wall.*
>*Show me secrets. Show me all."*

Her eyes widened.

"You are blessed, Jack Spriggins," she rasped. "Dark Lell lives in your shadow."

Jack glanced at the mirror. A veiled likeness of the Dark Spirit looked back at him through Ganzil's entranced face.

Ganzil sounded humbled. "Shaded One, allow me to guide Jack through the caves of his mind that you hold so dear. No other spirit will reach him, if you wish."

She trembled, as if being throttled. The drops of water on the mirror rippled.

"Brave Jack. Such horrors you've seen of late. Ogre sabers at your throat. A village of slaughtered fishermen. Red scalps on a warrior's belt. Imps dancing around a fire ball, plotting to take your place. Betrayal from that liar, Allwise – a false wizard."

Hate blistered inside Jack as she pressed her hand over his heart. The mirror's image changed Ganzil's blue-green eyes to a marvelous blackish brown.

"Who's this, Jack? What female demon has invaded your heart? Is it a loathsome Fae?"

Ganzil pressed her face to the glass with a force that nearly cracked it.

"Show her again," she commanded. "Show me that man-stealing sylph."

Snow White's face flashed in the mirror.

The witch screamed in rage. "Tell me her name!"

"Snow White," said Jack. The words came as if pulled out of him. "Her name is Snow White Camlann."

A low cackle, like an ancient crow, escaped Ganzil's throat. She lapsed into rhyme:

> *"White as a snow fox weaving spells on men.*
> *Fair as a snowdrop, heaping weakness upon them.*
> *Red as blood, black as coal.*
> *Where does she dwell? Where is her soul?"*

"At the Orchard," said Jack, unable to bite his tongue.

"So, the general's missing daughter survived. Her eliminated faerie band no longer lives, but she has found a garden where she is the fairest of them all?"

Jack nodded.

Ganzil forced him over the mirror to see his reflection.

"You are under my spell, Jack Spriggins. You will act for me. Through your eyes, I will strike with your hands. My greatest desire is now yours. Yes?"

A feverish vitality coursed through him as Jack tensed. "Yes," he echoed.

She held him close and murmured in his ear. "And my will is the death of Snow White. I want her bleeding heart presented to me in a glass chest. I want it sliced out of her faerie body with your own knife. I want her last sight to be the satisfied smirk on your lips, for it will also be on mine."

"It'll be yers."

Ganzil's released him. "You'll speak of this to no one. The Fae cannot live. I am the real Beauty. Go back to the Orchard, Jack. Go to her. You are the greatest hunter in the woods. My soldier. And I am your queen."

Her spell began to take hold. He kicked at the floor in defense.

"Stop!" he yelled. "Stop it now!"

Ganzil did not look scared, but delighted. She clasped a hand over his mouth, digging her fingernails into his cheek, then repealed her incantation.

"Mirror, Mirror. Cease your call.
Keep your secrets. Back to wall."

A cool hush ran through the room. Ganzil pressed a finger to his lips. She rehung the mirror and then relit the lamp. Neither spoke.

It was well after midnight when Jack led Blackberry along the road out of town. The horse clomped his hooves in frustration, not being allowed to gallop. Jack was not steady enough to stay upright in the saddle. He held the reins tightly, feeling drained and guilty. There was no point spending the night in Rivercross.

"In one swoop I'm a lousy son, a lousy friend, and a lousy protector."

Jack's thoughts were his own again but he felt haunted by Ganzil's hex, real or not. She had pried information from him that the desert soldiers had not by the enchantment of her pretty face. He was confused by Ganzil's power. Would the power of Snow White be even more enfeebling? He checked his crossbow to make sure the trigger was locked.

"I've no idea what I feel about Snow White now. Is she safe around me? Am I safe around her?"

A lilting tune from Scratch's piano drifted out of the tavern.

> *"A red rose for the Beauty seen,*
> *A pink rose for a child,*
> *A yellow rose for Beauty aged,*
> *An orange rose for the wild.*
> *Yet save the white rose, fairest all,*
> *For Beauty one can feel.*
> *While others come and fade away,*
> *She stays forever real."*

"I'll trust my gut over the whim of a witch," said Jack. "Wish I had more of that cider, though."

Ganzil had tossed him a few apples as he left the inn but they looked a tad green. Blackberry refused them. Jack stuffed the rejected fruit in the saddlebag and trotted the horse from Rivercross toward the Orchard.

"And the Orchard *is* my home."

A red spark passed in front of his nose. There was a snap as a second one flared, just long enough to light up Tylo's telltale grin before the elf snuffed it out. Blackberry was startled and whinnied. Jack calmed the stallion with a few "shushes".

"Don't tell me, runt," he said. "Yeh tracked me into town."

"I did, Giant Killer," said Tylo. "If you can flee the Orchard, I can too. Tylo be bored and snake-stressed, just like you be."

The elf might have been a burden but he was also a needed distraction. After the evening's exploits, Jack needed one.

"So what trouble did yeh make in Rivercross?"

"A hotfoot or two," said Tylo. "But mostly I be hopping from sooty chibby to chibby."

"Yeh mean *chimney*."

"Chim-ney tops, while I be waiting for you to come out of Ma Spriggins' teahouse." Tylo hiked up his trousers, which never fit.

Jack looked back at the town behind them. "Why didn't yeh come in?"

"The lunks did not let me. They say, 'elfkind not welcome' and slammed the door."

"Since when did that ever stop yeh?" said Jack.

"Not welcome be not welcome," said Tylo. "It was too hot and clunky in there, anyway. And the rinky-tink music hurt my ears."

"Mine too." Only months before, Jack would have sided with the townsfolk. Now, he fumbled to excuse them. "If Ma had been there, the inn would've been open to yeh."

Tylo jiggled his tiny behind in a suggestive shake. "So, who did Giant Killer keep all his time with? Be it a curvy-wurvy girl? Hmm? Did you have smoochy smooches and tingles in your lunk-loins?"

"Shut up," said Jack. "Yer not old enough to ask me about such stuff. Ever."

The elf stood as straight up as his balance would allow. "I am a near-grown."

Jack was tempted to beat his own chest after the evening's adventure. There came another popping sound like fireworks.

"Sounds like their celebrating Green Mother's Day in fine fettle."

The sky flared and then burned a bright orange.

"Blarn. Is it already morning?" said Jack.

Tylo scratched his head, staring at the horizon. "Seems early to be early."

Blackberry nervously began sidestepping. A backwoods alarm bell rang out as plumes of smoke spilled into the sky. Jack and Tylo exchanged dreadful glances. The elfling shot up the nearest pine and swung through the trees towards the bedlam. Jack leaped onto Blackberry's saddle and spurred the stallion to bolt after him.

The Orchard School was on fire.

* * * * *

From the collection of Professor Tymothy Mason: palagot symbols etched on a strip of birch that had been tied to a messenger finch. Scholars presumed it sent by Hepkatee (Crone of the Woods), to a fellow witch, Viviyann Greygeese (Mother Goose), in Arborvale, on the eve of the famed "Siege of the Orchard".

(TRANSLATION)

"*Visions from my hearth flames. Ganzil practices dark arts in Rivercross. The soul of the Great Forest burns. Bring the Maiden to me at once. We will deal with Ganzil together, sister, to heal this fracture in the Power of Three.*"

Chapter **12**

DEFENDERS

The gate of the Orchard School was locked. The alarm bell clanged inside as plumes of smoke belched into the reddened, infernal sky. Perdur was atop the stone spire swinging a lamp to signal the students. He crossed his hand before the light in a code Allwise had taught them:

Ogres - on - west - grounds.
Archers - set - position - behind - stables.

He was directing a counter attack.

"Arrgh!" Jack shouted angrily for not being in the midst of the fight. "How's this possible?"

Perdur spotted him, circling Blackberry and waving. The fight master signaled:

Let - Jack - in - gate.

The ringing ceased and the gates swung open. Tymmy Mason stood in his nightshirt, holding a hammer and bell. His face was blackened with soot.

"Jack!" he exclaimed. "We're being attacked by ogres."

"Drop that bell and grab a musket," said Jack.

Tymmy bolted for the weapons shed.

The main house was in flames. Ogre soldiers were breaking windows and tossing lit torches inside. Amid shouts of shock and panic, Jack could only hope everyone got out. The stables were ablaze. His heart broke to see his home being destroyed.

How the ogre troops got in was anybody's guess. The outer walls were intact, the gate had been locked; yet a full platoon of warriors was raiding the place.

Jack loaded his crossbow and clung tight to Blackberry's reins. "Heigh!"

He spurred the horse into the fray. He saw Varlan and Barlan Wood run shirtless to free the horses from the burning stables. Ogre war cries were shouted as a group of warriors charged the boys with raised sabers. Barlan glanced back, horrified. The twins pushed the rolling doors open and disappeared into the smoke.

Jack fired arrows at the ogres, catching the front-runner through the neck, dropping him beside the water trough. Frightened stallions and mares charged out from the stable, trampling another warrior.

Varlan rode out bareback astride Thundersong, looking like a legendary sea-lord armed with a pitchfork. He clashed weapons with the nearest warrior. Using his training, he parried well and speared the Desertlander in the shoulder.

Barlan quickly trailed out of the stable on Greywick.

With a "heigh!" the brave twins galloped in a circle around the attackers.

The one Varlan had forked was a bull of a man. Without so much as a wince, he yanked the triton from his flesh and aimed to throw it.

Jack's next shot was lined up, but young Frog surprised everyone emerging from the water trough. He smashed the unsuspecting brute across the legs with a cosh-baton. The pitchfork fell as the ogre dropped to his knees. Frog pummeled him on the snakehead helmet. The huge man keeled over sideways.

Then the stable collapsed from the flames.

Jack and the twins marshaled their horses around the warriors like Redvere had taught them. With tightening passes, a pair of Desertlanders were crammed together. One warrior slashed Barlan in the leg as he leaned out to strike. The boy yelped but returned a swift slice. The ogre shrieked, clutching the side of his neck as he fell.

The other attacker swung a spiked flail at Jack, who ducked backwards as it skimmed above his cheek. A narrow miss. The ogre was pierced from behind by an arrow. As he crumpled to the ground, Jack looked up. Perdur had fired the shot from the tower.

They nodded to each other.

"Where's Allwise?" shouted Jack.

"I don't know!" shouted Perdur.

The old man was nowhere to be seen. His hound Micca was chasing an enemy warrior with a wolfish growl.

A fierce "Hee-Yo!" made Tylo's presence known at the greenhouse. Glass shattered and a slew of colorful birds flew out. The little elf gave the ogres big problems, leaping from the trees of the cherry orchard and firing shots with his twig bow. He led them to the spire and went up the ladder.

Two ogres followed the elf. Another pair of them shot flaming arrows at the wooden platform atop the tower, which caught fire. Perdur had devised an escape. There was a cord strung from the top of the spire to the trunk of a walnut tree below. The fight-master whistled down to Jack, signaling with his lantern:

Enemy - in - hedge - maze.

Jack knew why the ogres were there. *To kill Snow White.* His heart pounded. He understood the *sartyrian* shouts, *"Find the fae girl!"* Several warriors charged past the burning lodge towards the east garden.

He spurred Blackberry towards the maze. The horse whinnied and reared, causing Jack to lose control of the reins and fall hard to the ground. Gasping for air, he struggled to his feet. A large shadow loomed over the grass, enveloping him. A tall warlord stepped from the billows of smoke, brandishing bloody sabers in each hand. An array of elf scalps swayed from his thick belt. His imposing build and distinct jaw tattoos were all too familiar.

It was Bluebeard.

"Giant Killer Spriggins," he said with unnatural calm. "The Great Serpent has brought you before me again. You owe me a death. This time you shall pay."

"I'm here to disappoint yeh," said Jack.

Bluebeard twirled his sabers over his head, and said, "*Mrtyu Monghra!*" (Die mongrel.)

He charged at Jack, a blur of shimmering bronze as his blades whirled.

Jack hooked an arm into Blackberry's saddle strap and swung the horse round, blocking the warlord's attack. With a click of his cheek, Jack gave Blackberry a command. The horse lowered its head and bucked.

Bluebeard evaded the horse's kick but Jack ushered a second kick of his own and caught the warlord under the chin with his shopmades.

The ogre rubbed his jaw. "Take your strikes, boy. They are your last."

"Hee-Yo, Bluebeard!" shouted Tylo from above. The elf zipped down Perdur's line from the stone spire using his bow as a sheath. He landed at the foot of the walnut tree. Perdur fired arrows from the tower then zipped down as well with his long bow.

Both aimed their weapons at Bluebeard in a standoff. Manawydan emerged from beneath the Orchard's water tower. He was bloody, stripped to the waist and wielding a battle-ax. Rose Red joined him armed with a crossbow. Judging from the smock worn over her dress, she had been in the laboratory when the ogres invaded. Jack was relieved to see them alive and feisty as ever.

"No one bests Spriggins, lest it's me," said Manawydan to Bluebeard.

The students closed in for battle.

"Come, little mice," said Bluebeard, adding to Jack in *sartyrian*, "*Vigrah Saahk sama adya mrtyu.*" ("You will see your friends die before I kill you.")

Perdur countered. *"Yuddhu kor duun!"* ("You'll have to get through me first.")

He unsheathed his cutlass as Manawydan swung his battle-axe at the warlord.

Bluebeard's swordsmanship was masterful, meeting their efforts with staggering force. He caught Manawydan's stroke with one saber and outmuscled him. Perdur made several thrusts, only to have his blade knocked aside by the warlord's second saber. Both stepped aggressively around Bluebeard but could not outflank him.

More ogres rushed past the flaming trees to join their leader with a united war cry, *"Maj sutur!"*

Rose spun and fired an arrow. She pierced one of the warriors through his chest plate. Jack fired, giving her cover. Beside him, Tylo peppered the ogres with bulls-eyes from his scrappy twig bow. One ogre managed to swing his curved saber. Jack ducked as Tylo finished him.

"Gut and scalp the dirty imp!" shouted an ogre officer.

Tylo wisely bolted, making them chase him around the stone spire.

Jack reloaded and took aim at Bluebeard. The warlord had forced Perdur and Manawydan beneath the walnut grove. Each struggled to gain an advantage. Perdur lunged with hawkish strokes, forcing the warlord to slope and parry.

"You're skilled for one with so much lard on your bones," said Bluebeard. "But no match against a desert warlord."

Manawydan swung a powerful ax stroke that Bluebeard defended with an upward parry. He kicked the boy in the chest, knocking him back against the water tower.

Perdur gave a long thrust. Bluebeard kneeled with a backhand slice that knocked the cutlass aside while slashing his second sword across the fight master's exposed gut. The front of Perdur's white shirt turned red. He groaned and fell over.

"No!" said Jack, horrified.

Bluebeard ducked behind a walnut tree as Jack fired another shot. It was a near miss. The warlord's black eyes shifted to him, white fangs curling from his lips.

"I will cut off your shooting arm and keep it as a trophy," said Bluebeard.

He kicked Perdur aside and spun his blades. "*Hyn Pythava!*" he said, honoring his serpent goddess.

Jack charged.

A snapping boom erupted from the structure beams of the main house as it collapsed in flames. Billows of smoky embers shot out and engulfed them all. Jack covered his face from the searing haze, searching for the warlord. Waving at the acrid smoke, he stepped on Perdur's cutlass and picked it up.

Bluebeard laughed. Jack dived blindly as a saber swiped through the smoke. He sprang to his feet as the warlord's second blade sliced down, clashing the steel saber against Perdur's cutlass. The curved blade withdrew. Bluebeard laughed more. He was enjoying this.

Jack was too emotional, something Perdur had instructed him to avoid in combat.

"*Think. See the whole picture and act,*" the teacher had said.

The warlord's shape charged through the smoke slashing his blades. Jack was outsized and outmatched, so he dropped to the grass and swiped low with his leg. The heel of his boot caught Bluebeard in the crook of the knees.

The butcherer fell forward. Jack drove Perdur's cutlass through his shoulder.

Surprisingly, Bluebeard did not shriek nor writhe in pain. Instead, he struck Jack with a fist that might as well have been cast in iron. "I will squeeze the yellow from your eyes!"

His grip slid up to Jack's throat.

A harsh cadence of wood chops came from the water tower. Through the smoke, Manawydan cleaved the wooden supports with his battle-ax.

"Hu-hur-hurry!" croaked Jack, clutching with both hands at Bluebeard's grip.

Manawydan gave the fractured supports a guiding push. "Here it comes!"

The water tower toppled with a creaking groan. Bluebeard looked up. His strangle hold on Jack broke as the tank slammed on the yard. A massive rush of water swept them both away. Jack was splashed aside but Bluebeard got carried by the torrent out of the walnut grove. He yelled like madman.

Manawydan yanked Jack to his feet.

"Yeh saved me, Manaw."

"Just tryin' to put out the fires," said Manawydan. "But glad I did both."

The two rivals stumbled back to Perdur. Rose Red was bent over his body but it was too late. The inspiring, earnest fight-master was dead.

Jack looked away.

The orchard was unrecognizable. Trees were on fire. The collapsed buildings smoldered. The lawns and gardens were black with soot. Farm animals squealed, running here and there. Allwise was nowhere to be seen. Screams of terror winnowed from the root cellar. Mysslo was being dragged out across the lawn by ogre guards. The pathetic ground elf had less fight in him than a snared rabbit.

Tylo scampered after him. "I will save Mysslo's scalp." He pelted the enemy with darts from his bow.

"Can yeh believe, an elf's picking up our slack?" said Jack.

A war trumpet blasted from the Orchard gate. Heavy hooves stampeded as cavalrymen charged inside.

"That's Havensbend!" said Manawydan. "The Count's Men have come."

Count Corrobis led the charge with "Puss" seated on his shoulders. The riders' sword clashes and pistol-pops rang out from all directions as the ogres rushed to engage them.

"Ka Bur!" Corrobis spun his horse and pointed the cutlass at Bluebeard.

The drenched warlord staggered to his feet across the lawn. He jerked Perdur's broken blade from his shoulder as if brushing off a fly.

"The pretty-faced Count," said Bluebeard, splashing forward with his sabers ready. "After my blades change your appearance, the ladies will not wish to look at you again."

The cat nudged the Count's ear. Corrobis leapt down from his steed. "You and your savages will regret your actions here."

The Count's words sounded rehearsed, like a hammy actor from Rivercross Square. Not that it mattered because his swordsmanship was no fake.

Bluebeard attacked.

Corrobis elegantly swung the cutlass with smooth, precise strokes meeting Bluebeard's sabers blow for blow. Their swords clapped with peals of ringing steel. Bluebeard retreated with a backward step.

"You only have an advantage because I am wounded," he said.

The cat hissed.

"Your pride perhaps?" said Corrobis. (This comeback was so clever, the cat must have prompted it).

The warlord lunged. The Count's maneuvers were simple but his thrusts knocked his opponent's sabers in opposite directions, disarming him. Bluebeard cautiously raised his arms, the edge of Corrobis' cutlass poised at his throat.

He spoke smugly. "I would praise the victor but I cannot *mew.*"

The handsome Count nicked his blade across the ogre's jaw, drawing red blood from his tattooed "blue beard".

"That's for the Orchard."

"That's for Perdur Galles!" shouted Manawydan.

"Perdur!" echoed Rose Red and Jack.

The Desertlanders had faced similar defeats and were now retreating from the smoldering Orchard into the shadows like scared rats.

"*Korgaas!*" cursed Bluebeard. "Where are your backbones? Bring me Camlann's daughter! Turn and fight!"

Outmatched, Bluebeard shoved free of Corrobis and ran, hurtling over the wall following his men.

It was stupefying. "Gutless bully," said Jack.

"Jack!" shouted Rose Red, pointing at the maze. "Snow White."

They rushed towards the maze. Other ogres, who had not yet retreated, saw them coming. Rose and Tylo took positions and began firing arrows. Manawydan cleaved with his battle ax. Jack used their cover to bolt past the enemy and run inside the twisting hedges.

Following the rows, a melodic voice crept like a sultry whisper into Jack's head. The corrupting scent of cinnamon spread from his nostrils.

"Mirror. Mirror. Through Jack's sight.
Find the faerie. Find Snow White."

It was Ganzil. Jack felt her power burning in him with feverish effect.

"All that's spoiled, ruined by Fae.
Mirror. Mirror. Make her pay."

The young witch had him in her thrall.

"I'll find her," he swore.

The west side of the maze was burning. Rounds of musket fire racketed from further in. Jack took the familiar corners. *"Find her, Jack!"* said Ganzil. *"Find Snow White! Put an end to her."*

In a trance, he came to the hidden passage of Snow White's bower. The door was open. Before it, lay a heap of three slain ogre soldiers with muskets in their hands. From their positions on the ground, Jack could tell they had killed each other.

"What the blarn?"

He stepped inside the little pavilion. Two brawny ogres were pointing loaded pistols at each other.

"She's mine, you scale-less weakling!" shouted one.

"*Ubdain!* (Never!)" said the other, "I saw her first."

"You're unworthy, I outrank you. The faerie is my prize."

"No! I shall kill you for a fair glance at her unmatched beauty."

The ogres traded savage gunfire. Each slumped to the ground and succumbed to their wounds.

Snow White crept out from behind the oak at the center of the pavilion. She appeared untouched, even fearless; her hollow yew wand lifted in protection.

Ganzil's haunts pressed Jack further. *"See what the Fae make men do? How primitive, helpless you become. Do not be fooled. You cannot let her live."*

The young faerie brightened. She opened her arms to Jack and stepped over the warriors' corpses. Jack set his jaw against whatever charm Snow White might use. He subtly unlatched the safety on his crossbow, jiggling the quiver to loosen an arrow. With innermost grit, he summoned the hunter within to take charge.

"Do it," said Ganzil. *"End this strumpet's unnatural dance."*

Snow White paused. Her dark eyes watched Jack's bow as he aimed it at her. She lowered her protective wand. The faerie did not waver or scream. She simply spoke, using actual words.

"If you must, Jack."

It was not conniving like Ganzil or even knowledgeable like Rose Red. Snow White's voice was clear and guiltless, like a typical thirteen-year-old girl.

"Because that's what yeh are," said Jack. "Just a brave, lonely girl."

Cool sweat dripped from his temples and neck. The girl's simple smile brought him relief. He locked the safety and lowered his crossbow.

Ganzil's voice broke through. *"No! She's tricking you! No!"* Her furious chant pulsed in the back of his head:

"Mirror. Mirror. Kill the Fae!
You, Jack Spriggins, do as I say!"

Jack's anger took over. "Yer mirror is broke, witch. I ain't under yer spell no more."

Ganzil screamed as a strident red cardinal flew out from the pavilion and flapped into the smoke-filled sky. Her hold on Jack was shattered.

"I'm sorry, Snow White. I'm so sorry," said Jack, hoarsely. He turned his face away to hide the shame.

The girl put a finger to his lips in comfort. Jack felt the throb of his bruised eye and realized he must have looked like a beaten mess. Snow White did not mind.

Flames leapt from the south garden, streaking the hedge only fifty feet away.

"We gotta get outta here." He indicated the dead ogres. "There's plenty more where they came from. Yeh ain't too popular with wraiths and witches neither."

Her thin garment would be a problem outside.

"Yeh got anything that'll cover yeh from head to toe – maybe something of Rose Red's?"

The girl winked. She tore down a curtain of white mesh from the pavilion that had been used for mosquito netting. In a twirl, she enwrapped herself with it, resembling a bride under a long veil. To Jack's surprise, the netting actually dampened her Fae effect. No one could miss her but would not swoon with madness either.

"Fine, fine!" he said, ushering her into the maze. "Now, follow me out. One wrong turn and we get scorched."

Snow White grabbed his elbow with a trusting squeeze. They got through the maze and moved across the trampled lawn to learn what and who had survived the night's raid.

* * * * *

A rough list of casualty statistics for the Desertland Conflicts (popularly called the "Ogre Wars") compiled by 2nd Lt. Andrew "Slicer" Two-Leaves of the Forestland Army.

FORESTLAND SOLDIERS (MEN) - 5400 (served) - 2750 (casualties)
DESERTLAND SOLDIERS (MEN) - 11,500 (combatants) - 4700 (casualties)
FORESTLAND CIVILIANS - 550 (casualties)
OTHER FOREST RACES (ELF, FAE, DWARFS) - 29,000 (casualties)

Chapter 13

BROKEN PIECES

A mixture of heavy clouds and smoking ruins cast a murky pall over the Orchard grounds. All the brilliant shades of the summer blossoms were gone, replaced by black and naked orchard trees, or barren soil covered with soot and gray ash. Gone too were the birdsongs and eager hollers of students exercising before breakfast.

The siege was over but the grounds were unrecognizable. The stone spire was a lonely monument of blackened char, like a tower of Lell's underworld. There were no sleeping quarters or mess hall; the main lodge was gone. So were the stables and barn. Livestock was missing from their pens. The hens had been taken. A single wall of cracked glass was all that remained of Allwise's prized greenhouse. Neighboring farmers and townsfolk had arrived and were gazing at all the damage.

Only the infirmary still stood. It had lost a portion of its canvas roof and looked a bit lopsided but was otherwise intact. Most of the students and convalescent soldiers had gathered there. Jack led Snow White under the awning.

Everyone was busy. Rose Red had set up a small surgery in one corner and was sewing clean stitches in Barlan Wood's left leg. Several of Count Corrobis' wounded men were spread on cots, grateful to be cared for. One of them was Brion Bellows, the blacksmith turned tracker who had been so helpful to Jack in the woods. Manawydan and Geoff Greens had been bandaged, and rolled dice to pass the time. First-year students were salvaging an inventory of supplies. Tylo played his reed pipes in the corner. The lilting chords uplifted spirits that would otherwise have sunk.

The first to notice Jack was Manawydan, who roared with laughter. "Look at Spriggins! His bruised face is bluer than an ogre's."

The boys all dropped their work and clamored around their hero. "Jack! I saw you fight Bluebeard almost as good as Count Corrobis did." "Jack! I fought a real ogre." "Jack! I used the lasso throw you showed us." "Jack! Jack! Jack!"

Tylo leap-frogged over them. "Glad you be well, Giant Killer. Black eyes and a split lip suit your man-skin."

"Yeah, yeah," said Jack. "That bully Bluebeard slipped away."

Snow White reached her hand to Tylo from beneath her veil. He took it and bowed. "Spun yourself a pretty web, I see. Mistress Camlann. I can hardly see your lovely face."

Jack stepped in front of her. "Listen, y'all keep a distance. That thin net's the only thing keeping yeh from swooning."

Rose Red tied the last of Barlan's sutures and hurried over, embracing Snow White.

"I thought the Desertlanders had taken you. Or worse," she said.

Snow White smiled, indicating Jack.

"Jack, you saved her," said Rose, shifting a hug to him.

"Snow ain't safe yet," said Jack, fumbling with his arms. He felt sure he did not deserve the hug or the credit. "Where's Allwise?"

"Your bruises," said Rose. She carefully examined his face but did not answer him. "I can help get the swelling down. Bones feel intact."

"Where's Allwise?" he said again.

She teared up and appeared to avoid the question. "Frog and Timmy covered Perdur's body and laid him out back by the others. Lon, the groundskeeper is dead, and four of the Count's Men. Mrs. Linnie's badly burnt and Mysslo's missing. I fear the worst for him."

"Where's Allw—?"

She placed a hand over his mouth and nodded, indicating a hunched figure seated on a barrel under the shelter flap. The old man had his back to them and was staring blankly out at the ruins.

It was Allwise.

"What we knew of him is gone," said Rose.

Jack had seen plenty of hard things in his fifteen years but none stopped him cold like this one. He hesitated, and then walked over to his mentor.

Allwise did not notice Jack standing there. The sparkle had gone from his eyes. His lips twitched as if trying to form words, but no sound came out. The inspired energy that had kept him so vital and alert seemed drawn away. All that was left was a sad, bent husk of a man. Micca lay at his feet, still and heartbroken, awaiting a command from his master.

"Sir? It's Spriggins," said Jack, waving a hand before his mentor's face. "Yeh was just harping at me yesterday. Want to finish where yeh left off?"

"He can't hear you," said Rose.

Jack refused to accept this and leaned in closer. "Hey, old man. Yeh've always been real hard on me, saying I gotta step up to be my best version of me. We gave everything we had last night. Did all the things yeh taught us. We did it for this place, for each other, and for yeh. Maybe yeh could do the same too for us? I'll help yeh, if yeh want."

Allwise did not flinch, his attention caught by phantoms only he could see.

"What happened to him?" said Jack.

Rose Red dabbed the corners of Allwise's mouth with the handkerchief. "It had been coming for a while. You probably saw it too. I think the sight of Desertland soldiers storming our school was just too much. His brilliant mind just froze."

"I wasn't very nice to him," said Jack. "Ever."

Rose Red half smiled. "Neither was I. Neither was he, for that matter. Allwise doesn't see any value in 'nice'. He wants us to be fair and to keep on learning."

Drops of rain spattered the cracked pavement followed by a summer shower. Jack helped Rose Red move Allwise back under the tent where he could stay dry. They left him to his locked thoughts.

Frog stuck his head inside the tent. He was drenched (not unusual for the swimmer). "Good ol' Water Spirit. Rain'll put out the last fires."

"Too bad the Wet Codger didn't show up last night," said Manawydan with a grunt, crossing his arms.

Snow White darted about filling containers with rain water outside. Rose Red watched as her gossamer veil flitted behind her. All the boys were watching too.

"Jack," said Rose. "Snow's mosquito netting won't hold up much longer, not with all her activity."

"Yer right," said Jack. "Allwise told me yeh both planned to take her to the Dwarf Domain and ask the miners to watch over her? He figured their mountains would be the safest place to hide her from her enemies. Believe me, she's got a whole pack of them."

Rose shook her head. "That's not possible now." She turned to Allwise and to her patients on the cots. "Doctors are scarce. Plus, I can't leave *him* alone."

Jack agreed. "Yep. Yer the only sawbones left. The Orchard needs yeh. So, I'll take Snow to the Iron Hills myself."

"How, Jack?"

"On Blackberry."

She drew a handful of bean pods from a jar on a shelf and squeezed out a salve. She rubbed the balm on Jack's face.

"Even if you do get past the battle lines, dwarfs are difficult," she said, "Allwise would have done a lot of swift talking to get them to accept Snow White. That's not one of your strong suits, friend."

Jack's aches began to numb. He felt a surge of confidence. "Allwise said the same thing. But with him in a stare and Perdur gone, I'm gonna stack my deck and make the trip anyway."

He bowed under the tent flap and shielded his eyes against the rain. Through the downpour he spied the remains of what had been Allwise's study. The roof was collapsed but two walls were intact. He jumped off the platform and ran to the study.

"There's a slim chance what I need here didn't get burned up," he figured.

Two charred beams lay across Allwise's heavy stone vault. His desk and other cabinets had been crushed. Treasured volumes of knowledge were scattered amid the soot and debris. The books were rapidly being ruined by the rain. Jack looked mournfully at their blackened spines. As he started to climb over the slippery beams, somebody moved in the shadows. It was the young scholar, Tymmy Mason, crawling on his hands and knees, scooping the soaked books into his arms.

"What the blarn are yeh doing, Tym?"

"Hey Jack," said the thirteen-year-old through the rain. "Trying to save – I dunno – the last of our schooling? Whatever I can grab and put into Allwise's stone vault."

Jack could see Tymmy's innocent face was as wet from tears as it was from raindrops.

"Lemme help."

"Can you get the vault open? It's locked."

"That's one of my gifts," said Jack.

He swiped the drenched bangs out of his face, pushed his ear against the vault door, and began to work its embedded clockwork latch. Tracking the series of clicks reminded him of solving the hedge maze ("*half-turn right, full turn left, back...*") His old thief talents proved reliable as ever. The lock clicked open, and, with a bit of prying with his bone knife, he pulled the heavy door back.

Tymmy peeked in with a gasp. "Look! The rarest books and manuscripts are here, safe as ever." He fingered past some of the volumes. "*Tom Tailor's Trail Guide. History of Giantdom. Western Dialects. Morgan's Mathematical Theories. Great Sagas of the Forestland.* A bundle of scrolls and maps. It's not all gone!"

"That's a relief," said Jack, looking around.

He spotted the small cherrywood chest he had come looking for. Beneath the lid was a yellowed scroll with a cracked wax seal. It was *the Deed of Dynadin.*

"Yer right, kid. It's not all gone. Not by a long shot."

Jack slipped the deed inside his vest pocket. Then he helped Tymmy stuff the surviving books into the vault.

"We better take shelter," said Tymmy. "We can catch fever in this rain the longer we stay out here."

Jack slapped the younger boy on the back. "Let's git then. Race yeh back to the infirmary."

"No fair. Your legs are longer than mine!"

"I'll hop on one foot, Mason!"

The weather dwindled to a drizzle when they reached the tent. Varlan Wood rode his colt Thundersong up at the same time. The drenched twin slid off his tired horse and dodged under the flap to check his brother's stitches. Breathlessly, he turned to Jack.

"The Count's Men caught up to the ogres outside Rivercross," he said, pausing to gulp water from a ladle passed to him by Rose Red. "Those 'snake faces' didn't stand a chance. Saw it myself. Count Corrobis captured Bluebeard. They're going to hold him in a prison at Havensbend."

The sound of more hooves clomped outside. A mule-drawn wagon pulled up. Two women leapt out and tromped in for cover from the storm. One was scrawny, biting her bottom lip with a worried face. Jack recalled her name was Tilda, a cook from the Bean Tea Inn. The other woman was Ma.

"Look at us!" said Ma, shaking out her wet shawl and hat. "Soaked as boiled tators."

"Hey, Ma," said Jack, relieved to see her looking as robust as ever.

Ludi did not share the same sentiments looking at him. "Yeh got purple shiners all over yer face. But, my boy, yer still standing, healing, and no doubt fixing to stir things up elsewhere."

Jack grinned. "Don't know where I git it from."

She laughed heartily and nodded at the wagon. "Tilda and me brung supplies, mostly food and quilts from the Inn. A couple lanterns. Dry stockings and pairs of boots from Mister Scratch. We in Rivercross all heard what happened here. Such a shame, son." She peered past the mist. "Swee' Sleeping Beauty! Ain't a floorboard or roof shingle left, is there? And all them pretty plants be gone."

"Ogres took it all, Ma," said Jack.

Ludi put comforting arms around Frog and Tymmy Mason. "Naw. It was yeh boys and all yer learning that made this Orchard special and it still is."

Jack motioned the youngsters. "Y'all help Barlan unpack the wagon and find Thundersong and Ma's mule a dry spot."

They jumped off the sick deck, splashing about in the rain, happy to be useful.

"Look at yeh, Jacky," said Ludi. "I'd think yeh was running the place if I didn't know better." She looked around the tent. "Rose Red!"

The dark girl was enveloped in Ludi's embrace. "It's good you're here, Mrs. Spriggins."

"Now, now," said Ludi. "Put me and Tilda to work. We passed more of the Count's riders driving up, some looking worse for wear. Guessin' they'll fill these cots soon."

"I'm treating everyone who needs it," said Rose Red.

Tylo hopped on top of the table, clutching his right shoulder. "Treat me. The ogs did slam me against the spire. My shooting arm smarts."

Rose Red studied his injury. "Why didn't you say something before? Your joint needs to be put back in place, Tylo. It's simple, but will hurt."

"I trust you," said the elf.

With a "one-two-three" count, Rose Red gave his arm a firm thrust and snapped it back into its socket. Tylo groaned with a thin "Eee-yo-yo" between clenched teeth. Jack and Ludi winced but Tylo hopped up with wide bright eyes.

"Ah, Sparky, thank you for Rose Redness!" he sang. "My arm be happy. Thank you."

Ludi shook her head in amazement. "Yer a brave little fella."

"I am humbled to greet you with a healthy hand, Mistress Giant-Killer-Ma Ma'am," Tylo waved.

She waved back.

Snow White stretched some clean linen over the wooden work table.

Ma took notice. "And who's this lass under all the wrappings?"

Jack spoke cautiously. "This is Snow White Camlann, Ma. She's a—"

"A faerie, son. I know." If Ludi felt a typical woman's resentment towards the Fae, it did not show. "I seen 'em before in the woods. Not as young as this one, though, and not for a long

~ 167 ~

time. Let me help yeh, dear." She took one end of Snow White's sheet and they laid it out smoothly.

Jack spoke up. "Snow and I better git a move on. The more folks learn that she's here, the more danger she'll be in."

"Where to, son?" said his mother.

"North. That's all I'm gonna say."

Frog tugged on Jack's sleeve. "Jack, I can git yeh through the Swamps. That's my homeland, after all."

Jack was not about to bring an eleven-year-old into the center of the war. "There's something more important for yeh to do."

"What's that?" said the boy.

"Need yeh to go into the woods out west, find the Learning Twigs tribe, and fetch more elflings to come start their schooling."

Tymmy Mason said, "Who'll teach them?"

"*Y'all*," said Jack. "Rose Red. Manaw, Geoff, the twins. Everyone here can teach what they know best. Yeh got the books."

All the students perked up as if seeds in the soil had sprung new green buds.

"I can do that!" said Frog. "But I ain't been in the west forest before."

One of the soldiers stood up. "I'll go, Jack." It was Brion Bellows. "Give me a day to get patched up and I'll take the lads to the Learning Twigs glade."

"Obliged," said Jack, nodding to the boys. "Bellows knows the way."

Tylo slumped over like a miserable kicked ball. "Jack Spriggins thinks so poorly of Tylo that he will not even allow me to gather my own kin to re-grow the Orchard. Why?"

Everyone's eyes were on Jack, waiting for his reply.

"Because I need yeh to come with me and Snow White," he said. "Yeh can get through trees faster, see dangers faster, and yap yer way out of trouble faster. Will yeh?"

"Indeed, will I! We! Us!" A lit firecracker could not have exploded with half the thrill Tylo had. "Why do we dilly-dally? Let us go."

"Careful with your shoulder, Tylo," said Rose Red. "It'll be tender for a bit."

"We leave as soon as I can find Blackberry," said Jack.

The air lingered with a wet stickiness left behind by the rain. Blackberry and the other horses were found grazing in a meadow by the Orchard lake under a grove of fig trees that the fire had not destroyed. Jack called out. Blackberry trotted over, nudging his snout into the crook of his neck.

"You're already tacked up," said Jack, patting his mane. "Ready for a journey?"

The horse tossed his head and snorted.

"I'll take that as a yes. Good boy."

He grabbed a handful of figs and packed them in the saddlebags. Mounted atop Blackberry, he rounded up the other horses and drove them back to the common yard. Ludi was covering Allwise with a quilt as Jack and the team trotted up.

"It still makes me gush seeing yeh tall in the saddle like a Ranger," she said.

"I'll be itching saddle sores before this ride's over," said Jack.

Ludi spoke in a low voice. "Tell me truthful, son. Should yeh be the one leading this journey? Yeh never took a liking to elf or faerie-kind."

Jack leaned down. "Yeh neither, Ma. I reckon yeh told me a bunch of times when I was a kid the whole lot of 'em should've been run'd off or shot. Why'd did yeh change, Ma?"

Ludi slapped a hand to her cheeks and trilled her lips. "Yeh remember I was feeling poorly, don't yeh? Found it hard to like m'self, not to mention others. Them beans Allwise sent yeh home with shook my doldrums away. Everything started to shine after that. Folks too. Even m'self! T'were the biggest change of all. But yeh ain't sick like I was. Can yeh shake that hatefulness from yer core?"

"I dunno," said Jack. "But even if I got nothing but a heart full of hate, I promise I'll still see this through. I owe the old man for all he's taught me."

"We both owe him, Jack."

Allwise just stared ahead, his hands shaking lightly.

"Yer heading back to Rivercross, Ma?" said Jack.

"Naw. These kids need a ma for a while," she said. "Mr. Scratch is kindly watching the inn."

"About that serving girl of yers. Ganzil."

Ma shook her head. "She's gone, Jacky." Ludi smiled, enjoying the gossip. "Pretty thing took off in the middle of the night, prob'ly with one of her beaus. Didn't even say 'good-bye'. Yeh should've seen her room. Full of mirrors, it was. Hand mirrors, wall mirrors, even little pocket mirrors."

"Nothing good ever looked back at her from 'em, that's for sure."

"Yeh'll be back as soon as yer quest is done?"

"Reckon not." said Jack, determined. "There's a war and I been itching to fight. Soon as Snow White's safe, I'm gonna join the ranks. I can't be held back no more."

Ludi patted his hand. "Yeh got gumption, my boy. Always did."

Rose Red and Snow White came out of the tent and gave each other teary hugs.

"If you need me, Snow, send the petal of a white rose and I'll find you," said Rose Red.

Jack was struck by their bond. The black girl from Zan and the faerie from Lake Dream could not have looked more different, yet no one would question they were sisters.

Jack leaned out and offered his hand. "Climb on with me, Snow White."

She gracefully vaulted on to the back of the saddle without so much as a billow from her net veil.

"Didn't see that coming," said Jack. "Nice move."

Rose Red dried her eyes. "I'm going to miss you too, Jack."

"Where's that tawny runt of an elf?"

A shrill whistle came from the Orchard wall. Tylo was on top of it, pacing impatiently on his hands. "Hee-yo-yo, Giant Killer! Why do lunkheads take so long? Any elf would have gone to the dwarf mines and back again in the time you've taken to get on your horsey."

Jack rolled his eyes and spurred Blackberry. "Heigh!"

The hound, Micca, suddenly bound from Allwise's side, barking and running to keep up. Jack started to shoo the dog back but saw there was no changing his mind.

"Guess we got another on our crew," he said. "C'mon, Micca! If yeh can keep up, yer welcome."

The other students lined up to see them off and sang a plaintive farewell.

"Fire blazes. Water falls.
Still our apples grow.
Voices silenced. Axes swung.
Trees bend to and fro."

"Orchard seeds are planted deep.
Roots reach far below.
Let the Darkness keep on digging.
Still our apples grow."

Blackberry cantered out the Orchard gate. Jack felt Snow White's grip tighten around his waist. Tylo leapt in the trees above. Micca panted alongside. The singing voices of home faded behind them as the road took new turns ahead.

Jack took stock of his crew. "I'll bet Redvere's leading a troop of archers into battle right now, like a knight in a picture book. Here I am, the Giant Killer, with an elf, a crazed hound, and a faerie draped in mosquito net."

He snickered.

"At least no one's going to write about this. History is for the heroes."

* * * * *

From a brochure for the Havensbend Museum (a century and a half after the Siege of the Orchard).

"New to the permanent exhibits in the Corrobis wing, THE OGRE WAR COLLECTION is most popular with our visitors. Among the artifacts on display:

HILT OF THE SNAKE-BITE DAGGER - Historians agree that Jack the Giant Killer must have gained this bronze weapon from a mystic temple and used it to slay five hundred monster ogres in a single battle. The exact translation of 'Snake-Bite' is up for debate among language experts.

BRIDAL VEIL OF SNOW WHITE - A fragment of netted lace thought to be from the wedding gown of a Forestland princess who had no doubt been rescued from peril by a handsome prince.

ELF'S FEATHER COLLAR - A holiday garment worn by merry, simple-minded elf workers over tunics, hose, and pointed boots when they were not making toys or mending shoes.

HERO'S BATTLE AX - A weapon likely wielded by Jack the Giant Killer himself to tame fire-breathing dragons. The northern word 'Manawydan' (translated as 'Strong Wind') crudely carved on the handle must be a nickname for Jack as it describes him perfectly.

Most of these priceless finds were discovered on an archaeological dig at an apple orchard near the 'Wizard's Stone Pillar', a tourist attraction of Forestland Park. Museum curators have labored with fairy-time scholars to authenticate the items' histories. **Any corrections or additions to their research, however, is welcome.**"

Chapter 14

ROAD RABBLE

Jack did not steer his party straight into the deep woods. Instead, he chose to visit *Whispering Vine*, home of his friend, Ella Vintner. It was a notable vineyard a few miles from town, where they could stock up on vittles and other necessities for the journey north.

"Tylo will be the happiest to make acquaintance of Red Riding Hood," said the elf clambering from the boughs. "She be almost as famous as Jack Giant Killer."

"Her name's just Ella," said Jack.

Snow White was silently seated behind him on the saddle. Tylo bound through the trees beside the road. Micca panted keeping apace, nearly mad with devotion at their side. After traveling a fair stretch, the hound growled suspiciously and then began barking.

"Whoa!" said Jack, rearing Blackberry to halt. "What is it, boy?"

Up ahead, a stick snapped at the roadside. The dog charged into the underbrush.

"Micca, heel!" said Jack. The angry hound did not obey the command.

There was a rustle of branches as a critter fled. To everyone's surprise it was Mysslo, the ground elf, who suddenly emerged on the road waving his skinny arms, begging in sloppy elfspeak for Jack to stop. "P-p-please! Do not harm m-m-me!"

The charging hound pounced on the ground elf with a ferocious growl. Mysslo shrieked, trying to bury himself in the dirt for protection. Jack leapt off the saddle. Tylo alit from the branches. Both of them grabbed ahold of Micca before the ground elf was mauled.

"What's wrong with yeh, boy?"

The dog continued to growl.

"It must be the ogre scent Micca smells," said Jack. "Mysslo's probably covered with it."

Mysslo cried out, "Y-y-yes! Yes! That be so. Don't let the mad dog eat me."

"No scratch on you," said Tylo, checking him. "The hound knows the stink is not yours, Mysslo. Go back to the Orchard and be not chomped on."

"No-no-no," said Mysslo, trying to dig a deeper hole with his gnarled fingers. "O-o-ogres be there."

"The ogres were run off," said Jack, keeping hold of the dog. "But I saw them drag yeh away last night. Thought yeh was a goner."

Tylo grabbed the pitiful ground elf firmly by the shoulders. "Mysslo, we be your friends," he clicked in elfspeak. "You've survived the ogs. They be gone. Now be an elf! Show Sparky's courage and make jokes, not fraidy tears."

Jack silently wondered, "Was that why elves always laughed and played pranks? Was it being brave, not cheeky?"

Mysslo sucked strands of drool up his nostrils and mouth. "I c-c-cannot go back to Orchard. It's not safe for me there. N-n-not safe."

Tylo shrugged. "Where we go be not safe either. There's Snow White Fae we have to save."

"I could keep eyes on S-s-snow White too," said Mysslo, cracking a bashful grin at the faerie.

Tylo looked at Jack like a pathetic dog begging for scraps. Snow White encouragingly touched his shoulder.

Jack shook his head. "Naw. We ain't bringing Mysslo. Blackberry's already got a full saddle and he'll just slow us down."

"No-no! Keep me. You must," said Mysslo. "Don't leave me behind."

"I could put him on my shoulders like an elf tyke," said Tylo, who scooted under Mysslo as the ground elf jumped onto his sinewy shoulders. "See, Giant Killer? I be robusty like Manawydan. He weighs very little."

Jack released Micca. "Bring him. But if he gets dropped, we ain't stopping to pick him up."

"Fine be fine," said Tylo, scaling up an oak with Mysslo clinging to him.

"Y-y-yes," said Mysslo meekly. "H-h-hooray."

The hound whimpered at Jack, seemingly disgruntled.

"I feel the same, boy," he said, remounting Blackberry. "Heigh!"

Micca ran alongside Blackberry at a brisk trot until they reached Whispering Vine.

Ella Vintner had become famous at the same time Jack did. She was known forest-wide as "Red Riding Hood" who had escaped the clutches of Likov Fen, the villainous wolf trainer who was slain before he could devour her, thanks to Jack's heroics. In the two years since, she remained secluded in her family's chateau near the Green River at the forest's edge, after her mother had passed away. Life should have been very lonely for the thirteen-year-old; home-schooled and forbidden to leave the vineyard by her protective father. But that was not the story, as Jack well knew. Ella had countless devoted friends to laugh, sing, and talk with. They just happened to be *animals and birds*.

The ability to talk with woodland creatures was regarded by Ella as her "spirit gift". Jack had scoffed at such nonsense until he saw it up close and knew it was no hoax.

He secretly admitted, "Her chats with wrens, foxes and wolves saved me more than once." As did her friendship, which was always faithful and devoted.

It was past sunset and yet the vineyard had an air of chaos about it. Workers and house servants were loading wagons, hitching up horses, and dashing about in a hurried manner. Jack did not understand what the fuss was about. So, rather than ride up the front lane of the chateau (with his unusual companions), he took them to a concealed grove of blue fir trees nearby. It was a favorite spot for Jack, where an array of soft blue needles shone on the branches in a way usually reserved for shimmering lakes. He always got a solemn feeling that the eyes of spirits were watching them.

"Don't stir up trouble," he said, looking mainly at Tylo. "I'll be back in a hare's minute."

Jack hopped off Blackberry and handed the reins to Snow White. Rain began to sprinkle as he crept around to the back entrance of the chateau by the kitchen. Not surprisingly, another crafty visitor had come calling. A rusty fox was rapping its paw on the door.

Ella opened it. "Hello, Bright Grin," she said to the lively pup.

Jack stayed hid behind a rain barrel under the storm drain. In the doorway, Ella had grown an inch or three. She still had the glow in her gray eyes that was so engaging. Her long, auburn locks were pulled back from her face; a stray curl dangled on her forehead as always, refusing to stay tied. The blue-checked dress and sash she wore did not fit well and her bare feet were covered with ash from hearth cinders. She was the kind of girl who liked to pitch in with household chores (despite her wealth), so these were likely work clothes.

The fox kept its head low. Ella bent down to put an ear closer. She suddenly straightened up and looked Jack's way.

"Are you sure it was Jack Spriggins you saw?" she said.

The fox fidgeted, spun around, and then sat with a yip.

"His yellow eyes looked like a raccoon's with dark rings around them? Oh, what's Jack gotten himself into?"

She ducked into the kitchen a moment and returned with a morsel of bacon, which Bright Grin gratefully devoured.

"I understand the sow that provided this was a kind soul who had grown so big she couldn't move."

The fox could have not cared less. It licked the grease off its jowls.

Ella shooed Bright Grin away with a knowing glance. "Better be off, little pal. Papa's foreman isn't as sure as I am that you've been staying clear of the henhouse."

With a yip, Bright Grin ran off.

The rain went from a sprinkle to a downpour. Ella poked her head out in the rain, looking toward the fir grove.

"Jack?" she called with a pitched whisper. "Are you out there, Jack?"

He stepped into the light. "I reckon so."

Ella's face lit up and she took his hands with a warm clasp, shuffling him indoors.

The Vintner kitchen was as comforting as ever; a large, brick room with a stately hearth. There was an iron stove, overhung with copper pots and skillets and a wood-burning oven. Assortments of bread, fruit jars, and grapes in bunches rested on a large maple countertop. Ella's scarlet cape was draped on a peg by the door.

"Jack Spriggins! I've missed you," she said, pulling him closer to the fire. "Oh, you *do* look like a raccoon around the eyes. It must've been a miserable tussle."

"Ogres," said Jack. "They attacked the Orchard."

"Yes, we heard the news," said Ella. "A messenger came from Rivercross. How awful. That's why we're packing up here to take refuge in Havensbend in case the attacks spread."

Jack nodded. "It ain't a bad idea."

"Come with us. Papa won't be all 'happy hand-shakes' but gaining you and your crossbow would certainly make you more welcome."

"I can't," said Jack. "Got a big favor to ask yeh."

Ella smiled. "Well, ask away."

"I'm leading a journey up north. Can yeh spare some food, drink, and clothes for a friend?"

"You're going to the war?"

"Around it actually. This 'friend' was hiding at the Orchard because the enemy wants her dead. And Ella? She's a faerie. The last one living. They even killed her ma."

"The poor thing. She must be terrified."

"Y'know, she ain't, somehow." Jack helped himself to a ladle of water from the indoor pump.

"It's just the two of you?"

"No. I got Blackberry, Micca and—" Jack stalled.

"What is it?"

"And two elves."

Ella giggled. "Jack Spriggins with elves? I am so delighted."

"Yeah, yeah."

"Where are your friends?"

"Out back in the fir grove." Jack helped himself to some grapes.

"Why, Jack!" said Ella. "You left them out in the dark rainy woods, as if I wouldn't welcome them inside? I'm horrified."

Jack reached for her arm. "And I knew yeh would be. But yeh have to understand, nobody can know about the faerie. With all the fuss here, somebody might—"

The door to the stairway flew open. A sleek woman dressed in a jade satin jacket and long skirt burst in. She had an icy expression that turned colder when she saw Jack.

"Ella! What is the meaning of this? Answer me, you selfish girl."

The lady spoke as one who was used to ordering servants about. She grabbed an iron poker from the hearth grate and pointed it at Jack.

"Who is this vagabond in my kitchen? I'll summon the sheriff and have you hauled off."

"That'd be a first for Big Bill," said Jack.

Ella calmly stepped between them. "Why, no need for that, Mother. This is our good friend, Jack Spriggins."

"Jack Spriggins?" said the woman, obviously familiar with his name.

"Yes," said Ella, turning to Jack. "This is my stepmother. She and father were wed last spring when he went back to the Coastlands for a visit. I'm afraid I didn't get around to writing you about it. Stepmother and her two daughters have come to live here at Whispering Vine so I won't be lonely."

Jack recalled Ella's sweet, late mother and knew at once that this second Mrs. Vintner was not a kind person. She had severely coiffed red hair and a face of cold beauty with black-lined eyes. Her smile appeared painted upon her pursed lips.

"*You* are the Giant Killer?" she said, lowering her weapon.

"That's what they call me, Mrs. Vintner," said Jack.

"It is *Madame* Vintner, if you please," she insisted. "And, of course, your burglaries of the Giantdom are well-known, even in the Coastlands. Perhaps your battered appearance is not what it seems."

Ella spoke up. "He was defending himself against the ogre attackers we were warned about."

Madame Vintner returned the poker to its stand. "And now, he's here." Her skirts swished as she crossed the floor with sharp clicking heels.

"Papa said Jack is welcome here anytime, Mother," said Ella.

"And our door will stay open to him, child." If possible, Madame Vintner's politeness was more threatening than her harshness. "Unfortunately, today we are fleeing for our lives. You must understand, young man, how inconvenient it is to entertain guests at the moment."

"I just dropped in to check on Ella," said Jack. "Don't mean to cause any trouble. Unless, Ella, yeh wanna come with?"

"Why, Jack," said Madame. "I *need* Ella. Her father is ill and my own daughters would be lost without her." She brushed at Ella's loose curl with a swipe of manicured fingernails. "But it is so good to know our little family has a capable, famous protector to watch over us among all the Forestland boors we meet."

Micca the hound barked outside from the grove, interrupting her.

"Whose dreadful dog is that?" she said. "It had better not be one of ours."

"Mine," said Jack, who glanced out the door. "I'll see to it on my way out, ma'am."

"May I please see Jack away, Mother?" said Ella.

Madame Vintner sniffed with displeasure. "Be quick about it. We've lost so much time already." She shifted back up the stairs, the kitchen door shutting loudly behind her. Jack imagined the slam of a dungeon gate could not have sounded as gloomy.

"So, yer pa got hitched again," he said. "Sorry."

Ella waved off the apology. "Your instinct to keep the elves and faerie away from the house was for the best. Let's be quick and fetch food for your journey. Then I can meet them."

She packed loaves of bread, some jars of tomato soup, a block of cheese and some cherries and grapes into a basket. Once regarded by Jack as a rich little pest, Ella had grown full of purpose.

"I should've been in touch with yeh more, Ella."

"You wrote," she said, pumping a jug full of water.

"I sent a single lousy postage card from Ma's inn over a year ago. Kind of shameful when I think of the pages and pages yeh used to write me every week. I kept them all in my desk at the Orchard."

Ella's gleeful smile returned. "That card from you is one of my prized possessions. Like my cherry-red cape."

She stretched on tiptoes for a tin of butter biscuits. Jack easily reached up to the shelf and handed them to her.

"We've been friends since the first moment we met, Jack, and always will be whether we hear from each other every day or not."

Jack hefted the heavy basket on his arm. "When the war dies down, I'll come around more. I promise."

"Oh dear," said Ella, taking inventory of the food she had loaded. "I just realized I've no clue what a faerie eats."

"Same stuff we do. And don't bother about the elves. Yeh don't wanna know what they eat."

Micca continued to bark outside.

"I better go check that dog," said Jack.

Ella frowned. "He's confused. Going on about digging, a storm cellar, and a pit of snakes. It's hard to make out. Dogs lose their words when they get too excited."

She stepped into a pair of slippers and tied on the red cape to accompany Jack outside. The rain had let up. Jack lifted a low hanging bough for them to cross under into the grove.

"Where's Micca?" he said. "I heard him yelping all the way from the house."

Tylo sank to all fours and acted like a rabid hound. "Feisty-Furry got upset, gnashing fangs and ready to bite Mysslo."

"Mad dog, mad dog," muttered Mysslo.

"I snapped elf sparks from my fingertips to scare him off," said Tylo. "He ran thataway."

Blackberry sidled up to Ella, affectionately nuzzling her.

"Sweet Blackberry," said Ella. "There's feed and water in our stables. You know the way."

The horse snorted and trotted out of the grove as if at home.

Tylo's eyes bugged open. "Berry-Hoofer knew just what you told him?" He skipped around in excitement. "You be Red Riding Hood! A person who can talk to all manner of beasties."

Ella curtseyed. "That's me, more or less. The stories get so big, I don't recognize *me* in them most of the time."

Tylo play-acted, pulling the hem of her red cape around his head. "*Oh, Grandmama! Your eyes are so big!*" He removed the cape and gnashed his teeth. "*All the better to see you, child.*"

The little party burst into laughter, timid Mysslo highest-pitched of all.

Ella gasped for air, turning to Jack. "Did I really sound like that?"

Jack pressed a finger and thumb together. "A tad."

Tylo went down on one knee. "I, Tylo of the Learning Twigs, vow to be Riding Hood's most treasured suitor when we both be grown enough for such things."

Jack grunted. "Rose Red'll be mighty relieved to know yeh moved on *from her.*"

Ella folded her arms in mock-jealousy. "I've a feeling you'll only break my heart, Tylo."

The tree elf blew several sweet notes on his pipes.

Jack nudged him. "Stop it. Git some blood back in yer elf noggin and hush up before everybody knows we're out here."

Ella shyly approached Snow White. "There's food in the basket if you get hungry."

Snow White gestured gratefully.

"I've met your father," said Ella. "You have his kindness in your eyes. And I'm sorry about your mother. I lost mine too. In fact, she rests in peace right beneath that very tree."

She indicated a fir of darkest blue. The faerie dismounted and took respectful steps towards the grave, then spun perfect circles around the spreading roots in tribute.

"Thank you. Mama would've loved that." Ella then took note of the net veil. "You don't need this silly thing," she said, lifting it off. "I'll fetch you some practical clothes that will disguise you, not draw more attention."

Snow White shook out her long black hair, clearly pleased to be free of the drape.

In the shadows of the pines an animal growled. Jack and Tylo drew their bows. Micca had returned, now barking madly. His threatening barks were directed at Mysslo.

Tylo put his hands on his ears. "Yippity yip yip!"

"Stop, Micca!" said Jack. "What're yeh so afraid of?"

Ella ignored Micca's bared teeth and knelt beside him. The dog kept steadily barking while she pet the scruff of his neck, listening carefully. "Micca's not frightened for himself." she said.

"W-w-what's Riding Hood doing?" Mysslo came forward. "Make her stop. S-s-stop."

The dog lunged at the ground elf.

Jack caught hold of Micca's collar. "What's with you, boy?"

"He's been trying to warn you, Jack," said Ella carefully. "He doesn't want what happened at the Orchard to happen to any of you."

Tylo aimed his twig darts out at the wilderness. "Are the ogs out there?"

Ella shook her head. "No, I'm afraid that's not it. Micca saw it all. Someone let them into the Orchard. Someone who was already inside."

"Who?" said Jack, struggling to hold Micca still.

Ella pointed to Mysslo, the ground elf.

"*Him.*"

* * * * *

A letter from Allwise of the Orchard found in the archives of the Vintner estate at Whispering Vine. It is dated two years before the infamous "Siege".

My good Mister Vintner,

I would like you to consider sending your daughter, Ella, to my school at the Orchard west of Rivercross. She would attend on full scholarship. As you know, we teach youth of exceptional abilities. Her considerable gifts of communication would be nurtured and trained along with her bright mind in a manner that could not be understood even by the finest private institutions of the Coastlands.

Ella would not be the only female student in our care. My own ward, Rose Red of Zan, is a medical prodigy who has advanced her exceptional talents. She is only a few years older than Ella and would willingly embrace her as a sisterly mentor. The experience would be enriching to both girls.

I know your household must be lonely since the passing of your admirable wife. We would offer her the finest curriculum for education, health and friendship. Please consider.

Allwise
of the Orchard
There is no record that any response was sent.

Chapter 15

GOBLIN BITES

Jack clasped Micca's collar, holding the hound at bay.

"L-l-liar!" said Mysslo. "Riding Hood be liar!"

"Ella ain't got a lying bone in her body," said Jack.

Tylo shook his head in disbelief. "Mysslo. You let the ogs into the Orchard?"

Mysslo squirmed. "No-no. Never! H-h-how would a maimed wretchling like me even do such a thing?"

"Micca says you dug tunnels," said Ella.

Mysslo twitched. "Gardens. N-n-not tunnels."

"Naw," said Jack, who instinctively unhitched the crossbow from his belt. "Reckon it adds up. All that time down in the root cellar yeh was digging an entry right under our feet."

"Bugs!" said Tylo. "Dribbly Mysslo was working for Bluebeard?"

Mysslo's grimace turned to a smirk as his hunched little body straightened.

"Why no," he said, without the stutter. "Bluebeard works for me. He does what I tell him to do. That ink-stained prince may call himself a 'warlord' but he's only a weapon in my arsenal. *All* ogres are under my thumb."

The change in behavior was shocking.

"I recognize yer voice," said Jack, taking aim. "Yer one of the wraiths. The short hood from the Briars."

He let go of Micca and loaded his bow.

The ferocious dog pounced on Mysslo. They rolled on to the grass in a flurry of growls and flailing limbs. The ground elf did not cower or scream. There was a ghastly gleam in his eyes as he bared his rotten teeth at the dog – AND TOOK A BITE. The hound yelped; a bloody chunk went missing from his side.

Mysslo chewed. "Oh, how I've longed to do that. Until the big stomping horse left us, I did not dare. Come, Tylo. You cannot be surprised."

"Mysslo," said Tylo, his bow trembling in his hands. "This jest be not worthy."

"No jest," said Mysslo swallowing with satisfaction. "I am, indeed, the purest of goblins. Devoted to the screams of the terror-stricken."

Ella hurried over to the fallen dog, covering him protectively with her cape. "You wicked fiend! No spirit will protect you now."

"I shall try to remember that, Mistress Vintner," said Mysslo, "When I am devouring you."

Jack took aim with his crossbow. "Yeh ain't touching a hair on her head."

Mysslo let out a false sigh. "I suppose I could leave her hair intact. It smells yummy but is not as satisfying as the flesh."

"No, no, nope," said Tylo, in disbelief. "Mysslo just be a groundie from Trusting Claytoes tribe. That is all."

"Before the wraiths sought me out, I *was* of the starving Claytoes," said Mysslo. "Then I ate them all. Who knew it would also be so pleasant?"

The tree elf slumped. "Oh, Mysslo. Such a liar. Such an actor. You were never hurt by ogs when Corrobis found you."

Mysslo picked at his teeth with a finger. "Those self-made wounds were my way inside the Orchard. Oh, how I resisted gobbling that fetching Count and his men. All but the cat; I hate the taste of feline."

Of all the foes Jack had ever faced, none scared him more than this four-foot goblin. His slightest movement, his shrewdest glance, made the heart skip a beat. The wraith snake seemed less dangerous in comparison.

"The gob conned us all, even Allwise," said Jack. "Ain't it clear as spit now?" Without waiting for an answer, he pulled his crossbow trigger.

The arrow shot glanced Mysslo on his bony shoulder. The goblin shrieked in rage and charged at Jack with hair-raising speed. His lean strength was a shock and he wrestled the bow down before Jack could load it again.

"You're quite a shot, Spriggins," said Mysslo, savagely twisting Jack's wrist. "If you hadn't done that, I might've spared you. We wraiths could have used a heartless murderer like yourself."

Jack hollered in pain and tried to jab the fiend with his knee. Mysslo hopped back with hideous grace. Then Tylo fired a dart from his bow. The goblin caught it in his bare hand without even looking up. He then sprang at the tree elf, landing with a brutal thud against Tylo's chest, wrapping his legs around him like a vice.

"Alas, cousin," hissed Mysslo. "I'd rather hoped you would join me."

"I will never be a goblin!" said Tylo.

"Why not?" said Mysslo. "Once you've tasted the power, you'll see. Spriggins hates you but *fears* me. Let's start by feasting on these three lunkhead spawn."

"No!" said Tylo. "Sparky's flame, help me!"

A sharp whisk of three pings whistled in the air. Mysslo was struck in the back by a trio of thorns. He screamed as if pierced by spears and hobbled off Tylo. Jack looked to see who had shot the prickers.

Snow White lowered her yew wand from her lips. Apparently, it was also a dart shooter. The thirteen-year-old faerie wore the stern expression of a young warrior ready to make a kill.

No one had expected this.

"Snow?" said Jack, gawking.

"I thank you, Mistress Camlann," said Tylo, rocking clear of the villain.

Mysslo weaved and bobbed. "Ah, struck by the odious Fae." He addressed Snow White with a leer. "You brought the attack upon the Orchard. It would not have been necessary had you just died with your mother. Now, your friends will die too. All because of you."

Snow White raised the yew wand and swung it in loops over her head. A hollow, beckoning note blew from the instrument, so deep and penetrating, it made Jack's ears ache. The hum summoned a stronger buzz from the crook of a large fir tree. The buzz grew louder, wilder, and somehow angrier with each pass of the wand.

Ella pointed. "There's a hornets nest up there."

A cloud of angry hornets swarmed out of the fir branches and flew around Mysslo who began screaming in agony as he was stung repeatedly.

"Curse the fae! Curse the fae! Curses!"

Jack was thrown by the frenzied sight. "There's a lot about faeries and goblins I got to get caught up on."

The swarm spread out, flying madly through the grove.

"Jack," said Ella, yanking his sleeve. "I think Snow White's wand can only call hornets, not control them."

"Meaning there's stingers for all of us too?"

He pulled Ella away from Micca and they tumbled for protection under a cluster of evergreens. Tylo scurried up a pine trunk. His yips betrayed several hornets were on his tail. Snow White stood motionless with not so much as a blink. The ornery insects passed her by.

Mysslo had a different defense. Covered in welts, he issued the bloodcurdling *palagot* bane: "ACHIX-SKRIIT-OTAAK-ACTIS!"

It was more dreadful and effective coming from the goblin than Tylo's imitations had ever been. It made Jack feel woozy and weak. Horses neighed from the vineyard stable. Jack covered Ella's ears. Tylo howled. Every hornet dropped dead from the air, littering the forest floor with writhing insects. The ancient curse carried a truly evil force.

Jack held his nausea in check and rolled out from the evergreens. He advanced with his crossbow aimed at Mysslo. "Surrender and I won't kill yeh."

Despite Mysslo's obvious pain, the goblin managed to giggle. "Am I to be turned over to noble General Camlann? Huh-ha!" He pawed the earth with his leathery arms and legs, sending a blinding spew of mud into Jack's face. "Dig, dig, dig! Like the Trusting Claytoe I am."

Jack swiped the blinding muck from his eyes, "Jits!"

Mysslo leapt over a log on crackling knuckles and toes. He dove between two gray firs like a demon into the darkness.

"We can't let him get away," said Jack.

Tylo was already hurtling through the trees in pursuit. Jack tore out of the grove onto a backwoods road that ran between the forest and the vineyard. He could see it stretch out before him. A rumble of fast-beating horse hoofs came approaching around a bend with ogre yells of "*Hyn Pythava!*"

The flash of an elf spark from the treetops caught Jack's attention. Tylo clicked in elfspeak, "Enemy riders!"

There were too many riders to take on, so Jack ducked back under the trees and hunched in the shadows to stay hid. Tylo disappeared and hid in the treetops as well.

Mysslo's hunched form plummeted out of the brush onto the road. He began waving his arms at his allies, hailing them with a jig of triumph as the horses got closer. "*Hyn Pythava! Hyn Pythava!*" he crooned, pointing at Jack and Tylo. "Kill them! I win, I win! The blades of chaos will fall swiftly on Jack Spriggins and—"

That was the last thing Mysslo said. The horses did not slow down and ran over the goblin. The six ogre soldiers on stolen steeds never even saw him. Mysslo squawked as he was trampled by the heavy hooves. A hideous knob of flesh was all that remained of him after they went by. Even if he had survived, the second band of horses that sped through definitely finished the job. It was Count Corrobis and his cavalry in relentless pursuit of the enemy. None were aware of the bony gristle they had trampled. Except for the Count's cat. Jack swore the tabby nodded to him as they passed. The chase went on and the clamor faded.

Jack stepped onto the quiet road and warily crossed to the mutilated goblin.

Tylo dipped down from a redwood. "Now, Mysslo *really* be ground elf."

"Ground meat," said Jack, grimacing. "We gotta get rid of this mess. If ogres find him, they'll do to Ella's home what they did to the Orchard."

He doused Mysslo's corpse with the vial of lamp oil he always carried.

"Do yer thing," said Jack, faking a finger snap.

Tylo popped three elf-sparks from his thumb and charred the remains.

"Fire is better than you deserve, goblin," said Tylo in elfspeak.

Jack gave him a sideways glance. "Goblins weren't even real to me 'til tonight."

"Goblins were once elves," Tylo explained. "Elder Learning Twigs say the gobs were hunted from the woods many ages ago, never to return. Mysslo proved them wrong. Horribly wrong."

"He called yeh 'cousin'," said Jack with suspicion.

"He called you 'murderer'," said Tylo. "Am I to believe that?"

~ 194 ~

"Naw. I guess he was trying to turn us against each other. Pack of lies."

Tylo lifted his chin. "And that is why you never call an elf a goblin."

They returned to the vineyard and found a stable boy was brushing out Blackberry's sleek coat. The horse had been fed and the saddlebags filled. It was not until Jack offered thanks that he recognized the stable boy was *Snow White*. Ella had ingeniously dressed her in boy's work clothes.

"You wanted a disguise?" said Ella, entering the pen. "Well, no one's going to recognize a faerie dressed like that. Autumn's chill will come by the time you reach the north. I've packed warmer garb for you and Tylo."

"Where's Micca?" said Tylo.

Ella sighed and took Snow White's hand. "Snow and I pet him until his breath stopped, barely a minute after you left. We buried him beneath a silver fir near my mother."

"Trusty barker knew it was Mysslo," said Tylo.

"He was a good dog," said Jack.

Somebody rang a steel triangle from the front of the chateau. An impatient rattle of loaded wagons and tethered mares echoed back.

"Time for us to part," said Ella.

"I kinda hate to leave yeh," said Jack. "That Madame Vintner ain't decent enough to be yer ma."

Ella squeezed his palm. "Your adventures are taking you to the far corners of the Great Forest. Mine are here with my new family. We'll have plenty to share when we meet again. And Jack, I know that we will meet again soon."

"Be safe," he said.

"I'll be fine, I always am," said Ella.

Tylo took her hand, kissing it like a gentleman. "Best Learning Twig wishes to see you again too, my beloved Red Riding Hood."

She blew them all a goodbye kiss and raised her red hood before gliding off to the kitchen. The elf piped several sweet notes after her before Jack nudged him to quit.

"Pipe down, yeh red-headed tomcat."

He mounted Blackberry and extended a hand to Snow White. The faerie secured her wand in her boyish new belt and accepted his help onto the saddle. Tylo bolted ahead. The horse was frisky for a run and they were away, heading north; a trio of halfgrowns trying to keep a step ahead of danger.

* * * * *

From "A Handbook to the Forestlands" 2nd Edition

GOBLIN - A deviant scion of woodland elves; goblins shunned the Fire Spirit and devoted their existence to spiritless chaos. Perhaps the most horrific race of creatures in Great Forest lore, they sank to cannibalism ("goblin" meaning "gobbling"), and turned on their forebears with wicked terror, destroying many innocent elf tribes. It is said, that the Fire Spirit rewarded the elves with the gift of fire, to ward off and defend their kin against this sinister race of goblins. Some of these tribes bandied together and helped drive the black threat of goblins away from the Great Forest. The goblin culture may have been eradicated before the Great Wars, yet sightings and encounters were cited by unverified reports. Most likely, these were exaggerations of many a campfire tale.

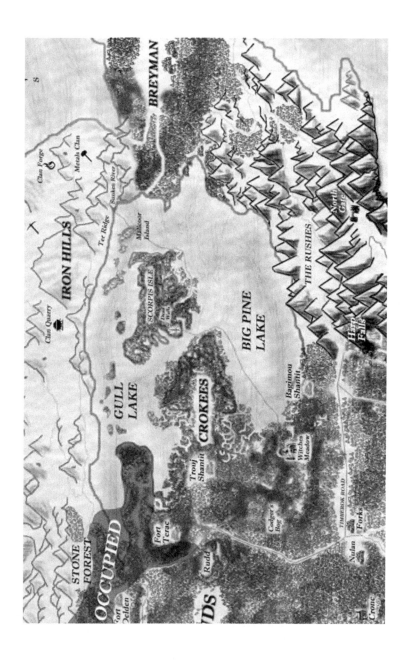

Chapter **16**

THE DREAMERS

Most of Allwise's maps of the Great Forest had been lost in the Orchard fire. Fortunately for Jack, one of his favorite pastimes had been poring over them in the old man's study. So, a picture had formed in his head of how to smuggle Snow White to the Dwarf Domain.

A typical journey to the Iron Hills would take them up past Fort Delden through the Stone Forest and would last only a few days, but with war raging along the upper Timberok Road, that route would prove impassable considering the ogres held the territory. The easiest thing would be to catch a ride east to Bends Ferry and hike along Big Pine Lake toward Breyman, but maintaining the faerie's secrecy was an issue. Somebody on the ferry would ask too many questions. Besides, Tylo was bound to stir up trouble with common folk given any opportunity. So, Jack charted a tedious route through the woods, east of Forks. They would skirt around Breyman, avoiding any main thoroughfare and villages.

One advantage of his party was that all three had spent much of their young lives in the wild. Tylo and Snow White had no attachment to the comforts of "civil life" and were even more at ease in the wilderness than Jack. Tylo was especially helpful, scampering over the treetops to scout ahead. He was swift and had a sharp eye for danger. Jack noticed the elf still favored his injured arm, even after Rose Red had popped it back into joint. Not that the elf ever groused; he taunted Jack regularly, bouncing the occasional acorn off his noggin.

Jack chose to be thicker-headed and not retaliate.

It was a hot day, one of the last of summer. The little group had ventured for three days into the lower Crokee swamps past Bagimou Shantit. They stopped for a breather in a tree-covered cove by the lakeshore.

"We can splash water in our pits and cool our heels for a bit," said Jack.

He helped Snow White from the saddle. She eyed the trees with an instinctual wariness that reminded Jack of the way deer approached an open field. The whistle of shoreline birds caught her attention as did the wind's way of bending the trees. Confident the place was safe, she took a deep breath.

"That's Big Pine Lake," said Jack, looking around. "We've come a good stretch."

Tylo had been unusually quiet but now made a sudden splash as he leapt off a tree branch into the water. "Hee-Yo!"

Jack scowled at him over the ridge. "Noisy elf."

Another splash followed, this one made by Snow White. She popped up from the lake with a refreshed smile. Her long black hair glistened in the sunlight and her thin shift rippled round her. Jack averted his eyes. It was different traveling with a girl. That she was Fae brought troublesome distractions, but those Jack could handle so long as he kept his thoughts clear. Small spaces for privacy had to be set. Of course, the water did seem inviting.

"Aw, why in tarnation not?" said Jack. He stripped down to his trousers and jumped in. "Yee haw!"

The three swam in the cove for near an hour without care, soothing their aches.

Tylo splashed over to Jack who was backstroking in a wide circle beneath an overhanging willow. "I have been thinking, Giant Killer," he stated. "I need a sword."

"Huh?"

"A blade forged for someone just my size. Elf bow and darts will no longer do. I want a sword."

"Well, yeh ain't gonna find one on me just now."

"I mean to ask the dwarf smiths to make one for me as a gift."

"A gift? What're yeh gonna give them in exchange?"

"My respect."

"Yeh do that, elf. I'm sure it'll go over great. Dwarfs hate elves more than anyone."

"So then, maybe Jack the Giant Killer will ask for me?"

"Listen. Stow yer screwy ideas. In fact, plan on saying nothing to the dwarfs. Get it?"

"I would do so if there was a promise of a sword for me at the end."

"Forget it," said Jack. He splashed water at the elf. "Hobble yer lip and *I promise* – I won't use yer tawny head for arrow practice."

"Giant Killer would not do that."

"Wanna bet?'

Tylo grinned. "I will bet a short, perfectly edged dwarf-forged sword."

Snow White was frog-kicking towards the middle of the lake.

"I fear the dwarfs won't even take her. This whole trip might be for nothing."

"They will," said Tylo. He grabbed the willow branch and lifted himself above the surface. "They be a stout and hairy kind, even more grumbly than Lunkhead Spriggins. But they also be as weak-kneed when it comes to Fae." He spun from the willow, imitating a lovesick dwarf. "Ooh, a faerie! Be still my heart. Let me slick my beard, pick my teeth and stand upright so that Snow White likes me best."

"She's still a kid," said Jack, climbing out of the water. "We all owe General Camlann a lot. I just want to protect his daughter."

He ducked behind a bed of weeds to shake dry, wringing out his buckskin trousers. Wriggling into his boots, he saw that Snow White had drifted farther from the shore.

"I reckon she's swam far enough," said Jack, waving his arms.

No sooner did he say this when a black skiff emerged on the water rounding a point along the lakeshore. It was rowed by half a dozen men, a quarter of a league from where Snow White was swimming. Tylo saw them and whistled to the faerie in a manner of lake loons. His long screeches carried a warning in elf-speak. She must've heard him because she duck-dived under the surface. A minute passed. Then another.

Jack was about to swim out when Snow White reappeared in the cove beside them. The faerie had swum the full distance underwater. Perhaps only Frog could have covered the same stretch with a single breath.

Tylo had crawled out of the water and was watching the rowers from behind a rock.

"Tylo, get up here," said Jack, who climbed atop the cove. "Swimming was a bad idea."

He grabbed a spyglass from Blackberry's saddlebag and peered across at the rowing party. They were not ogres but forestland soldiers wearing the sigil of Breyman on their chest plates. They still had to be avoided.

The Breyman leader also had a spyglass. The man stood at the bow of the skiff, panning the cove. Tylo and Snow White were clambering up the escarpment when he saw them. The rowers veered the boat towards the cove, their strokes beating a quicker rhythm.

"We gotta git," said Jack, folding his little telescope.

Snow White donned her boy's clothes over her shift and joined Jack in the saddle. He trotted Blackberry under the trees. Tylo clambered up the boughs and reported down using bird-like chirks. *"Soldiers nearing the shoreline."*

Jack nodded and galloped Blackberry southeast towards the foothills of the Rushes. The Breyman soldiers would not be able to pursue them but were likely to report Jack's party to the rest of the army. It had been a close call. He would travel more carefully now.

"How did yeh swim the distance like that?" he said to Snow White. "Yeh didn't even come up for air."

She removed her wand from her sash, placed it to her lips, and drew a deep breath through the hollow.

"Yeh poked yer wand up for air?" said Jack. "Handy."

Snow White clasped Jack's waist with a gentle grip, resting her head against him like a little sister. He did not glance back but wondered how the faerie could have such trust in him after he aimed his bow at her during the Orchard siege.

They rode the foothills until night fell. Jack led Blackberry upslope to a low-lying ridge and viewed the lakeshore. Tylo caught up with them beneath an outcropping of rock.

"Were we followed?" said Jack.

"Yes," said Tylo.

Jack looked at him, "How many?"

"Just me."

"Blarn elf."

The imp elaborated. "I covered our tracks then hit a tall lunkhead soldier with a pinecone. This tricked him to go west. I believe Giant Killer Spriggins will benefit by thanking this best elfling of the Learning Twigs."

"Yeah, yeah."

Jack watched below as glowing firelights dotted the shoreline.

"Lots of campfires down there," he said.

"The lunkhead army be using Sparky's flame to roast their meat and sing manly songs."

"Jits," said Jack, folding up his spyglass. "We can't scoot by them, not even in the dark."

"No, we cannot," said Tylo. "What does Giant Killer wish to do?"

"How bout we turn pirate? There are canoes tied to rocks down there. We can grab one and make up time by crossing the lake directly."

Tylo cocked his head with a mischievous smile. "Giant Killer be thinking like an elf."

"Naw, I'm thinking like a thief from Thin Creek. Our deep-winded faerie could be a help here too." Jack watched Snow White feed Blackberry the last of the oats. "But it's time we let my steed go."

He sauntered up to Blackberry and tenderly stroked his black mane. "I know yeh can't understand me like Ella, boy, but yeh've taken us as far as the woods will let yeh. Yeh need to git back to the Orchard now."

Jack removed the bit from the horse's mouth and dropped the saddlebags. A pair of green apples rolled out. They had a vaguely familiar scent of cinnamon cider. Snow White picked one of the apples up and offered it to Blackberry. The horse turned away with a snort.

"The oats were enough, I reckon," said Jack.

He felt woozy for a moment. What was it about those apples?

Snow White motioned with her wrists making precise shapes with her fingers. Jack gathered the meaning as best he could.

"Yer right," he said. "Blackberry knows how to git back home."

The faerie patted Blackberry's nose.

Tylo scooted closer. "You be catching on to her dream-speak. That be rare for a lunkhead."

"Just taking stabs, really," said Jack. "It ain't a speech I'll ever truly crack. Why'd yeh call it dream-speak?"

"By a faerie's way of thinking, life be a dream of the Sleeping Beauty," said Tylo. "When the Beauty wakes, all life will be gone – snap!" He snuffed a dancing spark off the tip of his thumb. "You, me, everything will pass like a vanishing light."

"That's why she's so bold and hopeful," said Jack. "Every grief is part of a dream."

"And someone else's at that," added Tylo. "Do you think she is correct, Giant Killer?"

"Dunno."

Tylo began cracking his knuckles. "I dream of being taller. Even Learning Twigs say I be too small to do big things. So, I dream of tallness."

"Yer a big enough talker," said Jack.

"Was your pap tall, Giant Killer?"

"Ma tells me he was. He moved on before I knew him. Folks in Rivercross say he was a dark-haired, sharp-eyed hunter. A Crokee native, lean and mean."

"What be his name?"

"Jodd Spriggins."

"Do you think he be fighting in the war now?"

"Doubt it."

"What be your dreams, Jack?"

"Dunno," said Jack again.

In truth, he had terrible dreams, all of which started with the second gold apple falling off Lell's black tree. This led to images of Bluebeard; Allwise trying to speak; snakes; wraith drums; and – *Ganzil.*

"The green apples came from Ganzil!" he said.

There was a thud. One of the apples rolled in front of Jack. Snow White had taken a bite. The pupils of her dark eyes shrank and she staggered, clutching her throat for breath.

Jack caught the faerie in his arms. The color drained from her cheeks as if she were dying.

Tylo cried out. "The soul be flying out of her!"

Jack was not having it. Once at the Orchard, he'd taken too big a bite of some tough bison and, ashamed, pretended he was not choking to death. Fortunately, Rose Red saw through it and squeezed the stuck meat from his gullet, saving him. Now, Jack did the same. He wrapped both arms around the faerie's waist and with three upward thrusts forced the poisoned apple from her mouth. She was still not breathing. He lowered her to a bed of leaves.

"Rub her feet briskly," he told Tylo.

While Tylo did this, Jack pressed his lips to Snow White's bluish ones and blew short bursts of air into her still body. Once. Twice. On the third, she coughed and opened her eyes. He could not recall a better sight than her smile of recognition as a healthy pink glow returned to her face. She reached up, meekly stroking his chin.

Tylo pranced about in a happy fit. "Your kiss brought Snow White back, Giant Killer! It was your kiss that did it."

"Weren't no kiss," said Jack, helping Snow White to a seated position.

"Kissy-kiss, kiss!" said Tylo.

Jack's knees wobbled. Death had come for Snow White but he had denied it. Fearful thoughts flooded him: "*What if I hadn't?*" "*How did I know to?*" "*Why didn't I see it before?*"

There wasn't any of the dark guilt that came after a kill but no soothing pride either. Jack wondered if General Camlann, Gwachmai and Ootan ever felt the same way?

A red cardinal alit from a nearby tree and screeched into the air. Jack pitched the green apples into the brush.

"This was Ganzil's doing," he said. "The witch from Ma's inn. She wants Snow White dead."

Tylo nodded. "She be the female wraith from the Briar too."

The elf's truth was an eye-opener. Jack felt dense for not seeing it sooner.

"Yer darn toot! Pretty women can be just as deadly as goblins if yeh fall under their spell."

"Goldy Ganzil be a bad apple," said Tylo.

Jack checked the saddlebags to make sure there were no more surprises as he prepped Blackberry to say good-bye. Snow White patted the horse gently. Tylo kept a distance (as all elves did around horses) but spoke words of encouragement.

"Just think of all the good oats there will be back home, Stomp-berry."

Jack whispered to the steed, "I only feel like a real hero when I'm riding yeh."

With a smack on the rump, he sent Blackberry off. The horse went hesitantly at first, then picked up speed as if remembering the way.

Jack looked at Snow White. "We'll stay put for a day. Yeh can't be in any shape to set out just yet."

The faerie stood defiantly and spoke out in the common tongue, carefully choosing her words. "I have lived, not died. Trust I am my father's daughter. I am strong. I will go with you now while the night screens our passage."

Jack and Tylo exchanged glances.

"Reckon we're ready," said Jack, hoisting the saddlebags over his shoulder.

"A'pirating we go!" said Tylo, smacking his chest.

The night trek along the coast of Breyman was cautious. Not a critter stirred as the three crept closer to the soldier encampment. Fires had mostly dwindled as the Breyman troops retired into tents. An armed guard was posted. Dozens of miles away, sounds of muffled cannon fire echoed across Big Pine Lake. The western sky glowed from the battle.

A row of canoes was tied off at the shore. Jack and Tylo inched closer to the guard, concealed by reeds. Jack stooped low, within range with his crossbow. He was in good position to provide cover for Snow White.

He watched a silent ripple curl on the water. A rod of yew wood poked up against the magenta sky. It was Snow White's wand. She grabbed a breath and approached the canoes under the surface of the lake. Jack watched her loosen one of the lashes that held the boat in place. The guard glanced in her direction but the timely croak of a toad drew his attention away.

"*Rib-bid*," sounded Tylo from his position in the reeds.

It was all the cover Snow White needed to unhitch one canoe and swim away with it unnoticed. Jack and Tylo retreated like muskrats.

The trio of halfgrowns boarded the vessel a safe distance down shore from the soldiers' camp. Jack dipped the oars and rowed across the dark water. It was a tiring paddle past Scorpis Isle to the foot of the Iron Hills. He was grateful for the windless night, which provided them silent and swift passage. They beached on the rocks below the mining village of Ter Ridge.

After disembarking and stowing the canoe, Jack led his companions into the settlement. They passed under a huge, black stone arch and were greeted by an iron statue of Ter, the Earth Spirit. A curving uphill street lined with precisely cut stone houses stood with nary a light glowing inside. No watchmen roamed the streets. The entrance to the mines at the end of the lane was blocked off with boulders.

"Ter Ridge looks abandoned," said Jack.

He chose an empty dwelling on the cobblestone street for them to settle for the night. The stone apartment had bunks carved right into the rock walls. There was no other furniture. Jack selected a bunk at the top of the stairs for Snow White.

"Yeh settle there," he said. "Me and the elf will bed down by the doorway."

He and Tylo took bunks opposite each other. The elf fell fast asleep. Jack curled up so he could fit, keeping his crossbow in hand. He sighed. They had reached the Iron Hills of Dwarf Domain. Whatever was to come during this adventure should have kept him awake but he dozed off. For the first time in weeks, he had no bad dreams.

* * * * *

From "Old Deities of an Older World" compiled by noted traveler Kathlena Gabell.

THE EIGHT GREAT SPIRITS OF THE FORESTLANDS

GREEN MOTHER (*Green Ma, Na-La*) Her symbol: a green leaf. Often visualized as a friendly matron, she was the beloved Spirit of All Living Creatures and Plantlife.

EARTH ONE (*Ter*) His symbol: a rock. Seen as a handsome, muscular warrior. The Spirit of Strength, War, and Masonry. Dwarfs were his most loyal patrons.

WATER ONE (*Old Codger, Mar*) His symbol: a blue wave. An old sage with a beard and robes of water. The Spirit of Wisdom.

LIGHT ONE (*Shaina*) Her symbol: a yellow butterfly or the sun. A beautiful, fair-haired maiden, she was the Spirit of Beauty and the Arts. The Fae were devoted to her.

DARK ONE (*Lell*) Her symbol: a black raven or the moon. An exotic cloaked lady, twin sister of Light. The Spirit of Shadow, Mortality, and Primal Instinct.

FIRE ONE (*Master Red Eyes, Sparky*) His symbol: an orange/red flame. A charming imp who is the Spirit of Wit, Heat, and Song. Elves considered him their own.

WIND ONE (*Mad Mariah*) Her symbol: a harp. A wild, dancing nymph in veils of lavender and gray. Spirit of Storm and Adventure. The Giants built her a massive temple.

SILENT ONE (*Whisperer*) His symbol: an empty white circle. He was the invisible Spirit of Conscience, Morality, and Humanity among men and women.

The Eight played a large role in Forestland lore of the Sleeping Beauty, a princess of ancient times they had once cursed, then protected in eternal slumber to awaken in Paradise.

Chapter **17**

OLD TIMERS

A cock crowed. Jack woke with an icy shudder, curled up on his stony bunk of the Ter Ridge dwelling. He heard the huff and snort of a braying donkey, followed by the rattle of squeaky wheels and a wobbling shadow that rolled by the window.

Jack looked out. A splintery coach loaded with dirty bags and a couple of clanging pots went rocking down the cobbled road, pulled by a pair of old mules. Tagging behind it was a female hound with four pups, a goat, a rooster, and three goslings. Jack could only see the back of the driver's weathered top hat.

"Who do yeh think that crazy coot is?" said Jack to Tylo.

Only, Tylo was not there. His stone bunk was empty.

Jack fumed. "Don't know why I'm surprised. That elf lives to make trouble for me."

He went upstairs to check on Snow White. She too was nowhere to be found.

"Jits! I'm captain. Why am I left behind?"

Gearing up with his crossbow, quiver, and vines, Jack hustled out to the street. The rickety carriage and animals were gone. A vee of honking geese flew by. Otherwise, Ter Ridge looked as empty as it had the night before. Frustrated, he ascended the lane. There were no side roads or alleys.

"What's the story here?" wondered Jack.

There was no evidence that any raid or revolt had befallen the village, just that it had been cleared out and vacated with no afterthought. The cool air, beautiful mountains, and neat stone buildings suggested it had been a pleasant home for the dwarf miners. He could imagine them bustling off to the quarry for daily work or tending to their children and chores.

"What made them leave?"

A short wall of sandstone ran beside the lane, artistically etched with markings in the stonework. Old world symbols Jack recognized from Allwise's books narrated pictures of the patron spirit, Ter, and the serene Sleeping Beauty. Carved with great care by the dwarfs, it was obvious their spirits were deeply revered.

"Even more so than men worship," Jack supposed. "Not like a flighty, spark-popping, no-account elf. Where is he?"

"Hee-Yo!" Tylo called out.

The elf waved eagerly at him from the top of a bell tower in an old church made of smoothly rounded sandstone. "Look, Giant Killer! This belfry was built for ringing but there be no ringer."

"The town don't need a bell with a noisy elf up there," said Jack, bristling. "Did yeh see that old carriage with the animals pass by?"

"No. There be nobody here."

"Where's Snow White?"

"She be inside." Tylo scooted down the steeple. "Follow me."

"Wait!" said Jack, but Tylo had already dashed into the church.

Jack stalked in after him.

The dusty cathedral was spectacular with a dais approached by rows of smooth stone benches. Long arching panes of stained glass stretched to a rounded ceiling. The morning rays filled the sanctuary with different colors, cast from many depictions of the brawny Earth Spirit. In one, Mighty Ter was shone digging ore of dazzling red gems and blessing dwarfkind with a bounty of gold coins. Above the pulpit, an even grander image showed the patron waking the Sleeping Beauty with a kiss, framed by tinted azure glass.

Jack grew impatient to find the faerie. "Where is she?"

"Snow White be there," said Tylo, who pointed mischievously at the likeness of the Sleeping Beauty.

Jack marveled at the resemblance to Snow White – the fair skin and pink cheeks, black eyes and hair. It was as if the faerie had posed for it.

"What do yeh know?" he said, grinning. "Even the Earth One's got eyes for Snow. Now, where is she for real?"

"Within every dwarf's heart," a man's hoarse voice chimed in. "I cannot help thinking you both were meant to see this."

Jack and Tylo nearly swapped heartbeats as they jumped.

Seated in the back of the cathedral was an old dwarf. He looked to be Allwise's age, maybe older, with a voice that indicated a learned mind, though his vagrant appearance said otherwise. Like all dwarfs, his disproportionate upper body was average-sized, like a man's, but his stunted legs made him a dwarf. His head was crowned with a battered top hat and his grubby feet were bare. Knotted white hair and an overgrown beard covered his hunched body, which was clothed in tan leatherwear nearly identical as the shade of his wrinkled skin. He was feeding a pair of ducks, tossing seeds on the stone floor for them to pluck. A mutt was curled asleep by his feet. A goat even trotted down the aisle.

Jack recognized him as the coot from the wagon. "Who are yeh, old timer?"

"Don't you know me?" said the dwarf. "I am Orr Terson. We've met before, eh?" Then he shook his head, arguing with himself. "Ah nay. Nay. Perhaps not, I must know you from when you are older, but this is likely the first time you have met me."

Tylo crept closer with a teasing smile. "Tell us more, moldy sir."

Orr Terson nodded. "You are a good friend, tree-elf. Rare indeed. Do you know my brother, Bronze Terson, head of the Metal Clans?" Orr patted Tylo's hand, then he disagreed with himself again. "Nay, nay. You don't know him *yet*. I am here to relay that very information for your journey."

"We ain't met before," said Jack. "How come yeh talk so backwards?"

"Ah, that is exactly what I do," said Orr, clapping his hands over a snicker. "You two lads exist from birth to death but I have chosen to live my life from its end to its beginning. This way I am traveling toward much happier times than what your future brings. See?"

Tylo jumped up, excitedly. "I do! I do!" He skipped forward a few paces to demonstrate. "This be you and I, Giant Killer." Then he skipped backwards. "This be him. What lays in front of us be already behind him."

"Aye." Orr widened his eyes, which were the color of polished ambers; even more yellow than Jack's. "Such a bright elfling. So well-trained."

"He ain't," said Jack. "And I ain't got time for fool-talk."

Orr pointed up at the likeness of the Sleeping Beauty. "You bring with you an awakened damsel and a scrolled deed, do you not?"

"Maybe," said Jack, uneasily. "How'd yeh know that?"

"You haven't been listening." Orr broke into another laughing fit. "I know it the same way that I know you'll be having fish for breakfast. It's old news to me. I have lived it, boy."

"Yer the only dwarf left in this village," said Jack. "Why's that?"

"Someone had to look after all the stray animals left behind," said the old timer. "And the mines never suited me."

"So, the dwarf villagers live in the mines now?"

"Now and then," said Orr, who fished through his beard and pulled out a long clay pipe, stuffing it with dried smoking leaves.

Jack glanced at Tylo. "We gotta git. Let's find Snow White."

Orr pointed at them. "Beware of the deed you carry with you. That piece of paper will cause nothing but grief. Do not hand it over freely. Only an honest dwarf can wield its scribed promises properly. Now, where did I put my matches?"

Tylo flicked a spark off his calloused finger and lit the dwarf's pipe.

"Oh, mind my beard, little fella." Orr smacked his lips and sucked the glowing leaves. "Handy trick."

Tylo twinkled with a scheme. "Old Hat, it seems you know we have Dynadin's Deed and you know we have the damsel. Do you know of my sword?"

"Hehe," said Orr, through a billow of twirling smoke. "Indeed. It will be a great general's sword."

Tylo stood up taller than Jack had ever seen him, his face glowing with pride. "You hear, Jack Spriggins? A dwarf sword I shall have." He leapt on to the bench beside Orr. "And a general I shall be! You know much, Old Hat. More than Belly Bounce did I think."

"Who?"

Jack explained. "He means Allwise of the Orchard."

Orr's shiny eyes crinkled as a toothless smile spread under his whiskers. "Allwise. The Sage Calculator, as my brother and I call him. Allwise is one of the few upright men we dwarfs can respect."

Jack waved the cloud of smoke out of his face. "Yeh know him then, do yeh?"

"Aye. Nay. Perhaps not yet. I remember him and the lovely lady from Breyman. Her name is Viviyann. Do you know her?"

"Viviyann Greygeese?" said Jack. "I've seen her. She runs an orphanage in Arborvale."

"Mother Goose!" The old fool bent forward in a fit of laughter, coughing and drooling.

"I didn't reckon she was from Breyman," said Jack.

"Indeed, she was. Well, she *will be*." Orr took a confused puff. "A northern heiress of Castle Brey. Dynadin the First was her uncle. A goodly baron. He willed the noble deed to Viviyann."

"Why her?"

"She was the only family member he could trust to honor it. Certainly not his villainous son."

"Dynadin the Second?" Tylo chirped, absorbed by the tale.

"By Ter's Mighty Fists, aye, that's the one!" said Orr. "A dastardly tyrant. He claimed the deed never existed and, with one stroke, destroyed all the goodwill between the men of Breyman and we dwarfs."

Jack knelt down beside Orr. "Yeh mean, Dynadin the First was gonna give the dwarf clans ownership of the mines?"

Orr groaned like an old mule then resumed smacking on his pipe. "Aye. The mountains, the mines."

"That's why dwarfs be so nasty," said Tylo. "Deed say 'yes', men say 'no'."

"Deed or no deed," said Orr, "The Barons of Breyman will not honor it."

Jack steered the goat away from gnawing on his beanstalk vines. Then snuck a look at the deed safely stashed in his pocket. "Why didn't ol' Viviyann just hand the scroll over to the clans then?"

Orr became oddly lucid. "Because she knew the other Forestland territories would never challenge Breyman's claim for fear of civil war. And, of course, her life was in peril the moment Dynadin the Second, her cousin, came to rule. Small wonder she ran off with her lover, and the deed."

Tylo pondered the romance. "And who would that loving lunkhead be?"

Orr winked once more. "Calculator. Belly Bounce. Allwise."

"Naw!" Jack cried. "Can't be. The old geezer was her lover? Or, *anyone's* lover?"

"Everyone has a younger self to cherish, boy," said Orr. "I can hardly wait to be that age again."

"So that's why she trusted Allwise with the deed," said Jack. "But he must've known she had it. Over fifty years now. Why did he keep that secret for so long?"

"Allwise the Calculator," sighed Orr with a puff. "Playing the game from every side."

"Will giving up the Deed get us inside the mountain?" said Jack.

"No," said Orr, "Keep quiet about it. Those Hoodies will only use it to break the clans."

"Hoodies?" said Tylo.

"Yeh mean the wraiths?" said Jack.

Orr's crazed laugh filled the sanctuary. He stood and scooted his filthy feet along the floor, hobbling through the colored rays of the window reflections. He paused to look up at the stained glass Sleeping Beauty. "She will help you. The damsel in men's clothes whose face is white as snow."

"Snow White," said Jack. "Yeh know where she is?"

"That's her," said Orr, nodding at the glass portrait. "She's right there."

"Yeah, yeah," said Jack. "I get the picture. But how will Snow White ever—"

Orr Terson ducked into a deep purple beam and shifted from sight.

"Where in tarnation?" said Jack. He and Tylo ran toward the dais, scanning down the rows of benches. The hairy hermit had seemingly disappeared. The animals were all gone as well.

The elf cocked his head. "Maybe Orr Terson has walked back into last summer."

"I think we breathed too much of his wacky smoke," said Jack.

Outside the church, the rattle of squeaky wheels scraped over the stone street. Jack pushed open the door. Orr Terson and his herd were riding down the lane.

Tylo rubbed his stomach. "Old Hat promised we'd have fish for breakfast."

"Naw," said Jack. "He's too touched in the noggin to take serious."

"Those smoky words do give a clue where Snow White be," said Tylo looking over the road side wall. "There."

The elf pointed to a lush ravine behind the buildings. It was some hundred feet down, reached by carved rock steps. A continual churn of water flowed from the Iron River, shielded by groves of sugar maples, their leaves already changing red for fall. Snow White, in her boy's attire, was walking along the rocky strand of the riverbed looking like a country bumpkin with a string of freshly caught salmon.

"And she's caught a string of fish," said Tylo, glancing at Jack.

Jack was irked. "No thought for her own safety. Let's get her away from there. I've a feeling this place ain't as deserted as it seems."

They marched to the ravine. The faerie was kneeling beside the river adding another salmon catch to her string. She noticed them and showed off her catch.

"Snow," said Jack. "Yeh can't just traipse off without me."

"And catch more fish than Giant Killer, me, or the whole lunkhead army," said Tylo.

"We're here to protect yeh—" Jack would have gone on but three dwarfs stepped out from the maples, armed with longbows. Two others cut off the path to the river. Jack's party was caught in their crosshairs.

The stern hunters were young and fit with a lot of muscle in their upper bodies. None were as tall as five feet. One had black skin like Rose Red's, another was as light as Jack, and the others were tanned somewhere between. They wore trousers and vests of animal skins, and boots made of fine leather with silver trim. All had beards close-cropped to their faces and wore round, smoked glass spectacles to shield their eyes from the sun.

Jack raised his hands in surrender. Tylo did the same (more in mimicry). Snow White merely held her fish line, looking amused and fascinated by the grim dwarf faces.

One dwarf warily approached Jack, bow poised. "I am Shard Smith, captain of this hunting company." The bearded captain was a she-dwarf, as her womanly voice revealed. "You are not welcome here, forest lad. And that pesky tree elf even less so. Be gone from this valley."

"Can't," said Jack. "We've come too far to meet yeh."

Shard Smith kicked Jack between the legs, causing him to double over. "You've gone too far, talking back to me."

"It's only fair yeh hear us out," said Jack between gasps. (The blow really smarted.)

The dark-skinned dwarf placed a short sword to Jack's throat. "Fair is what your kind has never been to us, chap," he said, in a deep voice. "I am Smoal Klub of Clan Iron and I shall judge you with edge of this blade, fair or not."

Shard Smith agreed. "We dwarfs decide the laws on our lands."

Jack strained to stand with dignity. "I can't speak for my kind, just for me. We ain't leaving 'til we meet with yer clan leaders."

Tylo laid his charm on the she-dwarf, Shard. "Dwarfess Shardy, know you not that this rude, but righteous, lunkhead you have kicked be Jack the Giant Killer Spriggins?"

"Watch your lying tongue, elf," said Shard Smith, training her weapon at his head.

Tylo ran behind Jack. "Serious female makes a point," he said, cowering.

Captain Smith raised her smoky spectacles to see Jack more clearly. "You're the lad who conquered the pompous giants?"

"The same," said Jack.

Tylo leaned out behind Jack's leg. "See his coil of beanstalk vines? And I be Tylo, Brightest Learning Twig and Smacker of Ogres."

The dwarfs were not impressed.

"My answer is 'no'," said Shard. "Return now to your war and spare us from making further violence on you."

"But Shardy," said Tylo, "We bring you the Sleeping Beauty. Awake and in person."

"Insolent elf!" said Smoal Klub, outraged. "Speak falsely of the Beauty and I'll put an arrow in you right here."

Shard eyed Snow White standing by the river's edge in her manly togs and string of salmon, wearing an expression of honest curiosity. "Teach the young poacher the penalty for his crimes," she said. "Take him. Hold old out his arm."

The obedient hunters took Snow White, while another held her arm out straight. Shard Smith raised her short sword.

"Don't touch her!" shouted Jack.

The dwarf captain stopped. She drew closer to Snow White and removed the boy's cap and scarf from her head. Unmasked, the faerie's dark flow of hair cascaded to her shoulders, framing her lovely face. This was the only defense she needed.

"You see?" said Tylo. "This be the Sleeping Beauty, Her Majesty of all the Great Forest. She honors dwarfkind with the rarest tribute of her *very real presence.*"

Even Jack had to admit how striking Snow White appeared in the amber sunlight reflected off the water. Tylo's ploy was not bad. The dwarfs collectively gasped, lowering their weapons and dropping their heads to kneel before the beautiful faerie. She looked unsure how to react, still holding the string of twitching fish.

"Bless the Beauty," they whispered fervently. The dwarfs touched their palms to the ground and moved their mouths collectively in prayer.

"The prophecy has come true," said Smoal. "Praise the Awakened Princess."

As ridiculous as this all seemed to Jack, Snow White's mistaken identity was playing out just beautifully. So, he rolled with it.

Shard Smith finished with her devotions and humbly spoke.

"Forgive me, Beauty. We have waited for you, as did our fathers, and our fathers' fathers. That you make yourself known to us – mere hunters of dwarfkind – and you be even more beauteous than our artists have depicted, is an honor I shall cherish to the grave."

"Praise the Awakened Princess," repeated the dwarfs.

Tylo pressed his advantage. "Jack Giant Killer and Best Learning Twig be Her Majesty's trusted guardians, appointed to guide her to this hallowed place. Now the Awakened Princess must be presented to your honored leaders in the Dwarf Underground, to await the arrival of bold Ter to claim her hand."

Captain Shard Smith nodded to the dwarfs. "It shall be so."

The hunters rushed forward, competing to reach Snow White first. Smoal Klub muscled ahead and nobly offered his arm. "Allow me to escort you across the rocky strand to our boat, my princess."

Snow White's engaging smile caused the dark dwarf to blush.

They boarded a birch-bark canoe loaded with elk and deer carcasses and rowed up the Iron River. Snow White was seated in the center, a bouquet of maple leaves placed upon her lap (next to the salmon). Tylo and Jack rode behind the carcasses in the stern, waving at the flies.

The boat passed inside the Mouth of the Mountain, an immense earthen portal sculpted to resemble the fierce likeness of Mighty Ter, the Earth Spirit. Beefy dwarf sentinels were stationed along the torchlit walls within the gaping entrance, ready to pierce any intruder with their trained bows. Their judging glares made Jack wary of leaving sunlight behind in favor of this dark grotto of Dwarf Domain.

Tylo spoke in elfspeak beneath a clenched smile. "Have you any wise notions how we can leave this dwarf pit if my Sleeping Beauty jest sours?"

"I'm working on it," said Jack.

The elf simply replied, "I need a sword."

*****

From "A Handbook to the Forestlands" 2nd Edition

DWARF - An offspring of seven mining clans that dwell in the mountainous highlands of the northern Forestlands. Most are descendants of migrants from distant countries like the Dragonlands or Zan. Smaller in size than an average person, a typical dwarf is extremely muscular, hard working, and productive. Crafters of the finest blade-ware, they masterfully negotiate for commodities rare to their surroundings in exchange for precious metals and weaponry, of which they have plenty. The Earth Spirit dominates their religious lives.

Chapter 18

AMBASSADORS

Word had spread among the dwarfs about the arrival of the "Awakened Princess". A large retinue was already gathered at an underground quay lit by torches when Snow White disembarked the hunters' canoe with Jack and Tylo. Their greeting was ceremonious. An assembly of worshipers knelt before her. The dwarfs hummed a low, monotonous chant, which droned throughout the cavernous domain.

"Shouldn't there be more smiles, Giant Killer?" said Tylo, with a nudge to Jack's thigh.

"They're serious about this princess stuff," said Jack. "We'll be branded like calves when they learn Snow ain't the real deal."

"The dwarfs need not know."

"Yeh'd best reckon they'll figure it out."

Shard Smith guided them out of the grotto to a resplendent stone rotunda. The floor was ornamented with a marble design that was interlaced with veins of copper. Above it hung a giant stalactite carved in the likeness of Mighty Ter. His face was highlighted with brass, his eyes set with many gemstones.

"Any one of them stones could make us richer than the Count of Havensbend," said Jack.

"The Earth Spirit looks mean, though," said Tylo. "He can keep his eyeballs."

"Welcome to the Domain," spoke a stern voice. "I am Bronz Terson, Head of the Dwarf Metal Clans."

Tylo nudged Jack. "That be Orr Terson's bro-bro?"

"Reckon the old hermit spoke true," said Jack.

Bronz Terson stood on a grand stairway that was chiseled into the bedrock. He looked down with amber eyes that resembled his brother, Orr the Hermit, but without the smile. His leather chest plate was inlaid with copper (and a shimmering blue metal Jack did not know) over which he wore a sleek brown mantle.

"Bronz be combed and mean-mad," said Tylo, "Where as his brother, Orr, was messy and mad-mad."

Dwarfs did not need spectacles inside the caverns. Their eyes reflected the torchlight like gleaming jewels. Pairs of malachites, amethysts, topazes, and azures blinked in reverence at Snow White and her companions.

A second company of dwarfs entered the rotunda led by a tense dwarf who was both broad shouldered yet lean and taut. He was younger than Bronz Terson and had a nasty sneer. His ceremonial chest plate was forged of sleek gray metal bearing the imprint of a flame.

"Pewtr Smelt!" hailed Terson. "Head of the Forge Clan."

An attending guard lifted a copper horn to his mouth and blew a triple blast that echoed inside the mountain.

"Three blasts for our sturdy Earth Spirit," said Smelt. "Forge Clan has answered the call. He eyed Jack's trio with grumbling disdain as he filed past them to greet Bronz Terson. The clan heads raised their arms like hammers and hooked them together in an intense salute.

A third clan entered from another tunnel, marching to a chant. They carried polished long chisels, which they stamped with a thunderous beat until they came to a halt. The leader was a she-dwarf, nearly five feet tall, in silver armor and a midnight blue mantle. Her clipped beard complimented aquamarine eyes that flickered as she peered at Snow White.

One of her guards lifted a silver horn to his mouth and blew a triple blast.

"Three more blasts for the awakened Bride of Ter," she said. "We are with you."

"Welcome, Azur Cutter!" said Bronz. "Head of the Gems Clan."

Jack observed that only the Clan Heads wore formal attire. The masses were a mix of soldier-workers wearing sturdy leather and forearm braces. Azur Cutter climbed the stairs and greeted Bronz Terson with the same arm-bracing salute as Pewtr Smith.

Terson began. "I was led to believe the Beauty is in our midst, Captain Smith. You present these outsiders before us?"

"Do not fret," said Shard Smith, motioning to the faerie. "We are indeed blessed."

Snow White moved lissomely up the staircase. One by one, dwarfs knelt on their thick knees as she passed. The faerie lowered her head but Bronz Terson extended his hand to her chin.

"No, child," he said. "We must honor you."

The three Clan Heads bowed.

Tylo poked Jack's thigh. "Would now be a good time to ask for my sword?"

"Don't push yer luck," muttered Jack.

Bronz Terson rose. "Captain Smith, have your Iron Guard escort the outsiders to the council chamber."

He offered Snow White his arm and escorted her through an entry way framed with molded iron. Two dwarf guards armed with quarterstaffs stepped forward. Each wore a silver brooch, etched with a black fist on their leather chest plates. They pushed Jack and Tylo behind the procession.

The council chamber was perfectly round with walls of deep, gray crags that reached up beyond sight. Massive iron girders buttressed every curve. A window had been sliced in the rock that beheld a distant view of Big Pine Lake. On the floor was a tiled mosaic depicting Ter by the Sleeping Beauty's bier in soft rose hues. Four stone lecterns were situated at the center. Each was dwarf-size and bore soldered symbols for the clans (pickax for Gems, maul for Metals, flame for Forge, and cart for Quarry). Bronz Terson took his place behind the pickax stand.

"So tell me, forest lad," he demanded of Jack. "Why do you bring the Beauty before us dressed like a woodland yokel?"

"Cause she ain't who yeh think," said Jack. "She's Fae. Truth is, she's General Ardus Camlann's daughter. We had to keep her hid from the enemy. That's why she's in them clothes."

The Clan Heads exchanged grimaces of disbelief.

"Do you mean to tell me that this vision is not the Awakened Princess but a commoner?"

Shard Smith paled. "My lords," she protested, with a shriveling glare at Jack, "I was misled. The fork-tongued elfling lied. They led us to believe she was the Promised One."

Bronz lifted a hushing hand. He cocked his head with interest at Snow White. She was standing on the Sleeping Beauty mosaic. "Remarkable resemblance. If only it weren't—"

"A lie!" broke in Pewtr Smelt. "What makes you think we clans would house an outsider in Dwarf Domain?"

"Because she's the daughter of yer ally," said Jack. "General Camlann ain't no commoner. He is the leader of the Forestland Army who's out there fighting to keep ogres from yer mines. Yeh owe him for that."

"We forged the weapons that Camlann's Army uses for that war," said Pewtr. "The Dwarfs owe him nothing."

Tylo boldly stepped forward. "Snow White Camlann be the last Fae."

"Why do you speak, elf?" said Azur Cutter. "It is unfortunate the faerie race has fallen but I am certain they held no influence over dwarfkind. Fae are average females to our senses, nothing more."

Snow White smiled and began to whirl innocently around the chamber. Tylo accompanied her on his pipes. The same dreamlike enchantment Jack had felt when he first saw her now captivated the Clan Heads. Pewtr Smelt and Bronz Terson appeared as smitten as schoolboys.

"Av-er-age females," repeated Tylo, cheekily between tweets.

"Speak more," said Bronz, in a daze.

"Allwise of the Orchard sent us," said Jack. "He told me you could protect her."

Bronz Terson tried to sober. "Did he, now? Allwise and I knew each other when we were young. Why did the Calculator not come and make the request in person?"

"He ain't well," said Jack.

"I am sorry to hear that. Allwise Calculator gave us trusted council when he chose to. Our stance against the Breyman men who oppressed us was inspired by him."

"And look where it got us," said Pewtr Smelt. "Fine words for a man who turned his back on us when he could have done much more."

"Men simply cannot be trusted," said Azur Cutter. "And elves are never welcome."

"Azur, you speak truly," said Bronz Terson, looking at Snow White with disappointment. "I regret to say, the outsiders shall be granted no sanctuary."

"Indeed, stubby dwarfs!" said Tylo. "I, Best of the Learning Twigs, demand a Melding of the Mines."

The Clan Heads looked taken aback as did Shard Smith and the attending guards.

Pewtr Smelt fumbled for words. "A Melding? It's— no. It is not practical."

Tylo interrupted with obvious glee. "That be no matter!" He placed one hand in the crook of his back like a little statesman and strutted across the chamber floor, launching into a word-for-word recital of the ancient dwarf law that he had learned from Rose Red.

"The Dwarf Rules for the Meeting of the Meld state that the four Clan Heads of Dwarf Domain must gather together and discuss a resolution for any proposal that challenges the tenets of Dwarf security.

*Heads of each Clan – Forge, Metals, Gems and Quarry –
must debate, defend and decide the most reasonable answer to the
problem presented. Whatever the council concludes will be accepted
without question.*

*This tried and true method of judgment by Dwarfkind stands
in perpetuity, to deliberate issues within our community, with
neighbors of the Great Forest, or with foreigners. The four Clans
have sworn by oath to Father Ter, the Earth Spirit, that any request
for a Meeting of the Meld shall convene without fail to safeguard the
status and Security of Dwarf Domain.*

See Footnote Forty-two for sources."

"Of course, there's more," said Tylo, sucking in a belly of air
for the next stanza.

"That's quite enough," said Bronz Terson. "We know our
own decrees, elf."

Jack took the floor. "Then yeh gotta honor it and keep us
safe til yeh do."

Azur Cutter stroked her beard thoughtfully. "Long it has
been since a Melding has gathered."

"For this? Preposterous!" said Smelt. "The Head of Quarry
Clans, Gravl Smoothstone, is far too busy to be pulled from his post
in the West Domain to come here. It is an effrontery that this
rapscallion was ever allowed to speak."

Bronz Terson patted the walls, upon which was inscribed
several passages in ancient lettering. "The elf has recited a law on
which our community has stood for more than a century, exactly as
our forbearers set it down. Hearing it aloud, which of us would deny
it?"

Pewtr Smelt resigned with a bitter twitch. "Very well. The
Melding stands. Word shall be sent to Smoothstone."

Tylo lifted his chin in triumph. "I believe I will take this room while we wait. It has a fine view."

"You are not guests," said Smelt. "You came to us uninvited. It will be several days before the meeting can be assembled."

"So we're yer prisoners then?" said Jack.

"You will earn your keep until the Melding convenes," said Bronz Terson. "You shall labor in the mines and study like all dwarf youth. Snow White Camlann will tend the root gardens and aid in cookery under the supervision of Captain Shard Smith." He motioned the guards. "Take Jack Spriggins and the tree elf to the lower depths directly."

Jack did not like the wicked smirk that appeared on Pewtr Smelt's face.

Two of the Iron Guard led Snow White from the chamber. Jack reached out but was forcibly blocked. "I'm sworn to protect her," he said.

Captain Smith placed her fist against her chest plate. "I will honor that in your stead. She is still the Promised One to me."

Snow White waved confidently to them as they parted.

* * * * *

Old Dwarfish Proverb (translated from a stone carving by Professor Tymothy Mason)

"Only Snow White could tame an angry Dwarf."

Chapter **19**

SWORDSMITHS

It was a considerable march down to the iron mines following the short-legged dwarfs whose strict, steady gait challenged Jack and Tylo to keep up. Twisted paths entered tunnel after tunnel, leading into caverns the size of grain fields. There was no sun, but thousands of glass beacons brought light to the far corners. Teams of fit dwarf miners pounded mauls into granite crags. Ore was loaded onto railcars and hauled away. Most of the workers wore round spectacles with magnifying lenses that made their eyes look buggy. No one laughed or shouted, yet there was a calming rhythm in their hammers and pickaxes. Labor made them whole.

As the mines became deeper and vaster, Jack realized what a secure hiding place they could be for Snow White. As for himself and the elf, it might prove less accommodating. The foreman of the Iron Clan was Smoal Klub, the same black dwarf from the hunting party. He gave Jack a hammer and long pry nail and Tylo a withering look.

"You'll work for me now with no tall tales." He handed Tylo a much smaller hammer. "This one's better suited for children. Or devilish imps."

He showed them to a busy grotto.

"You'll mine this wall," he said. "Granite is tough work. It won't make dwarfs of you but will keep you honest. Be the first to work and be the last to rest."

The dwarfs chanted as they hammered, keeping a beat with each strike:

"Strong Arm Ter with veins of ore.
Swing and strike! Swing and strike!

Mine Ter's Earth unto the core,
Swing and strike! Swing and strike!

All for one! Sink the nail.
Swing and strike! Swing and strike!

Woo the Maid; drink the ale.
Swing and strike! Swing and strike!

When She wakes She'll find us hale,
Swing and strike! Swing and strike!

Jack and Tylo were housed with typical teenage he-dwarfs and thrown into their vigorous routine. Each morning they had to be roused from sleeping berths and shuttled by rail trolley to assigned spots in the mines. There, they divvied up tools, bowed to Spirit Ter, and started the day's dig.

Swing and strike! Swing and Strike!

Jack had never worked so hard. His muscles strengthened from the constant strokes of hammer into rock, repeated until a relief horn sounded.

"Drop your sledges," Smoal would order. "Meal time. *Now.*"

In the dining grotto, the youth ate large broiled steak and root vegetables. Even if the food had not been delicious (which it was) there would not have been a morsel left on the earthenware.

They were then trolleyed to an arena for afternoon recreation. He's and she's alike threw themselves into a game called "tersbol". A field was marked out in the shape of a triangle and they were divided into three teams that shuffled an oval rock across it. The object was to keep the "bol" away from one's home goal and score more than the opponents. There was no limit on tackles, tripping, and strikes with flat shale sticks. Jack's long legs and gutsy play gave him a reputation as a strong player. The tight-lipped dwarfs offered no praise but always chose him first for their teams.

Tylo, on the other hand, was not valued on the game field or any place else in the mines, try as he might. Dark circles appeared around his eyes and there was a stumble in his usually sure gait. Not that the elf ever let on. He kept a grin on his sunken cheeks and jested even in the most strenuous of chores.

"Knowing that my sword be inside this stone keeps me digging," he kept saying. "You will see, Giant Killer. You will see."

Daily schooling occurred after tersbol. The young dwarfs squatted on the sports field and were instructed by an elderly cleric called Father Tassl Cryst, who taught them theological lessons and mathematics. He was a pleasant, white-haired soul in a black kilt and ruffled vest with a bronze pendant of Ter's fist around his thick neck.

"Add, add, and add some more," he taught. "Subtraction is only a theory. Once a thing is brought to Ter's earth, it never goes away but can always be added to. So add, add, add."

Jack and Tylo listened with interest.

"We only add up," said the elf.

"Why didn't Allwise teach it this way?" said Jack.

Jack regularly asked Father Tassl about Snow White. He always returned that she was "a rare flower in the garden", tending roots and also minding dwarf toddlers in the Metals region.

"Dwarfkind has warmed to her presence," said the cleric. "She is a fascination among us, so like the revered Beauty."

"Does that mean the Meld will let her stay?" said Jack.

Tassl drew them in closer. "It is in stone scripture that if a faerie weds a dwarf, their child will be born whole. Tis a wish of us all to be as tall and striding as men and claim our place in the Great Forest without dispute."

Jack did not like this account. "Y'all know Snow's just a kid? She's far too young for bridal talk."

"Aye," said Tassl. "But perhaps by the war's end, she will be of age. The prophecy may go far to keep her safe in our mines."

Tylo looked puzzled. "Why do we forestfolk always wish to be tall?"

Father Tassl patted the elf's shoulder (one of the few dwarfs to show him kindness). "To be accepted, naturally, in the image of Mighty Ter."

"I'd like to see Snow White," said Jack. "She's still my responsibility and it's been days."

"A visit can be arranged," said Tassl, "If couched as an educational endeavor. Leave it to me."

"Add, add, and add some more," quoted Tylo.

Smoal Klub broke up the exchange. "Rinse time," he announced.

The class was taken to a steaming cavern where craters bubbled with mineral baths that were warmed by the earth itself.

Jack covered his nose. "What's that stink?"

"Sulfur baths to cleanse the toil and ache off your freakishly sized frames," said Smoal. "Do us all a courtesy and have a dunk."

The dwarfs eagerly stripped down and slipped into various pools. Tylo hid behind a row of stalagmites but Jack jumped in. The fizzling water engulfed his sore body like a comfy blanket. It was a soothing finish to the day's labor.

Then the daily grind began anew. Jack lost track of the days. On the fourth, maybe fifth day, the earth shook with a tremor. "Ter's temper", as the miners called it.

"It makes me want to run all ways at once," said Jack. "But if y'all ain't breaking a sweat, guess we'll come through all right."

The swaying waned and the dust cleared.

"Where's Tylo?" said Jack.

"Buried?" said Smoal. "If we could be so lucky."

"Tylo!" called Jack.

A weak moan answered, "Jack." Then Tylo's voice strengthened. "Giant Killer! I have found it!"

"Where are yeh?"

Tylo was half-covered under a stone pile, his right arm pinned beneath the heavy granite. Jack and Smoal used a fallen beam for leverage and rolled the stone away.

Tylo managed a chuckle. "I have found it," he repeated, pointing at the toppled wall.

Jack held up an oil lamp to see. "Found what, Tylo?"

"My sword is in that stone."

"Think yeh got knocked too hard on the skull," said Jack.

Tylo staggered to his tiny feet, clutching his pickax with his good hand. He took a swing at the wreckage. A gleam of silvery-blue rock dislodged from the gap and landed with a thud at his feet.

"There! It is my sword."

Smoal examined the shiny wodge. "This is terzerok ore, most rare," he exclaimed, tracing its path up to a shimmering vein in the cracked cave. "The largest deposit ever I have seen."

"And this particular chunk be mine," said Tylo.

"Breyman men would claim it as their own," said Smoal. "But dwarf law says that a find belongs to the finder. If you can carry it, whelp, 'tis yours."

Tylo's legs wobbled as he lifted the magnificent rock, which was over half his size, and slung it on his back. "O, that I had a free hand to play an ode on my flute."

Smoal grunted. "How you plan to form a sword from the stone is folly for an elf. Back to digging now. And I do mean *now*."

Jack was mindful of Tylo's lame arm. He stayed by his side for the rest of the work day, lending a hand to keep the terzerok from flattening the Best Learning Twig.

After school time, Father Tassl proved true to his word. He took Jack and Tylo on a ride up the mountainside in a pulleyed cage to visit Snow White. The ascent was slow and nerve-wrecking. It was best not to question the cage's mechanics so long as it reached the top, where they hastily disembarked. A stone barrier was furled aside revealing the welcome outdoors.

To Jack's surprise, it was night, not day. The stars almost scratched his head, they seemed so close. The air was cool and there was grass underfoot. The famed root gardens were layered in terraces down the cliffside.

"Heee!" said Tylo. "How I have missed the smack of a breeze."

He carefully rested his rock, and then began rolling around on the grass. Soon, he was doing flips, digging up earthworms, and eating them without care. The she-dwarfs tending garden exchanged disgusted looks.

"Father Tassl," greeted Captain Shard Smith. "You and your 'followers' wish to see Snow White?"

"Twould bring gratitude of plentitude," said Tassl.

Shard gestured and Snow White came toward them from another terrace. Goosebumps charged Jack's body as she embraced him. She wore a dwarf's long night shirt. Girdled with strands of garnets, it made a perfect faerie gown.

"As I vowed, Jack Spriggins," said Shard, "She has been well cared for."

Snow White shuffled Jack and Tylo around the terrace gardens for a tour.

Jack nodded. "She's been tending these?"

"She spends productive hours here," said Shard Smith.

"I'm grateful," said Jack. "So, no hard feelings then?"

"You and the elf lied to us," said Shard, "But Snow White has become my friend in her short time here and praises you both. I understand the reason for the deception. By the tolerance of Mighty Ter, I am willing to withhold my grudge, unless you prove her wrong."

"That's a fair shake."

A shock of white steam escaped a brick funnel on the next mountain over.

Tylo rolled onto his feet. "What be that, Fair Bearded Shardy?"

"It's *Captain* Shard Smith," she said sternly.

"Why, it is the Forge, of course," said Father Tassl.

Shard beamed with pride. "My younger brother, Hamr Smith, labors there. He's a craftsman of uncommon worth."

Tylo let out an 'eeee' of excitement and rolled the terzerok forward. "By Sparky's spark, my sword will come to me as simply as a carrot plucked from this garden spot."

"That terzerok is enough for a blade," said Shard. "When forged it can slice through stone."

"Naw!" said Jack.

"Aye. There are few smiths with the skill to mold it," said Shard. "But my Hamr is among them."

"Then, I bid you, Smithy-Sis," said Tylo. "Take us to meet your noble bro-bro so he may craft my sword now."

"I am not to do the bidding of an elf," she scoffed. "Never."

There was an awkward silence. Snow White looked angrily at the dwarf captain.

"Very well," said Shard, softening. "We go for Snow White, though. And I cannot speak for my brother's acts when we find him."

As she led the party to a railcar, it dawned on Jack that a faerie might have more charm over dwarfkind than they were willing to admit.

"How miraculous," said Father Tassl. "Outsiders are rarely permitted in the Forge."

Shard Smith released a rusty brake and started the railcar down a steep descent.

"I've been on bucking colts that felt safer," said Jack, gripping the side with white knuckles. Wind stung his face as the tram took a sharp dip to the bottom.

Father Tassl seized the opportunity to educate. "Of all the dwarf clans, the Forge is the only one we are not born into. Only those who can master Ter's rocky flesh and shape it to finest metal are chosen to belong."

"That is how Hamr was called to serve," said Shard.

The rails entered the mouth of a rock-covered hillock. Through the tunnel, the railcar came to a jarring halt at the furnaces of Clan Forge. A torrid blast caused the riders to cover their faces. Three master grates spurted with molten ore. Dwarfs poured cauldrons of orange and white smelt into stone casks. Swords and armored chest plates, metal shields and tools, were produced with rhythmic precision by the smiths. Jack noticed that they were all clean shaven (beards would have been a hazard amid the fiery metals). They pried out the casts while the ore was still malleable using tongs.

The artistry of the dwarfs was on full display as they hammered and chiseled the smelt. Sparks flew with each stroke like a symphony of angry bells.

Tylo tapped his feet. "That be the music of dwarfs."

The smiths lifted their metalwork and tossed them into cooling pools. Steam clouds hissed from the water. Only Hamr

Smith kept honing a blade on his anvil, pounding it with exact strikes until he was satisfied, which seemed to be a long time coming.

"My brother," said Shard.

He was close to Jack's age, no older than sixteen. Tan skin, like his sister, and powerfully built from the waist up, his short sturdy legs were bowed. He was handsome with cropped curly hair and a strong jaw. His thick lips were set in a stoic line. The constant heat kept him stripped to leather trousers and a workman's apron.

Hamr waved off his sister and the outsiders. "Stand back," he yelled between deafening blows of his sledge. "This saber on my anvil is having a difficult time taking shape."

Tylo jiggled in excitement. "It knows *my* sword be next, that be why!"

The young smith's next wallop landed only inches from Tylo's head. "Say again?"

"*My sword.* The sword that you will hammer to life."

Hamr came down harder on the quivering steel. "There is no way an elf like you will ever wield a blade of my making."

Tylo weaved closer to being flattened, buzzing, "Wham, wham! Trimmer, trimmer! Sharp, sharp, sharp!"

Between the heat and rage, Hamr's temples turned deep red. "Ter give me strength!" he yelled, delivering the saber a last blow and pitching it into the pool.

"Now move on to mine," said Tylo.

The teenage dwarf turned to Shard. "What have I done that you bring this menace before me, sister?"

"It was a mistake to guide the Beauty's companions here," said Shard.

Hamr lifted his visor revealing azure blue eyes. "The Beauty is welcome. The man's son less so, though he does honor in the tersbol field. But this halfgrown hobgoblin—"

Jack tried warn him. "I'd walk that back."

It was too late.

Tylo raised his voice. "You, Smith, will be stabbed the moment you've finished my sword for calling me 'goblin'!"

Hamr replied, "If you could even manage to lift a blade, I'd still sleep soundly at night."

"I be stronger than you think." Tylo heaved the chunk of terzerok, which rolled to the smith's feet.

Hamr picked it up. He addressed two of his fellow smiths. "What say you, cousins?"

Anvl and Chizl Smith came over from their lathes. They might have shared the same surname but were likely distant cousins for their skin was shades darker than Hamr's and their eyes orange like agate moonstones.

"Impressive," said Anvl. "Pure terzerok."

"Which dwarf found this?" said Chizl.

"No dwarf" said Jack. "The elf did. And it's all his, by yer laws."

Expressions of displeasure showed on the dwarfs faces.

"You be disturbed, Hamr-Smither," said Tylo. "Perhaps such a metal is beyond you?"

With a smug grin, Hamr opened his palm and motioned with his fingers. "If I agree to forge this terzerok, what will you give me as payment?"

"Pay-ment?" Tylo sounded out.

Jack made it clear for him. "Dwarf-work ain't free."

Tylo thumped his head thoughtfully. "My payment will be my noggin."

"Noggin?"

"Up here," said Tylo. "My brain basket. My elfin head. This copper topper will be yours, Smither, when my sword be in my hand."

"Stoke the fires and stand back," said Hamr. "I'll pound out the finest short sword ever seen."

The smiths cast the terzerok in the fiery grates. Chizl pumped air from the bellows while Anvl stirred the melting ore. The cavern glowed orange-red as the liquid took shape. Hamr struck it with focused fury that only heroes of lore might have done.

"*Swing and strike!*" chanted Tylo. "*Swing and strike!*"

Anvl forged a hilt of copper on his metalworking lathe, then wound it with strands of leather for the grip. Hamr tossed aside his sledge and gripped a sharp chisel. He guided the tool along the sword's heated edge. It was cooled, fit with the hilt, and topped with a blue azurite pommel.

"Perfectly balanced," said Hamr, waving the new short sword above his sweaty head, "Enough curve to make the edge lethal from any angle."

The terzerok had a mystic blue sheen. Hamr sliced through a boulder in the cave wall like a hot knife in a brick of butter. Jack had never seen such a remarkable weapon.

"What name shall it bear?" said Chizl, brandishing a burin for engraving.

Tylo hopped from foot to foot. "Burn!" he said. "By Sparky's fire, my sword will be named 'Burn'."

Hamr nodded in consent.

Shavings of terzerok fell as Chizl carved the inscription into the blade: *BURN*.

Tylo twitched in glee. "I will cling to this short sword with all the importance I will soon forget."

He reached for Burn but Hamr took it.

"Your head's removal shall be done with this very edge, then?" he said.

It was a sobering reminder of what was owed.

"Alas," Father Tassl whispered to Jack. "It appears your elf friend will lose his head."

"I wouldn't be too sure," said Jack. "Tylo's got more luck than a fool under a rainbow."

Hamr Smith was impatient. "Well?"

"Very well, Smithy," said Tylo. "I owe you my head?"

"You do."

Tylo knelt before Hamr and lowered his tawny head with surprising resignation.

Jack quietly unsheathed his bone knife, though doubted Hamr would actually take the elf's life. The young dwarfsmith cast conflicted glances to his kin as he raised Burn like a novice executioner.

"Just remember," said Tylo, with a devilish wink. "Only my head was promised. You may not touch my neck."

* * * * *

From "Knives, Guns, and Me" by Joss Jamie Abe Gareth, weapons expert of the Thunder Country.

TERZEROK STEEL

For as much steel as I done shot and stabbed with - t'aint nothing that compares with the strains smelted from forges of the Dwarf Domain in what used to be called the 'Great Forest'. This were iron, copper, tin, even slate, mixed with ores called Terzerok that could only be found in the region's Iron Hills. They were bluish in color and lighter to hold, sharper to cut with, quick to fire, and darn near impossible to break. Some claimed the purest steel could slice through stone. Bullets crafted from the stuff changed warfare as it was known.

School-smart types that study rocks told me (more than once) that meteor stars fell in those northern woods long before folks kept calendars and mountains grew out of them. That's why the metal mined there was so rare. Only Dwarfs ever got the knack of making alloys from it. That, added with their skill to mold weapons, made them the finest smiths in the world.

Pieces from that period, especially swords, spears, and shields forged before the Ogre Wars, are near priceless in value. The Terzerok pistols developed round the same time can be regarded, in this shooter's opinion, as works of art. They rival anything we Thunderers came up with and rammed gun powder down during them wild pioneer days.

Chapter 20

THE SWING AND THE STRIKE

There was no way to cut off a head without disturbing the neck. No doubt Hamr Smith felt furious, humiliated, and defeated all at once but he did not strike out or even bang on the anvil. He just tucked the terzerok short sword in his belt and ran off.

Tylo made a move to go after him. "Smithy, Burn be my sword!"

Snow White stopped the elf with a reproachful look.

"I'll go instead," said Jack. "Reckon I know best what it's like to be hoodwinked by a tree pest."

There was a network of narrow passages connecting the forge caverns. Jack tracked these until he came to a small grotto that served as a stable for elk and deer that toted heavy carts through the mines. Hamr was seated by the pen of a docile-eyed buck elk with shorn antlers. Jack squatted beside him.

"The elf cannot have the sword," said Hamr.

"Yer going back on yer word," said Jack.

"He tricked me. My word was never respected."

"That's yer business. I ain't stepping in lest yeh make me."

"Men always step in where they do not belong. What makes Jack Spriggins any different?"

"Dunno. I ain't the forestland's favorite son. Not by a long shot."

"Who is?"

"Well, there's a fella named Corrobis. He's already captain of his own troop and a big war hero. Girls all swoon for him because they think he's good-looking and he's always making news in the village squares."

"He sounds like a bore."

"He *is*. But he's the favorite. His pet cat has more smarts if yeh asked me."

Hamr gave the elk a handful of bark through the slats. "This is *my* pet. I feed him and trim his antlers so he can move easier through the tunnels. He's never been above ground."

"I got a horse back home," said Jack. "His name's Blackberry."

"Dwarfs do not name our animals. This one is simply 'Hamr Smith's Elk'."

"Ever think about taking him outdoors for sunshine?"

"The sun would likely blind him," said Hamr. "As it would me."

Jack stared at the lone light; a blue glass lantern. "How long have yeh been in these caves?"

Hamr appeared reluctant, then sighed. "Longer than most my age. My father was a glassblower in Ter Ridge. My mother and sister were hunters. I had an older brother named Hilt Smith who dug wells in the mines. A cave-in ended his life. I welded him a tombstone from the metal of his shovel. The work was admired by Clan Forge. They honored my family by calling me to serve here. Ten years of age was I. Now I am sixteen."

His voice was soft and low but full of purpose. No nonsense, the same as Jack's.

"Can yeh ever leave?" said Jack.

"Leave my work?" said Hamr. "Even if I could, where would I go? All dwarfkind is underground now."

"Why? Yeh dwarfs got so many skills. I wish I could clobber out a blade as perfect as that short sword yeh just made. But living down here in the dark, never seeing the sky. Reckon I'd probably just run away."

"That is a thoughtless statement only a forest man would make. We dwarfs love our labor. We love our mines. We love to fashion the finest wares ever known. What we do not love is being owned. Inside the mountains we reign with Ter's blessing. Outside, we are slaves. We hide in the underground because it is the only place we can call our own."

The elk bayed. Hamr soothed him by offering a radish root.

Jack chose his words carefully. "Yeh say '*we dwarfs*'. But what about Hamr Smith?"

Hamr looked at the dark rock walls and then down at his calloused hands. "I should like to see Ter Ridge again someday. Maybe the woods too. Tell me. Do all woodland females look like Snow White?"

Jack twittered his lips. "Course not. But there's plenty worth knowing, and a few yeh'd rather not."

"It's the same with dwarf girls."

Jack stretched his sore arms. "Sitting here, side by side, I'm thinking we're a lot alike."

"You do not feel that you men, being taller, are better than us?" said Hamr.

"Me? I'm just a no-account kid from Thin Creek with a thief's luck."

"Pardon?" Hamr looked shocked. "I did not think men could be modest."

"That's because yeh've only known lowlifes, like the ones that forced yeh to work for their gain."

"The Barons of Breyman," said Hamr. "The Dynadins."

"Yeah, them. Most forest men just want dwarfs on their side. We're getting licked out there without yeh. Yeh got muscles, smarts and know-how. It's yer craft that keeps us better armed to fight the ogres."

"And what will happen when the war is over, Jack?"

"Whatever yeh choose. Yer as free as anyone else as far as I'm concerned. And General Camlann would say the same. And if the dwarfs protect his daughter, he'll back yeh up with his whole army. Yeh can count on him. He's the best of us."

"Does the general wear a black hood?"

This shocked Jack. "Naw. He's no wraith. They want Snow White dead. It's why we're here."

Hamr clutched the terzerok sword as if to defend the faerie. "Forgive me. I've heard whispers that wraiths give council to our clan heads."

Jack stood, bumping his head on the low ceiling. "Ow. If that's true, we're all in trouble."

"I have an instinct to trust you, Jack Spriggins. Though it goes against all I was raised to believe about mankind. Perhaps Mighty Ter sent you here so I'd learn otherwise."

"What's inside makes yeh what yeh are," said Jack, rubbing his bruised noggin. "Reckon I'm learning too. But I ain't a backstabber. Same goes for Tylo."

"The elf!" Hamr's temper returned. "How can you ally yourself with that swindling, rusty-haired burl?"

"C'mon," said Jack. "Yeh weren't really gonna cut off his head. I saw it in yer eyes."

"True, I would have spared the blade the trouble."

"Y'know, elves get treated worse than any dwarf does," said Jack. "Sure, they'll drive yeh crazy like an itch on the butt, but Tylo's stayed all these days in the mines because he promised to look after Snow White – no sun, no trees, and hurting something awful. I ain't gonna lie, I never liked elves. But this one's so brave he makes me feel small."

Hamr kicked the dirt. "The elf cannot have the sword."

"He just wants it to feel like he's holding his own in a strange land."

"Nay," said Hamr, stubbornly.

"Keep it then," said Jack. "I'll protect him myself."

He gave Hamr Smith's Elk a last pat on the neck and turned to go. Tylo was there in the way, hanging upside down from a stalactite.

"How long yeh been there?" said Jack.

If the elf overheard what had been said, the only hint he gave was an ear-connecting smile. "Come! Clans be crowded in the big hall. The Melding of the Mines be ready. They wait with Snow White to take us there."

"Bout time," said Jack.

Hamr Smith pushed by Jack. "I will attend with my fellow smiths, Chizl and Anvl."

He passed by Tylo and paused a half-step beyond. Hamr then handed Tylo the terzerok short sword.

"Burn!" said Tylo, embracing the azure hilt. The elf stowed the silver-blue sword in his bow quiver. "Thank you, Fire-Smither, for the world's best sword."

"What changed yer mind?" said Jack.

Hamr glanced at him. "You did, Giant Killer."

Jack extended his palm to shake Hamr's hand. He nearly buckled from the strong grip he got back.

"Lead on," Jack nodded.

Tylo crawled along the craggy wall guided by the trail of blue glass lanterns, singing.

"*Swing and strike. Swing and strike. I'll be the swing if you be the strike.*"

Jack patted the *Deed of Dynadin* in his inner pocket then took long strides through the spiraling caves.

"Try to keep up with Hamr Smith," he told Tylo. "He knows the way."

* * * * *

ODE TO HAMR SMITH'S ELK

(Anonymous)
You knew only darkness. You knew only toil.
The soot and buried chore,
Were normal to you.
It is doubtful you could see,
Or hear beyond the clip-clop of your hooves,
Hauling carts through holes,
Alone and unguided.
Forgotten.
A crown of antlers cut to nubs,
To better fit the paths you trod.
Overlooked despite your size.
Despite your worth.
Forgotten.
Yet, to rub your nose,
Or stroke your sides,
I felt only love, true and friendly.
I think back on that unashamed affection,
From one so passed by,
And sob the only tears left in me.

Chapter **21**

DOMAIN DEBATERS

The Hall of Metals was packed to its iron girders by the horde of dwarfs eager to attend the Melding of the Mines. Captain Shard Smith halted Jack and Tylo before the entrance. "I am to hold all your blades, bows, and quivers before you go inside, and deliver them to the armory."

"Are we gonna get them back?" said Jack.

"This is a council of thought, not warfare." she said.

Father Tassl offered a rolling cart. "I shall spare you the trouble of taking the armaments to the armory, noble captain. You wish to see this Meld and stand by the Fae lass. I can stow them for you."

Shard agreed. Jack reluctantly placed his crossbow, arrows, and lasso into the cleric's cart.

Tylo's skinny fingers seemed fused to his new short sword. "Burn be more family than sword to me," he pleaded.

"Then it shall be at home under Ter's watchful eyes," said Tassl, handling the terzerok weapon with care.

Jack noted how Snow White's wand was ignored. The yew stick stayed tucked in her garnet belt without mention.

The Four Clan Heads were already convened. The crowded hall fell silent as Shard guided Jack, Tylo and Snow White to the circular mosaic in the hall's center. Hamr Smith and his cousins had slipped into the tight gallery behind.

Gravl Smoothstone, Head of the Quarry Clans, was the new face in the chamber. He was the handsomest of dwarfs; dark-skinned, beardless with a groomed mustache and amethyst eyes. He wore a simple white mantle draped over a leather chest plate, looking more like a laborer than a statesman. His natural smile was rare among the glowering dwarfs.

"You've summoned me from the quarries in the west," he said from his lectern. "I'd still be holding a gritty pickax if it hadn't been confiscated at the door."

Smoothstone's humor gave Jack some hope.

"We are grateful you are attending," said Bronz Terson of the Metal Clans.

"And standing here is the reason for our Meld," said Smoothstone as he advanced to Snow White. "I see why the clerics proclaim her the 'Awakened Princess'. Truly, she mirrors any likeness to the sleeping princess I have seen."

Snow White demurred with a coy smile.

Bronz Terson held to an efficient tone. "The issue before us is that Snow White Camlann, Last of the Fae, seeks asylum in our Domain. Allwise Calculator of the Orchard has made the request through his messenger, Jack Spriggins, of Giant Killer fame."

A reaction droned through the chamber.

"No dwarf should act on orders from any man," said Azur Cutter, Head of the Gems Clan. "I, for one, would like to hear from Snow White, herself."

"Nay," said Pewtr Smelt. "She will only bewitch us with the charm of the Fae."

"Let Snow White speak!" said Hamr Smith from the gallery.

A hubbub of dwarf voices agreed.

"Lass," said Bronz Terson to the faerie. "Put your claim before us."

Snow White stepped forward like a moonflower at eventide. Her hands spun in slight gestures at her sides as she turned on her toes, gracefully circling the chamber.

"Use words that you speak, Mistress Camlann," coached Tylo.

Snow White stopped dancing. "A faerie dreams while a dwarf digs," she said. "But I've learned I'd be happy as another pair of hard-working hands in these mines. Not a Sleeping Beauty. Not a general's daughter. Just an honored guest among friends. Could you all feel the same and accept me as such?"

Her hands made Fae symbols prompting her spoken words.

"I do not wish to cause strife," she went on. "Your clans have faced too much already. I've moved from bower to bower in my thirteen years and will find another home if you cannot keep me. The Great Spirits will provide. You've taught me to be useful in the hours I do not dream and have treated me as one of you. For that, I'm ever grateful."

There was not the slightest cough, gasp, or stray breath from the hundreds of dwarfs gathered in the hall as she finished speaking. She rose on her toes, turning slowly, and returned to Jack's side.

"Bet that's the most yeh've talked in yer life," said Jack.

"Too much?" she whispered.

"Naw. Just right."

Hamr Smith was so touched he began to sing a wordless ode to the faerie. The gallery promptly joined him. Jack was astonished by the beauty of the dwarf voices, which rose in precise bold harmonies that filled the chamber.

"Singing be not fun to a dwarf," said Tylo, "It be holy."

"Snow White," said Gravl Smoothstone. "Your words have moved us all. I myself am without reason or speech."

"I am not!" said Pewtr Smelt. "Her father leads the forestland army. Accepting her would suggest an alliance between us, one that we dwarfs have strived to distance ourselves from. Breyman will certainly levy further sanctions and possibly attack us if we do."

"Some of Breyman's ranks fight alongside Camlann's," said Smoothstone. "What is the problem?"

Pewtr Smelt pounded his lectern. "The war will end and men will divide once more. We will be in the middle of their disputes, charged with this faerie refugee, and suffer the more for it."

"I agree," said Azur Cutter of the Gems Clan. "Our history proves any dealing with forest men to be costly to dwarfkind."

Bronz Terson then added, "The Hooded Ones did warn us of making such compromises."

"Yeh mean the Wraiths?" said Jack. "What kind of fools are yeh to listen to their twisted lies?"

"You are not a speaker of this Meld, Jack Spriggins," said Pewtr Smelt. "Talk out of turn once more and you will be removed from the hall."

"Let us think more of Snow White," said Smoothstone. "She is innocent of our politics."

"Very well," said Smelt, sneering as if he'd found a worm in a half-eaten apple. "Let us banish her at once."

"Or let her stay," said Smoothstone. "And prove Ter's courage runs through every dwarf."

"Hear, hear!" agreed Hamr Smith and other encouraging voices from the gallery.

"We have enough freedom," said Pewtr Smelt. "Right here. Inside the mines. It has always been so. Harboring *her* threatens that security."

"Are we free?" said Smoothstone. "Cowering under the earth for fear of Breyman?"

"Freedom and ownership of the mines was given to all dwarfs by Dynadin the First," said Bronz Terson. "It was the better part of a century ago when he willed it to us."

"Bah," said Pewtr Smelt. "The myth of a promise that never was. The *Deed of Dynadin* is a falsehood. The baron's successors deny it was ever penned. Have you seen it?"

Bronz Terson sighed. "No one has. It was stolen."

Jack took the deed from his vest and waved it over his head like a flag. "Yeh talking about this?"

The Clan Heads returned a variety of looks: shock from Azur Cutter; sentiment from Bronz Terson; hope from Gravl Smoothstone; outrage from Pewtr Smelt. Smoothstone accepted the document and examined it.

"Tis the wax seal of Dynadin the First, true enough," he said, unrolling the parchment and reading aloud:

"Tis my intention, in spite of fierce opposition from fellow landowners, and mine own ungrateful sons, to grant these northern Dwarfs the ownership of the Domain Mines of the Iron Hills ... "

Gravl Smoothstone paused reading and gave Jack a bewildered look. "This appears to be an original copy. There are signatures of our forbears. It has the signature of Dynadin the First and the dwarf mark of our forefather, Orus Strok."

Pewtr Smelt snatched the deed and read it, the color draining from his face. "How came you in possession of this, Jack Spriggins?"

"Well," said Jack. "Near as I can figure, Viviyann Greygeese smuggled the deed from Castle Brey after her uncle, the first Dyn, died. She gave it to Allwise and he was fixing how to give it back."

Bronz Terson steadied himself. "Why did you not present this when first we met?"

"I was told this deed ain't nothing but trouble," said Jack. "Reckon they got that right."

"Withholding state property is treason," said Smelt.

Jack rolled his eyes. "Quit squabbling over where the deed's been. It's here now."

"It is," said Bronz. "And it proves the mountain domain is truly ours."

"Do not be a fool," said Smelt. "It's a forgery."

Azur Cutter rubbed her beard. "Aye. The current Dynadins shall never accept it."

"Jits!" said Jack. "Breyman ain't the only army in the woods. Show that deed to General Camlann. He'd back yeh."

Pewtr Smelt considered this. "Mankind's most famous warrior? How interesting. We also have his daughter to ensure his cooperation."

"But as a kindness, not a ransom," said Smoothstone cautiously.

"Be it not the same thing?" said Smelt. "The words of men mean precious little when penned on parchment. Only when they fear real loss do they act."

"You suggest that Camlann's soldiers will back us against Breyman?" said Azur Cutter.

Snow White cringed. Jack instinctively stood in front of her and felt Tylo climb up his shoulders to take a higher posture.

"This meld be taking a bad turn," said Tylo. "Shame to you, Dwarf Smelt."

"I'm with the elf," said Jack. "It was a big mistake to bring Snow White here. Allwise thought better of yeh."

"Are you above blackmail and deceit, Jack Spriggins?" said Smelt. "Your acts in Giantdom say otherwise."

Chuckles arose from the gallery.

"Noble Clan Heads," said Hamr Smith, pushing through the onlookers. "I am only a forge-worker but I beg you, be good to Snow White. Do not make her a prisoner. The deed is ours. We need only our virtues as dwarfs to uphold it. But sheltering her is a matter of decency."

"Youthful ideals, but acknowledged," said Bronz Terson. "Pewtr Smelt of Clan Forge has made valid arguments. 'Tis time we Heads deliberated in private."

Smoothstone clutched the deed as the Clan Heads removed themselves to an antechamber. Armed guards blocked the exit, keeping close watch of Jack and Tylo.

Hamr approached Jack. "You should know, the Clans will not allow you, the elf, or Snow White to leave the mines now."

Captain Shard agreed. "My brother speaks true."

"We didn't come here for Snow to be yer hostage," said Jack. "I know yeh dwarfs got grudges, but that ain't gonna solve them."

"Snow White has her champions among us, Jack," said Hamr, who shot him a meaningful look. He and his sister backed away into the throng.

Deliberations were brief. The four Clan Heads reentered the hall and took their places at their respective lecterns.

"We have a resolution," announced Bronz Terson. "Regarding Snow White, we shall take her into our care—"

An outburst of cheers erupted from the gallery.

Bronz raised his palms for silence, for he had not finished.

"And custody," he said.

The gallery fell silent. The Iron Guard clasped Snow White's hands behind her back and stamped their spears with loyal obedience. Captain Shard was missing from their ranks.

Bronz Terson finished. "The faerie girl's liberty shall be conditional upon military support of General Ardus Camlann and his Forestland army, securing the legitimacy of the Deed of Dynadin."

Pewtr Smelt took over. "As for Jack Spriggins and the elf, we hereby sentence you to fifty years hard labor in the limestone quarry for committing treason against this council."

Two sentries yanked Tylo's injured arm to bind his hands. The elf shrieked with pain. It took six guards to put Jack in iron clasps. An uproar swelled from the gallery, comprised mostly of jeering dwarfs.

"Down to mankind. Down to elves. Down, down, down."

Gravl Smoothstone watched with a grave look as the Iron Guard took them from the chamber.

"Now what, Giant Killer?" said Tylo.

Jack answered under his breath. "Now we gotta figure how to escape."

* * * * *

Quote on a scrap of antiquated parchment framed and mounted over the cash register at the Domain Gem Cave Tour gift shop.

"The muscular, misshapen race of immigrant dwarfs hath toiled without equitable compensation for their service, artistry and craft of highest excellence. This shall end hereby, with the swift stroke of my signature and the press of my seal. May it right the wrongs, which no soul, chaste or corrupt, can doubt. The only wrongdoing is to do nothing at all."

The actual fragment of paper is not for sale but printed facsimiles are available for five and twenty at the check out stand.

Chapter **22**

SEVEN STRONGER

The mines were darker than before. Jack and Tylo were being escorted away by a convoy of guards. Without weapons or a guide, no escape seemed possible. Jack honed all his senses, searching for any way to make a break. Snow White and her escort were within sight several paces ahead. He could tell she was doing the same. The entire company came to a halt at an intersecting fork in the tunnels near the boundary of the Metals Domain.

Captain Shard Smith appeared from an adjoining underpass. Behind her were three new guards armed with long bows, axes, and sledges; their faces masked by copper helmets.

"I shall take over delivering Snow White to her quarters," said Captain Smith, addressing the senior escort. "And will deliver the outlaws to the quarry."

"What is this?" said Gravl Smoothstone. The Quarry Clan Head had accompanied the dwarf convoy for reasons that were suspiciously unclear. "I was intending to lead the prisoners myself, Captain."

"Tis unnecessary," said Captain Smith. "I have selected my own sentries who shall not succumb to the faerie's charms, the elf's tricks, or the Giant Killer's wiles. We will take them, presently."

Smoothstone resisted. "That conflicts with my duty as Head of Clan Quarry."

The senior escort also opposed. "And mine," he said. "I am the commander in charge."

Tylo looked up at Jack. "We be so popular all the dwarfs vie to take us to our doom."

A low rumble from within the cavern walls stopped the argument.

Smoothstone held up a hand with caution. "Brace yourselves. Mighty Ter is angry."

The gangway began to sway beneath their feet. It was an earth tremor, the second in as many days, only this one was far more pronounced and violent. Boulders fell from the gray crags, making Jack's heart race. Tylo huddled close to him. Snow White covered her head. The dwarf guards were knocked into each other and the shaking batted everybody off their feet. The quake grew in intensity and noise until stone dust exploded from the portal.

Then all fell silent.

A mix of coughs, prayers, and shouts for order came in quick succession.

Smoothstone was the first to recover. He grasped Jack's irons and pushed him forward. "Now we truly cannot tarry. The Earth Spirit has provided a distraction for us to exit from the mines."

"Us?" said Jack.

"Aye," said Smoothstone. "I have come to lead you and fair Snow White to freedom."

"So have I," confessed Shard Smith, stumbling to her feet.

Her three chosen guards lifted their helmets. Naturally, they were Hamr Smith and his cousins, Anvl and Chizl.

Hamr patted his sledge. "As I said, Jack Spriggins, Snow White has her champions."

The broken glow from a cracked glass lamp became visible through the dust. Squeaky wheels warbled as Father Tassl Cryst rolled his cart onto the gangway. He passed the shaken enemy guards and tottered near Jack.

"Add, add, add," he said. "I trust no one is badly hurt? How is Snow White?"

The faerie waved at him, trying to draw closer to her friends.

"And Jack Spriggins?" said Tassl.

"My knees are knocking," said Jack, "But I'm still standing on them."

Tylo let his own status be known. "The Best Learning Twig only wishes for a tree to climb up."

Father Tassl shone his lantern on the contents of his cart. "May wishes add up to truths."

Jack could see the cleric still had the crossbow, Tylo's sword, and all their other weapons.

"Stop!" warned an approaching voice. "Go no further."

It was Smoal Klub, the mine foreman.

"The bridge is not stable," he said. "Do not advance. Damage is severe. Turn back. In fact, I will take charge of the prisoners."

From the glint in the crusty dwarf's onyx eyes, Jack could tell he was also an ally.

"Turn back," Smoal repeated.

The senior escort clustered with the enemy guards suspiciously, raising blades and arrows.

"A rot festers here," said the commander with a snide air. "Therefore, I will remain in charge of the captives until official word comes from Clan Head Pewtr Smith."

If Jack and the conspirators were going to escape, there would be a skirmish. The only surprise was that Snow White started it. She blew crippling thorn darts from her wand into the necks of the commander and two of his guards. As they buckled, Hamr and the cousins charged full tilt at the remaining foes.

"So much for diplomacy," yelled Smoothstone, withdrawing a maul from his belt. He smashed it into an attacking guard's chest plate.

Father Tassl pulled the terzerok sword from his cart and split Jack's manacles with a single stroke. "Ter support us," the cleric prayed. He kicked the shiny sword over to Tylo who made short work of his binds, then cradled the hilt.

"Simmer shiny Burn!" said Tylo, who hopped protectively to Snow White's side.

Jack grabbed his crossbow and quiver. Captain Shard Smith and Smoal stood at his flanks. There was half a minute of clangs, flings and curses. Then the skirmish ended as quickly as it began with the opposing guards spread out unconscious on the gangway.

"Y'all sprung us!" said Jack.

Snow White made heartfelt gestures of thanks.

Smoothstone bowed to her. "Fair Snow White, we seven dwarfs have risked everything this day to see you and your companions free of our brethren's misguided avarice."

"Aye," said Captain Smith. "And if we had to include the forest boy and elf, so be it."

Hamr Smith regarded the fallen guards. "Tis strange to fight my own kind. But the Meld was so un-dwarfish, how could we side against you? Right is right. Any good dwarf knows that."

His rebel fellows nodded in agreement.

"We must hurry," said Captain Smith. "Pewtr Smelt is no fool. He will realize his orders have gone awry."

"He'll send the Iron Guard after us," said Smoothstone.

Captain Shard Smith removed the brooch from her breast plate and tossed it over the gangway. "Looks like I've resigned."

Then, there was an aftershock.

The rumble shook the iron buttresses that held the underground together. Debris fell and more funnels of dust shot from the portal. The dwarfs did not panic but squatted for cover. Jack did the same, shielding his body around Snow White and Tylo.

"Mighty Ter persists," said Father Tassl when the rumble subsided. "If we do not leave the mountains, he will seal us in."

They rushed down the gangway but found the portal had caved in.

"Rugged Fate," said Smoal Klub. "The railcars are just beyond this barrier."

"Ain't there another way to them?" said Jack.

Hamr Smith raised his maul and struck the wall. "We will do what dwarfs do best. Swing and strike!"

The seven dwarfs got busy battering the large stones. The blockage crumbled under their quick hard strokes.

"We break walls eight times thicker every day," said Smoal Klub.

Jack pushed against a boulder with the help of Smoothstone.

"Ain't yeh giving up a lot by helping us?" said Jack. "Leaving yer whole clan behind?"

"I would be giving up far more if I did nothing," said the quarry head.

With a combined thrust, they shoved the slab aside. Stones of the pile shifted into new positions and a small hole opened at the top of the portal.

"Climb through!" said Hamr Smith.

He led the way, helping Snow White up and over the rock pile. The dwarfs followed with Jack and Tylo bringing up the rear. They were narrowly missed by a slew of arrows dispatched by Pewtr Smelt's guards, who were advancing on the gangway behind them.

"Traitors!" said Smelt. "Stop the traitors by any means!"

Jack boosted Tylo to safety and retaliated by firing his crossbow, disabling the lead marksmen. He then passed through hole himself, which Hamr collapsed with a blow of the sledge.

"Smelt's guard will break this wall apart as we did," said Hamr. "We need to launch those transports."

Straight ahead was the railcar terminal. Tylo sliced the chains apart with Burn as Jack helped push three cars into place with the dwarfs, who hitched their couplers.

A loud crumbling came from the portal as Pewtr Smelt's Guard broke through the rockfall. "No one escapes!" said Smelt, from a hole at the top. A captain quickly squeezed through, followed by others.

"Climb in," said Jack.

Shard Smith and Snow White got in the front railcar while Father Tassl jumped into the last and released the rusty brake lever. Jack and his fellow rebels pushed the railcars. The iron wheels screeched as the little train started to roll.

"Put more back into it!" shouted Hamr.

Smelt's guards busted a larger hole through the rock wall and scrambled over the pile, aiming their longbows.

The three railcars rolled forward, veering towards a low tunnel. Gravl Smoothstone leapt inside the first car. Tylo jumped into the middle with Smoal and Anvl. Jack got into the last. Chizl Smith was delayed as he smashed the front axles of the remaining cars.

Hamr ran back and stopped Chizl's hammer. "Get aboard, cuz."

They raced together and Chizl hopped in beside Jack. The tracks suddenly dipped as the railcars gained speed. Hamr charged after to keep up. Chizl yanked on the brake lever but the iron wheels only screeched and threw sparks.

Jack extended a hand. "Reach, Hamr!"

They barely latched on to each other. Hamr got dragged behind the railcar as arrows whizzed at them fired by the pursuing guards. The deadly shafts careened off the iron siding.

Hamr shouted. "I can't hold on!"

Jack felt their grip slipping and was being pulled out of the railcar as well. The wheels spun faster. He felt the supported grasps of Anvl and Chizl around his waist when Tylo's bare feet crawling up his back. The elf clung his legs around Jack's shoulders and extended Burn – hilt first – towards Hamr. Tylo's calloused little hands were wrapped with his work shirt, gripping the flat edge of the blade. Hamr clasped the hilt with a last surge of strength.

"Pull!" Tylo said to Jack.

"Pull!" Jack said to Anvl and Chizl.

As one, the team hefted Hamr and they toppled inside the railcar as it entered the low tunnel. A log jam of elbows and boots collided in the car. Jack felt the craggy ceiling skim the top of his hair and shuddered to think how close he had come to having his head knocked off.

Hamr's knees were scraped raw. He still held on to Burn but, after twisting the short sword two or three times, handed it back to Tylo.

"Still yours," he mumbled with cold respect.

Tylo winced as he took the azure hilt with his lame hand but then switched to his good one. His bright smile returned. "Smithy forged me a life-saber."

The railcars tilted left, then right, missing protruding edges of rock by inches. Jack could see Snow White up front beside Shard Smith, the wind whipping her dark locks. Noticing him, she gave a confident smile. The train dipped into pitch-blackness.

"Where does this tunnel take us?" said Jack.

"To the Grotto of the Sunken River," said Hamr.

The temperature dropped as the cars descended. Beads of water struck their faces. The momentum finally slowed. Anvl, Chizl, and Smoothstone forced down the brakes and the railcars came to jolting rest.

"If only we had some light," said Smoal Klub.

Tylo snapped sparks off his thumb. "Sparky's gift to you, Klubber."

The elf's flares were enough to get their bearings. Jack flopped out of the tram and put an ear to the tracks.

"There's a rumble on the rails," he said.

Shard Smith reasoned, "Then Pewtr Smelt is closing in behind us."

"The river lies a short way east," said Smoothstone. "Lead us with your flickers, elf."

Tylo took Snow White's hand and the group followed them along a corridor. The elf snickered when Jack and the dwarfs bumped into each other each time his illuminating sparks petered out.

"No more jokes, Tylo!" said Jack. "We're tripping all over each other back here."

Now Snow White giggled as well.

Several empty canoes were stacked beside the landing at the river's edge. The dwarfs launched two of them. Jack rode in the lead canoe with Tylo, Snow White, Hamr, and Shard Smith climbing in behind him. Smoothstone led Father Tassl and the other dwarfs in the second canoe. Jack pushed off the jagged walls with his oar and began churning the water. The grotto was cold and damp.

"I'm Jack Spriggins," he said, spontaneously announcing roll call. "Who's behind me?"   "Shard Smith here."

"Hamr Smith here."

"Snow White Camlann here."

"Father Tassl Cryst here."

"Smoal Klub here."

"Gravl Smoothstone here."

"Anvl Smith here."

"Chizl Smith here."

"Tylo, Best of the Learning Twigs and Finest Elf Sword Handler, here."

Jack returned, "And where are we rowing?"

"Forward!" said the crews.

They rowed in silence for a spell, meandering through the dark canal until Smoothstone hissed from the second canoe. "We are being followed."

A red light had appeared, deep in the grotto behind them.

"Pewtr Smelt and his crew," said Shard Smith.

"Git yer oars churning faster," said Jack.

They doubled their strokes. The tunnel widened and a sparkling gleam cut through the dark, welcoming them under a massive rock arch. Blushing orange clouds reflected off the water as the crew glided onto Gull Lake. It was near sunset and a shock for Jack, seeing the autumn colors along the shoreline after a long week inside the mines. So was the sudden chill in the air.

The dwarfs donned their smoky glasses and rubbed their arms for warmth. Tylo, Jack and Snow White squinted until their eyes adjusted.

Smoothstone drew a deep breath, taking in the expansive scenery. "My pledge to the Awakened Princess already feels rewarded. We dwarfs have denied ourselves a place in this outer world for too long."

"It is colder than I remember," said Hamr, pulling up his collar.

"You're too easily chilled brother," said Shard. "That is why I always did the hunting."

Hamr smirked and dipped his hand in the cold water, glancing back at the mountains. "This is a promising journey we set out on but I shall greatly miss Hamr Smith's Elk."

"This lake is war territory," said Jack. "Keep yer guard up. If Breyman soldiers don't spot us, ogre troops might. And they'll scalp us all."

Tylo clicked his tongue in warning. "If they do not, the frowny dwarfs coming at us surely will."

Pewtr Smelt's crew had oared to the lake from the grotto, obviously intent to overtake them. Jack rowed his party closer to the shores of Malicoor Island. The shoreline was overhung with amber willows and dogwoods.

"Use the leaves for cover," said Jack.

Hamr and Shard cut down branches and masked the sides of their canoe with them. Smoothstone paddled alongside while Anvl and Chizl covered their boat as well.

"Disguise," said Smoothstone. "Very clever, Jack Spriggins,"

"Blending in is a thief's oldest trick," said Jack.

Hugging the shoreline, they skimmed a southward heading along the island. Night descended with a purple sky, the air grew even colder. Snow White, Tylo, and Shard Smith huddled for warmth. Hamr and Jack kept rowing.

Glowing lamps could be seen bobbing from Smelt's canoes. Jack heard them calling out oar strokes.

"They must see us," said Jack.

Smoothstone pointed at the shoreline. "So can other foes."

Torches began to flare up amid the cypress trees on the island.

"Those be ogs," clicked Tylo in elfspeak.

"Jits!" said Jack.

The island torches clustered at the shore as the ogre soldiers uncovered several flat vessels. They swiftly launched four of them with piercing battle cries.

"We cannot out run them," said Smoothstone.

"We sure can't," said Jack. "Just lay your oars aside and be still."

"Play dead?" said Hamr Smith.

"Not too dead," said Jack, loading his crossbow. "Just keep yer aim ready if they discover us."

A crude war chant came from the ogre boats.

> *"Hiss, Serpent, splash and row!*
> *Cross the waters to our foe!*
> *Leave it red with rage and woe!*
> *Hiss, Serpent, splash and row!"*

Jack allowed their leaf-masked canoes to float from shore, resembling logs that were adrift. He and his crew peeked through the boughs as the ogres rowed past them. Smelt's canoes were not as fortunate. The ogres issued bloodcurdling war cries as they rowed directly at them. Smelt's canoes veered away.

"Smelt is fleeing!" gasped Hamr.

"The ogres will cut them down," said Smoothstone with a tone of sadness.

"We must lend aid to our kin, aye?" said Anvl Smith.

"Nay," said Father Tassl. "The Great Spirits teach us not to change our course once it is set, only press forward with courage. Terspeed to Smelt and his crew but we must leave them to their fate."

Hamr agreed. "Aye. We are Snow White's champions now and dwarfs second."

"Aye," said Shard.

Chizl and Anvl Smith seemed resigned to the decision. They took up their oars and rowed with the others.

Jack called out for roll call once more.

"I'm Jack Spriggins. Who's behind me?"

His companions answered in turn, Snow White followed by each of the seven dwarfs.

Tylo finished with, "Tylo, the wettest, coldest, and most grateful elf ever."

Clashes and shrieks of the grisly battle on the lake echoed in the distance. It was not long before the pursuant dwarf canoes drifted from the ogre flotilla, hulls ablaze.

"I'm grateful too," said Jack.

* * * * *

An excerpt from *"The Great Forest - Volume Six : Chronicles of War"* by Professor Tymothy Mason.

THE BATTLE OF GULL LAKE

A decisive turn of the tide in the Great Ogre War of the last century occurred on the shores of Gull Lake three years into the conflict. It brought the population, power, and metal-working resources of the **Dwarf Clans** *(previously declared as neutral) into alliance with the Forestland Army. The shifted an influx of strength and unparalleled weaponry in favor of the northern woods.*

Gull Lake was located near the northernmost boundary of the Great Forest. Conjoined by Big Pine Lake, and surrounding the legendary **Scorpis Isle***, it was on these waters that the Dwarf troops, led by Clan Head,* **Pewtr Smelt***, advanced into what had become Ogre territory and struck a mighty blow to drive the invaders out. The Desert Army was taken by surprise and, though forceful in their* own right, completely underestimated the strength and numbers of the dwarf miners.

Motive for the dwarfs' sudden alliance with Forest men has been attributed to **Snow White Camlann**, daughter of **General Ardus Camlann.** A young maiden at the time, she had come into contact with the Seven Clans and (though accounts vary) inspired them with her beauty, grace, and spirit to take a stand against the Desertlanders' expansion and dominance before it reached their mountain fortresses. (Modern geologists pinpoint that recurring seismic tremors in the Iron Hills during the same period may have contributed the exodus of the dwarfs from the mountains.)

The attack at Gull Lake occurred both on water and on land. Deadly ogre sabers were met blow for blow by superior dwarfin blades, arrows, and improved musketry. Tremendous loss of life was inevitable on both sides as the battle raged for days. On the morning of the third, **Captains Gwachmai Camlann** and **Ootan of Zan** joined the Dwarf Clans with hundreds from their own ranks, subduing the Desertlanders by the evening of the sixth day.

This campaign was far from the last in the war, and relatively minor compared with the historic battles of Fort Hedgewall, the Timberok Road, and the Mist Hills. Many shifts of territory and senseless tragedies would follow. Gull Lake, however, is rightfully remembered as a uniting action that gave the wavering Forestland a boost in both vitality and morale when it was most needed.

Chapter **23**

DEAD WALLS

The island of Malicoor sat under an ashen moon with more torch flames cropping up on its coast. Ironically, Pewtr Smelt had ruined the ogre's surprise attack and they were forced to put into the water early.

"The ogres have played their hand," said Smoothstone. "There will be war at Ter Ridge."   "Ain't nobody living there to defend it," said Jack.

The dwarfs glanced at each other and chuckled.

"Ter Ridge is a trap," said Shard Smith. "The ogres will find it is heavily guarded."

"Yer kidding?" said Jack.

"Are you surprised?" said Shard. "You spent a night there with the elf and Snow White. You thought it deserted, did you not?"

"Kinda figured something weren't right," said Jack. "Like eyes were always on us. Guess they were."

Through his spyglass, Jack watched the dwarf ranks spill out of the mountain caves and roll cannons into positions at Ter Ridge. Before long, the Iron Hills lit up orange as the Clans opened fire upon the approaching ogre flotilla. There were explosions and swells of battle cries as the enemy stormed the shores. New ogre vessels launched from Malicoor. Two headed straight at Jack and his rebels.

"They've spotted us," said Shard.

"Reckon so," said Jack, putting down his spyglass.

They tossed the tree cover off the canoes and rowed until their arms were numb. The ogres had larger vessels and more oarsmen. It was only a matter of time before Jack and their two small canoes would be overtaken.

Within sight lay Scorpis Isle; a much larger body of land than Malicoor. It had desolate bone-gray cliffs and was rumored to be haunted. Fog crept along its coast. Jack and Smoothstone navigated their crafts through the brume, skirting a seawall of humongous boulders that fed into a firth. Rowing into its straight, a cold gloom foretold of perdition ashore.

"Scorpis Isle," said Smoothstone. "Only the dead dock here."

"Death's everywhere out on the lake," said Jack. "Let's take our chances here with the spooks."

The two canoes moored at a stone portal beneath a grove of eighty-foot black cypress trees that swayed like upright corpses. Beyond were the ruins of a man-made courtyard lined with crumbled pillars. A splash of waves deadened as they docked.

"It is said Scorpis is where the Sleeping Beauty's ancestors entombed their dead," said Father Tassl.

"Ain't hard to believe." Jack climbed out of his boat to help the others. The moment his feet touched the cold stone landing, he felt dread. "We're not staying long."

Tylo's teeth chattered. "A floating graveyard. Mysslo would've loved it."

"Ganzil too," said Jack.

Even with an injured arm, Tylo clambered up the cypress trees to scout. Shortly, he clicked down in elfspeak. "Two ogre flatboats coming."

"Jits," said Jack, figuring a plan. "Then we'll haul our boats through these ruins and come out the isle's south point. From there, we row out to Big Pine Lake and make the crossing."

Smoothstone took hold of his arm. "Not even bootleggers dare go into those tombs."

Jack lifted an end of his canoe. "Don't have much choice," he said. "I'd rather face a ghost than be one."

Hamr agreed. "As long as Snow White is safe, I am good with it."

He and Shard hoisted the back of Jack's canoe. Smoothstone relented, following with Smoal and the cousins as they toted the second boat. Snow White took Father Tassl's arm, although it was unclear which one was supporting the other.

Tylo leapt across the cypresses clicking wildly. "Ogres be here!"

Boots stamped from the rocky beach and *sartyrian* curses carried over the dead wind.

"*Boor saad, molthena saad!*" (*Find them, kill them!*)

The desert army's torches blazed. Jack hustled to keep his party ahead. They shouldered their canoes up a stairway of thirteen steps that led to a black corridor framed by two broken columns.

"A hallway of crypts," said Father Tassl. "Bless our path, O Spirit Guides."

Tylo hastened down the trees and perched on Jack's canoe as they crossed inside the catacombs. Thanks to his flickering thumb they could see. The corridor was thick with lichen and midnight green ivy. Tombs lined the walls, most of which had crumbled, revealing black niches and remains of forgotten kings and queens; knights, and sorcerers; races of men, giants and dwarfs. Faded symbols were etched above their stone sarcophagi.

"Anyone know what those say?" said Jack.

"*Do not disturb?*" said Smoothstone.

"We ain't disturbing, just passing through."

"Do not assume a specter will know the difference."

A torch shone at the end of the corridor. An ogre sentry had caught up with them. His *sartyrian* call brought more ogres. They carelessly fired warning shots from pistols and kicked strewn skulls aside, bearing down on Snow White and and her champions.

"*Taan zool*," said the ogre leader, demanding surrender.

Oddly, the floor beneath Jack's feet grew colder. Mist spilled out of cracks in the walls. Deep groans spread from every direction. The ogre commander halted, then waved his soldiers back in retreat. A gust of suction drew the mist back and extinguished all the torches and lamps. Whatever they had angered was not going to let them go peacefully.

"Run!" said Jack.

He pushed his party forward into the suffocating darkness. Ogre screams for mercy and sounds of ripping and crunching were swallowed up in the abysmal crypt. The coldness itself seemed to be pursuant down every blind turn. Tylo tried to snap sparks but only bluish flits popped from his thumbs, dying instantly.

The rush of adrenaline kept Jack's legs from buckling until he felt an icy touch on the back of his neck, which caused him to stumble to the floor. He was certain he would be trampled by the others, or crushed by crumbling walls. He curled up for protection. Scraping sounds rasped against the stonework, gradually fading. Then Jack could see nor hear any others around him.

"Don't leave me behind in the dark," he uttered. "Please."

A strong hand reached down through a shaft of white light that appeared above him.

"Hamr? Is that yeh?"

He took hold of the wrist and was pulled to his feet. The figure was not a dwarf but a man. There was a comforting smile on the pale face and a whiff of fresh cut hay. It was Perdur Galles, Jack's murdered combat teacher.

"How?" said Jack.

He crossed through the light, reaching out. Nobody was there after all.

Jack shook his head, confused but suddenly peaceful. He guided himself along the tomb walls, following more rays that eked around each turn until he came to a jagged opening that spilled out on the far end of Scorpis Isle.

Snow White, Tylo, and the dwarfs sat or lay next to the canoes near the edge of a seawall. They had been waiting for Jack to emerge. Big Pine Lake spread out to the south, free of battle with a welcoming forest on the opposite shore.

Everyone was noticeably shaken from the catacombs and did not speak. They tethered the boats by the lake with the intent of sailing off but none could bring themselves to leave.

Snow White moved closer to Jack. "My mother came to me in those tombs," she said, breaking the silence. "She led me out here but disappeared as soon as there was light."

"I saw my friend, Perdur," said Jack. "He gave me strength."

Hamr Smith overheard them. "For me it was my dead brother. He mussed my hair as he always used to. Then he was gone."

"He came to me as well," said Shard, taking his hand.

"I was guided by a lost love," said Gravl Smoothstone. "Not a word from her lips, but a kiss that reminded me of Shirwood where we had once planned to settle."

"Shirwood?" said Jack.

"It's a deeply wooded country across the southern sea," continued Smoothstone. "There are pioneer colonies of dwarf loggers, miners, and farmers there. They have been separated from the clans of the Iron Hills for generations but are still our cousins."

"Hamr and I have kin there," said Shard.

"We all do," said Smoal Klub.

"I know about the place," said Jack. "Studied it in school."

Smoothstone stood. "It would be a safe refuge to bring Snow White. Tis far away from wars and assassins who might seek her out. I propose we dwarfs take her there."

Jack shrugged. "How would we make the trip? Shirwood ain't close."

"*You* would not," said Smoothstone. "Nor the elf. You are too well-known, Jack Spriggins. Her secrecy is better served by us dwarfs alone. We seven have the will and grit to bring the general's daughter to the safety of Shirwood."

Jack shifted his feet uncomfortably. "Dunno. Ogres ain't likely to find Snow White in that far-off place, but keeping her safe is my quest. I ain't keen on giving it up."

"The Clan Head's proposal is reasonable," said Shard Smith. "Have you a better one?"

Snow White crept away from the group, stepping into the first canoe where she sat alone. Waves rocked her gently and she shivered from the cold, staring at the lake.

"We're some thoughtless blowhards," said Hamr. "We should have asked what Snow White's wishes are."

"I will," said Jack. "Can y'all spare us a moment?"

The company left them alone and started gathering what supplies were left for the trip across. Jack stepped to the first canoe and drew closer to Snow White. Water lapped against the hull as he wondered if he should speak first.

"Where am I to go?" said Snow White.

"Someplace where yeh'll be safe," said Jack.

"I don't want to leave the Great Forest and go to Shirwood," she said. "What's the point of keeping me alive if I'm sent far away?"

"When yeh put it that way," said Jack. "It don't seem smart."

"I know how selfish I'm being."

"Yeh really ain't. Yeh just know what yeh want. Like Tylo and his sword."

Over in the courtyard by the seawall, Tylo swung Burn about, growling at unseen ghosts. The dwarfs stared at him, dumbfounded.

"Now that's probably the funniest sight on Scorpis Isle for a thousand years," said Jack.

Snow White laughed.

"Jits," he said. "If yeh told me last spring I'd make friends with an elf, a faerie, and seven dwarfs, I'd have spit. Now look at me. So turned around if I saw myself in a mirror I'd say, 'Who the blarn's that?' Pardon my language."

The faerie leaned her head on her hand. "I like it when you curse, Jack."

"Just don't start doing it yerself," he said. "I can hear yer pa blaming me for giving yeh bad manners."

She rubbed the scar on his eyebrow. "How did you get this?"

"When I was a kid on Thin Creek."

"Is that where you're from?"

"Yep, good ol' Thin Creek. Wait a sec!" Jack stood, nearly tipping over the canoe, then sat again full of ideas. "That's where I'll take yeh til the war ends. My old shack from when I was a tike on Thin Creek. Ma fixed it up real nice and nobody, I mean *nobody,* ever goes there."

"You'd stay with me?"

"For a while. I reckon Rose Red would be better than me, or even Ella. She'd get every critter in the woods, bears, wolves and bobcats to watch after yeh if she was there. Even owls."

"But why not you?"

"Let's face it," said Jack. "The older yeh git, the more yer Fae charms are going to yank at me the wrong way. Yer like a little sister to me now, and that ain't right."

Snow White's shoulders sank. "I guess not."

"Yeh don't want me tripping at the sight of yeh," said Jack. "Like them lovesick dwarfs."

"Ahem," coughed Hamr Smith. He was standing on the dock and had overheard every word. "Your elf is not well."

"Tylo?"

The elf was still parrying the air, wild-eyed and sweaty.

"Stay back, Mysslo!" he shouted to an invisible phantom. "And get back you wicked snake! Wraiths! Ogres everywhere!"

Jack entered the courtyard, disturbed by Tylo's frightening behavior.

"What's wrong with yeh?" said Jack.

"Get back, wraith," said Tylo to Jack. "I'll not let you hurt Snow White!"

"Tis madness," said Smoal.

"We must stop him before he hurts himself," said Father Tassl.

"I will do it," said Hamr, bracing for a wrestle.

"And I," said Chizl, approaching as well.

Jack uncoiled his vines, prepping a lasso. "Just don't hurt him."

The armed dwarfs took wary steps towards Tylo. He stepped back, not recognizing any of them.

"Back, ogres, or I'll slice you!"

"We ain't ogres, Tylo," said Jack, circling him.

"He has a fever," said Snow White. "His poor arm looks blue and swollen."

Tylo looked at her with tears in his eyes. "You be safe, fairest one?"

Snow White calmed him. "Yes, Tylo. Put faithful Burn aside. You're among friends here."

"But I saw Mysslo in there," said Tylo, looking back at the tombs. "And his snake."

Jack moved in closer. "They weren't real."

"Yes," said Hamr, pressing a finger to his lips. "The snake has left the isle. Shh."

Tylo's eyes flared suspiciously. "It hisses!" he cried. "There it be, coiling to strike you!"

The crazed elf flung the short sword at Hamr, who ducked. Burn arced over the courtyard and stuck a large boulder with a shimmering vibration. The sword was sunk in the stone to its hilt. Jack seized the chance and lassoed Tylo to the ground with his beanstalk vines, and then rushed forward.

"Be the snake dead?" said Tylo.

"Yeh got it," said Jack.

Tylo collapsed in his arms.

Snow White knelt beside them. "Our poor hero."

Father Tassl took charge. "Make a fire, Chizl. Shard, fetch water from the lake. I have hawthorne leaves in my satchel to brew a tea for the elf's fever."

Smoal Klub tried to withdraw Burn from the boulder. The sword did not budge. He tried yanking it with two hands and failed again. Finally, he stepped up, braced his feet upon the rock, and heaved with all his muscular might. The sword did not move an inch.

"Scorpis Isle seems to have ahold of the terzerok blade," said Smoal.

"Let me try," said Jack.

He took hold of the blue gem hilt and spent the next minute grunting and straining before giving up. "There's bigger muscles than mine here. Y'all have at it."

Chizl Smith attempted next. The mighty-armed dwarf placed his bowed legs on the stone with a smug grin. His swell of pride soon faded as the weapon stayed put. Anvl also failed. So did Anvl and Chizl pulling together.

"As I said," said Smoal Klub. "The sword and stone are now one."

Jack nudged Hamr Smith playfully. "Yeh forged it too good. Think how impressed Snow would've been of the champ who pulled it free."

Hamr blushed, accepting the challenge. "None of you tried hard enough."

The sixteen-year-old smith strode up to Burn, wiping flop sweat off his beefy palms with a hardened focus. He bent his thickset knees and contracted every tendon and sinew of burgeoning muscle. A deep growl escaped his clenched teeth as he pulled the hilt. Hamr might have been able raise the entire boulder off the ground but Burn would not be withdrawn.

He backed away and fell to the ground. "I have failed you," said Hamr, gasping at Snow White.

She tilted her head. "No one could've tried harder."

"You've failed *me*, Smithy," cried Tylo. "I've lost Burn!"

Tassl's tea had brought the elf back to consciousness but he appeared weak and pale. Snow White made a sling for his arm from the hem of her gown and Jack carried him to the canoes.

"We be not leaving this charming isle?" said Tylo. "Can I not stay with my sword?"

"Nope. Yer Burn's staying put," said Jack. "We need to push off."

Tylo stretched his neck to view the sword once more. "Farewell, my shiny edge! Whoever frees you will have the world's finest weapon. Farewell, Scorpis Isle. You are the most terrible place I have ever visited."

"And thus, our adventure to Shirwood begins," said Smoothstone.

Jack shot Snow White a wink that said, "*Not really.*" She smiled in relief.

Even as Jack and the dwarfs rowed their canoes across Big Pine Lake, Tylo rambled on. "Farewell, Lady in Black. I cross the sea, but not yet to thee."

"*Lady in Black?*" Jack glanced over his shoulder at the misty shore. The veiled shape of Lady Lell stood amid the lapping waves. She held the third golden apple, which dropped into the lake. A ripple of black crossed the water, jostling the canoes. Tylo's eyes shut and he fell quiet and still.

"Yeh ain't taking him, Spirit," said Jack. "So, keep yer dang apple."

He leaned down to check Tylo. The elf was snoring.

* * * * *

A child's ghost song still sung on grade school playgrounds.

"There's a sword on Scorpis Isle,
Where ghouls and gloom take ev'ry smile."

(CHANT) : "There's a sword on Scorpis Isle."

"The sword is stuck in blackest stone,
It sticks out like a splint of bone."

(CHANT): "There's a sword on Scorpis Isle."

"Take a boat and sail there,

~ 290 ~

Find the sword, yet then beware."

(CHANT): "There's a sword on Scorpis Isle."

"Pull free the sword with your hand,
And all the souls there you'll command."

(CHANT): "There's a sword on Scorpis Isle."

"But if the sword stays in its stone,
The Dead will rise and take your soul."

(CHANT:) "There's a sword on Scorpis Isle."
"There's a sword of Scorpis Isle."

AAAAAHHHH.

Chapter 24

TOWER WATCHERS

Snow White's champions crossed Big Pine Lake before midday. They beached the canoes some leagues west of Bagimou Shantit, a Crokee settlement. Tylo's fever had spiked. He was muttering hallucinations about dark spirits and wraiths.

"He's gotten worse," said Jack.

The party was uneasy about bringing the elf to the Crokee settlement for care; it would put Snow White at risk and expose their whereabouts to potential enemies.

The faerie objected with impassioned gestures. "Tylo's life is what matters now."

All agreed, there was little choice if the elf was to survive. So, they charted a course to Bagimou Shantit. However, a strange event got them turned all around.

"We ain't headed the right way," said Jack, squinting as afternoon rays broke through the clouds.

Smoothstone's compass had misdirected them. It read west but led them an hour's hike *away* from Bagimou Shantit. Shard Smith double-checked with her own compass. Both got the same reading and neither instrument was correct.

"These woods are cursed," said Smoothstone.

"Or we are," said Shard.

"Yer gadgets don't know east or west," said Jack. "But I do." He rerouted, marching the party along another track through the woods. He and Hamr took turns carrying Tylo on their backs to make better time. The elf was too ill to move on his own.

By late-afternoon, the woods were so overgrown they could go no further. On one side was an impassable ravine and on the other, a ridge covered by a wall of vegetation. The only option was to turn back.

"Jits!"

"Tylo's infection is as bad as I've seen," said Father Tassl. "Even if we make it to the Crokee settlement, tis unlikely his poor soul will survive the journey."

There was nothing that could be done.

"Stay with us, Tylo," said Snow White, stroking his tawny hair.

Jack took a few paces apart from the others and shut his eyes. "*Yeh there, Spirits?*" he whispered. "*I know I don't talk to yeh much but Tylo needs yeh and I need yeh too. Just a path or a sign. Give us a push and I'll do the hard work, whatever that is.*"

No words of wisdom came. Jack felt foolish. He was about to swear off spirits forever when a spicy scent wafted between the trees.

"Does anybody else smell incense?" said Father Tassl.

"Tis unmistakable," said Smoal.

The scent came from the vegetation wall, over which loomed a great tree shaped like a crescent moon. Long strands of ivy fluttered off its branches. Jack trounced waist deep across the overgrowth and pushed the vines aside. Hidden behind the vegetation was a cavern with tree roots climbing up the sides. Through it was framed a clear view of a meadow with a small barn, homey cabin, and large garden, all nestled in a hidden nook of the woods. There were cows and pigs grazing the pastures, and a gaggle of geese plucking the grass with nosy bills.

Jack's party stepped into the meadow, their faces full of wonder.

Two old women in green wool dresses were harvesting the last fruits and vegetables of autumn. Bushels of gourds, yellow corn, and late-sprouting berries were spread in neat rows. Jack recognized the first woman. She was neat as a pin under a pointed sun hat, plump with a welcoming smile.

"Hello, children," she said. "I am Viviyann Greygeese."

"Mother Goose," said Tylo weakly, drooped over Hamr's shoulders.

"That's right," she said.

The other woman was Hepkatee, Crone of the Woods. She was much older, near-blind, her sparse white hair wound in a knot, and had no smile whatsoever. Jack knew her as well. When they saw each other, Hepkatee turned even uglier.

"Nyeahh," she scowled.

"Vicious old crank," said Jack. "Last person I'd want to run into."

"Why, it's Ludi Spriggins' boy, Jack," said Viviyann kindly. "We were beginning to doubt you'd find us."

"Milady?" said Smoothstone. "How could you have known we were coming, when we ourselves knew it not?"

Viviyann lifted her hat, revealing one of her eyes was dark brown and the other pale green. "The Great Ones speak to us. Your journey was guided by the Green Mother. Your coming to our bower farm was no accident."

"What she means is, they're witches," said Jack.

The crone barked out impatiently, "Enough wasteful chitterchat! Where be the faerie?"

The seven dwarfs closed in protectively around Snow White. Jack stood with them.

"Keep yer distance, Old Ugly," he said.

Hepkatee pointed a gnarled finger at him. "Mind yer tongue, Yellow Eyes, or I'll make ugly things ooze out of yeh."

"Spell-casting biddy!" said Jack.

"Thievin' pickpocket!" said the crone.

The dwarfs drew their weapons.

"Now, now," said Viviyann soothingly. "Let's keep keep things civil. Jack and Hepkatee don't always see eye-to-eye but, I can assure you, this is a safe haven for all."

Snow White stepped out shyly from behind her protectors. "I am here, Mother Goose."

Both witches were relieved to see her. Hepkatee hobbled nearer.

"Power. Youth. Innocence," she uttered. "She'll do."

"It's wonderful you're here, little dear," said Viviyann. "The last of your kind – and the first."

Snow White's eyes broadened as she soaked in the elderly women and their surroundings.

Jack nodded at Tylo. "Can yeh help the elf?"

Viviyann sighed. "Tylo, is it? Brave soul. Hepkatee will have a look at that arm of yours."

The old crone abruptly beckoned Hamr to carry Tylo to the cabin, so he followed her.

"Hepkatee will do all she can," said Viviyann. "Now, there's clean water in the barrel over there. Why don't y'all make good of it and I'll fix you a hearty breakfast. Fresh eggs, sausages, porridge with honey, and Hepkatee's gingerbread."

The scrub and grub acted like magic on the journeyers. Escaping the mines had taken its toll but now they sat around a large table outdoors, eating hot food while the morning rays strengthened their weary souls.

Smoothstone knelt to the two witches in respect. "'Tis rare we dwarfs find such hospitality among forestlanders," he said. "Permit me, Lady Greygeese, to give you a special thanks for what you did for dwarfkind."

"What do you mean, good sir?"

He produced a familiar scroll from under his mantle. "This *Deed of Dynadin*. We are grateful you kept it safe these many years and then sent it with Jack Spriggins on his quest."

Jack nearly choked on his tea. "Yeh smuggled it out, Smoothstone?"

"Indeed," said the dashing dark dwarf. "As you would have, Jack."

Viviyann looked grave. "Well. This is unexpected."

"I shall safeguard it til a free Dwarf Domain can be declared," said Smoothstone, "After the dust settles from our sudden departure and the corruption of our clans is struck down."

"Then I'm grateful it landed in your good hands," said Viviyann.

The cabin door opened. Jack tried to catch sight of Tylo laying inside but his view was obscured by Hepkatee who glared at him with a fiendish leer.

"What d'yeh want?" said Jack.

"Do yeh like yer gingerbread, Yellow Eyes?" she cackled.

He shot her a dirty look and took a deliberately large bite, smacking his lips with a showy "mmmm".

The crone squinted. "The worms add flavor, don't they?"

Jack stopped chewing. A white grub squirmed in the middle of his half-eaten bun. He spit in disgust, dropping it. The dwarfs chuckled and went on munching theirs.

"Delicious!" said Hamr Smith.

The others nodded enthusiastically.

When Jack reexamined the gingerbread, there was no worm after all.

"Just a witchy illusion?"

The crone hooted in amusement at her prank.

"Darn hag!" said Jack. "That the best yeh can do? Where's the third sister in yer coven – the young goldilocks? She's been casting far meaner spells."

Viviyann answered plainly. "You're referring to Ganzil, Jack?"

"Speak not her name," said Hepkatee. "Yet, show her to him."

"Ganzil's here?"

Viviyann rose from the table. "She is. The naughty girl left us little choice."

She walked out toward the meadow and motioned for Jack to follow. The whole company got up, including Snow White.

"Stay here, young sylph," said Hepkatee. She took Snow White's hand in her gnarled fingers. "It's best yeh keep out of her sight. Let the others go."

Shard folded her arms defiantly. "I stay at Snow White's side."

Smoal agreed, placing a hand on his maul. "So shall I."

"Bah," said the crone. "Stubborn, distrusting dwarfs."

Viviyann led Jack and the others over a grassy pasture into a copse of redwoods.

"That incense smell again," said Father Tassl. "What is it?"

Viviyann looked amused. "An oil from a wild plant called Lell's Thistle. We burn it to soothe the wayward senses of the young sorceress we've locked away."

"Where is she?" said Smoothstone.

The heavy woman pointed to a sixty foot redwood, or so it appeared at first glance. The structure was covered with vines and moss but as Jack stared more closely, he realized it was not growing out of the earth. It was actually a man-made tower of stone brick and mortar.

"Who made that?" said Jack.

"If I am not mistaken," said Father Tassl. "This is the last of the giants' treasure towers."

"Indeed, it is," said Viviyann. "Do you know the history, sir?"

Tassl cleared his throat as though delighted to educate. "Centuries ago, giantkind dwelt here in the Forestland before they retreated to the eastern mountains. They hoarded much of their wealth inside these towers, which are said to be impenetrable."

"There's not a single door," said Hamr Smith, examining the masonry.

"There's a window," said Jack, pointing up.

From a semi-circular window at the top hung a shimmering golden tassel that waved gently with the breeze.

Smoothstone marveled. "What golden banner drapes from yonder window?"

"Tis a braid of lovely hair," said Anvl.

"It glimmers like the sun," said Chizl, shouldering against his brother for a clearer view.

Jack scowled. "That's Ganzil up there."

"Does the maiden require rescuing?" said Smoothstone.

"By no means," said Viviyann. "She's imprisoned in a room that no ladder or stairway can reach, where no champion can be seduced to do her dark bidding."

Jack shuffled his feet uncomfortably, feeling a sting of guilt. Viviyann gave him a sympathetic smile, which only made him more insecure. *How much did she know of his encounter with Ganzil in Rivercross?*

Ganzil leaned out the window, reaching for a red cardinal perched on the sill. Her stunning features immediately won the dwarfs over. Collectively, they "oohed", adjusting their smoked glass spectacles.

"Those eyes," said Hamr. "Like blue-green gems."

"And such perfect nose and lips," said Chizl Smith. "Worthy to be a bride of Ter."

"Forget it," said Jack. "That's just the trimmings. She would murder Snow White in a heartbeat."

"No!" exclaimed the dwarfs.

"Truly," said Viviyann. "We had better hopes for Ganzil but she is ill with jealously. She wields enough sorcery to be a dangerous threat. That is why Hepkatee and I set her apart until she can regain her reason."

"She seems fairly content up there," said Smoothstone.

"She is comfortable," said Viviyann. "And I visit her with encouraging words each day."

"There is a door then?" said Hamr.

Viviyann chuckled. "The giants *did* provide a way to get up to her chamber but it must remain a secret."

"How wise," said Father Tassl.

"Must've been a hassle getting her to stay put," said Jack. "She's full of tricks."

"So is Hepkatee," said Viviyann. "The crone presented Ganzil with a butchered sow's heart, claiming it was the heart of Snow White and that *Jack Spriggins* had slain the faerie."

"Well, that takes the bacon," said Father Tassl.

Jack felt tickled. "And the old hag blamed me? Ha! It's a cheat even I'll whistle at."

"Well, I have seen enough," said Smoothstone. "Let us return to young Snow White's side. She remains the fairest of them all."

"Aye," said the Smith cousins.

Ganzil hissed and withdrew from view.

The dwarfs tromped back to the meadow. Viviyann went along, lifting her long skirt above the ankles to keep up. Jack lingered by the tower with Hamr Smith, who apparently had a similar fascination. They sat on a fallen redwood log, staring up at the tower window.

"You know this Ganzil well, do you?" said Hamr.

"Too well to trust," said Jack. "She cast a spell on me and I want to make sure it's over and done. It would be better for all of us if this tower were twice as high."

Ganzil reappeared in the window sill, lackadaisically braiding her long, golden hair.

"Females are *complicated*," said Hamr.

"Just the ones that toy with yeh."

"Have you known many?"

"Enough to know they're trouble. Yeh?"

Hamr nodded. "She-dwarfs are a distraction, even the ones *I* wish to be distracted by."

"Seems they ignore us, or won't let us alone; no in between," said Jack. "Last spring, an uppity farm girl named Belinda visited the Orchard with her father, a farmer from Havensbend. She was kinda my age, kinda pretty. Kinda flirty. Y'know?"

"Sure," said Hamr.

"My roommate, Tristano – a real ladies man – talked me into giving Belinda a tour of the gardens. Turns out all she wanted was to roll in the hayloft."

Hamr raised his eyebrows. "That sounds lucky."

"Sure," said Jack. "Til I learned that Tristano gave her the same tour the summer before. And Manawydan before him."

"And how did *that* feel?"

"Still lucky. But nothing special. Embarrassing, I reckon. And—"

"Complicated?"

Jack blew his bangs out of his eyes. "Yep."

Up above, Ganzil gave them a long, pleasant smile. She mouthed a chant that seemed to travel down the tower wall. It reached Jack as if whispered in his ear.

> *"Mirror. Mirror. Far from sight,*
> *Take the heart of Fae Snow White.*
> *Little boys and little men,*
> *Find your manhood, do her in."*

"Did you hear that?" said Hamr, raising his smoked glasses.

"It's how her witchcraft gets inside yer head," said Jack.

Ganzil glared at Jack, closing her fists tightly until blood dripped through her fingers. She tossed the pig's heart that had been given to her by Hepkatee, which landed with a thud beside the log.

Hamr jumped to his feet. "Why, she's a genuine harpy!"

Ganzil flashed her bloody palms at them and then withdrew from the window.

"Ain't pretty, is it?" Jack wiped blood spatters off his sleeve. "And, deep down, neither is she."

The two youths walked away from the tower. Before either knew why, they were running.

* * * * *

A descriptive passage from "Tom Tailor's Trail Guide", respected journal of the Great Forest penned over a century before the Ogre Wars.

TREASURE TOWERS OF THE GIANTS

"If an adventurer is fortunate enough in their travels, ye come by a round citadel locked amid the trees of marvelous masonry, nigh on sixty to ninety feet from ground. Look fondly at its ancient stones but trespass not within. This be a Treasure Tower of Giantkind. That race of oversized beings stashed bushels of gold, priceless artwork, and illuminated manuscripts within these towers. However, the notion of entering and pilfering the contents yields a fruitless and gruesome end to the intruder.

Some of the Giant structures are surrounded by moats. Others have lethally sharp brambles. The rare tower built without such impediments is constructed with nary a door nor visible entrance. A window may be carved at the highest point but cannot be reached by ladder or stairwell.

These doorless treasure towers are mysteriously locked, intricate puzzles; secured with such measures of gory death that generations of thrillseekers have failed to solve. The skeletal remains of those madcap adventurers have borne the marks of spear thrusts, decapitations, crushed bones, corrosive decay and charred remains. I warn ye, there be no chartings that vouchsafe harmless passage – not in any book, this volume included.

It has been said, the Giant Barons of old possessed the knowledgeable keys that gave them unhindered access to the riches of their towers. It can be concluded that the treasures were heretofore emptied during the great Exodus of the Giants, many generations past. Only treacherous booby traps and empty towers remain for would-be-treasure-seekers, who dare to enter the Treasure Towers of the Giants in the wake of said history."

Chapter 25

AT ARM's LENGTH

While Tylo was confined to bed within the cabin, Jack pitched in with the dwarfs and helped harvest the farm's crops. Viviyann was grateful for their help. Jack was threshing in the wheat field when a raven cawed above. The black bird was not a welcome sight.

It landed on Hepkatee's outstretched arm. "Sersi," she said, stroking its feathers. "Yeh be back, faithful friend."

Jack leaned against the sickle. "And what terrible news does yer crow bring? More lost battles? More fires? More ogres?"

"Bah!" said the crone, pointing at the bower's edge. "Yer mouth outruns yer brain, Yellow Eyes. Sersi brings others who can somehow stand the sight of yeh."

A clip of horse hooves galloped out of the passage beneath the Tree of the Crescent Moon.

"Blackberry?" said Jack, disbelieving his eyes.

The black stallion ran into the bower with a well-seated rider wearing a gray hood. As they cantered closer, Jack recognized she was Rose Red. Behind her rode Varlan Wood, seated on Thundersong.

Jack reached up to help Rose off the saddle. "How did yeh know where to find us?"

"The Crone's raven. Sersi came with a message tied to a white rose petal, so I came as fast as I could. Varlan volunteered to accompany me."

Snow White ran up to greet them. The two girls embraced.

"Where's Tylo?" said Rose.

"In the cabin," said Jack. "Yer here to help then?"

"If I can." She squeezed his hand.

Jack realized Tylo's health situation had grown more serious.

Varlan stood gawking at the hidden farm, the dwarfs, and the disagreeable crone.

"Varlan?" said Rose.

"Oh, yes!" He handed Rose a familiar black haversack, which Allwise had used to hold surgical instruments. "You'll be needing this."

Rose Red braced herself. "Please take me to Tylo, Jack."

He led her inside. Viviyann was seated by Tylo's bunk. The elf's small form lay eerily still except for a slight rise and fall of the chest. His face was turned away from the door.

"Ah, Rose Red," said Viviyann. "How good you've come."

"I hope I have the skill needed, ma'am," said Rose, at the daunting sight of her sick friend.

"You can do more for the little fella than Hepkatee or I, my dear. Allwise set store by you and what Tylo needs most is *your skill.*"

Viviyann smiled with complete confidence, and then steered Jack out to the porch, gently shutting the door between them.

He ambled over to the little barn where Varlan had brought the horses.

Snow White was lovingly patting Blackberry's sleek mane. She had donned a simple green cotton gown that transformed her into the likeness of a peasant girl (A fetching one, whom Varlan could not keep his eyes off). Only the yew wand tucked in her apron gave any hint that she was a faerie. She had bonded considerably with the witches in the short time since arriving, especially Hepkatee. They spoke together in Faespeak, signing with hands aflutter. Their connection made Jack uneasy.

"Old Ugly's acting like a granny to Snow, all sweet and kind. Jits. Ain't fooling me for a second. She's got a plot twisting in that wrinkled brain of hers."

It was not long until he learned what it was.

"Snow White is to become the Maiden in our Coven of Three," said Hepkatee, when supper was set that evening.

The faerie stood by her side. Rose Red and Viviyann still tended to Tylo in the cabin, but Jack, Varlan, and the dwarfs were all seated at the picnic table. They dropped their bread in their stew and gawked.

"Yer making her be a witch?" said Jack.

"The rune stones say 'aye', Thief," said the crone. "She'll take the place of wayward Ganzil."

"She will not be safe here," said Shard Smith.

"Bah, of course she will," said Hepkatee. "No one can step in this thicket that we don't let. Green Mother shrouds us with Her wilderness."

Smoothstone looked betrayed. "Nay, withered crone. We dwarfs are sworn to protect Snow White. She will travel with us to Shirwood."

Hepkatee glowered. "Yeh be all doomed if she does."

"Is that a threat?" said Smoothstone, who stood.

"Both of yeh is way off," said Jack. "Snow's coming with me to Thin Creek."

Now Smoothstone gripped the hilt of his maul. "We never discussed that course, Jack Spriggins."

Jack stood. "Well, we just did."

"Again, I say nay."

Only Hamr Smith's strong grip on Jack's elbow kept him from advancing on the Quarry Clan Leader.

"Hold your tempers," said Shard Smith. "Snow White wishes to speak."

The faerie lifted her hands, calming them.

"I'll be safe in this meadow and put none of you at risk," she said. "Mother Goose and Old Gran offer me a home here in the Great Forest, where a faerie belongs. Where I can grow and learn. They understand me, as my mother and sisters did. In ways no one else can."

Hepkatee stirred the soup cauldron over the fire grate. "We can teach Snow White how to tame her siren charms and use them for service to all."

Jack sank onto the bench, glaring at the crone. "This is some spell yeh put on her. Yeh tricked her into it."

The crone cackled. "That's so like yeh, Yellow Eyes, to raise a ruckus 'cause yeh don't like the answer yeh hear. Tis the Green Mother's will, boy, plain and true."

"Do not forget Mighty Ter," said Father Tassl. "Twas his strength that guided Snow White here."

"The Earth One's underfoot, as always," said Hepkatee.

Smoothstone sank on the bench as well. "Very well."

Jack addressed Snow White. "Yer sure this is right for yeh, kid?'

Snow White looked fondly at him. "I knew the second we got here, Jack. It was meant for me."

"Well, if dragging yeh across mines, woods, and a haunted isle got yeh here, then I guess it ain't all for nothing," he said.

"You know, there's a Fae saying," said Snow White, whose fingers deftly spun out the words as she spoke aloud, '*Don't doubt the dream. Shaina knows where the dreamer goes.*' "

Jack tried to echo the movements, causing a pleasant smile to enlighten the girl's face. Between her gladness and the beauty of the bower farm at dusk, he knew she was in the right place.

"Allwise would pitch a fit at me leaving yeh here," said Jack. "But I'm guessing there's things even he didn't know."

Snow White raised her wand and twirled it over her head, making the same low hum that had drawn out the wasps.

Jack ducked. "There ain't a hornets hive nearby, is there?"

Instead, dozens of fireflies lit up the dusky meadow and flitted above the grass, going to and fro in glowing circles. All the dwarfs gasped with delight.

"I must say, the light spirit got it right," said Father Tassl. "This place fits a faerie's dream."

Jack turned to Hamr Smith. "Girls. When they're right, they're right."

"Complicated," said Hamr.

Despite the enchanting fireflies, Shard Smith was not convinced. "What of us? Are we dwarfs to surrender being Snow White's protectors?"

"Nay," said Smoothstone, his voice resonating with deep conviction, "Our vow is everlasting and I shall honor it so long as I have breath in my body."

Snow White danced through the streams of lightning bugs, addressing the seven dwarfs. "You've given me so much. You can all protect my spirit knowing my flesh is safe."

Hamr removed his smoked spectacles, bowing. "In your name, I feel inspired to explore this forestland. Perhaps allow myself some schooling beyond the forge before I am full grown."

"Tis Shirwood for me," said Smoal Klub.

"And me," said Father Tassl.

"I will preserve your memory at Shirwood for now," said Smoothstone. "We all dream of starting anew. Thank you for that, Snow White."

Snow White kissed his dark forehead. "For my dream with all of you, I'm honored."

Anvl and Chizl Smith stepped forward, keen to receive kisses of their own.

"We shall join the army ranks and fight alongside your father, General Camlann," said Chizl.

"Men be less terrible in the company of dwarfs that know you, Snow White," said Anvl.

Both cousins got the desired soft pecks on their cheeks. Their faces blushed like the sky.

Shard began to sob. "If I am forced to part from you, sweet faerie, and my brother at once, I cannot bear any life."

"Then stay," said Snow White, looking to Hepkatee for approval.

"Fine," said the crone, begrudgingly. "The she-dwarf can do all the tasks my sore bones can't. And she'll be some help guarding the tower."

"I thank you, crone," said Shard, kneeling before her.

Hepkatee rudely turned away with a "bah."

Supper resumed. Snow White poured out new bowls of stew. The fireflies continued dancing over over the meadow as the night took on a surprisingly pleasant mood. Jack sat beside Varlan, truly enjoying the meal. He and Smoothstone acknowledged each other with an agreeable nod. Midway through his second helping, it dawned on Jack that his mission was over.

"I can leave here and go with Anvl and Chizl to the front," he realized. "I'll be a forestland soldier at last."

He wolfed down a few more hunks of cornbread, then hurried to the barn to brush down Blackberry.

"We're gonna be rangers, boy," said Jack to the steed. "All grown, fighting alongside Redvere and Smoke. I bet the elf will join us too, when he's rested."

Viviyann slid open the barn door. She looked careworn, turning a sprig of violet between her fingers.

"Jack," she said. "A word?"

The look on her face did not bode well for Tylo.

Jack swallowed hard. "Tylo didn't make it. Yeh've come to tell me he's dead."

"No, he's alive," said Viviyann. "His fever broke and he's resting from the surgery. Rose saved him."

"What do yeh mean?"

The tired woman leaned against the stalls. "His right arm. It was diseased with putrefaction and would have spread throughout his little body. She had to remove it."

Jack did not know where to look or what to say. He started for the door but stopped when he saw Rose was now seated outside at the picnic table. She met his eyes with a look of loss and failure. Snow White was wrapping her arms around her for comfort. Varlan and the dwarfs all stood. Hamr Smith waited on the cabin porch as if reluctant to enter and see one-armed Tylo.

Blackberry and Thundersong sensed the sadness and neighed mournfully. Jack trudged back to the horses.

"His shooting arm," said Jack. "He ain't ever gonna be the same."

Viviyann managed a smile. "No. That doesn't mean he'll be worse off. Just different."

Jack looked at his own arms, trying to imagine life without them. "It's my fault. I brought Tylo here when he should've stayed at the Orchard."

"Nonsense," said Viviyann firmly. "You're Tylo's hero, Jack. Never have I seen an elf who's strived so much to adopt the nature of a – what's that word – a 'lunkhead'? That's because of you, Jack. And I'm sure he's admired you since the moment he met you."

"But I hated him," said Jack. "I hated all elves."

"And do you still?"

"Since knowing the little runt? How could I?"

"Good, because the only thing you should hate is 'hate'."

"Hating's just been my way of not looking at myself. And yeh can't do that once yeh know a person, no matter where they come from."

~ 311 ~

Viviyann sat on a bale of hay with a puff of relief. "Your journey to the Dwarf Domain was fruitful if only for learning that. Never forget the words you just spoke, Jack."

He plopped next to her. "Yeh don't think they're wasted on a mean, thieving kid from Thin Creek?"

"I can't tell you to love yourself. Or anyone, for that matter. It's beyond my gifts. What I *can* do is look ahead." She held the violet to her pert nose and inhaled its scent. The whites of Viviyann's eyes widened.

"*I see a man. Tall, lean, quiet. Hazel yellow eyes. A few scars and wounds. Not handsome, perhaps, but he attracts. Always striding. Striding through new lands and old. He's turned a great darkness of his soul – the mistakes, temper, and evil doubt – into strength. Into courage and decency. This man doesn't choose to lead, but others follow him. He mends what he finds broken, then moves on with a coil of vines on his shoulder.*"

"Sounds like a good fella."

Viviyann trembled as the sight left her. "Doesn't he? Jack, if you can't be fond the half-grown lad you are now, maybe you can find some love for the man you might become. The one Tylo already thinks you are."

Misery hit Jack hard. He sobbed, unashamedly for the first time in his life. Tears swelled his cheeks. Mother Goose held him until he calmed. No one's embrace, even ma's, ever felt as warm.

"What now, dear boy?" she said. "Are you still on your way to the army?"

"Depends on what Tylo needs me to do."

"Well, he's been drifting in and out of sleep but did say he wishes to go home."

"Reckon I'll get him back to the Learning Twigs camp as soon as he's ready."

Viviyann gave him the violet sprig. "In truth, Jack, Tylo told me home for him is now the Orchard."

Jack paused, then lifted Blackberry's bridle onto the hook. "That's the home we'll go to then. Our home."

* * * * *

From "A Handbook to the Forestlands" 2nd Edition

*THE THREE WITCHES - A trio of women that serve the Great Spirits, particularly the Green Mother, and keep the power of the Realm rooted in nature. They have always consisted of a **crone**, a **mother**, and a **maiden**. The Three are seldom related by blood but bonded in their cause. The roles are traditionally inherited by succession as the youngest ages into the elderly; maiden to mother, mother to crone. Most Forestlanders regard the witches suspiciously; as soothsayers but also as healers. For this reason, their visions and methods are often shrouded by fear, seldom understood or respected by common folk.*

Chapter 26

TYLO AND JACK

As Jack, Tylo, Rose Red, and Varlan Wood rode their horses out of the bower farm past the Tree of the Crescent Moon, the discord of the outside world came rushing back. War cannons echoed in the north; herds of scavenging beasts roamed the countryside, scattered from war-torn farms; frost lingered beyond noon and made for a cold, hard journey.

Tylo stayed silently on the saddle, seated in front of Rose on Blackberry. Bandages covered his right shoulder, revealing a blatant gap where the arm ought to have been. He did not climb trees, scout ahead, or toss mud balls. Jack rode tandem with Varlan astride Thundersong, casting concerned glances at the elf. It was as if Tylo's spirit had been taken along with his arm. They quickened to a trot alongside the Green River, following the Timberok Road back to the Orchard.

Autumn's arrival had exploded in fiery hues but the changes Jack found through the gates of the Orchard School were far more dramatic. The grounds were bustling with people full of chores and purpose. Workers hauled wheelbarrows of charred debris to waiting wagons. Most of the wreckage had been cleared and the last remnants of the old main house were being tossed aboard. Frames had been erected for a new stable and carpenters hammered the boards into place. Young women in nursing smocks came out of large tents where the sick bay still stood. They guided wounded men in wheelchairs to a hot meal served outside. It smelled delicious.

Excited laughter from youngsters and grownups alike brightened the air, as did the pleasant smell emanating from the ground following an autumn rain shower. While no trees, flowers, or anything green had survived the attack, there was still growth; it was just on faces, not in blooms.

"How'd all this happen in just a few weeks?" said Jack.

"The townsfolk of Rivercross," said Rose Red. "Your mother brought them to help us rebuild. And we students have carried on."

"Like Allwise taught us," said Varlan.

Tymmy Mason and Frog ran up to greet them. They tackled Jack with rambunctious excitement as he climbed off Thundersong.

"You've come back," said Tymmy.

Jack cracked a smile and rolled to his feet. "Did I shrink or have yeh gotten taller?"

"We've taken on a lot of responsibility," said Tymmy, sounding like a scholar ten times his age. "It's possible I'm standing straighter than I did."

Frog was soaking wet.

"Jits, yeh been swimming in this weather?" said Jack. "The water must've been freezing."

The eleven year old shook out his damp curls. "Naw. Once I start cutting cross it, I just keep telling myself, '*It's as warm as it was yesterday.*' Maybe when winter comes, my shivers will listen."

Varlan helped Tylo climb down from Blackberry's saddle. The one-armed elf did not greet them. Tymmy and Frog tried not to stare.

"Tylo," said Frog. "Can I get a 'hee-yo?'"

The elf gave them a nod, smiled slightly at seeing the Orchard, then hobbled off towards the lake.

Tymmy finally spoke. "We heard Tylo got hurt, but his whole right arm's gone."

"Ain't like him not to joke," said Frog.

"Give him time," said Rose Red, stroking Blackberry. "He's young, only three. He'll pull through."

"*Three years old?*" said Jack.

"Three of *our* years, Jack," said Rose Red.

Tymmy added, "An average elf ages close to six and a half years for every one of ours."

Jack did the math. "That makes him older than me. You too, Rose."

Rose Red collected Allwise's black haversack. "It does."

To Jack's shock, fifteen new elflings sprang into view. They giggled and gamboled through a regime of tumbling maneuvers on the field where Perdur Galles used to teach. Only, it was muscle-laden Manawydan who sprinted after them, shouting harsh instructions mixed with some choice north-country swears.

"More Learning Twigs?" said Jack.

"Fetched 'em, just like yeh asked," said Frog.

Rose Red laughed. "After word of Tylo's heroics got out, it's been hard to keep them away."

"But Manaw don't speak their clicks and chirks," said Jack. "How'd that bragging beefhead get them to fall in line?"

Frog guffawed. "With plenty of mudballs chucked at his noggin."

Tymmy answered more astutely. "Elves have seen their tribes thinned out by the enemy. Manawydan is one of the strongest, most fearless warriors they've ever seen. He fought Bluebeard and lived to tell about it. They took to him just like we always did to you."

Jack watched his former rival challenge the squirrelly trainees to fire from strategic positions. Many hit precise marks with their twig arrows. Manawydan's once smug grin was replaced by a humble look that seemed confident and pleased.

"He's forming an exceptional crew of elfin archers," said Rose Red.

"Good for him," said Jack. "Good for all of them."

By now, Barlan Wood reached the gate to exchange an elaborate greeting with his brother (fist bumps, double handshakes, elbow knocks, and a hug).

Jack smirked at the twins. "Sometimes I don't know how yeh tell each other apart."

"Our folks say the same thing," said Varlan.

"Did you see Tylo's brothers, Togo and Tuko, out there?" said Barlan.

Jack scanned the practice field again. Two lively four foot elves stood out. They had similar tawny hair as Tylo's and were cheekier than the rest, but neither had the same wit and spring.

"Still," said Jack. "Maybe they'll help Tylo feel like himself again."

The reunited students made their way to the infirmary tent, the only spot on the grounds Jack still recognized. Near thirty recovering soldiers and civilians were spread out on the cots. A slender doctor in his late twenties checked each one, writing notes and listening to their chests with a newfangled instrument called a sterno-scope.

"Who's the new doc?" said Jack.

"Dr. John Appleseed," said Rose Red. "He gave up his practice in Havensbend to come here. He even brought his sweet wife and their two youngsters, Seamus and Vivi. I've learned a lot at his side."

She waved and the doc nodded in a friendly manner, apparently relieved that she had returned.

"I reckon yeh were missed," said Jack.

Rose eagerly tied on an apron. "Maybe I'll help finish the rounds before I rest."

Jack winked. "Doubt yeh could sleep if yeh didn't."

She winked back, then joined the new doctor.

Jack tip-toed out. Tymmy and Frog were sitting by the tent waiting for him.

Frog jumped to his feet. "Jack? Did yeh really chase the dwarfs out of their mines to fight for our side?"

Jack hemmed and hawed. "Well, I already ruined the giants so I guess the dwarfs were next."

"It states in 'Tom Tailor's Trail Guide'," said Tymmy Mason, "That dwarfs are dangerously stubborn zealots, well-armed and robust. Is it true?"

"That's bunk," said Jack. "They're the hardest workers yeh'll ever meet. And all their praying keeps them strong-hearted. Don't ever forget it."

Tymmy and Frog's eyes widened. "We won't."

Jack softened. "Yeh two runts are reading '*Tom Tailor*' now?"

"Rose Red assigned it," said Frog. "We seniors study a few hours after supper from books that didn't get burned up."

"Think I'll join yeh," said Jack. "Been starved for some book-learning."

The boys were thrilled.

"We could read some now!" said Tymmy.

"I could use some grub and shut-eye first, yeh eager beavers," said Jack. "Rose too, I'll bet."

Frog ran off towards the dining tent. "I'll brew you and Rose some tea."

Tymmy was fast on his bunkmate's heels. "I'll get yeh a pillow. And a book."

Suddenly alone, Jack began to venture over the old grounds he as once knew so well. A measured sound of sawing drew him to a villager who was dividing a stack of perfectly cut pine planks. The carpenter was stout but not flabby, stern but not sour, elderly but not withered. Jack had a notion who he was.

"Yer Perdur's pa, ain't yeh?"

The man looked up. "Yes. I'm Perdur Galles Senior. And you must be Jack Spriggins. The yellow eyes gave you away."

"I miss yer son," said Jack. "He was my teacher. And my friend."

Galles Senior smiled. "I came from Weaver's Corner to bury him. Now I've stayed on to help rebuild the orchard that he loved. Did Per ever tell you his pa could build houses?"

"Well, he did fix up my ma's cabin in the woods, so it makes sense. He did a fine job building up the students here too."

Jack took a gander at the construction drawings for a new main house assembled over the frame of the old one. Sturdier and larger yet as pleasant as before. It would be a daunting job to finish before winter set in.

"Need a helper?" he said, rolling up his sleeves. Jack lifted a fresh plank between the carpenter's sawhorses.

Rebuilding the main house became an assignment for the whole Orchard School. All the students contributed, utilizing geometry, woodcraft, and artistic skills guided by Galles Senior. Tymmy Mason redrafted room plans. Jack and Manawydan chopped pines from the forest and hauled them on wagons to a local sawmill where the foreman cut them into planks. Frog and the Wood twins worked with the masons, bricklaying a massive stone chimney and fireplace. Geoff Greens and Rose Red varnished and sealed the floor boards. After a week, the main house roof was raised.

Nurse Tilda (formerly ma's cook at *Ludi's Bean Tea Inn*) took to sitting old Allwise outside his tent in an oak rocker for a daily view of the progress. The stricken man never raised an eyebrow but the stillness in his ever-trembling hands seemed to signal approval. It was enough to keep the boys and Rose Red singing.

"Orchard seeds are planted deep.
Roots reach far below.
Let the Darkness keep on digging.
Still our apples grow."

The building was where Jack and the others welcomed new students. One was a ten-year-old spitfire named Alais Swan from the farm community of Sunvale. She was little sister to five soldiers serving in the Forestland Army and was the best shot with a long rifle anyone had seen. Alais could also curse a blue streak that rivaled Jack. Naturally, they got along well.

To everyone's surprise, sixteen year-old dwarf blacksmith, Hamr Smith, arrived to join them at the Orchard School. "The best way for me to serve Snow White is to learn what man's world can offer," he said. "And what I can offer it."

Hamr set up a forge near the lake. He taught students about geology and mining. They unearthed raw deposits from the neighboring Boulder Caves. Turns out, they were rich with minerals. Hamr taught them to artfully design all manner of steel and fortify the new buildings, craft innovative farming tools, and restock the armory with the finest weapons in these parts.

"*Swing and strike!*" became the favorite chant of the new Orchard School.

In turn, the dwarfsmith became a voracious scholar. He was schooled in poetic verse by Tymmy Mason, life sketching with pastels by Rose Red, and horseback riding by Varlan Wood. He bonded so well with a honey-hued pony called Cai's Heart that it was renamed Hamr Smith's Horse. The two were seldom apart.

One afternoon, Jack and Rose Red watched them canter by the infirmary.

Jack teased. "Hamr! Yer starting to look like one of those mythical beasts from forest lore. Y'know, the ones whose top half is a man and bottom is a horse?"

"It's called a centaur," said Rose Red.

"A centaur! That's the one," said Jack.

"Four long legs are better than two short ones," said Hamr, patting his horse's mane.

"Bet Tylo would find that funny," said Jack.

The elf was a sore subject for Jack. Tylo still avoided him, a whole month since their return.

"Yeh reckon he blames me for his arm?" said Jack.

"Listen to yourself, Jack Spriggins," said Rose. "It wasn't too long ago when you begged to be rid of Tylo. Now, you miss him."

Jack cracked his knuckles in frustration. "But it ain't like he's run off. He's still at the Orchard. Sometimes I spot him with the other elves or by Hamr's forge. I caught him sitting with Allwise once or twice and the old geezer can't even talk back. But Tylo won't give me a single look. Like he's hiding."

"He probably is. Hold strong to what you just said, Jack. Tylo's still here. He's still part of our story, it just hasn't unfolded yet."

"Speaking of stories," Jack reached into Ma's latest basket of goods and fished out the *Rivercross Crier,* the town newspaper. "Yeh caught up on what locals read these days? The front-page headline reads: '*Victories at the Front led by Snow White Inspiration*'. What bunk! If folks take time to print something, yeh'd think they'd print what's true."

Rose tried to keep a straight face. "Isn't dwarfkind joining General Camlann's army a good thing?"

He crinkled the paper in his fists. "First off, it's all about Snow White and the dwarfs. I'm barely mentioned and Tylo ain't in it at all. Not that Snow ain't important. She is. But she was supposed to be kept a secret."

"Good stories don't stay secrets long, Jack," said Rose, taking the basket. "Oh! Look what your mother knit."

She tossed him a green muffler scarf and took a long red one for herself.

Jack wound it around his throat and kept ranting. "They call Snow the fairest *woman* of them all. She's just *a girl*. Only thirteen. And all that bunk about poisoned apples, dead sleep, and wicked stepmothers. That's all mixed up. Even worse, they're saying that she was wakened with a smooch from – get this – Count Corrobis! Jits, he weren't even there."

Rose Red stood, staring towards the Orchard entrance. "But he is *here*. Look, coming through the gate."

Handsome Count Corrobis rode in astride his magnificent brown steed without fanfare (not that he needed it), outfitted in a tailored blue wool jacket. As always, his tabby cat was perched on the saddle in front of him. A troop of six cavalrymen galloped behind, Brion Bellows among them. They were guiding a prison coach. It held one captive, Bluebeard, cuffed in chains. He had grown actual whiskers while in the Havensbend jail that shaded his blue tattooed chin.

"Wait here," Jack told Rose Red, as he hustled to the gate.

Hamr, Manawydan, and Alais Swan met Jack as he reached the cavalcade; sledge, ax, and rifle drawn and poised. The wall was lined with Learning Twig archers, their loaded bows aimed at Bluebeard from every angle.

Corrobis visibly gulped and climbed off his mount. "Hello, Jack. We just stopped over to water our horses. Ka Bur is my prisoner of war. His troops are defeated. It's a great win for us."

Jack's eyes never left Bluebeard. "It weren't smart to bring him here."

Corrobis let his cat crawl around the back of his neck. "I'm escorting the chieftain to the front. He is to be exchanged for a pair of our captains, who were taken alive. We negotiated the terms with the Desertlanders."

"Who's we?"

"General Camlann, Captain Ootan, Captain Gwachmai, and myself."

Wounded soldiers and workers had joined the students, Galles Senior among them. If Bluebeard was intimidated, it did not show.

Corrobis continued. "Last month's earthquakes originated in the Desert Empire. Two of their cities were decimated. So, many ogres are returning home."

"The war's over then?" said Jack.

"Almost," said Brion Bellows, from the water trough. "But not quite yet."

Jack stalked over to the prison coach and locked eyes with Bluebeard. "Yeh thought yeh destroyed this place, didn't yeh? This is the Orchard. Look. It's still standing and it always will."

Bluebeard thrust his arms through the bars, fast as a trigger snake, looping his chains around Jack's throat. The count's cat let out an ear-piercing yowl. Corrobis drew his cutlass.

Jack caught the manacle and dropped his weight before Bluebeard garroted him.

The students advanced but Jack twisted free, pressing his legs against the stepping board. Bluebeard was yanked forward; his face mashed against the bars. Jack waved the students back.

"I always reckoned fighting a downed man wasn't fair," said Jack, unsheathing his bone knife and pressing it against the ogre's exposed throat. "Yeh taught me otherwise."

"Kill him, Spriggins," said Manawydan.

"Do it," said Frog.

"That black-hearted devil'd do yeh worse," said Alais Swan.

Corrobis gripped Jack's arm. "Stop. He's not worth a murder charge."

Jack sought out Galles Senior in the crowd. The man shook his head 'no'.

"Fine," said Jack, seething.

He released Bluebeard, who fell backward in the coach, gasping for air. The mighty ogre forced himself to stand.

"You think you love your home more than I do mine, Jack Spriggins?" he said hoarsely. "Soldiers have no say about who and where we fight. Do you know why?"

Corrobis rapped the bars with his cutlass. "Keep your fangs shut, Ka Bur."

"Naw, let him talk," said Jack.

Bluebeard laughed. "I am the heartless warrior I was raised to be. So are you, Giant Killer. We both serve the shadows that toy with us."

Jack spoke in *sartyrian*. "Wraiths, yeh mean?"

"That is an apt description of them. You are too smart for your own good. You should not have let me live, boy. Only death will give one of us victory."

Corrobis had heard enough. "You're lucky Jack is the hero he is."

A blaze of tawny red swooped down in front of the coach. "I be only *half* the hero Giant Killer is, at least in height."

It was Tylo. He twirled a mudball in his fling and thwacked Bluebeard in the face.

Jack burst into laughter.

"Urchin!" said Bluebeard, wiping his face. The warlord lifted his shirt and displayed a belt of bloody elfin scalps. "Many imp scalps have I taken in your honor, Tylo of the Learning Twigs. I will add yours to the collection when I am free."

Tylo's lips stretched to a wrathful smirk. He snapped an elf-spark that he flicked at the grisly belt of scalps. The red tufts of hair burst into flames.

Bluebeard leapt, frantically swatting the fire. Jack gawked as Tylo sprang one-armed into a handstand, unsheathed his bone knife with his left foot and pitched it to his right. With remarkable aim, the elf flung the whirling blade into the coach, severing Bluebeard's burning sash from his waist. The blaze spread over the floorboards.

"Corrobis! Release me before I am burnt alive!" said Bluebeard.

Jack and Corrobis scooped buckets of water from the trough and chucked them on the fire. Bluebeard coughed from the smoke. The elves on the wall hooted and joined in, filling buckets and tossing more water at the smoking coach while chittering elfin taunts at Bluebeard.

They mocked his coughs. *"Horf! Ach! Blargh!"*

When the smoke cleared, Bluebeard was drenched but still held his head high. "Well done, striplings," he said shaking his manacles. "When next we meet, I will attire myself with your innards."

Brion Bellows signaled the driver and the Count's Men trotted the prison coach out of the yard. The students and soldiers cheered, "Away with Bluebeard!" The elves chirped like thrilled mockingbirds.

Corrobis prepared to mount his horse, "I am sorry for the disruption," he said. "We should have watered our horses in Rivercross."

The Count froze when he saw the cat missing from his saddle. Thick blonde hair drooped over his eyes as he anxiously looked this way and that. The tabby was rubbing up against Jack's shin, as if deciding whether to stay or go.

"Puss?" said Corrobis.

"Go on, mouser," whispered Jack, scratching the cat's ears. "Corrobis is lost without yeh." The animal returned a bored expression but pranced to his master's arms. A relieved Corrobis climbed back on to his brown stallion. With a click of boots, he and his cat were gone.

Hamr Smith picked up the bone knife, shaking his head in disbelief. "Never have I seen such knife business like you did there, Tylo. It worked well. Ter is honored by you."

Tylo bowed, jesting with humility. "I give you my finest one-armed salute, Smithy."

"I might be persuaded to craft another short-sword on my forge," said Hamr. "Would it be wielded?"

"Yes," said Tylo. "Til Burn be mine once more."

Hamr rolled his jewel blue eyes. "Best of luck with that." He tottered off, twirling his sledge.

A chilling gust blew at their backs.

"Brrr," said Tylo. "It be so cold. Have you another neck-wrap of sheep's wool, Giant Killer?"

Jack smirked. "Ma knit a special one just for yeh. Of course, it would help if yeh bothered to wear a shirt once in a while."

"I shall note that."

"C'mon then."

He and Tylo veered away from the path and hiked over to the infirmary tent. They came to Ma's basket, still on the bench outside. Jack dug out a lengthy blue muffler and tossed it to the elf.

"Elf-sized scarf. From Ludi Spriggins' own knitting."

Tylo was able to wrap it around his throat twice and still have enough slack to trip on. "Ah, blueness! My newest favorite color, after Sparky orange."

"Ella's making yeh another scarf about that shade."

"You spoke to my true-love Red Riding Hood?"

"Well, I wrote to her. A real long letter. And one to Redvere too. The stagecoach came and both wrote back. Ella asked me to visit Whispering Vine for the Winter Holiday."

"Am I to go as well?"

"Like I could stop yeh." Jack paused to find the right words. "Reckon yer feeling better?"

Tylo itched his shaggy head. "I am feeling new."

"I thought yeh was mad at me. Or worse."

"*Naw,*" said Tylo (imitating him perfectly). "I just wanted to be sure my one arm be as good as two. I do not wish to be left behind."

"I reckon your aim is even better now," said Jack. "That swipe yeh took at Bluebeard was real handy."

"Real footy!" said Tylo, leaping into another handstand and wiggling his toes, "Hee-Yo! Do you like elves now?"

Jack had to be honest. "Well, I like *yeh,* Tylo, and I'm proud of that. As for other elves, I'll have to take them one at a time."

"As I do with lunkheads," said Tylo.

"Me too," said Jack. "Y'know, I ain't all that friendly with anybody."

"And if we pretend all folks be good, then we miss the bad ones. We end up with a lot of Mysslos."

"Or wraiths."

"Then we never make real friends."

"Like Tylo and Jack."

"Hee-yo!" hollered Tylo.

"HEE-YO!" Jack hollered back. It was such an amazing yell, every head in earshot turned.

Then it started to snow.

Lacey crystal flakes fell, the first the Orchard had seen in years. Rose Red emerged from the sick tent, her arms spread in delight. Tylo danced over to her playing a tune on his reed pipes. Hamr Smith joined them. Jack stuck out his tongue to catch the snowflakes. Within a few minutes the flurry covered the grounds in a soft, healing blanket of white.

"Does this make anyone else miss Snow White?" said Rose Red.

"Everything that causes wonder does," said Hamr.

"It be like a dream!" said Tylo, watching the snowfall.

"Then I ain't waking up any time soon," said Jack.

Tylo shook the snow from his hair and spun his arms in a circle, as Snow White would. "Now, we have something to wake up to. We had only days but we grew them into forever."

* * * * *

"Tell a tale a thousand ways,
It never sounds the same.
Half grown heroes take on quests,
Some journeys, foes, or name."

"Yet, spin it all through eyes anew,
The old lore always keeps.
Each generation has its Jack,
And still the Beauty sleeps."

Made in the USA
Middletown, DE
20 November 2020

24642729R00189